Joseph Arnould

Memoir of Thomas

First lord Denman, formerly lord chief justice of England

Joseph Arnould

Memoir of Thomas
First lord Denman, formerly lord chief justice of England

ISBN/EAN: 9783337423087

Printed in Europe, USA, Canada, Australia, Japan

Cover: Foto ©Raphael Reischuk / pixelio.de

More available books at **www.hansebooks.com**

MEMOIR

OF

THOMAS, FIRST LORD DENMAN

FORMERLY

LORD CHIEF JUSTICE OF ENGLAND

BY

SIR JOSEPH ARNOULD

LATE JUDGE OF THE HIGH COURT OF BOMBAY

IN TWO VOLUMES

VOL. I.

LONDON
LONGMANS, GREEN, AND CO.
1873

PREFACE.

Tʜɪs Mᴇᴍᴏɪʀ has been principally compiled from materials placed at the writer's disposal by various members of the late Lᴏʀᴅ Dᴇɴᴍᴀɴ's family; by his old friend, Sir Jᴏʜɴ Tᴀʏʟᴏʀ Cᴏʟᴇʀɪᴅɢᴇ ; and by Mr. Hᴇʀᴍᴀɴ Mᴇʀɪᴠᴀʟᴇ, the son of a friend still older.

It is intended as much for general as for professional readers : for Dᴇɴᴍᴀɴ, though of a high order both as an advocate and a judge, was of a still higher order as a man and a citizen; so that a record, however imperfect, of his noble and virtuous life may, it is hoped, be found interesting and useful even beyond the comparatively narrow limits of exclusively legal circles.

TABLE OF CONTENTS

OF

THE FIRST VOLUME.

CHAPTER I.

DESCENT, PARENTAGE, BIRTH, AND CHILDHOOD.

A.D. 1779 TO 1788.

CHAPTER II.

ETON AND CAMBRIDGE.

A.D. 1788 TO 1800.

CHAPTER III.

LAW STUDIES—SPECIAL PLEADING—MARRIAGE.

A.D. 1800 TO 1804.   ÆT. 21 TO 25.

Denman commences his legal studies, April, 1800—In chambers with Merivale at Featherstone Buildings, Holborn—A pupil of Charles Butler—Works hard at real property law—Separate chambers at 25

CHAPTER IV.

CALL TO BAR—EARLY MARRIED LIFE.

A.D. 1804 TO 1811.   ÆT. 25 TO 32.

Special Pleading—Periodical literature (the 'Monthly Review'), 1804–1806—Cambridge election for Chancellor—Lord Henry Petty—Fox-Grenville administration, Jan. 1806—Denman's devotion to Fox—Letter to Sir F. Burdett shortly after Fox's death—Denman called to the Bar, 1806—Change of residence to No. 5 Queen's Square, Blooms-bury—Joins Midland Circuit and Lincolnshire Sessions—Leading

CHAPTER V.

PROGRESS AT THE BAR.

A.D. 1811 TO 1815.   ÆT. 32 TO 36.

In 1811 Denman's practice on circuit and sessions much increased—Takes chambers at No. 5 Old Square, Lincoln's Inn—Extracts from Midland Circuit Book—Brougham specially retained at Lincoln in Spring Assizes of 1811 for defence of John Drakard, of the '*Stamford News*' —Merivale disappointed that Denman was not retained—Dangerous illness of Merivale in October and November 1811—Extract from letter from Merivale to Denman, Nov. 22, 1811—Death of Denman's uncle, Dr. Joseph Denman, in 1812—Disposal of his property—The

CHAPTER VI.

DEFENCE OF BRANDRETH AND OTHERS FOR HIGH TREASON.

A.D. 1816, 1817. ÆT. 37, 38.

CHAPTER VII.

PARLIAMENT—M.P. FOR WAREHAM AND NOTTINGHAM.

A.D. 1818 TO 1820.   ÆT. 39 TO 41.

CHAPTER VIII.

THE QUEEN'S ARRIVAL—DENMAN HER SOLICITOR-GENERAL.

A.D. 1820.   ÆT. 41.

CHAPTER IX.

THE QUEEN'S TRIAL—EARLIER STAGES.

A.D. 1820.   ÆT. 41.

CHAPTER X.

THE QUEEN'S TRIAL CONTINUED AND CONCLUDED.

A.D. 1820. ÆT. 41.

CHAPTER XI.

THE QUEEN'S DEATH.

A.D. 1821.   ÆT. 42.

CHAPTER XII.

FROM DEATH OF QUEEN TO DEATH OF CANNING— DENMAN, COMMON SERJEANT.

A.D. 1821 TO 1827.   ÆT. 42 TO 48.

CHAPTER XIII.

DENMAN IN HOUSE OF COMMONS FROM 1821 TO 1826.

A.D. 1821 TO 1826. ÆT. 42 TO 47.

General estimate of Denman's Parliamentary career for this period— *Session of* 1821—Presents petition from Thomas Davison, fined 100*l.* for contempt, by Mr. Justice Best, on his trial for blasphemy, February 23, 1821—Speech on Mr. Lennard's motion for repeal of Seditious Meetings and Blasphemous Libel Acts, May 8, 1821—On Sir F. Burdett's motion for enquiry into the Manchester Massacre of 1819, May 15, 1821—On Sir J. Mackintosh's bill for abolishing death punishment in cases of forgery, June 4, 1821—Observations on the proceedings of the Constitutional Association, July 3, 1821. *Session of* 1822—Speech on the proceedings at the Queen's funeral, March 6, 1822—On Lord John Russell's motion on the state of the Representation of the People, April 25, 1822—Against renewal of Aliens' Regulation Act, June 5, 1822— On same subject, July 19, 1822. *Session of* 1823—Speech on petition from Richard Carlile, fined and imprisoned for blasphemous libel, May 8, 1823—On motion of Mr. John Williams for enquiry into delays in Court of Chancery, June 5, 1823—Instances of delay cited by Denman in his speech. *Session of* 1824—Speech on Mr. George Lamb's motion for leave to bring in a Bill for allowing counsel to prisoners charged with felony, April 6, 1824—Against farther renewal of Aliens' Regulation Act, April 12, 1824—Speech on petition of James Silk Buckingham, May 25, 1824—On trial and capital conviction of Missionary Smith at Demerara, June 11, 1824—On Government bill for the suppression of insurrection in Ireland, June 14, 1824. *Session of* 1825—Passage in King's speech as to the Catholic Association, February 2, 1825—Denman's speech in debate on the Address, February 4, 1825—Speech on Government bill for suppressing unlawful societies in Ireland, February 10, 1825—Attack on Lord Eldon as the chief opponent of Catholic Emancipation—Speech on petition against re-enacting the Combination Laws, May 4, 1825—Speech on Chief Justices' and Judges' Salaries Bill, May 16, 1825—Denman's views in 1825 on the position and status of Puisne Judges—Income of Lord Ellenborough while Chief Justice of King's Bench—Sums realised by Chief Justice Eyre by sale of offices in Common Pleas—Salaries of Chief Justices and Judges as fixed by Act of 1825, and as subsequently reduced by Acts of 1832 and 1851—Speech on proposed increase of allowances to the Duchess of Kent and the Duke of Cumberland, May 27, 1825—Quarantine Laws—Dr. Baillie's opinion, June 3, 1825— Speech on Sir F. Burdett's motion for producing the evidence taken before the Chancery Commissioners, June 7, 1825—Damaging attack on Lord Eldon as Chancellor. *Session of* 1826—Denman's observations

CHAPTER XIV.

DENMAN'S EXERTIONS OTHERWISE THAN IN PARLIAMENT FOR THE AMENDMENT OF THE LAW.

A.D. 1824 TO 1828.   ÆT. 45 TO 49.

Denman's article in the 'Edinburgh Review' for March 1824, on Law Reform—Defects of the English law of evidence pointed out—Exclusion of testimony on the ground of interest—Exclusion of prosecutor's evidence as to genuineness of signature in cases of forgery—Interest ought never to exclude testimony—Query as to the case of parties— Protected cases: 1. Case of Catholic priest and confessing penitent. 2. Legal adviser and client. 3. Husband and wife—Remarks as to testimony of Husband and Wife—Present state of English law (1873) as to testimony of husband and wife—As to confidential communications between client and legal adviser—Denman's criticism of defects then (1824) existing in our criminal law procedure—Question as to the superiority, or the reverse, of the French system of interrogating the prisoner over the English system of non-interrogation—Denman's objections to the French system as it affects both the prisoner and the tribunal —Balance of advantages and disadvantages pretty even—Passage from the article relating to the slow progress, but ultimate triumph, of the criminal law reforms of Romilly and Mackintosh—Peel's criminal law codification of 1823, abolishing death punishment in above 100 cases—Encouragement to law reformers to persevere—In 1828, in consequence of Brougham's great speech of February 7, a commission appointed to enquire into and report upon the proceedings in actions at law—Denman's answers to questions submitted by the Commissioners suggesting various measures of legal reform, all of which have since been carried out—Denman also publishes a pamphlet on Law Reform under the title of 'Considerations submitted to the Commissioners, &c.,' urging, *inter alia*, that *no* evidence should be excluded on the ground

CHAPTER XV.

FAMILY AND SOCIAL LIFE, HOLLAND HOUSE, ETC.

A.D. 1821 TO 1828.

CHAPTER XVI.

KING'S COUNSEL AT LAST.

A.D. 1828. ÆT. 49.

CHAPTER XVII.

DUKE OF WELLINGTON'S MINISTRY—DENMAN M.P. FOR NOTTINGHAM AGAIN.

A.D. 1828 TO 1830. ÆT. 49 TO 51.

CHAPTER XVIII.

LORD GREY'S MINISTRY—SIR THOMAS DENMAN, ATTORNEY-GENERAL.

A.D. 1830 TO 1831.　ÆT. 51 TO 52.

Opening of the New Parliament, November 2, 1830—Brougham's notice
of motion on Parliamentary Reform for November 16—The Duke of
Wellington's declaration in the House of Lords against any reform in
Parliament, November 2, 1830—Denman's first speech in the new
Parliament, in debate on the Address, November 3—His reference to
and condemnation of the Duke's declaration—Effect of the Duke's
declaration—Panic in London—The police maltreated and the Duke
himself mobbed—The King and Queen prevented from going to the
Lord Mayor's banquet—Lord Macaulay's description of the panic—

Denman's speech on November 8, condemning the attacks on the
police, and the outrage to the Duke—Peel's compliment to Denman
on his speech—Denman's letter to Mrs. Wright of November 12, 1830
—He is of the 'young party'—Believes the Duke's position to be un-
tenable—Had expected him to take up Parliamentary Reform as he
had Catholic Emancipation—The Duke of Wellington resigns on
November 16—Earl Grey's Ministry formed—Brougham, Chancellor
—Denman, Attorney-General—Magnanimity of William IV. and its
effects on Denman—His reference to it in the House of Commons—
Denman's re-election for Nottingham—The Duke of Newcastle, in the
House of Lords, complains of his speech on being re-elected—
Brougham explains, and the Duke takes nothing by his motion—
Denman's appointment as Attorney-General highly popular—Letter
of congratulation from W. W. Pepys—Denman resigns the office of
Common Serjeant—Thanks of the City for the manner in which he
had discharged it—Testimony to the same effect of the Old Bailey
Bar—Denman's opinion expressed in Parliament as to vote by Ballot,
November 22, 1830—As to Lord (then Mr.) Campbell's bill for registration of deeds, December 16, 1830—Defence of Brougham from an
attack by Sugden, and eulogies on him—Denman at close of 1830 and
beginning of 1831 conducts the prosecution against the agrarian
rioters, tried before the Special Commissions at Winchester and Salisbury—His humane and able conduct of the prosecution—Interest of
the King in the proceedings—Correspondence thereon between Denman and the King through Sir Herbert Taylor—Sense of House of
Commons as to value of Denman's exertions shown on Hunt's motion
for an amnesty to all the convicts—Denman's speech on that motion,
February 13, 1831—Denman's prosecutions, *ex officio*, against Carlile
and Cobbett for stirring up the peasantry to insurrection—Passages
selected for prosecution in Carlile's case; in Cobbett's case—Carlile
tried on January 10, 1831—Convicted and severely sentenced—
Cobbett's trial postponed till July 1831—Cobbett's able speech in his
own defence—'The lank and merciless Whigs,' &c.—The jury
cannot agree and Cobbett is discharged—Denman, in consequence of
this trial, in bad odour with the advanced Liberals—This was the last
of Denman's *ex officio* prosecutions, though frequently afterwards
pressed to prosecute at the instance of the King—Letter from Lord
Grey on the subject, May 4, 1831—Mr. (afterwards Sir) Fowell
Buxton's resolutions of April 15, 1831, for the abolition of Slavery—
Denman's speech in favour of them—Letter from the venerable
William Wilberforce introducing his son Samuel to Denman *Page* 315

CHAPTER XIX.

THE REFORM BILL—SESSION OF 1831.

A.D. 1831.   ÆT. 52.

CHAPTER XX.

THE REFORM BILL—SESSION OF 1832.

A.D. 1832. ÆT. 53.

Early in January 1832, Denman, as Attorney-General, prosecutes the Bristol rioters before a special commission—The House re-assembles on January 19, and the Bill again goes into committee—Croker in his glory—Macaulay and Croker, on March 19, in the debate on the final third reading in the Commons—Parallel between Cholera and Reform —Croker in the smoking-room of the House—Denman's letter thence to Mrs. Wright—Denman speaks on third reading, March 20—Bill, as amended, sent up to the Lords—Read a second time there, April 14— Bill in committee in the Lords—Majority against ministers on Lord Lyndhurst's motion, May 7—Grey and Brougham go down to the King at Windsor, May 8—The King accepts the resignation of the Reform ministry, May 9—Popular excitement—Duke of Wellington unable to form a Cabinet—The Grey ministry reinstated, May 18— Consequence to Denman, at this time, of permanent loss of office. His letter to Mrs. Wright, written between the 9th and 18th of May—Contents: His feeling of anxiety for the country, and of disappointment as regards the King—Professional prospects—The Bench—The Speakership—Loss of office, how received by his wife and family—His son Joseph—Intrigues by which the fall of the Whig ministry was brought about—Lord Lyndhurst, Mephistopheles—Baring—Peel—Denman's satisfaction that the whole Cabinet had resolved on resignation— Legal gossip—Revenue case before Lyndhurst as Chief Baron—Mr. 'Rat'—Scotch appeal case before Brougham—'Poor as a rat'— Another case before Lord Lyndhurst, 'When rogues fall out, honest men come by their own'—Jeffrey (Lord Advocate) taken by Denman to see his mother—Debate on Lord Stormont's motion on the 'Conduct of the Press,' May 21, 1832—Article in 'Satirist' of May 13 brought to Denman's attention—He declines to prosecute *ex officio*—His reasons—Peel misrepresents his speech—Denman explains his views of the duty of an Attorney-General in regard to Press Prosecutions— William IV. writes to Lord Althorpe to ascertain Denman's real views on the subject—Lord Althorpe, in consequence, writes to Denman on May 23—Denman prepares and sends on May 24, 'A Memorial on *ex officio informations*'—Its contents—Explanation of what he said on the subject on Lord Stormont's motion—The real question one not so much of feeling as expediency—Prosecution gives publicity to what might otherwise pass unnoticed—The Attorney-General should never take action without specific instruction in cases of personal libel— Inconveniences of having publicly to state objections against proceed-

CHAPTER XXI.

CLOSE OF SESSION OF 1832—STONY MIDDLETON—DENMAN'S POLITICAL CONFESSIONS TO MERIVALE.

A.D. 1832.   ÆT. 53.

CHAPTER XXII.

APPOINTMENT AS CHIEF JUSTICE.

A.D. 1832. ÆT. 53.

CHAPTER XXIII.

SIR THOMAS DENMAN, CHIEF JUSTICE.

A.D. 1833.   ÆT. 54.

MEMOIR

OF

THOMAS, FIRST LORD DENMAN.

CHAPTER I.

DESCENT, PARENTAGE, BIRTH, AND CHILDHOOD.

A.D. 1779 TO 1788.

The Denman family—Great-grandfather and grandfather of Lord
Denman—His paternal uncle, Dr. Joseph Denman—His father, Dr.
Thomas Denman—His mother, *neé* Miss Elizabeth Brodie—His
maternal uncle, Rev. P. B. Brodie—His first cousins, William, Peter,
and Sir Benjamin Brodie—Marriage of Dr. Denman and Miss E.
Brodie, 1770—Happiness of the union—Lord Denman's twin sisters,
Margaret and Sophia—Their husbands, Sir R. Croft and Dr. Matthew
Baillie—Agnes and Joanna Baillie—Birth of Lord Denman, Feb. 23,
1779—Place of birth—Narrow escape from fire when an infant—
Childhood of Lord Denman—Sent to Mrs. Barbauld's school at
Palgrave in 1782—His progress and improvement there—Mrs.
Denman as a mother—Her belief in the power of early training—
Love of the child for his parents—Early and life-long piety of his
character—Dr. Denman as a father—Takes the child with him on his
professional excursions out of London—Letter from him to his wife on
one of these—Burke's house at Beaconsfield—The boy taken from
Mrs. Barbauld's and sent to Dr. Thompson's at Kensington in 1786—
Remains there till 1788.

A FAMILY of DENMANS had for many generations been
settled in Lincolnshire and Nottinghamshire. They
were persons of reputable condition as early as the

days of the Third Edward; intermarried, in later times, with several county families of distinction ; and in one of their branches became progenitors, in the female line, of Anne Hyde, the first wife of James the Second, and mother of the two queens, Mary and Anne.[1]   A more characteristic, if not a more honourable, circumstance in the family story is that a Rev. William Denman, rector of Ordsall, near Retford, in Nottinghamshire, refusing in the evil days of Queen Mary to renounce his Protestant principles, was ejected from his living, to which, however, he seems to have been restored under Elizabeth.

It is probable, but, from defect of parish registers, not provable, that Thomas Denman of Bevercotes in Nottinghamshire, the great-grandfather and first known lineal ancestor of Lord Denman, was of this family. Thomas Denman of Bevercotes died about the year 1740, at the age of 96, and was born, therefore, in the early years of the great civil war.

Lord Denman's grandfather, John Denman, the second son of Thomas of Bevercotes, settled as a general practitioner at Bakewell in Derbyshire.   His family was large, his practice very small (averaging only from 50*l.* to 100*l.* a year), and he died in his fifty-eighth year, leaving behind him two sons and several daughters very slenderly provided for.

---

[1] The connexion was sufficiently remote : the second wife of the great Lord Clarendon, and mother of Anne Hyde, was a daughter of Sir Thomas Aylesbury, Master of Requests in time of James I., by a Miss Frances Denman, daughter of the Rev. Francis Denman, Rector of East Retford, and of Anne Blount, one of the Blounts of Eckington in Derbyshire—a county family of high repute.

The elder of his two sons, Joseph, a person of strong original character—shrewd and frugal—succeeded to and soon improved his father's business; he married a lady of some property (including the small estate of Stony Middleton, near Bakewell), used to practise a good deal at Buxton in the season, and, in his later years, was a frequent visitor at Chatsworth, being a great favourite of the fifth duke of Devonshire—the friend of Fox and husband of the beautiful duchess.

The second son, Thomas, father of Lord Denman (born in 1733), went up to London in the twenty-first year of his age with 75*l.* in his pocket: 50*l.* bequeathed by his grandfather, and 25*l.* as his share of what his father was supposed to have been worth at the time of his death.

In his autobiography (a well-written work), Dr. Thomas Denman has given an interesting and animated account of the struggles of his early manhood, from the time when he ' passed as surgeon to a ship of sixth rate,' to the period when, after ' a wandering but not generally disagreeable life of nine years,' as a naval surgeon, having managed to scrape together 500*l.*, he first settled himself in London as a medical practitioner in Oxenden Street, Haymarket, with a single maid-servant for his whole establishment.

From this modest commencement his progress, though for some time by no means rapid, was steady and continuous, until he ultimately became, and long remained, conspicuously known as the first accoucheur in the metropolis.   He early devoted himself almost exclusively to that department of practice, and having in 1770 (the 38th year of his age) become, jointly with Dr. Krohn, professor of midwifery to the Middlesex Hospital, and being, moreover, in the receipt of about 300*l.* a year from his private practice, he determined to marry.

The lady he chose for his wife was a handsome and engaging young gentlewoman of Scottish descent, Elizabeth, the youngest daughter of Mr. Alexander Brodie, then established as an army accoutrement maker in Brewer Street, Golden Square.

Mr. Brodie came of a good Scotch family — the Brodies of Brodie in Morayshire—and he had a son, a clergyman in the Church of England, the Rev. Peter Bullinger Brodie, whom, immediately on his taking orders, the second Lord Holland had presented to the rectory of Winterslow, near Winchester.

The rector of Winterslow, Lord Denman's maternal uncle, became father, in due course, of Mr. William Brodie, afterwards a banker at Salisbury, and for many years member for the borough, of Mr. Peter Brodie, a well-known conveyancer, and of Sir Benjamin Brodie, who for some years held the highest rank in the profession of surgery, while his first cousin, Lord Denman, was presiding in Westminster Hall, as Chief of the Common Law.

Miss Elizabeth Brodie, at the time of her marriage with Dr. Denman, which took place on the 1st of November, 1770, was in the 24th year of her age. ‘ It would have been impossible,’ writes her husband, in his autobiography, ‘ to have chosen a wife more suitable to my disposition and circumstances ; her manner was amiable, her disposition gentle, her understanding, naturally good, improved by reading and the conversation of reasonable people, and she has that regard for truth and propriety, that I am firmly persuaded no human consideration could induce her to depart from them.   She is frugal, without meanness, temperate and cheerful, and it is impossible for any two people to have lived together with more harmony and affection than we have done.'

Within a year after the marriage of Dr. and Mrs. Denman, on the 9th of July, 1771, twin daughters were born to them—Margaret and Sophia.

Of these Margaret, in 1789, was married to Mr. (afterwards Sir) Richard Croft (the seventh baronet of his family), who first assisted, and after 1815 succeeded, Dr. Denman in what had then long been the most extensive midwifery practice in London.

Sophia, in 1791, became the wife of the admirable and eminent Dr. Matthew Baillie, the first physician of his age, brother of Agnes and of Joanna Baillie, the gifted authoress of the ' Plays of the Passions.'

Thomas, Lord Denman, the third and last child, and only son, of his parents, was born on the 23rd of February, 1779, when the twin sisters (afterwards Lady Croft and Mrs. Baillie) were in the eighth year of their age.

The place of his birth was Queen Street, Golden Square (now called after his name, Denman Street), in a house to which Dr. Denman had removed, two years after his marriage, from his original quarters in Oxenden Street.

Although Mrs. Denman was still quite young, and her husband in the full vigour of mature manhood, they seem to have regarded the birth of another child as an event scarcely to have been anticipated.[1]

From the first the infant, as might have been expected, was the object of the most anxious and devoted solicitude and affection.   Before completing his third year he had almost perished in a fire, which utterly destroyed the house in Queen Street, and he was only rescued from the flames by the calm intrepidity of his father, who saved the child's life at the imminent risk of his own.   Immediately after this providential escape Dr. Denman established himself in Old Burlington Street, where he thenceforth continued to reside during the most active portion of his distinguished professional career.

. The parents had not long recovered from the shock of this appalling danger, when, fearing that the child, who had now become more than ever the pet and plaything of the family, might be spoiled by excessive indulgence, they, in the exercise of an almost Spartan self-control, sent the little creature away from home, when only about three-and-a-half years old, to be brought up by the well-known Mrs. Barbauld, who then kept a school for young children at Palgrave, near Diss in Norfolk.[2]

---

[1] 'The birth of this child,' writes Dr. Denman in his 'Autobiography,' 'was an inexpressible blessing, as I had given up the hopes of having any more children, my daughters at that time being more than seven years old.' Mrs. Denman was only thirty-two and the Doctor forty-six when their son was born.

[2] The school was at this time fashionable and highly patronised : Miss

The principal motive to this act of self-sacrifice, and the struggle it cost the mother, were expressed by her in a few artless and homely lines, written in answer to a friend who had enquired, with some natural wonder, how she could possibly have consented to separate herself so early from so beloved a child.

> Love only could the thought suggest,
> Love tore the darling from our breast:
> So much our child we prize,
> Patient our pleasure we resign
> That he in future years may shine
> And be both good and wise.[1]

There was something prophetic, as it turned out, in the aspiration. The lady to whom the mother entrusted her little treasure executed her task admirably, drawing out all the child's natural powers, especially those of memory and elocution. He seems to have been a forward little child. In June 1783, when in his fifth year, Mrs. Barbauld encloses to his mother 'a little piece of verse which, with great applause, he spoke at our play.' 'The dear boy,' she reports, 'has already begun Latin; he has an excellent memory, and delights in learning.' In August of the same year she writes, 'he is going on with his Latin, and reading English books of amusement.' He was an engaging little fellow, affectionate and generous: 'I do not know a sweeter child,' writes Mrs. Barbauld, and she duly

Aikin, in her 'Life of Mrs. Barbauld' (published in 1825), gives a long list of the children of the nobility whose early years were spent at Palgrave. Among Denman's little companions there was Sir William Gell, of antiquarian celebrity.

[1] Mrs. Denman was fond of expressing herself in verse, an accomplishment in which she had a fair amount of proficiency.

records, for his fond mother's gratification, his generosity in sharing his cakes and his other home presents among his little schoolmates.

There can be no doubt that the three or four years spent with Mrs. Barbauld were exceedingly well spent; the fearless advocate and upright judge of the future owed much, beyond a question, to the simple homely training in truthfulness, honour, and self-denial which he received at Palgrave; while, as regards acquirements, Lord Denman always attributed to the judicious care of his first instructress much of the retentiveness of his memory, of his fondness for literature, and of the force and clearness of his elocution.[1]

Mrs. Denman was herself always most assiduous in the moral and intellectual training of her son. Her own tastes were strongly literary, and she knew how to make literature attractive to the young. Many of her verses were very creditable productions, and a MS. essay of hers, on the 'advantages of robbing orchards,' which formed one of the delights of her children, has a great deal of the grave humour and clear telling style of Miss Edgeworth. Like many other clever people of the generation immediately preceding the French Revolution, she had a somewhat exaggerated belief in the efficacy of strict moral and intellectual training and constant self-introspection. A copy still exists of forty-six rules carefully drawn up in her own

---

[1] Lord Denman always spoke in the most affectionate terms of Mrs. Barbauld. On the publication of Miss Aikin's memoir in 1825 he expressed his gratification that so much had been done to preserve the memory of ' my dear old instructress.'

handwriting for the regulation of her own conduct in all the minutiæ of daily life ; the precise extent to which she was to permit herself to indulge in dinner parties and morning visits, in cards and in theatricals ; the exact mode and form in which she was to demean herself as a wife, a mother, and the mistress of an establishment. A school of thought then fashionable had infected the reading world with notions of human perfectibility as the result of careful training, which, with so many other illusions of that sanguine time, have passed away, under the disenchanting influence of a sad and terrible experience, till the pendulum, it may be, has swung too far in the opposite direction, and we are now as much too lax as we were formerly too strict. Dr. Denman and his wife both held firmly to the belief that it was in their power, by constant and careful supervision, to make their son, as the Doctor expresses it in a letter hereafter to be quoted, one of the wisest and best men that ' ever lived ; ' and the degree of success that attended their strenuous endeavours may no doubt in some measure seem to justify the system they pursued.[1]

The boy grew up deeply attached to both his parents : his love and dutiful regard for his mother more especially seemed throughout life to grow with his growth and strengthen with his strength.

His second daughter, the Hon. Mrs. Hodgson, in some notes kindly supplied by her for the purposes of

---

[1] Lord Denman himself always deprecated an over-anxious watchfulness in the training of children, and was never fussy or fidgetty with his own.

this memoir, relates as an instance of this pious regard, a promise which he made to this beloved parent in his early boyhood, to read daily a chapter in the Bible, and which he never failed inviolably to observe throughout all the busiest periods of his after life.

'No one,' adds Mrs. Hodgson, 'ever had a more intimate knowledge of the Bible, or ever acted more thoroughly on Christian principles, in all the relations of life, than my dear father, though his horror of hypocrisy and cant made him very reserved in speaking of such subjects : one of his favourite texts was " Overcome evil with good." ' [1]

Dr. Denman's attachment to the child was not inferior to the mother's. He was never tired of devising schemes for his mental or physical improvement, and was never happier than when he could take the little fellow with him on his occasional professional excursions into the country.

The following passages are from a chance-preserved letter written by the Doctor to his wife while on one of these excursions when the child was in his eighth year.

Oxford: October 13, 1787.

My dear Love,—I am sitting by a good fire in the bedroom, and Thomas is in bed, though not yet asleep ; and we both think that it would not be disagreeable to you to hear something of our transactions during the day.

We arrived at Southall at the time mentioned in our first

---

[1] This was the text he chose for the first sermon preached by his youngest son, the Hon. and Rev. Louis Denman, who entirely confirms his sister's statement as to the deep and unaffected piety of their father.

note, and proceeded with all the expedition which prudence would allow to Beaconsfield, where we got soon after four. While our veal cutlet was dressing we took a walk of a short mile to see Mr. Burke's house, which is the most elegant thing of the kind I ever saw. I had an idea of its being a farm, or something between a farm and a gentleman's house, but I was quite mistaken. In the centre there are seven windows in a line, and from the two angles of the front, there are colonnades, consisting of seven or eight columns each, which lead to two considerable masses of building, which are, in proportion, as elegant as the centre. All the ground, and it seems a considerable domain, is well planted, and with much taste, and the whole you and the girls will have a good idea of, according to your old estimate, by my saying it would suit Sir Charles Grandison.

It appears to have been partly from anxiety about the child's health, but still more, no doubt, from a desire of being able personally to watch over his physical and intellectual progress, that Dr. Denman removed him, when in his seventh year, from Mrs. Barbauld's at Palgrave to Dr. Thompson's at Kensington, at which latter place he remained till his tenth year, when he was sent to Eton.[1]

---

[1] Dr. Thompson belonged more to the old school than Mrs. Barbauld but he was a very respectable teacher.

CHAPTER II.

ETON AND CAMBRIDGE.

A.D. 1788 TO 1800.

Denman at Eton from 1788 to 1795—Few records of his Eton career—
Notice of him (æt. 13) during an Eton vacation at Winterslow—Early
love for music—Early politics and talent for speaking—Burnt in the
leg for not ' making a speech '—Greek and Latin scholarship—English
verse translations—Denman at Winterslow 1795 to 1796—Rambles in
North Wiltshire—Stonehenge, Essay on—Thorney Down, Verses on
—Denman goes into residence at St. John's College, Cambridge, Oct.
1796—His pursuits and friendships at the University—Merivale—
Shadwell—Hodgson—Drury—Bland—The ' Greek Anthology' and its
contributors—Byron's praises of in ' English Bards and Scotch Reviewers'—Denman's translation ' With myrtle my sword will I
wreathe' praised by Byron in note to third canto of ' Childe Harold'—
Denman's undergraduate life at St. John's—Merivale's Diary—Walk-
ing tour with Shadwell in Wales 1797—Plan for a winter excursion
to Snowdon—Walks with Merivale in neighbourhood of Cambridge—
Literary talk—Lord Levaine—Denman's readiness at capping verses—
His memory and love for poetry—Akenside and Beattie—Hamlet—
Similarity of tastes and pursuits in Denman and Merivale—Denman's
fondness for romances of chivalry—His admirable Greek scholarship—
Denman's correspondence at Cambridge with his sister Mrs. Baillie—
Extracts from letters to her—Description of Dovedale—And of Dorset
and Devon coasts—Early admiration for ' Lyrical Ballads'—For Joanna
Baillie's dramas—Mrs. Baillie's memoirs of her brother—His early
love of theatricals—A taste that never left him—Denman's political
sentiments—An ardent ' Foxite'—His unswerving political constancy
—Early admiration for Dr. Parr as a staunch Whig—Mrs. Baillie's
speculations as to origin of her brother's political opinions—Personal
advantages of Denman as a young man—Physical strength and activity
—Walks from Cambridge to London in twelve hours—His magnificent
voice—Air of distinction and refinement—Combination of sweetness and
force—Correspondence between Denman, while at Cambridge, and his

DR. DENMAN sent his son to Eton in September 1788,
and the boy remained there for nearly seven years,
till the summer holidays of 1795—from his tenth to
his seventeenth year.

The records of his Eton career are very scanty; a
few of his schoolboy letters have indeed been preserved
by the pious care of his relatives—principally of his
sister Mrs. Baillie, who was throughout life a constant
and favorite correspondent—but they throw no light on
his early pursuits or friendships, and, though creditable
to his good sense and intelligence, are none of them
of sufficient interest to justify transcription.

He was frequently in the habit of passing part
of his Eton vacations with Mr. Brodie and his
young cousins at Winterslow, and on one of these
occasions, when he was in his thirteenth year, we get
a glimpse of him in a letter from one of his maternal
aunts to her sister Mrs. Denman. 'He pleases his
uncle very much,' she writes, ' by going into the
school-room and sitting down with his cousins to
business. He is turning the Story of Sadak, the master
of the horse, into Latin verse: it was quite his own
suggestion, and my brother says he does it very well.'

Miss Brodie also mentions his love for music, and expresses some surprise at the extent of his accomplishments in singing. 'He has got together a choice collection of ballads,' she says, ' which he delights in singing for the amusement of his young cousins.' The taste for music, thus early developed, was a source of great enjoyment to Lord Denman throughout his life.

The boy's strong political opinions, which were even then of an ultra-Liberal cast, got him into many scrapes at Eton; but he held to them, though then exceedingly unfashionable, with characteristic tenacity, and did manful battle against the young Pittites and anti-Jacobins of the school. His talent for speaking was also known at Eton, and, as Mrs. Hodgson records, one form of bullying adopted towards him when a fag was to insist on his unpremeditated exercise of this talent, under the most inconvenient circumstances; on one occasion he was roused from sleep and ordered instantly 'to make a speech,' and on his obstinate refusal to comply, was burned on the leg with a red-hot poker, the scar of which branding he carried with him to his grave.

He was well grounded at Eton in Greek and Latin scholarship, and one of his English verse translations from the Greek, executed while at school, 'The Complaint of Danaë,' was of sufficient merit to be afterwards inserted in the 'Anthology.'

It is not known why Dr. Denman removed his son from Eton at an earlier age than usual—sixteen and a half; it may probably have been with a view to his health. A fever which had attacked him in his sixteenth year had a good deal weakened him, and the doctor

may have wished to set him up by the bracing air of
the North Wiltshire Downs.   At any rate, Denman
did not return to Eton after the summer vacation of
1795, but went instead to his uncle's at Winterslow.

Mr. Brodie was himself an accomplished scholar,
and the preparatory year that his nephew passed with
him before going into residence at Cambridge no
doubt tended to increase the accuracy and extent of
his classical acquirements.   At Winterslow, his great
amusement was to make long rambles on foot among
the breezy plains and uplands of North Wiltshire—
frequently extending his excursions as far as Stonehenge, the solitary grandeur of which struck him pro-
foundly, and set him at work among the antiquarians and
early chroniclers, to solve, if possible, the mystery of its
origin.   The essay he wrote on this subject has been
preserved, and is highly creditable to his early diligence
and acuteness.   At Winterslow also he indulged a
good deal in the composition of English verse, which,
as already stated, he had begun to cultivate with some
success at Eton.   Some of his translations from the
classics are above the average, and some original lines
on ' Thorney Down ' (a bold hill crowned with a clump
of wood, which rises to a commanding eminence over
Salisbury Plain), have a fair share of merit, though they
naturally enough show strong traces of a mode in
poetry which is less fashionable now than in the days
when Darwin (of ' the Botanic Garden ') was regarded
as a monarch of Parnassus.[1]

From Winterslow, in October 1796, being then well

---

[1] The lines to ' Thorney Down,' together with several translations
and original pieces in verse, will be found in Appendix No. II.

advanced in his eighteenth year, Denman went into residence at St. John's College, Cambridge, and he remained at the University rather more than three years —till February 1800, when, soon after taking his degree, he left it for London.

At Cambridge he devoted himself with considerable success both to scholarship and general literature. This is clear from the results, and, even in the absence of other proof, might be inferred from the nature of the friendships he formed or continued there. Merivale and Bland, the two principal writers, and the latter also the editor, of the 'Greek Anthology;'[1] Francis Hodgson and Henry Drury, their friends and coadjutors, the former afterwards known as a successful translator of Juvenal; Launcelot Shadwell, Chancellor's Medallist and Seventh Wrangler in 1800—all of them ripe scholars and young men of very considerable talent and literary culture—were among the most intimate of Denman's associates at Cambridge. Denman was himself a con-

---

[1] 'The Anthology' has great merits: its full title is 'Collections from the Greek Anthology, by the Rev. Robert Bland and others.' John Herman Merivale, as the initial M. prefixed to his translations indicates, and as Bland candidly states in his preface (p. xlvi. Edition 1813), was the most copious, if not the most gifted, contributor. It is strange that this admirable collection, now very scarce, has not been reprinted. Byron, who, as his earlier letters show, was on intimate terms with Bland, Hodgson, Drury, and Merivale, was a great admirer of the ' Anthology,' and in ' English Bards and Scotch Reviewers ' thus apostrophises the contributors :

> And you associate bards who snatched to light
> Those gems too long concealed from mortal sight,
> Whose mingling taste combined to cull the wreath
> Where Attic flowers Aonian odours breathe,
> And all their renovated fragrance flung
> To grace the beauties of your native tongue.

tributor to the 'Anthology' and his spirited rendering of the song of Callistratus, on Harmodius and Aristogeiton, is one of the best in the collection.[2]

From a diary kept at Cambridge by Denman's intimate friend John Herman Merivale, and kindly placed at the disposal of the present writer by his distinguished son Herman Merivale,[3] some notices may be gleaned of the future Chief Justice's undergaduate life at St. John's. The admiration for scenery and fondness for walking excursions which he had shown at Winterslow, had not diminished at Cambridge. In Merivale's diary, under date Oct. 26, 1797, the following note appears :

At supper I sate by Denman, who gave me a very interesting account of a walking tour he had just made with Shadwell through Wales. They traced the Wye from its source to the sea, and then, after going through the Southern Counties, got into Merioneth and Caernarvonshire, climbed Snowdon and Cader Idris, and returned into Shropshire. On their arrival at Shrewsbury they had just sixteen shillings left, having stayed out much longer than they intended. Driven to this extremity, they lived on bread and cheese till they

In one of his letters to Hodgson (Oct. 13, 1811), after his return from the East, he says, ' I always bewailed the absence of the " Anthology." Of the young men whose names are mentioned in the text, John Herman Merivale (Commissioner of Bankrupts, 1832) Launcelot Shadwell (Vice-Chancellor of England, 1827 to 1850), and Francis Hodgson (Archdeacon of Derby, 1836, Provost of Eton, 1840–1852), were life-long friends of Denman's; the last named also, in 1838, became his son-in-law. Bland and Drury were undermasters at Harrow. They and Hodgson married three sisters, charming and accomplished women of the name of Tayleur.

[2] Byron, in a note to the 20th stanza of the third canto of 'Childe Harold,' refers to this of Denman's as ' the best English translation.' Denman's ' Anthology ' and other verses will be found in Appendix No. II.

[3] Mr. Herman Merivale, C.B., Permanent Under-Secretary of State for India.

got to Oxford, where a fresh supply from a friend enabled them to pay their fare in the mail to London. To add to their misfortunes, they had worn out their shoes in climbing the mountains, and had not money enough to buy others.

A few days later the diary records—

Denman mentioned to me a plan he has formed of walking again to Snowdon at Christmas, chiefly, he says, ' to make observations on the people,' whose mode of living in the winter he supposes to be as different from their summer living as those of separate nations. He imagines that the scenery must also be wonderfully grand when the mountains are covered with snow, and the torrents and waterfalls round converted into ice.

Under date Nov. 13, 1797, Mr. Merivale writes:

I took a walk with Denman almost to Maddingly; we had a very pleasant conversation on literary subjects, particularly on poetry, and he appeared to show great taste and justice of observation.

On February 12, 1798, he writes:

To-morrow I take a long walk with Denman to a cottage about five miles from Ely, in order to give the produce of the fines we have imposed on one another for the last three weeks, for missing chapel, to a poor family that lives there. Denman says he never saw anywhere so great an appearance of poverty, and resolved when he next passed that way to do something for them.

February 13:

To-day at 12 o'clock, after going through our usual lectures, Denman and I set out on our walk, and were joined by Lord Lovaine, who was a schoolfellow [at Eton] and intimate acquaintance of Denman. We got back to St. John's at half-past five, which was pretty well, considering that our walk was upwards of twenty miles. Within two or three miles of Cambridge, on our return, we began to grow a little tired, and, to beguile the way, had recourse to the old school amusement of capping verses, in which Denman beat Lord Lovaine and myself all to pieces. He seems to have a remarkably good memory, and I believe there are few things he meets with, either Greek, Latin, Italian, French, or English —if they please him—but what he makes a point of being able to repeat. I have heard him say: 'It's an infamous thing to make extracts or write out anything that strikes you; if it's worth writing, it's surely worth learning by heart.' Akenside's 'Pleasures of Imagination' he thinks the finest didactic poem in the language, and I am sure he knows it from the beginning to the end. I believe he also knows all the first part at least of the 'Minstrel.' Some remarks he made on Hamlet pleased me very much. He considers as one of its great beauties the affection between Laertes and Ophelia. 'I believe,' he said, 'it is the only play in which Shakespeare has introduced the attachment of a brother and a sister, an attachment certainly the most pure and delightful of which I can form any conception.'

In the next year, under date March 8, 1799, Mr. Merivale writes:

Denman employs his time much as I do, and the frequent communications we have with each other on the subject of our respective labours are very pleasant, and, I believe, not unimproving to each of us; though the advantage is much more on my side, from the great abilities and strong understanding he possesses, of which every conversation we have affords me fresh instances. His superiority to me in classical attainments is another source of that advantage.

April 15, 1799:

Denman has been employing himself much lately in reading histories of the times of chivalry and romances, till he is become a perfect Quixote, and is almost ready to sally forth in quest of adventures. He also studies the classics a good deal, and has offered to read a play of Sophocles with me, which I think exceedingly kind, as he is a much better Greek scholar than I am, and all the trouble will therefore be his, and the advantage greatly on my side.

After making all due allowance for the characteristic modesty and self-depreciation of the amiable diarist, it must be admitted that the above is no mean praise from so accomplished a Grecian as John Herman Merivale.

From a charming sketch of her brother's life by Mrs. Baillie, which will often be quoted from in the course of the present Memoir, and from passages in his correspondence with her while at Cambridge, a few additional illustrations may be given of the pursuits and literary tastes of young Denman while at the University.

One of his letters to her, written in August 1798, while on a vacation walking tour among the Derbyshire highlands, contains the following description of Dovedale—the beautiful valley from which he many years afterwards took his title as Baron Denman of Dovedale.

Dovedale I traversed yesterday: all its beauties begin on my father's estate. I am sure that you never saw a more astonishing or romantic place. The descent to it is through my father's enclosures, till the ground becomes so steep and craggy as to defy all enclosures, and to be incapable of being ploughed, mown, or reaped. But there is good pasture, and the cattle acquire address and courage enough to walk among the rocks with ease, and graze with security. Some were reposing in the cool and oozy caverns, and others standing in the river. The Dove, indeed, is not quite such a river as I should have wished for; but then I saw it at a disadvantage, for it had lately subsided from a flood to its former channel, so as to want both the rapidity of a large stream and the clearness of a small one. It runs in this part of its course almost directly southward, separating Derbyshire from Staffordshire; the hills of the latter county, which form the western banks of the Dove, are higher and more wooded; those belonging to Derbyshire are bolder and more rocky, more various and grotesque. On both sides they stand almost perpendicularly above the river, and sometimes close it in so completely that there is no path except over large stones thrown into the water.

A later letter to the same correspondent, giving an account of a passage by sea from Southampton to Dartmouth, sketches with a firm, clear touch some of the features of the south-west coast:

We went on board the passage-boat at one, and sailed soon after three. The breeze was for some time pretty fresh and favourable, till we came towards the western extremity of the Isle of Wight, when the sea looked like glass, and we got on very slowly indeed. I stayed on deck most part of the night. Between the Needles the tide ran very strong, and the motion almost made me sick; but I escaped, though rather narrowly. Yesterday morning we were again becalmed for near two hours off the coast of Dorsetshire, and some of the crew went on shore for provisions to the neighbouring small town of Swannage. [How oddly this reads in these days of steam and scramble!] From Swannage to Portland the range of cliffs is exceedingly fine. There are many lone farm-houses thrown in very peculiar situations among these hills; they are all surrounded with trees, and a few cornfields are seen running along the summit. Weymouth is too far within a creek to be seen from the main sea. The rock was pointed out on which Captain Pierse and his family were destroyed in the 'Hallswell.'[4] The day was exceedingly clear, and a small fleet of East Indiamen at no great distance looked very pretty. A little before sunset the sky was beautifully illuminated, and I hoped for one of the most splendid natural objects that can be seen, but dark clouds, hardly distinguishable from distant mountains, intervened. The moon rose in obscurity; but a fresh breeze sprang up, and continued till this morning, when some other passengers and myself landed at Dartmouth. I am not very dainty; but I was heartily glad to quit the vessel. Dartmouth stands at the extremity of a narrow winding harbour, which is, however, very convenient for small craft, and is guarded by a castle at its entrance. The town stands on a steep hill, and is surrounded by others equally steep. Gibbon might call it a 'diffuse' town. The streets are very dirty, but there are many good houses at the outskirts, and the gardens on the side of the hill are pleasant, and give an appearance of great plenty—I walked about till seven, when, not finding the people at the inn stirring, I took a boat for Totness, and was rowed up the Dart, which runs between very fine high banks, with a great deal of wood and pleasant villages scattered round. This town (Totness) is about ten miles up the river, which is deep enough to admit very considerable merchantmen; it is surrounded by a good country, which does not, however, answer the descriptions usually given of Devonshire. I shall walk about eight miles on the road to Exeter this afternoon, and take my chance for a conveyance for the other sixteen.

His correspondence with Mrs. Baillie supplies some further information as to his literary tastes in his college days. He was an early admirer of Wordsworth. In a letter to his sister of November 1798 he writes:

[4] The wreck of the 'Hallswell,' East Indiaman, is recorded in 'Shipwrecks and Disasters at Sea.' It took place in 1786 and created a great sensation at the time.

Have you yet met with 'Lyrical Ballads,' from which 'Goody Blake' is taken.[5] They would, I think, delight you extremely; they consist of very pleasing tales and reflections, which are made doubly interesting by a simplicity of style, at once dignified and impressive. I can hardly help copying out two or three short passages for you, but you must buy the book.

He took a great interest in all the productions of Joanna Baillie. 'Are we,' he writes to his sister in the same letter, 'soon to expect the Play " On Hatred," and the others. I hope they will come out before I have left Cambridge, because I flatter myself with the thought that I could be of some little use to them here, which I can expect to be nowhere else.'

'He delighted,' says Mrs. Baillie in the admirable sketch of her brother's life already alluded to, 'in poetry and especially in dramatic writings; above all in Shakespeare, whose works were the constant study of his father, and whom from childhood he had constantly heard quoted and admired. He was also extremely fond of theatrical representations; indeed, his admiration of the more eminent performers of those times (Mrs. Siddons and the Kembles) was carried so far as at times to occasion his parents much uneasiness.'

This taste for the drama he never lost: he never failed, if possible, to be present on the first night of any new play which had raised the expectations of the public (as at Talfourd's ' Ion,' ' Athenian Captive,' &c.)

---

[5] The first volume of the 'Lyrical Ballads' was published in the summer of 1798 by Joseph Cottle of Bristol. The ballads were published anonymously, and Denman had been at first inclined to attribute their authorship to Coleridge.

and when presiding as a judge on circuit used always himself to patronize, and to engage the young barristers who attended the judge's dinner also to patronize, the local drama at the various assize towns.

In his political opinions Denman, in youth as in later life, was an ardent 'Foxite,' what would now be called an advanced Liberal. 'Many difficulties did he get into,' writes Mrs. Baillie in her memoir, 'even as a boy at school, by his love of political discussions, and many were the sacrifices he made in after life on this account; but he held fast his opinions on the subject through good report and evil report, never swerving to the right hand or the left.'

In one of his letters to Mrs. Baillie from the University, written in 1799, occurs the following passage, which shows that he held firm to the faith at Cambridge, as he had done at Eton, and as he did throughout the whole long course of his public life. 'The great Dr. Parr,' he writes, 'has been here lately, and received a great deal of attention from all the heads of houses, &c. It is a great comfort to see a man of such pre-eminent learning and intellectual ability still attached to rational liberty, and to the principles of the *praised and undermined* British Constitution.'

Mrs. Baillie is inclined to attribute some portion of his steady and decided Liberal tendencies to the influence of his first teacher, Mrs. Barbauld; and it is certainly possible, in the case of so forward and thoughtful a child, that even at that early age 'the seeds were sown,' as Mrs. Baillie expresses it, 'of that love of liberty and abhorrence of political oppression which he felt so strongly in after life,' but, as she sensibly adds, ' it should also be remembered that my brother's nearest connexions had almost universally adopted the same principles. His father was a staunch Whig, and his maternal uncle, the Rev. Mr. Brodie, always supported similar political opinions. Mr. Brodie, indeed, was not only politically but personally attached to Mr. Fox (Lord Holland, it may be remembered, had given him his living of Winterslow), and it was probably from him that my brother acquired that warm admiration of this great statesman that he never afterwards ceased to feel.'

To the mental and moral characteristics of Denman as a young man should be added the physical. He possessed in youth, and, indeed, throughout life, very considerable personal advantages. Mrs. Baillie says ' he greatly resembled the mother he loved so much, and the beauty of whose old age will so long be remembered.' His countenance was very expressive; the features high and strongly marked, but well-formed and handsome, the whole face conveying an expression of sweetness combined with power. He was about five feet eleven inches in height, spare and strong in frame, capable and fond of vigorous exertion, as is proved by his having more than once while at Cambridge walked thence to London, with his friend Shadwell, in little more than twelve hours, including stoppages—thus keeping up for the whole distance of somewhat over fifty miles, an average rate of more than four miles an hour. Among his physical advantages must not be forgotten his possession of a voice magnificent in its depth and compass, singularly musical in its modulations, and capable of adapting itself to all moods, whether of pity and tenderness, or anger and scorn.

The principal thing that struck you in his personal appearance was his remarkable air of distinction ; ' on his unembarrassed brow Nature had written gentleman.' 'His appearance,' says Mrs. Baillie, and what she says is quite free from exaggeration or the over partiality of a sister, ' was that of *a gentleman in a remarkable degree;* and I really do not think he could have been placed in any situation or in any circumstance where that would not have been at once perceived and acknowledged.'

The next thing most striking about him was a certain very winning combination of gentleness and power, sweetness and force. ' Always quite simple and unassuming,' writes Mrs. Baillie, ' and free from all affectation, he had in youth a degree of diffidence, sometimes even of shyness, which is often found with sensibility of character.' [6] ' But,' adds his sister, 'gentle and unassuming as he was, there was about him a *striking expression of one born to command.*' He was in fact a man that almost everybody liked, and that nobody could take an unwarrantable liberty with. Among men, though frank and cordial with his intimates, his manner with those not so well known to him was apt to be reserved and somewhat stately; but in

---

[6] So much was this the case that an old Chancery barrister, meeting him once at Rockingham Castle, shortly before his call to the Bar, declared that he could never succeed in his profession ' as he had not brass enough.'

the society of women he had uniformly a manly and chivalrous gentleness of demeanour, which, without effort, was sure to charm.

Of the correspondence between Denman while at Cambridge and his parents a few relics have been preserved, from which the following passages may be extracted.

In a letter to his mother, of February 19, 1799, he writes :—

You must attribute my delay in answering your letters to the old cause, viz. want of materials. College life is at the best too uniform to give any scope to the powers of invention; and now that the snow blockades us so that we can hardly creep out of our rooms we really have nothing to tell. It is, as my father used to say, excellent weather for study. I work all day, and in the evening play chess with Merivale—that is the entire history of my proceedings.

Some time ago a proposal was made to the Senate that degrees in honours should be conferred in this university for knowledge in other subjects besides mathematics. The proposal, without being even debated, was immediately rejected by the Caput.[7] This is all the news of the place.

The violent agitation which the question of our union with Ireland seems to have excited elsewhere has had but little effect upon the torpor which reigns here; and the destruction of Naples[8] is listened to with perfect indifference; but a good deal of curiosity is excited by the mail, owing to the snow, being drawn by six horses.

In the summer of the same year (June 25, 1799), he writes to his father in a way which shows how eager

[7] The Classical Tripos at Cambridge was not established till 1824.

[8] Downfall of the Parthenopean Republic and restoration of the Bourbons in 1799.

and personal an interest the excellent Doctor continued to take in the progress of his son's studies :—

I have, according to your desire, read 'Paterculus' History,' which I found a pleasing and spirited compendium of the history of Rome from its foundation to the sixteenth year of Tiberius. This history, however, in which nothing is related but bare facts, without much attention to their causes, and in which their connection is less noticed than their order, necessarily seems very meagre after the full, liberal, and manly details of Tacitus : who had besides the advantage of living so much after the times of which he wrote, that information was more plentiful, and impartiality less dangerous.

I believe that the particular passage to which you refer in Paterculus is an anecdote which throws a strong light on the ignorance and want of taste of Mummius, the commander under whom Corinth was destroyed. Observing that the ancient vases found there were very much valued, he gave orders that any one who broke any of them should provide a *new* one in its place.

I flatter myself I have profited by the 'Diversions of Purley,'[9] in which I think I see enough to make me admit the author's system, though I regretted very much my ignorance of the Anglo-Saxon language and others connected with it, which prevented my discovering the force of the proofs in many of the particular instances. If you are not acquainted with his general doctrine and mode of reasoning, it will give me great pleasure to make an abstract of the work for your perusal. Whenever I read a Scottish ballad (in which dialect the Saxon element has been much less contaminated than in our own), I always find some additional confirmation of his theory.

In the course of the same year the good Doctor writes to his son a letter which places in a strong light the

---

[9] Horne Tooke's celebrated work.

yearning of the father for union in taste and sympathy with his son, and his ardent desire to make that son, as he frankly admits, the 'wisest and best of mankind.'

Commencing with some disparaging observations on Goldsmith's 'flimsiness' as an historian, which need not be reproduced, he continues thus :—

When you talk of Horace, you take me somewhat out of my element, but I must confess to you that I think him the most instructive, the most elegant, and—what word shall I use besides ?—the most apposite writer that ever lived. The line you quote is beautiful. His 'Fortuna sævo læta negotio:' his 'Quoties me reficit gelidus Digentia rivus' and many, many others, show how much he strove to compose his mind, and the proper estimate and use he made of the means of human happiness. They are delightful reflections, but the only thing I should fear would be that those sentiments may have too great influence on *young* minds. Old age may be and ought to be contented, and it is a proof of want of understanding in an old man, if he has not got all he wants, not to suit his mind to what he has, ' *sit mihi quod nunc est, etiam minus,* &c. ; but youth is to acquire, to improve, to exert, to persevere, to keep in constant view the means by which the human mind may be made as perfect as possible, and when made thus perfect, to be exercised in all its excellencies, to learn the best methods of using its power, to bear disappointments and misfortunes with becoming fortitude, to check its appetites for personal indulgence, to correct its errors in their very beginning, to carry ourselves, if we are fortunate, with equanimity and proper condescension. For every one of these things there is a rule in Horace expressed in the happiest manner; but this you know better than I do.

Our correspondence is founded on the basis of this expectation, that you by your acquirements and by your conduct are to repair all the errors I may have committed, and all the deficiencies I have had. You are to be my proxy. The very reflection is pleasant to my feelings. *I wish it were in my power to make you the wisest and best man that ever lived;* but as that is not in my power, what is offered by me is not to be in the way of dictation or direction, but as submitted to your own consideration and judgment.

It is impossible not to be touched by the simple-hearted and single-minded sincerity with which this kind and good father seeks to give his son the benefit of his wisdom and experience, with the frank bearing of a friend, and somewhat even of the humility of one conscious of the inferior advantages of his own education.

Towards the close of Denman's university career it became only too evident to him that he should be unable to take such mathematical honours as were necessary to entitle him to compete for classical distinctions.[10]

He had, unfortunately, an extreme distaste for the study of pure mathematics; and his inability to overcome this was the cause of his leaving Cambridge, greatly to his father's disappointment, with only an ordinary degree. It was not only that he wanted head for mathematics (as he probably did), but he despised and disliked the study of them, as repulsive in itself, and alien from all the purposes of practical life.

Writing to his sister, Mrs. Baillie, in the latter part of 1798, he says:

You need not be afraid of my applying too intensely to mathematical studies. I was never fond of them, and it

---

[10] No one could then compete for the Chancellor's Medals who was no at least a Senior Optime.

seems to me rather preposterous that the whole of the ensuing year should be entirely given up to that which will be of no use in future life, and which must prevent me from attending to other things highly useful. Academical honours are perhaps too dearly bought at such a sacrifice.

His friend Launcelot Shadwell, who took his degree in the same year with himself (1800), was seventh wrangler and second chancellor's medallist. In a letter written to his sister soon after the publication of the Tripos, he thus adverts to his friend's position in it.

Shadwell, whom we all expected to be first or second wrangler, had not read enough pure mathematics (i.e. *free from all alloy of usefulness*), and has studied only Newton, so he is but seventh.

The following passage from the same letter will serve to show the manly spirit with which he bore up under his own failure:

You have heard, my dear sister, by this time that your wishes and exhortations have all been fruitless; it is in vain that you have decked with golden hues your ' castles in the air.' All my views of ambition are at an end, and you must be content to see poor Tom Denman merely as a brother, without any medal to adorn him, or any honours to recommend him.

I must own that I feel this disappointment more on their account whose expectations I have (perhaps imprudently) raised too high, than on my own, for I had but little right to hope for success where mathematics were in any degree concerned. As it is (he continues), I shall see you so much the sooner, and be free from a long suspense and a disagreeable residence after my friends are gone; but (he adds), I fear that my father will be very much mortified by the recital I have sent him without any reserve ; and as to *you*, I shall be afraid of looking you in the face for some time yet.

Dr. Denman *was* mortified, but like a wise man and a kind father, he at once resolved to make the best of the inevitable.

The following passage from a spirited copy of verses, composed by Denman just before he took his degree, shows the same feeling of dislike and contempt for mathematics, and indicates the nature of his own favourite studies and pursuits while at the University:—

> Where Dulness reigns despotic and serene
> And willing Seniors bow before the Queen,
> While youthful slaves with baneful labours pine
> And delve for dross in mathematic mine ;
> Where the grave gownsman sleeps o'er Dido's love
> And, yawning, asks what Virgil meant to prove ;
> Where all the truths divine by Plato taught
> And all that Horace sung and Tully thought
> Are doomed in close obscurity to lie,
> Scorned for the withered forms of x and y ;—
> I love the bold excursive thoughts that stray
> Where joyous Fancy points a fairer way ;
> I love the soul which free and unconfined
> Roams o'er the world and feels for all mankind,
> Which dares untutored to reflect, nor shrinks
> Bribed or subdued from uttering all it thinks.—
> Though the young censure, and the sages sneer,
> In Reason's cause undaunted persevere,
> Though they should blot thy name with deepest dye
> Of the foul charge of Singularity ;
> Though no snug fellowship shall be the meed
> Of thy exertions, dreadless yet proceed ;
> Nor think that fame and profit can atone
> For the sad ruins of a mind o'erthrown.

In another copy of verses written about the same time, after mentioning his failure to secure University distinctions, he refers with pride to the success with which he had hidden

> Each bitter sigh that rose
> For disappointed friends and joyful foes,

and to the elasticity with which his

> Long-pent soul more nimbly rose again,
> Broke college chains and burned to mix with men.[11]

His longing to mingle in the real scenes of life, in the tumult of action, was soon gratified. Immediately after taking his degree he left Cambridge for London, there to commence the career which, after arduous but successful labours, conducted him to the highest honours of his profession, and earned for him a name which the world ' will not willingly let die.'

[11] Both the copies of verses from which the above are extracts will be found in Appendix No. II.

CHAPTER III.

LAW STUDIES—SPECIAL PLEADING—MARRIAGE.

A.D. 1800 TO 1804.   ÆT. 21–25.

Denman commences his legal studies, April, 1800—In chambers with
Merivale at Featherstone Buildings, Holborn—A pupil of Charles
Butler—Works hard at real property law—Separate chambers at 25
Old Square, Lincoln's Inn—Pupil of Dampier, and of Tidd—His diligence as a law student—In 1803 begins practice as a Special Pleader
—His first legal employment—Denman keeps up his school and
college friendships—Merivale—Shadwell—Bland—Hodgson—Drury,
&c.—The Rev. Robert Bland—His talent and wild wit—His intimacy
with Byron—His marriage—Richard William Vevers—The serio-
comic 'training of Vevers'—Letter from Bland to Denman, 1803—
Bland at Old Burlington Street, 1803—Dr. and Mrs. Denman on the
virtues of their son—Epistles in verse to Denman from Hodgson and
Drury—'Dear lawless democrat with dreadful brow'—Hodgson and
Drury both friends of Byron—A dining club established by Denman
and his friends—Letter from Bland at Eton to Denman, 1804—John
Herman Merivale the most intimate of all Denman's friends—Early
letters from Merivale to Denman—Merivale in love with Miss Louisa
Drury—Denman falls in love at first sight with Miss Theodosia Vevers
—Parentage and family of Miss Vevers—Her maternal connexions—
Lord Sondes of Rockingham Castle—The Anderson family—Age of
Miss Vevers at marriage—Merivale to Denman on the prospects of his
courtship—A young lawyer's notion of wedded bliss in 1804—'Plain
living and high thinking'—Dr. Denman consents—Extracts of letters
from Denman to Miss Vevers—They are married at Saxby Church,
Oct. 18, 1804—Honeymoon spent at Rockingham Castle—'Aunt
Annie's account of the wedding—Congratulatory letters—Note from
'Fanny Anderson,' born Nelthorpe—Letter from Denman's mother to
his bride—First London residence of the young couple—Dr. Denman's
allowance of 400l. a year—Dr. Joseph Denman displeased at the match
—Correspondence on the subject betwen him and Dr. Baillie—Dr.
Baillie's letter to Dr. J. Denman of Oct. 15, 1804—Dr. J. Denman's

ON leaving the University, Denman resided for some little time with his father and mother in Old Burlington Street. In April 1800, he took rooms with his friend Merivale, in Featherstone Buildings, Holborn, and commenced his legal studies as pupil of the eminent real property lawyer Charles Butler, not unknown in literature as author of ' the Book of the Catholic Church,' and of the ' Lives of Bossuet and Fenelon.'

Here the ex-Cambridge student worked hard and honestly in mastering the elements of our intricate systems of land-tenure and conveyancing, at ' Coke on Littleton,' Gilbert on Uses, the rule in Shelley's case, and the subtle refinements of Contingent Remainders —studies certainly not less abstruse and arid than those mathematical ones which had repelled him at the University, but possessing for his sound and practical understanding the recommendation, which the others wanted, of being directly and visibly connected with the business of his future professional life.

In 1801 Dr. Denman purchased for him a set of chambers at 25 Old Square, Lincoln's Inn. In the same year he became a pupil of Mr. Dampier, an excellent lawyer, afterwards a Judge of the Court of King's Bench,[1] and, in 1802, he was admitted into the

[1] Mr. Dampier said of Denman that he was the only pupil he ever had who studied ' Coke upon Littleton ' of his own accord and with liking.

chambers of that famous pundit in the science of
Special Pleading, the veteran Tidd, author of the
opus magnum 'Tidd's Practice,' and teacher of a long
line of pupils afterwards illustrious in the law, including at least two future Chancellors—Lord Cottenham and Lord Campbell.

His industry and zeal during these three years of
legal study are attested by sundry manuscript folios,
filled not only with forms and precedents, but with
painstaking abstracts and summaries of various branches
of the Common Law.

In 1803 Denman took a clerk and commenced
practice as a Special Pleader on his own account.
His mother, from whose careful and exact memoranda
the above particulars have been obtained, has recorded
with characteristic punctuality, and natural gratification, the date of her son's first legal employment. 'On
December 13, 1803,' she writes, 'Mr. Alexander, an
attorney with whom Mr. Croft was connected in
business appointed Thomas Denman the younger his
Special Pleader; this was a joyful event to himself
and all his friends, and we humbly trust that the
opportunity he now has of making his talents known
will secure him the good opinion of his employer, and
lead him to a reasonable share of business.'

It is probable that Mrs. Denman, mother as she was,
was hardly sanguine enough to hope that she should
herself yet live to see the young protegé of Mr.
Alexander presiding in Westminster Hall as Lord
Chief Justice of England.

Denman, though working hard at his profession, kept up a close and constant intercourse and correspondence not only with Merivale and Shadwell, who were, like himself, 'apprentices at the law,' but also with those other joyous and congenial spirits, such as Bland, Hodgson, and Drury, who, with their wit, merriment and learning, had enlivened his days and nights at St. John's, and who were now, with an ultimate view to orders, either engaged in the drudgery of tuition at Harrow or Eton, or still enjoying the pleasures of literary lounging at the University. It is a matter of regret that none of Denman's own letters of this period have been preserved, but a few passages may be given from those of his friends.

Bland—'Anthology Bland'[2]—an erratic character full of fun and talent, is the liveliest of all these correspondents. The following passage in a letter written by him in 1803, from Harrow (where Bland was then one of the under-masters), illustrates the characters of many of Denman's early associates, and introduces us to one of his college friends not yet named, Richard William Vevers, the brother of the lady who soon afterwards became his wife. It is of course hardly necessary to observe that the whole passage is a grave

---

[2] The Rev. Robert Bland, editor of the 'Greek Anthology.' He was one of the under-masters of Harrow, while Byron was at the school. Byron, as his diaries of that date prove, was in the habit of frequently seeing Bland, even after 'Childe Harold,' in 1812, 1813, and 1814. Bland published several poems by no means without merit: 'Edwy and Elgiva,' 'The Four Slaves of Cythera,' &c., &c. Bland, as elsewhere mentioned, became by his marriage with one of the Miss Tayleurs a brother-in-law of Hodgson and Drury.

piece of irony, and that all the characters are to be taken *per contra.* The serio-comic suggestion of the writer is that the whole set should interest themselves in the moral and social development of Vevers, who was evidently a great favourite with them all.

You (Denman) shall be head and director of everything, leaving the minor points to me, Hodgson, Drury, &c. Suppose you teach him loyalty and respect for the king and every person placed in authority under him; Hodgson, a regard to the opinion of the world; Drury, dancing and moderation in wine; Hawtrey,[3] good-natured remarks on men and manners; Paley,[4] respectability and a deference for respectable people; Merivale, profound contemplation, and how to give a decisive opinion of his own on every subject; myself, innocent hilarity, and how to come into and go out of a room before any number of people; and all of us together, *punctuality in money matters !*

The same letter contains a few words which throw a transient gleam of light into the interior of the house in Old Burlington Street.

I dined at Dr. Denman's on Saturday : you have no idea how he launched out on your character, and Mrs. Denman too; how you were the best, the wisest, the most this, the most that. Had I not possessed the sweetest of tempers, I must have died with envy on the spot. I insinuated a few things, such as that youth, however wise it may seem to age, acts under a screen, and under that screen does many wry actions. It wouldn't go down : I was fairly hissed off.

---

[3] Head Master and Provost of Eton—the latter in succession to Hodgson. Hawtrey's refined fastidiousness made him, as a young man, somewhat censorious.

[4] Author of a book well known to lawyers, ' Paley on Convictions.'

Francis Hodgson[5] and Henry Drury[6] are frequent correspondents, occasionally in Latin and English verse, for which both had great and almost equal facility. A line from one of Henry Drury's rhyming epistles is characteristic. He addresses Denman as

thou
Dear lawless Democrat with dreadful brow,

thus happily enough hitting off the known latitude of his friend's political opinions, and that lofty severity of expression which in moments of just indignation would suddenly darken like a thunder-cloud over the brow of the ardent young Liberal.

The friends, after the cheerful fashion of those days, got up a dining club, which seems to have met generally in London, but sometimes at Harrow, and occasionally even at Eton, and of which the symposia, judging from the references to them in the letters, would appear to have been sufficiently joyous. Bland, with his fantastic wit and frolic, was generally the animating spirit of the company. The following passage from a letter of Bland's to Denman, dashed off by him while on a visit to Eton, where Hodgson seems then to have been engaged in tuition, will show the mettle

---

[5] Translator of Juvenal and author of several poems; Archdeacon of Derbyshire 1836; married, as his second wife, to Denman's second daughter, 1838; Provost of Eton 1840. Hodgson was on most intimate terms with Byron, who, on an occasion mentioned by Moore, behaved to him with princely generosity. It is to Hodgson that the great poet, on leaving England, addressed the well-known lines:

' Huzza, Hodgson, we are going.'

[6] One of the under-masters of Harrow, and also a friend and correspondent of Byron's. He was brother-in-law, through his sister, to Merivale, and also, through his wife, to Bland and Hodgson.

of the man, his normal state of indebtedness, his wild and reckless spirits, and the boundless affluence of his literary projects:

Eton, March 18, 1804.

With the very little drop of ink remaining in the horn, after the two epic poems, the six periodical papers, besides several epigrams, anagrams, and other things ending in '*grams*,' and an infinite number of songs, sonnets, rebusses, pasquinades, and some things 'unattempted yet in prose or rhyme,' which Hodgson has written since breakfast up to this hour—twelve o'clock—(not forgetting construing his boys, and answering duns)—with that very little drop of ink remaining, I have to request of you, Denman, to order Merry's (Merivale's) rooms to be opened, with sheets aired and a fire, on next Tuesday. You know not how many devices I have formed for ridding myself of encumbrances. Besides writing in journals, for which I intend to be paid three guineas a day, which, you know, at eight and fourpence per column would only amount to about seven columns and a half, I am seriously thinking of a scheme which would bring me in a clear 2,000*l*. For it is as clear as day that if I publish 'Edwy'[7] by subscription, and have 2,000 subscribers at one guinea the copy, I shall have gained 2,000*l*., after allowing 50*l*. for expenses in publishing. Hodgson is writing opposite to me in measured English, and has absolutely distanced me, who write almost in a desultory style. But then you must take into consideration the depth of accounts and calculation which must have impeded the progress of my pen. Oh! had you seen my father yesterday, musing in silent astonishment and with a countenance more in sorrow than in anger, over the dilapidated state of my finances. Let me hear from you if Burdett[8] and Vevers will let you write. Adieu,

R. B.

[7] His poem, subsequently published, though not by subscription, of 'Edwy and Elgiva.'

[8] Sir Francis. His career as an ultra-Liberal had begun two years

But of all Denman's early friends, the nearest and dearest was the accomplished John Herman Merivale, who, in town, was his constant companion, and who had for a time, as already mentioned, shared chambers with him before Denman took up separate quarters in Old Square. Merivale's letters during his occasional absences from London, in the Long Vacations and on circuit (for he had been early called to the Bar), are frequent and amusing, though, being written with the freedom of the age, the profession, and of the times, they are occasionally not of a kind to bear extensive quotation in these more decorous days. Towards the close of the Long Vacation of 1804, however, they began to take a graver tone, and to be occupied with subjects of a more romantic interest. Himself in love with the lady he soon afterwards married,[9] Merivale is in correspondence with his more ardent and impetuous friend on the rapid progress of that friend's attachment to the beautiful sister of their intimate college companion, Vevers.

The 'lawless Democrat with dreadful brow' had become entangled in the toils of love. Having gone down, in the course of the summer, to spend a few days at the house of his young friend's father, the Rev. Richard Vevers, of Saxby, near Melton Mowbray, in

before this with the Middlesex election of 1802, when he was unseated on petition. Denman was, at this time, much interested in his political doings.

[9] Louisa, daughter of Dr. Drury, the Head-master of Harrow, and sister of Merivale's and Denman's old friend Henry Drury. Death has only recently removed this excellent and accomplished lady. Dr. Drury had a country residence near Exeter, not far from the seat of the Merivale family at Barton Place.

Leicestershire, Denman had fallen in love at first sight with the beautiful eldest daughter of his host, Miss Theodosia Anne Vevers, a young lady rich in virtues and graces, well—indeed on the mother's side rather highly—connected, but with little or no fortune, either in possession or prospect.[10]

'To no one,' writes Merivale to Denman in September 1804, 'have I given a hint of your situation except to her who is *plus quam dimidia mei* [that is of course to Miss Lousia Drury]: she enters warmly into your interests; quite romantically approves your love at first sight (about which I sometimes dispute with her against you), and always augurs success. You are frequently the subject of our *tête-à-tête* discussions, and we often draw delightful pictures of large bonnets in the pit, and *parties quarrées* of whist in Chancery Lane.'

Pleasant indications these of a homelier and happier time, when 'plain living and high thinking' had not yet gone utterly out of fashion, nor the progress of luxury made early marriages with portionless brides all

---

[10] The mother of Miss Vevers (Theodosia Dorothy) was daughter of Sir William Anderson, of Lea Hall, near Gainsborough, in Lincolnshire, the sixth baronet. Miss Vevers' grandmother, Sir William's wife, had been a Miss Maddison, sister of the first Lady Sondes of Rockingham Castle: hence the friendship between Rockingham Castle and Saxby Parsonage. The Andersons are a good old family; one of the stock, Sir Edmund Anderson, Knt., was Lord Chief Justice of the Common Pleas, in the days of Elizabeth and James, from 1582 to 1605. His grandson, Sir Edmund Anderson, was created a baronet at the Stuart Restoration, 1660; and an uninterrupted line of heirs male has since continued the race: the present is the ninth baronet. Lady Denman, born in November 1779, the same year as her husband, was in her twenty-fifth year at the time of her marriage.

but impossible for young men of the higher professional classes.

' I am impatient,' continues Merivale, ' to know what will be your father's answer to your important communication [the ardent young lover had lost no time in taking his father into his confidence], but, unless I much mistake him, he will in a short time be rather pleased at your having formed a connexion of this kind, than dissatisfied with the poor prospects in point of fortune that it presents.'

Mr. Merivale was perfectly right in his anticipations ; Dr. and Mrs. Denman soon gave their cordial consent to the union. On October 3, Denman writes to Miss Vevers, after returning to town from Saxby :

I have now seen all my immediate connections. Nothing can be more cordial than their conduct on the occasion. My father and mother, from whose house I am writing, desire to be most kindly remembered to your family, and they are all as impatient to be acquainted with you as I am to introduce you to them. I shall write to Mr. Vevers as soon as I can fix a time for returning to Saxby, which you may be sure I shall accelerate to the utmost.

Ever yours, with the truest affection,

THOMAS DENMAN.

A few days later he writes again :—

My own feelings make me confident that we shall love one another well enough to live very happily on a little. It seems a difficult matter to find a proper house, which, if we fail to do, there is the alternative of living in lodgings or living for some time at my father's. It is needless to give any opinion on these plans till we meet, but I shall strain every nerve, and employ several persons to prosecute the

enquiry after a house.   If it is not immediately in the neighbourhood of the Inns of Court, a little walk will be so much
the better.   All my friends will be willing to exert themselves in the kindest manner, and, indeed they have never
seemed to possess half so strong a claim to my affection as
since they have shown such cordial promptitude to welcome
you.   My business was fortunately of a nature that required
no very intense application, so I got through it yesterday,
and now nothing detains me but the possibility of some
commission from Saxby.   I shall stay till Monday, to give
the whole family a fair chance, and that evening take the
mail to Oakham, where your brother may bring the gig, if
he pleases ; if not, I shall walk over. I feel I have no business
to be anywhere but with you.   Farewell till we meet.   Give
my love to all your family, and believe me ever affectionately
yours.

All the arrangements for the marriage were pushed
forward by the young lover with characteristic energy ;
and before the end of the Long Vacation—on
October 18, 1804—Thomas Denman the younger and
Theodosia Vevers became man and wife.

The ceremony was performed at Saxby church, and
the honeymoon was spent at Rockingham Castle.[11]
Should this memoir be fortunate enough to find any
readers among the fairer sex, they may, perhaps, be
amused by the following recollections of the wedding,
communicated many long years afterwards by one of
the bride's sisters, Miss Annie Vevers (Aunt Annie), for
the amusement of her nieces, the daughters of the bride
and bridegroom.[12]

[11] The seat of Lord Sondes in Northamptonshire.   The connexion
between the Vevers family and the Lords of Rockingham Castle has been
explained in the preceding note.

[12] The communication was addressed to Lord Denman's third daughter,

I send you but a very hurried, brief sketch of your beloved father's and mother's wedding. First, the bride and bridegroom, looking so charming—the first attired in pure white, with train twenty-four inches long, and most costly lace cap sent by dear Lady Croft.[13] They were followed by six blooming young bridesmaids, the youngest under six years of age, attired in white, with white ribbons and cockades round their heads; then brothers dearest Richard and Charles. The former gave the lovely bride away, and dear father united them. The church door was locked, but crowds got wind of it, and peeped in at the church windows. It happened to rain a little just before the wedding, and the lovely bride was in the twinkling of an eye nipped up by the adoring bridegroom, and so carried to church. As they came out of church 'Good lack! what a handsome couple!' 'Good lack a day! what a beautiful bride!' came from all the church-yard, which was by that time brim full. Then, after luncheon, came the chaise and four with favours, and the happy pair flew off for dear old Rockingham Castle, where they spent such a happy fortnight—horses ready at the door to ride out upon, no housekeeping, and such sumptuous doings. After they left we girls (after shedding fountains of tears at parting) cheered up and began singing.

A few old letters of congratulation on this marriage of almost seventy years ago have been preserved; among them a kind one to Denman from Lord Lovaine, already mentioned in Merivale's diary as an old school and college friend; a glowing epithalamium in heroic verse from the ever facile pen of the warm-hearted Francis Hodgson; and a few lines to the bride from

Fanny, now the Hon. Lady Baynes. Its kindly and genial writer is still alive.

[13] Lord Denman's sister Margaret, Mrs. Croft in 1804, not Lady Croft till 1816, when her husband succeeded to the baronetcy.

Fanny, daughter of Sir John Nelthorpe, herself then recently married to the Rev. Sir Charles Anderson, of Lea Hall, one of the maternal uncles of Theodosia Vevers.[14] This note, by a young married lady of Miss Austen's day and school, seems charming in its natural grace and simplicity—the fresh young thoughts in strange contrast with the faded yellow paper on which they are traced.

Lea: October 4, 1804.

My dearest Theodosia,—The contents of your father's letter have indeed given us all the greatest pleasure, and most sincerely do I wish you every possible happiness this world can afford. I wish you may be as happy as I am, and I cannot wish you better, were I to wish for ever. We shall be delighted to see Richard and his friend. I think I once remember seeing him at your house in Gower Street. I shall expect to hear from you very soon, and let me know a little of your future plans. I write in great haste, but would not let a day pass without telling you how happy we all are. I do assure you I have not heard anything which has given me so much pleasure a long, long time. God bless you, my dearest girl! every possible happiness attend you! My kindest love and congratulations to all.

Ever yours most affectionately and sincerely,

FANNY ANDERSON.

I am going on very well. I *tell you this* because I *know* you will be *glad to hear it.*

The following from Denman's mother, written two

---

[14] This lady was mother of the present (the ninth) baronet, Sir Charles Henry Anderson, born at Lea Hall soon after this letter was written. Sir Charles (Lady Denman's uncle), the eighth baronet, was the youngest son of his father, and succeeded to the baronetcy after the death of his elder brothers, one of whom, Sir Edmund, was the seventh baronet. Sir Charles was not more than ten or twelve years older than his niece, Lady Denman. While still a younger son he had taken orders.

days after the marriage, and addressed to the bride at Rockingham Castle, is very characteristic :

Mount Street, October 20, 1804.[15]

Accept, my dear daughter, our very sincere and most hearty congratulations on your marriage with our dear son. We hope and trust he will acquit himself well in his new relationship. Hitherto he has certainly conducted himself in such a manner as to secure the esteem and love of all his connections, and therefore I must needs say your prospect is a good one. We are very busy putting your house in order, and hope by the beginning of next week to have it a comfortable habitation for yourself and your good husband, and then we hope you will soon take possession of it. Pray tell your husband that he has had business from two quarters sent to him on his wedding day, and this we consider as a happy omen. On the first of next month [16] we hope yourself and husband will join our festive meeting; it is a day from which we date our choicest blessings, and its value will be greatly enhanced this year by the addition of your presence. I look forward with the greatest pleasure to our meeting, and am, with the sincerest regard,

Your truly affectionate mother,
ELIZABETH DENMAN.

The house referred to in Mrs. Denman's letter was a small one in Gloucester Street, Queen's Square, Bloomsbury, which, for a few years, formed the first London residence of the young couple. Dr. Denman made them an allowance of about 400*l.* a year, which in those days of heavy taxation and high war prices, was,

---

[15] Dr. Denman had shortly before this time changed his quarters from Old Burlington Street to Mount Street, where he continued to reside till his death.

[16] The anniversary of the wedding-day of Dr. and Mrs. Denman : they had now been married thirty-four years, and were aged respectively seventy-one and fifty-eight.

notwithstanding the far greater simplicity in the style of living, by no means an income which in any way dispensed with the necessity of vigorous professional exertion.

Dr. Joseph Denman, the uncle of the bridegroom, who, by care and frugality, had got together a fair amount of wealth, which, as he was without 'lawful issue' himself, it might naturally be supposed would ultimately be divided among his brother's children, appears to have been by no means too well pleased with the match. His brother, Thomas, seems to have written to him with a view of ascertaining whether he was disposed at once to do something for the young couple; and in consequence of this communication Dr. Joseph wrote to Dr. Baillie, the husband of his niece Sophia, expressing, as it would appear, in strong terms his sense of the imprudence of his nephew's marriage.   This letter has not been preserved; but the two following, from Dr. Baillie to his wife's uncle, do so much honour to the writer, and show so clearly the then position of the family and of the young people, that they are reprinted without abridgment.

The first, which is dated three days before the wedding, is evidently in answer to the letter from Dr. Joseph Denman, to which reference has just been made :—

October 15, 1804.

Dear Sir,—I received the favour of your obliging letter a few days ago, and I cannot help being highly gratified by the expressions of your good opinion, and the confidence you are disposed to place in me.   I shall endeavour not to abuse that confidence, but will reply to the subject of your interesting letter with the utmost sincerity.

There can be no doubt that your nephew, from his situation, his education, his prospects, and his talents, had a fair claim to marry a lady of good connections, of accomplishments, and with a fortune of ten or even fifteen thousand pounds. In such a marriage he might have been fortunate with respect to the good qualities of the lady herself, and he might have begun life in a higher position.

It is very doubtful, however, under such circumstances, whether he would have been sufficiently stimulated to exertion—whether he would not have rested too much upon his present ease and his future prospects.

In his present choice we trust that he has been fortunate as to the lady herself. From every quarter we hear a decidedly good account of her, and she is related to people of higher rank and fortune than the children of clergymen commonly are. There appears, therefore, in this marriage to be no defect but that of fortune.

As your nephew has chosen her entirely from his conviction of her merits, and for her personal appearance, his attachment is likely to remain more steady, and he will have every motive which can influence an honourable mind for making exertions in his profession. This feeling may lead him to much more professional eminence, and ultimately to more fortune than if he had begun life under more easy circumstances.

I am well aware that he ought to feel some difficulties, so as to be an uniform stimulus to his activity; but they should not be such as to depress his mind, or as to be unsuitable to the respectable position in the world which all his immediate relations fortunately hold. The allowance which his father intends to make him is, I understand, 400*l.* per annum. It can be calculated that this sum is not more than enough to cover the bare expenses of his house, even in the most frugal way of living, without clothes or the accidental daily expenses which must inevitably take place. The gains of his profession for the first two or three years must be very trifling, and therefore your nephew must be exposed to struggle with difficulties which are not suited to the situation which he holds.

I forbear to say any more on this subject. I know your attachment to him, and the generosity of your disposition when any proper occasion calls it forth. Your brother was certainly a little premature in writing to you upon this very delicate subject, but he was led to it in some measure by what you had said to him in one of your letters a few months ago.

You have gratified me exceedingly by the very affectionate manner in which you have expressed yourself with regard to my wife. Indeed, she deserves it all, and every day convinces me more and more how fortunate I have been in my choice. Both she and her sister would always put a high value upon any proof of your affection which you might be pleased to bestow upon them; but they would be extremely hurt if this should affect in any material degree the situation of their brother, who is the representative of the family, and to whom they look up not only with affection, but pride. In these sentiments I hope it is not necessary to say that Mr. Croft [17] and myself most entirely concur.

I have nothing more to say upon this interesting and delicate subject. In reply to your letter I have expressed my sentiments with frankness and sincerity, but I hope in a manner not unsuitable to the relative situation which we hold with respect to each other. Mrs. Baillie sends her most affectionate regards to you, and I remain, dear sir, with much esteem,

Yours most faithfully,
M. BAILLIE.

In answer to this, Dr. Joseph Denman, on October 27, after stating in general terms that he did not feel disposed immediately to alter in his nephew's favour the disposition he had already made of his property, inti-

---

[17] Afterwards Sir Richard.

mated his intention of at once bestowing in free gift upon Dr. Baillie and his wife the fee simple of a small estate, worth about 2,000*l*., adding, ' I feel highly gratified at the reflection that I have had it in my power thus to show my great attachment to and sincere affection for two persons who are an honour to their friends and a blessing to society.'

Dr. Baillie's answer is as follows :

Oct. 30, 1804.

My dear Sir,—I will not attempt to express the feelings which your last letter has excited in me. It is not enough to say that I feel most grateful for your uncommon liberality towards me; but I am more particularly affected by the motive from which it has arisen, and by a display of character on your part of which there have been few examples. I sincerely hope that no part of my future conduct will dispose you to repent of this uncommon instance of liberality towards me. It is infinitely beyond what I could have expected, and therefore I request that you will forgive me if I should express a wish that your nephew should in future feel that he is the great object of your benevolence.

I cannot avoid auguring well of this marriage. We have now seen the young lady. She has so much sweetness of manner and loveliness of person that I am sure you would forgive, if you saw her, your nephew for yielding to her charms. If you do not trust to my account, I beg that you will come and see, and then you would give Sophy and myself the highest gratification in thanking you personally for your extraordinary beneficence towards us. Sophy means to express by a letter from herself her sense of your liberality and affection. I shall therefore only add that I remain, dear sir,

Your most grateful and faithful
MATTHEW BAILLIE.

These letters throw great light on the noble character of Dr. Baillie, who, on another occasion, refused to accept of an estate which had been left to him by his relation, the celebrated Dr. John Hunter, because he would not stand in the way of other and still nearer relatives, who were more in need than himself of the testator's bounty.

The event proved the sagacity and correctness of Dr. Baillie's anticipations. The young lady, whose ' sweetness of temper and loveliness of person ' he records, became one of the best wives that man was ever blest with. The union endured for eight and forty years with uninterrupted affection on both sides, and with a rare preservation, even beyond the confines of old age, of a warmth and delicacy of mutual sentiment which to colder and more worldly natures would, at any age, have seemed romantic.

It would, indeed, have been difficult to find a human creature more attractive in person, or more charming in character and manner, than Denman's bride. In youth and early womanhood her beauty was remarkable—of the pure and noble type of Raffael's Madonnas ; light brown hair, large grey eyes of the deepest tenderness, face exquisitely oval, nose slightly, but only very slightly, aquiline. She literally adored her husband—believed in him as the best and wisest of men, and always encouraged him in his firm and noble acts of resistance against what he deemed oppression and wrong ; for, with all her exquisite gentleness, this lady had a high and resolute spirit, not less prompt than her husband's to show itself when a fitting occasion came to call it forth. She was well accomplished after the fashion of that time; had an exquisite taste for music, and no mean skill as a performer on the piano. She did not belie her Leicestershire breeding, and was an admirable and courageous horsewoman. 'It was told me of her,' writes her youngest son, the Hon. and Rev. Lewis Denman [18] (who amid all the duties of a parish priest most admirably performed, has not quite forgotten his old love—hereditary, no doubt—for horses), 'it was told me of her that as a young woman, gentle and quiet though her character was, she could ride hunters belonging to her father which none of the grooms dared mount.' She came of a good and gentle race, and had the qualities and habitudes generally to be found in the well-descended. She was fond of telling her children stories of her ancestors, which she did in a manner that riveted and spell-bound their young attention. 'She was,' says her youngest son, 'a loving, generous, noble character; and, as a mother, we all deeply loved and honoured her.' Her piety, like that of her husband, was deep, sincere, and genuine; not obtrusively showing itself in words, but abiding in the heart, purifying the sentiments, elevating the thoughts, and moulding the life.

The incentives to exertion derived from a numerous and rapidly increasing family were not absent from this auspicious and most happy union. No less than fifteen

---

[18] Rector of Willian, near Hitchin, in Hertfordshire.

children (born between 1804 and 1824) were the fruits of the marriage. Of these four died in childhood; eleven—five sons and six daughters—still survive.[19]

---

[19] For convenience of reference, a table of the late Lord Denman's family, with the respective marriages of his sons and daughters, will be found in Appendix No. I.

CHAPTER IV.

CALL TO BAR—EARLY MARRIED LIFE.

A.D. 1804 TO 1811.   ÆT. 25 TO 32.

Special Pleading—Periodical literature (the ' Monthly Review '), 1804–1806—Cambridge election for Chancellor—Lord Henry Petty—Fox-Grenville administration, Jan. 1806—Denman's devotion to Fox—Letter to Sir F. Burdett shortly after Fox's death—Denman called to the Bar, 1806—Change of residence to No. 5 Queen's Square, Bloomsbury—Joins Midland Circuit and Lincolnshire Sessions—Leading members of Midland Circuit—Mr. Serjeant Vaughan—Mr. Clarke, K.C.—Mr. John Balguy, K.C.—Denman's friends—Reader—Dwarris—Empson—Copley (Lyndhurst) and Francis Horner—Denman's regret at Copley's political apostasy—Denman's early position and progress on Circuit—Extracts from Midland Circuit book relating to him—His first retainer in town—Letter to his wife from Circuit, July 17, 1808—Denman's connexion through Merivale and Bland with the ' Critical Review '—Extract from his notice of Chief Justice Marshall's ' Life of Washington '—Dr. Denman suggests legal publication as a means of professional advancement—Denman's reply, July 6, 1808—Letter of Denman to his wife from Circuit, April 2, 1810—Copley and Denman at Miss Linwood's ball—Walcheren expedition—The money runs short at home—Money difficulties of Denman's earlier professional life—Never famous for prudence or economy—Mrs. Baillie's testimony—Mrs. Hodgson's account—She rather blames Dr. Denman's parsimony—Homely and frugal ways of Dr. Denman and his wife—' One luxury is enough '—The yearly allowance doled out in weekly instalments—Fondness of Dr. and Mrs. Denman for their grandchildren—Mrs. Hodgson's recollections of them—Prizes for being gentlewomen—Primitive simplicity of Dr. and Mrs. Denman's household—Denman as a husband and a father—Mrs. Baillie's recollections—His elevating influence on his daughters— Mrs. Hodgson's recollections of her mother and father—His romps with his girls when children—

FOR about a year and a half after his marriage Denman continued to practise as a special pleader, occasionally picking up a few stray guineas as a contributor to the 'Monthly Review,' which, until superseded by the 'Edinburgh,' had for some time been the leading literary organ of the Whig party.

In the winter of 1806 he went down to Cambridge to vote for Lord Henry Petty (afterwards the third Marquis of Lansdowne) as Chancellor for the University; and on that occasion wrote as follows to his friend Henry Drury, then an under-master at Harrow:

January 27, 1806.

Dear Drury,—At Lord Henry Petty's committee to-day I had news which (considering that both his opponents are Harrow men) is, I fear, too good to be true, viz. that you had promised him your vote. If it be so, *do* exert your influence on the occasion, and let us meet strong at Cambridge, where I rejoice to find that, through a mistake in not taking off my name when I desired it, I still have a vote, and shall certainly go down with Shadwell, Paley, and many others—all for Lord Henry.

I believe it is undoubtedly true that a new administration is formed: Lord Grenville, First Lord of the Treasury; Fox and Grey, Secretaries of State; Lord Spencer to go to Ireland; auspicium melioris ævi.

Pray send me a line by return of post to say we shall meet

at Cambridge and vote for the same able and honourable
man.   Remember me affectionately to Bland, and believe
me

Ever your sincere friend,
THOMAS DENMAN.

I have had a very kind letter from Hodgson.

Denman continued as staunch as ever in his political
devotion to Mr. Fox, and was an ardent supporter of
the new ministry whose formation he had announced
in the preceding letter.   The nature, at this period, of
his political sentiments may be judged of by the following lines, which he wrote to Sir F. Burdett in the
November of the same year, a short time after the
death (Sept. 13, 1806) of the great statesman, of whom
Sir Francis, in a then recently published address to the
electors of Westminster, had spoken in a manner which
Denman could not forgive.

Lincoln's Inn: Nov. 5, 1806.

Dear Sir,—The active part I took at the two last elections
would so naturally produce an expectation of the same
conduct now that I cannot feel justified in adopting a contrary resolution without apprizing you of it.   But the sentiments declared in your advertisement are so completely at
variance with mine that it is impossible for me to vote for
you on the present occasion.

That firm attachment to the principles of Mr. Fox which
first impelled me to the exertions I made in your cause I
still retain, and am convinced that there is no chance of
those principles being acted upon but by the continuance of
the present ministry.

I cannot, therefore, give my vote to a candidate who
grounds his claim on hostility to the present ministry, and
who can, at such a moment, speak lightly of the services and
memory of Mr. Fox.

It is with the most sincere regret that I feel called upon to make this declaration, being as fully satisfied of your integrity and good intentions as I am at this time decidedly hostile to the principles you have assumed.

I have the honour to be, sir,
Your most humble servant,
THOMAS DENMAN, jun.

On May 9, 1806, Denman was called to the bar by the Honourable Society of Lincoln's Inn; and shortly after, moved from Gloucester Street into a neighbouring but considerably larger house, No. 5 Queen's Square, Bloomsbury, where he continued to reside for the next ten or twelve years, until his increased practice enabled him to remove to Russell Square, which in those days was, in point of residence, the ' ne plus ultra ' of a successful barrister's ambition.

Denman, as he naturally would, from the local connexions of his own and his wife's family, joined the Midland Circuit and the Lincolnshire Sessions.

He was introduced to the circuit mess by the well-known Serjeant Vaughan,[1] who with Mr. Clarke the King's Counsel (generally called ' old Clarke,' to distinguish him from his son, then ' young Nat,' since Mr. Serjeant Clarke and County Court Judge for Wolverhampton), was, in those days, one of the leaders of the circuit.[2]   Vaughan was equally celebrated for possess-

---

[1] Born 1768; called to Bar 1791; Serjeant 1790; King's Serjeant 1816; Baron of Exchequer 1827; Judge of Common Pleas 1834; Died 1839, æt. seventy-one.

[2] The celebrated Sir Samuel Romilly had also been, and still nominally remained, a member of the Midland Circuit, but owing to the vast extent of his practice in Chancery for the ten years preceding his death (in 1817) he scarcely ever went round the circuit.

ing not the slightest notion of law, and a bold, rough and ready style of address, which made him a great favourite with juries and a most successful practitioner at Nisi Prius. Of his peculiar kind of eloquence an admirable specimen has been preserved by Mr. Robert Walton, author of an amusing little work, called 'Random Recollections of the Midland Circuit,'[3] to which the present writer is glad to express his obligations. The story shall be given in Mr. Walton's own words :—

In the course of his general reply in a cause tried at Warwick, Vaughan was commenting on his adversary's evidence, the last of whose witnesses was remaining in the box, standing at his ease with his hands in his pockets, apparently enjoying most heartily and laughing at the serjeant's jokes, when, Vaughan's eye lighting upon him, he exclaimed, ' And then we come to Brown ! Ah, there the impudent and deceitful fellow stands, *just like a crocodile, with tears in his eyes and his hands in his breeches pockets !* '[4]

Vaughan having held undisputed sway for more than thirty years in the lower class of Nisi Prius causes, both in town and on circuit, was, in 1827, made a Baron of the Exchequer, mainly, it was thought at the time, from the court influence of his brother, the celebrated physician, Sir Henry Halford ;[5] so the bar joke ran that Vaughan was a baron by *prescription.*

[3] First Series, 1860. Second Series, 1873: printed for the author, 62 Chancery Lane.

[4] Walton's ' Random Recollections,' first series, p. 13.

[5] The physician was the eldest of the family ; he took the name of Halford on succeeding to the Halford estates, which descended to him through his mother. He was court physician to George III., George IV., William IV., and Victoria (see life of Mr. Justice Vaughan in Foss's ' Lives of the Judges,' vol. ix. p. 280).

The elder Clarke, contemporary and rival of Vaughan, is described by Mr. Walton as a remarkably fine old man—a lawyer of a school and class now almost extinct, punctilious as to the accuracy of his professional costume, the unwrinkled fit of his black silk stockings, the powder of his wig, and the starch of his bands. He was, moreover not a bad lawyer, with a great fund of dry good sense, sometimes discomfiting his younger and more ardent antagonist, Denman, by saying confidentially to the common jurors, in answer to his opponent's eloquent flights, 'If such stuff and nonsense, gentlemen, as this is to prevail and get the better of you as men of sense, good God, gentlemen! where are we?'[6] Another very respected member of the Midland Circuit in those days was John Balguy.[7] Balguy, who was of an old and highly respectable Derbyshire family, led the life of a country gentleman and never practised or resided in London, though in the country he diligently attended Sessions and Circuit. Denman had a very high regard for him as a man of the most estimable qualities, and of very considerable talent. He had immense success with Derbyshire juries, by whom he was familiarly known as 'John Bogie.' Mr. Walton tells a story in connection with this which occurred on one of Denman's earlier judicial circuits, and might have puzzled a judge less familiar with the ways of the 'Old Midland.' In a cause in which Balguy had appeared for the plaintiff, the jury, being ready to give their verdict, were asked the usual

---

[6] 'Random Recollections,' first series, p. 19.

[7] Q.C., Recorder of Derby, afterwards Commissioner of Bankrupts at Birmingham ('Random Recollections,' first series, p. 24).

question whether they found for plaintiff or defendant, upon which, says Mr. Walton, the worthy foreman, having first scratched his head, replied, ' We knows nought about your plaintiffs or defendants ; we find for John Bogie there ' (pointing to Balguy). ' That will do, gentlemen,' quoth Lord Denman, with a good-humoured smile ; ' you find for the plaintiff.' [8]

Among Denman's more immediate contemporaries were Reader, Empson, and Dwarris, with all of whom he was on terms of affectionate intimacy. William Reader, Recorder of Northampton, with an honest pride in his brilliant friend's successes, helped him materially, as will afterwards appear, in his earlier Parliamentary contests, and was always the first, and certainly not the least sincere, in congratulating him on every step by which he rose to eminence. Dwarris (afterwards Sir Fortunatus Dwarris, and a Master in the Court of Queen's Bench by the appointment of his old friend Denman, when Chief Justice), was an accomplished scholar, and a very fair jurist, though he wanted the push and audacity which are almost necessary to commanding success in practice.

William Empson was another circuit friend of Denman's, whose professional success was not commensurate with his abilities. His health, in fact, which required frequent absences in milder climates, was too delicate for the rough work of the bar, but his literary and social reputation in the best circles was always considerable. He afterwards became the son-in-law of Jeffery, succeeded him for a time as editor of the ' Edinburgh

<hr>

[8] ' Random Recollections of the Midland Circuit,' first series, p. 25.

Review,' and was for some years Principal of Haleybury College.

Two greater names remain behind—those of Copley, afterwards Lord Lyndhurst,[9] and of Francis Horner,[10] soon to become famous for his exertions on the currency question, who were both members of the circuit when Denman joined it.

With Francis Horner Denman had some unexplained quarrel, which must have taken place very soon after his first becoming a member of the circuit mess, as in 1814 (as will be seen hereafter) Denman speaks of it as a ' seven years' grudge.'

For the commanding talents of Copley, who was seven years his senior, but who had only been called to the bar and joined the circuit two years before him, Denman had a very sincere admiration, which Copley returned, and a cordial liking sprang up between them, increased by the circumstance that they both at that time entertained and frankly avowed sentiments of what in those days was regarded as extreme political Liberalism ; sentiments to which Denman remained faithfully devoted throughout the whole of his career, but which Copley profligately abandoned in order to take office as Solicitor-General in 1819, under Lord Liverpool's ministry.   Denman, though he always remained outwardly on good terms

---

[9] Born 1772; called to Bar 1804; Solicitor-General (of the Tories) 1810; Attorney-General 1824 ; Chancellor and Lord Lyndhurst 1827; Chief Baron 1830; Chancellor a second time in 1834 ; a third time in 1841; died in 1863 in his ninety-second year.

[10] Born 1778; 'Bullion Report' 1810; died of consumption at Pisa 1817.

with his old circuit friend, never could forget or forgive this dereliction of principle.

'I remember my father,' writes Mrs. Hodgson, 'coming home one day in deep dejection at the acceptance of office in 1819 by his friend Copley under those who were in direct opposition to his known principles. He never could feel the same friendship for him in after years. On one occasion, when asked by Copley for his support at a Cambridge election, my father answered, " If saying that I know your real principles are the same as my own will help you, I will do so." '

It will be seen hereafter how, more than sixteen years after his original acceptance of office under the Tories, Lord Denman took occasion in the House of Lords bitterly to taunt Lord Lyndhurst with his political profligacy.[11]

While his charming temper and convivial qualities soon gained friends for Denman at the bar, his legal knowledge, talents, and local connections early procured for him a fair share of such business as on circuit and sessions usually falls to the province of junior barristers. In the year after his first joining (1807) he reports to his wife that he had had a 'prosperous sessions,' and in the spring assizes of the next year, 1808, he writes that ' he had four briefs at Derby.' He was never, indeed, from the first without a certain amount of practice. His legal acquirements were more than sufficiently extensive for the demands

[11] Debate of August 27, 1835. Hansard, Parl. Deb., vol. 30, N. S., p. 1042 et sq.

made on them, and his high character, commanding figure, magnificent voice, and vehement, earnest eloquence, soon earned for him a considerable share of local reputation.

When his son, the present Mr. Justice Denman, presided as judge in the spring of 1873 on his father's old circuit, he was good enough, with the kind permission of the circuit, to cause extracts to be made, for the use of this Memoir, from the old ' Circuit Book ' of the Midland, containing entries relating to Lord Denman's career while a member of that renowned legal consociation.

It may be needful to inform the uninitiated that among the contrivances with which the Bar on circuit is accustomed to enliven the compotations that succeed its mess dinners is that of holding a mimic court, in which fines (that generally go to swell the amount of the wine fund) are imposed on those who have in any way infringed the somewhat whimsical rules of circuit etiquette ;—who have done anything odd or eccentric within the limits of the circuit jurisdiction ; or who have even called down the *Nemesis* of mess table envy by being signally complimented by the judges, or being made the subjects of popular applause in Court, or by being retained specially to act as advocates on some other circuit,—by the accession, finally, of any legal honour, or the acceptance of any legal office.

It is to be hoped this explanation, given once for all, may enable the lay reader to comprehend the entries which will be copied from time to time from this ' Circuit Book.'

The only entries relating to Denman in the first four years of his circuit existence are the following :

1807. *July* 14, *Lincoln.*- -Mr. Denman was presented for wearing nankeen trousers at a circuit court [the proper costume no doubt on so grand an occasion being in those days a black dress suit].

1808. *April* 4, *Warwick.*—Mr. Denman presented Mr. Dayrell for saying in open court that no wise man would ever dream of going to law.

Also, Mr. Serjeant Vaughan for puffing the attornies of Notts in open court by saying, ' There are in this county in particular several most respectable attornies.'

[For this heinous offence a fine of one guinea was imposed, and paid.]

Also Mr. Reader, for lowering the character of the Bar by declaring in open court at Northampton that every one of his friends then sitting round that table would be glad to change places with an auctioneer.—One guinea.

1810. *August* 20, *Leicester.*—Mr. Perkins [12] presents Mr. Denman for accommodating an attorney named Hobbs with a seat at the green table [appropriated to the use of the Bar] to the inconvenience of the said Perkins.

Mr. Denman presents Mr. Reynolds for dancing with seven attornies' daughters at Derby ball.—One guinea.

Also Mr. Copley (Lord Lyndhurst) for an arrogant puff of himself in placing himself in competition with Lord Kenyon, saying in open court, ' Which is right, Lord Kenyon or I.'—One guinea.

Also Mr. Holt [13] for travelling the circuit in stage coaches, and without a servant.—One guinea.

Old Mrs. Denman carefully notes, and mention of

---

[12] Alfred Thrale Perkins, son of John Perkins, Mr. Thrale's head clerk, who became partner with Barclay in the great brewery.

[13] ' Reporter of Holt's Nisi Prius Cases ' &c.

the fact must not be omitted, that her son received his first retainer in London, in May 1807, when he was engaged to conduct Lord Cochrane's election for Westminster. Lord Cochrane and his colleague, Sir F. Burdett were elected, and young Denman, for his fortnight's work, received what then no doubt appeared to him the enormous fee of 150*l.*

On circuit and sessions it was his habit to write at least weekly, if not oftener, to his wife, and several of these letters have been preserved, together with Mrs. Denman's replies. Tenderer or more affectionate letters it is impossible to conceive, but concerned as they are with the small every-day details of professional and family life, they would have very little if any interest for general readers, while they frequently deal with intimate sentiments—the innermost secrets of the heart and the affections—on which it would be something like sacrilege to pour the broad light of posthumous publicity.

The following, a fair average specimen of the class, was written from Lincoln on the 17th of July 1808. It gives a passing notice of the Andersons, of Lady Nelthorpe, and 'Aunt Anne,' of whom mention has already been made in connection with Denman's marriage.

My dearest Love,—If there is any business it will prevent me from writing to-morrow; so I am determined to provide you with a letter for Monday morning to thank you for your good account of my dear boys [the two eldest, Thomas and Joseph], and tell you that I am extremely well, and have had a very prosperous sessions.

I was at Leá [Lea Hall, Sir Charles Anderson's seat] early
on Thursday morning, and found the whole family well.
Charles [the present baronet, whose birth was imminent
when his mother wrote to congratulate her 'dearest
Theodosia' on her marriage in 1804] is much grown, and
asked after Tom [the present Lord Denman, about a year
his junior]. As to the little girl, she really is an extraordinary
child—plump, strong, and healthy, sitting perfectly upright
in her nurse's arms. Between ourselves, she appears to be
rather a favourite, and the more so because Lady Nelthorpe
[Lady Anderson's mother] runs down her merit in comparison
with Charles'.

Lady Anderson said she should write to you in a few days.
Yesterday morning (Friday) Sir Charles, after struggling a
long time with his disinclination to leave home, set out to
ride with me to Kirton, which was fortunate for me, as some
of the gig tackle broke near Blyborough [showing the state
of the roads in those days], and so much time was lost in
repairing it that I could not have reached Kirton in time
for business without the loan of his servant's mare. On her
I galloped forward, and the groom brought the gig leisurely
after me.

This morning I arrived here [Lincoln], and have dined at
Lady Nelthorpe's, who desired her kind remembrances to you.
I have also received a joint letter from your father and Anne
[the 'Aunt Anne' who described the wedding], with a delightful account of the girls. He mentions, too, that I am to be
engaged at Leicester in a case from Melton.

I am not without hopes of a letter from you by favour of
Serjeant Vaughan this evening, and am in good spirits
from the certainty of hearing all about you from James
to-morrow. His arrival is now the most interesting object
I have to look forward to.

There is not a great deal of business expected, but perhaps
we may be agreeably disappointed. At Northampton there
were only three causes ; at Oakham no counsel went into
court, except Torkington, who only made two motions.

Give my best love to my father and mother. Ever with the truest affection, I am yours.

P.S. If you should be left bare by our numerous debts being paid, let me know, and I will send you a supply.

Though his professional progress was not un-satisfactory, Denman was glad to continue and extend his connection with periodical literature, in which his friend Merivale (then established with his wife in East Street, not far from Queen's Square) was about this time taking an active part. Under date January 11, 1808, Merivale writes to a correspondent:

My connection with the ' Critical Review' is really a source of great amusement to me. It has become still more pleasant of late from the circumstance that Denman has also engaged in it, and pursues it with great spirit. He formed his first connection with the 'Monthly,' and still writes occasionally in that review also. Mr. Fellowes [the then editor of the 'Critical'], through me and Bland, attacked Denman, who has, in consequence, engaged to furnish the political articles. The only one of his articles that has yet appeared is a review of Pitt's speeches.'

On March 19, 1808, Merivale writes again to the same friend :

You must not fear Denman; I beg you never to be afraid lest any 'virulent, intolerant, and dogmatic' paper in the ' Review ' should be his. I perfectly agree with you in your opinion of the article in question, but am perfectly ignorant who wrote it, except that he did not. 'Washington's Life' is the only article by Denman in the last number.

Reference has been made to the two papers thus mentioned by Mr. Merivale : they are of fair average merit, but there is nothing very striking about them. The following extract from the review of Chief Justice

Marshall's ' Life of Washington ' (the fifth and concluding volume of which had then recently been published)
will serve to show the style of Denman's early periodical
writing.

Considering the events of late years [this was written at
the height of Napoleon's power] it is impossible to refrain
from expressing a high admiration of Washington's conduct
at this period.   The acknowledged preserver of his country,
the founder of its independence, and by general solicitation
placed at the head of its government, attended wherever he
appeared by popular applause, and the sincere and heartfelt
devotion of his countrymen—none of these considerations
could make him deviate for a moment from the line he had
determined to maintain.

In his whole government no stain of avarice or selfishness,
or even of an undue desire to prefer his own family, can be
found; nor is there in any part of his conduct a single
instance of his assuming or affecting any personal distinction
as peculiarly due to himself.   When power was in a sudden
and irresistible manner forced upon him, he refused to hold
it except as trustee for the public ; and his self-denial in
the exercise of the supremacy entrusted to him forms
almost a singular instance in the history of man.

His father about this period seems to have been
anxious that he should endeavour to improve his
professional prospects by preparing legal reports or
compiling a legal treatise.   Denman, who felt very
clearly that his true road to success lay in a different
direction, sent an answer, of which the following are
extracts, to the good Doctor's suggestions :

Saxby : July 26, 1808.

My dear Father,—Though my hands are at present pretty
fully occupied, I will not any longer delay my acknowledgments for your very kind letters, which are principally

employed in recommending the publication of some legal writing.

I will tell you exactly my sentiments on the subject. If anything of that sort occurred to my mind as likely to be substantially good and useful, either to myself in the pursuit of necessary knowledge, or to the profession, I would not hesitate to undertake it immediately. But indeed it is much more difficult than could be easily conceived to find scope for literary exertion on any point of practical utility. The legal press is completely saturated with every production that can be wanted in every branch of the profession. As to your idea of displaying learning by a general review of the progress of law, either foreign or domestic, I seriously assure you that in my opinion (even if I had the learning to display) such a work would do a man much more harm than good in his prospects of advancement; for it would show that his mind had not been turned to what was immediately applicable to business, and he would be laid on the shelf like Hargrave,[14] as too much of an antiquarian to be worth consulting as a lawyer. It is certainly true that a man may make his name known, either as a publisher or as intending to publish, by appearing upon the wrapper of Butterworth's periodical reports, and announcing that he is about to publish some new work or edit some old one; and for this method of advertising one's self I understand a handsome premium is paid to the bookseller; and in the meantime it might happen that a few stray attornies would consult him on the subject to which his attention had thus appeared to be devoted. I should not envy business so acquired.

Denman then mentions incidentally, in answer to a question put by his father on another point, that his friend Copley was then engaged in publishing 'Reports of all the Election cases decided in the last Parliament,' and he then continues as follows:

[14] A very learned legal writer, author of several profound dissertations, and a well-known annotator of Coke upon Littleton.

You will stop here and say, if Copley publishes reports of cases why cannot you do the same? The answer is, in the first place, that the different courts are already furnished with reporters; secondly, that the office of reporter is much oftener a bar than an introduction to general business. Copley's superior powers, with the stand he has already made on circuit, are sure to bring him forward, notwithstanding that (as a reporter of election cases) he holds a position which is very commonly regarded as that of a clerk or register rather than of a counsel. Besides, reporting in one court prevents a man's attendance in all the others.

On the whole, I must conclude as I began, that I would cheerfully set about anything that presented itself *to my own mind* as useful and proper; but the general persuasion that publication might be advantageous is far from amounting to a motive for undertaking anything in particular, though it might be a spur to exertion when the subject was once selected.

Our sessions ended last Tuesday at Spilsby as prosperously for me as they had begun at Chesterfield. I had some guineas in my pocket after payment of all my expenses. On Friday I shall attend at Oakham, where I am retained on the part of the Harborough family in a tithe cause of considerable importance.

The letter just cited has referred to Copley as a legal reporter. The following, written by Denman to his wife from Warwick, on the spring circuit of 1810, presents the future Chancellor and the future Chief Justice as dancing till the small hours of the morning at a boarding-school ball :

Warwick: April 2, 1810.

This is the last letter, my dearest love, that you will receive from me on the present circuit, which, in fact, is now at an end for me. The business here has been lighter than usual, and will allow of my retreating in a day or two, so that I flatter myself with the hope of embracing you at the latest on Thursday night. Do let me find you and the dear children well, and all at home, though perhaps they will be in bed at the moment of my arrival.

I have been rather gay. At Leicester I was introduced by Copley to Miss Linwood, who had a ball and concert. She is well acquainted with my father, and desired her compliments to him. The dancing was kept up till between four and five in the morning, and then proceeded *without music*, the young ladies of her school, who formed the only band, being then too much fatigued to play any more. I retired at two.

To-day I had an invitation from an attorney in the town, but thought proper to decline in order to wait on the judges, which I have been too often prevented from doing. To-morrow I am going to dine with another circuiteer, who lives at a pleasant place near Kenilworth, and the next day again with the judges. This will be my last dinner (except on the road to London) till I have the happiness of sitting *vis-a-vis* to my dearest wife.

Your account of your brother rejoices me, but I blame myself extremely for giving you permission to visit him, without, at the same time, insisting on it that you should only go in a coach [not in a gig]. *This* I will still allow, but no other mode of travelling such a distance, either for that or any other purpose.

The honest part of the circuit is sadly disconcerted by the infamous conduct of the House of Commons in acquitting and even applauding ministers for their stupid and murderous proceedings at Walcheren.[15] After their escape it is horrible injustice to punish any man for any crime.

It gives me pain to hear that you have been distressed

---

[15] The wretched expedition in which

> The Earl of Chatham with his sword drawn
> Stood waiting for Sir Richard Strahan,
> Sir Richard, longing to be at 'em,
> Stood waiting for the Earl of Chatham.

for money.   Tell me in to-morrow's letter if that is still the case ; and if so, you shall have some without delay, for I cannot bear to have you in want even for an hour.   You must have been driven to extremities when you intercepted the purchase of poor Tom's pair of plaything horses [which Denman had no doubt meant to bring with him from circuit, as a present to his first-born, then about five years old]. My tenderest love to him and his sisters—to yourself my warm and unalterable attachment.

The reference to temporary money embarrassment with which the above letter ends recurs occasionally from time to time in the course of Denman's early letters to his wife.   Notwithstanding all his exertions, and the measure of success that attended them, there can be no doubt that the future Chief Justice, with a rapidly increasing family and a strong taste for social pleasures, not unfrequently experienced, in the earlier stages of his career, the inconveniences of a comparatively narrow income.   'Prudence and economy,' writes Mrs. Baillie in the sketch already so often quoted, ' were not predominating virtues in his character.   He was, indeed, always of a sanguine temperament, and disposed to take the most favourable view of his future fortunes, sometimes, perhaps, even more so than his more prudent friends might have desired.'

Lord Denman's second daughter, Mrs. Hodgson, writes, 'I have a very vivid recollection of the difficulties of my father's earlier life with regard to money matters.   Nothing but his own cheery, buoyant spirit could have kept him up through them.'   She is inclined to attribute some portion at least of these difficulties to the systematic caution of her grandfather, Dr. Denman, who always seems to have acted on the principle that in order to force a young man of social tastes and lively talents to work with all his might at the Bar, it was necessary to make him feel the perpetual stimulus of privation. In the main, the excellent doctor was no doubt right, but it is probable that he carried his system a little too far. The fact is, he himself had been brought up in the school of adversity, and belonged to a more primitive age. His habits of personal self-denial would now-a-days be thought somewhat ascetic. It is related of him by Mrs. Hodgson, that being asked one day at breakfast if he would not take some bacon, his reply was, 'Thank you, I have already had an egg, and one luxury is enough.' She mentions the curious circumstance that in the earlier years of their marriage old Mrs. Denman used to bring her daughter-in-law weekly 4*l.* for her housekeeping, and she justly remarks that 'such a mode of dealing with grown-up people was not likely to lead to real economy.' 'My grandfather and grandmother,' she adds, 'had lived a different life in a different age: they were really parsimonious, and expected the same rigid frugality which they themselves had practised. With his increasing family, and such slender assistance, it was impossible for my father to keep clear of debt, which a little more liberality in the outset might have prevented. I cannot help thinking that those good and primitive people made a mistake in tying him down as they did. He was launched upon a wider sea, and ought to have had more power to weather the storms of life.' There is a great deal of good sense in these observations, but the brilliant results of the treatment pursued by Dr. Denman seem to show that, if severe, it was, with a view to professional advancement, not injudicious.

Dr. and Mrs. Denman, with a certain tinge of old world formality about them, were very fond of and kind to their grandchildren. Mrs. Hodgson writes:

Dr. Denman I remember well—a fine old man with silver hair and teeth perfect to the last. He delighted in bringing us pottles of strawberries and teaching us to be gentlewomen, a point upon which he laid very great stress. I remember his giving my elder sister (the Hon. Mrs. Wright) a prayer-book because she had already become a gentlewoman, and promising me one when I should also have attained the same perfection. This was supposed to be the case on my seventh birthday, when I was presented with great ceremony by my grandmother with a large red morocco prayer-book, with 'Elizabeth Denman' in gilt letters on the back and a long inscription by my grandmother in the beginning. I have a vivid impression of a few days I spent in Mount Street with Dr. and Mrs. Denman. I was struck with their primitive simplicity, their frugal habits, and their somewhat rigid rule after the more indulgent dominion of my mother.

Of Denman as a husband and a father, both Mrs. Baillie and Mrs. Hodgson give a delightful picture. It was in his home and family that the rising but still struggling young barrister found the most quickening incentive to exertion and the richest reward of successful labour. 'Never,' writes Mrs. Baillie, ' was there a more indulgent husband or a more tender father. It was a pleasure to see him in the midst of his children, nursing the babies, playing with the older ones, and their friend and companion as they grew older still. None of their little pleasures and amusements were too trifling for him to enter into, and he also seized every opportunity which his professional duties would permit of assisting in their education. Certainly, there was but little of *actual teaching* in his power, but the interest he took in their pursuits encouraged his children to proceed, and their desire to please where they loved so much inspired them with a wish to improve themselves. Where this impression is once made,' continues Mrs. Baillie, ' perhaps the great object of education is accomplished, and not a great deal of positive teaching is afterwards required. Those who have had any opportunity of making the observation must have remarked how very much a little encouragement given by a kind and judicious father will tend to produce this effect, and I think its advantages are peculiarly noticeable in forming the characters of young women.'

Mrs. Hodgson's early recollections quite confirm Mrs. Baillie's more mature observation. ' My earliest recollection,' she writes, ' of my dear father and mother is of a very handsome couple, quite young; my father spirited, energetic, and delightful; my mother lovely, and sweetness itself. The devotion which we all felt for him, derived doubtless, from my mother's example of devoted love, never left us. I remember our delight at his return from work, our ecstasy when the nursery bell was rung for us to go down to dessert—then the being sent up stairs to find the ' Wedding

Coat,' a brown coat, carefully preserved, which he used to put on when he tossed us about on his shoulders. Then, as we grew older, I remember the reading of ' Alonzo the Brave and the Fair Imogene,'[16] to our great terror; 'The Idiot Boy,'[17] bits of Shakespeare, Milton, &c., all read in his deep sonorous voice, with dramatic effect. Then the first two cantos of 'Childe Harold,' 'Marmion,' &c., as they came out. I remember going to church with him at St. George the Martyr, and being taught to sing on his knee; travelling post with him the vacation, walking up the hills, learning the names of the trees and shrubs and plants, learning to admire the picturesque beauties of nature. I well recollect going once to spend the day at his Chambers at No. 5 Old Square, and thinking it one of the happiest days of my life, being taken out by the clerk to run down what I thought a formidably steep slope (the bank under the trees in Lincoln's Inn Gardens). On another occasion I remember, when very young, in a boat on the Thames, being asked by him whether I would follow another boat which had just shot London Bridge. On my delightedly saying, 'Yes,' he gave orders to the waterman accordingly, and we shot the bridge—a thing for which in after years he told me he had often reproached himself.

It was not only to his daughters that Denman showed himself the best and kindest of fathers : in his dealings with his sons, from childhood to manhood, he had equally the gift of making himself at once deeply

---

[16] Monk Lewis's terrific ghost ballad.
[17] Wordsworth's well-known lyrical ballad.

revered and sincerely beloved. He was their playfellow in the nursery, the companion of their rides and sports when boys, the considerate friend and kind elder brother of their maturer years. His fondness for his first-born son (a fondness pricelessly repaid in after years) amounted almost to a passion. He once told the boy that he was afraid to say how much he loved him; and as his other sons grew up they shared, without diminishing, the inexhaustible stores of his parental tenderness.

In connection with the above reminiscences of Denman's early married life, the following letter written from town to his wife, who was then with the children at Saxby, may find a place here, as showing the intensity of his home affections, the occasional difficulties of his exchequer, and the nature and extent of his social circle in London:

Queen Square: Friday, June 10, 1811.

My dearest Love,—If I could justly accuse myself of having been hitherto ignorant of your value, the loss of you at present would be a complete but painful mode of opening my eyes on the subject. You can form no idea from my occasional absences on the circuit of the melancholy difference I find in the house, the square, the town itself, and my own feelings, which you positively must consult by sending me a full account of yourself and my dear children three times a week at least. This surely is moderate, but I will not bind you to particular days, which might be inconvenient, only reminding you that if your letters are not sent in pretty good time in the morning to Melton, or if sent on a Saturday, they will be two days old when they reach me.

My friends are very good, and I have dined at home only on the day of my arrival.   They all desire their best remembrances.   Tuesday I was in Mount Street (Dr. Denman's); Wednesday in Grosvenor Street (Dr. Baillie's); yesterday in East Street (Merivale's); to-day I am going to Ben Brodie (afterwards Sir Benjamin), to take leave of my two aunts, who go to-morrow with Mr. Marsh (married to his cousin, Miss Brodie).   To-morrow I am to go to the Bishop of Rochester [18] at Bromley; and on Sunday I am to meet an Irish bishop at Massingberd's.[19]

You will be glad to hear that there is one circumstance which goes far towards reconciling me to your absence, but sorry to hear that that circumstance is—extreme poverty. There is such an extraordinary lack of money and the means of getting it that the daily expenses, had you all been here, would infallibly have run us quite a-ground, but I hope soon to be able to announce to you a turn of the tide.   Vaughan [20] good-naturedly asked me to spend to-morrow and Sunday with him at his villa, and offered to convey me.   But the two bishops, and the hope of obtaining a living from them,[21] prevent me from accompanying him.   Give my kind love to your father, mother, and sisters, and keep me in your own memory and affection, and those of your sweet children, as your and their most loving husband and father.

Denman still kept up his intercourse and correspondence with his old clerical college friends, Bland, Hodgson, and Drury.   Bland, under a pressure of debt and difficulty, had some time before accepted the appointment of British Chaplain at Amsterdam, whence he wrote about this time to his old friend a letter,

[18] Dr. King, Bishop of Rochester, an old friend of Dr. and Mrs. Denman.

[19] Of Ormsby, Lincolnshire.

[20] The famous Serjeant, afterwards Mr. Baron Vaughan.

[21] No doubt for his wife's brother, Rev. R. W. Vevers.

clouded indeed by painful depression, but lighted up every here and there with flashes of his former vivacity. It is not of a nature to be given entire, but a few passages may be selected :

Amsterdam : Saturday, March 31, 1811.

We have played at dumb show too long, my dear Denman. It is time that one of us should speak. It is only unfortunate it should fall on him who has least to say. These long pauses of deep and idle silence are fatal to friendship. To those who are happy in their own homes and the bosom of their families they are possibly by no means irksome. You have but little to gain by the renewal of our intercourse of old ; but I have too much to lose tamely to resign it. I saw, my good friend, I was becoming tedious and tiresome to all about me in England—my presence being like a dead weight on my associates. It is for this reason, and this alone, that I am inclined to view my separation from you in a favourable point of view. A temporary change of country, of companions, and objects of every kind, will, I hope, make me more supportable ; and from what I am going to tell you, should it really be realised, I entertain a hope of obtaining a stock of knowledge, and of recruiting my health. A friend here has advised me by all means, if possible, to go to the south of France. This plan I communicated to a French gentleman, one of our vestry, and the first character in this place for abilities. He is interesting himself to procure me a passport, and as our church appears at present to be abandoned from the pressure of the times, I propose to pass two months in those delicious regions, where my soul has been so long before me. Another gentleman lends me, should my hopes be realised, 50l. Something is due to me from England as minister of this place, something will be done by the vestry, and on the whole a sufficiency be raised to wind up my debts here, and support me for a short time in the plains of Languedoc or among the mountains of—God knows where. Hey! my friend, is not this something?

My father will not, I hope, quite abandon me, and from him I count on a trifle to convey me back to England in July or August. Yes, there are times when my heart is in my mouth in thinking of England.

The above summer sketch, Denman, is at present only in embryo. Three or four days will determine the vestry on the feasibility of opening or relinquishing our church—the latter appears the most probable from the sort of difficulties they have to encounter. In that case (child that I am to hope it) I shall be at Paris in a twinkling, stay three days, fall prostrate before the Apollo, the Venus, the Laocoon, give Talma my mite of approbation, wait my written orders from the surgeon, and then proceed on my route, which I already see to be the most this—the most that—in short, the only true land of Cockayne. Thus till July, when I shall expect wherewith to convey me back to England again. Well, my dear friend, suppose me by dint of quiet, serene skies, gay-looking people and self-satisfaction (worth them all) become a man again, mentally and physically, and returned to England, with my salary of 100*l.* a year remaining to me as a personage under Government—now could not another snug hundred be prepared for me in the West of England or Ireland by some curacy, or, in short, a something. My own opinion is that the Bishop of London, who is my rector, or Mr. Hope, will do something for me, merely on Sterne's admirable principle, that we love that which has already cost us trouble—you plant a tree, and because you plant it, you water it. Really, in sober verity, the future, though uncertain, is not hopeless.

Bland was back in England in the course of 1811. Merivale, writing to Denman, in October of that year, says :—

The news of Bland's return, which I had heard nothing of but from yourself, was kept from me for several days. His silence I cannot help considering as an unaccountable breach of old friendship. Nevertheless, I shall be glad to hear how and when he got over, how he does, and every other particular that you know concerning him.

In the same month of October, Byron, who had returned from the East in the preceding July, and who about this time saw a good deal of Hodgson, Drury, and Merivale, writes to Hodgson in reference to Bland :—

You have hinted, I think, that your friend Bland is returned from Holland. I have always had a great respect for his talents, and for what I knew of his character; but of me, I believe he knows nothing, except that he heard my sixth form repetitions at Harrow for ten months together, at the average of ten lines a morning, and those never perfect. I suppose he will now translate Vondel, the Dutch Shakespeare.[22]

Although Byron was at this time on intimate terms with Hodgson, Drury, Bland, and Merivale, it does not appear that he and Denman ever met except once. On that one occasion Byron, with the strange perversity that at times got the better of him, would talk of nothing but the grossest obscenity, raked out of the filth of old criminal law text books, to which he persisted in returning again and again, whenever an attempt was made to change the conversation.

[22] Letter to Hodgson, Oct. 13, 1811, in ' Moore's Life.' In a letter to Hodgson of Dec. 8, 1811, Byron writes: 'Bland dines with me on Tuesday to meet Moore ;' and again on Dec. 12: 'Bland did not come according to appointment, being unwell.'

This so disgusted Denman, though by no means in general more squeamish than the rest of his profession, that he declined again to lower, by personal intercourse, his ideal of the poet, for whose genius, as subsequently developed, he had the most unbounded admiration.

CHAPTER V.

PROGRESS AT THE BAR.

A.D 1811 TO 1815.   ÆT. 32 TO 36.

In 1811 Denman's practice on circuit and sessions much increased—Takes
chambers at No. 5 Old Square, Lincoln's Inn – Extracts from Midland
Circuit Book—Brougham specially retained at Lincoln in Spring
Assizes of 1811 for defence of John Drakard, of the '*Stamford News*'
—Merivale disappointed that Denman was not retained—Dangerous
illness of Merivale in October and November 1811—Extract from
letter from Merivale to Denman, Nov. 22, 1811—Death of Denman's
uncle, Dr. Joseph Denman, in 1812—Disposal of his property—The
story of the poisoned bottles—Impression produced by the occurrence
on Denman—Makes him cautious as to circumstantial evidence—
Letter from Denman to his wife on the death of her brother, Lieutenant Charles Vevers, R.N., at the storming of San Sebastian, August
31, 1813—From same to same, April 7, 1814—Delight at fall of
Napoleon—'Rooted success' on circuit—Defence, in July 1814, of
some of the associates of Lord Cochrane in the Stock Exchange Conspiracy—The trial before Lord Ellenborough—Partial summing-up
and severe sentence—After career of Lord Cochrane (Earl of Dundonald)—Denman, in August and September 1814, visits France with
his wife and children—Extracts from letters to Merivale describing the
trip—Meeting and reconciliation with Francis Horner—Horner's subsequent death by consumption—Public honours paid to; Mackintosh's
remarks on—Political speculations of Denman in 1814 as to Bonaparte
and the Bourbons—Theatricals in Paris; music and dancing—Column
of the Place Vendôme—Edmund Kean—Denman appointed Deputy
Recorder of Nottingham, 1815—Death of his father, November 1815—
Vigorous old age of Dr. Denman—His death sudden at last—His
character by his daughter, Mrs. Baillie—His treatise on midwifery and
lectures.

IN the fifth year after his call to the bar Denman's
practice on circuit and at sessions had already begun

very considerably to increase. Early in 1811 he entered a new (and final) set of chambers at No. 5 Old Square, Lincoln's Inn, and on this occasion his mother records, ' We had this day the pleasure of hearing that my son was overflowing with business at the sessions.' Shortly afterwards he himself writes to his wife from Derby, on the spring circuit, ' There was very little business at Nottingham, but I was in everything. Here at Derby there is a good deal, and I am in almost everything, and in most things have been applied to on both sides of the question.'

It may be as well here to throw together the few entries in the Midland Circuit book referring to Denman during the period comprised in the present chapter, and which serve to attest the progress he was making in the estimation of the judges, and of those still more powerful arbiters of a young barrister's fortunes—the attornies.

1811. *Summer Assizes, Leicester.*—Mr. Hudson presents Mr. Denman for rivalling Mr. Reader in candour, and for being puffed by Mr. Justice Grose in open court : ' Upon my word, you behave so candidly and fairly that I am much obliged to you.'—Fined one guinea.

1812. *Northampton.*—The Recorder presents Mr. Denman for advertising for business by informing an attorney in the County Hall at Lincoln where his lodgings were situated.

Mr. Reynolds presents Mr. Denman for puffing his great classical and etymological learning before divers—to wit 700,000—attornies in the Crown Court at Lincoln, in saying that *suesco* is evidently derived from *sus*, owing to the domestic habits of the sow, the chief evidence against a

prisoner indicted for stealing a pig being the animal's recollection of its own stye.

Mr. Reynolds also congratulates Mr. Denman on having
been three times puffed by Mr. Justice Vaughan [1] in *Rex* v.
Rhodes.

Mr. Reynolds further presents Mr. Denman for being
publicly puffed and encouraged by one Lockett, an attorney,
in open court at Derby, as deserving much more than a bad
eighteen-penny piece for a speech just then made by the said
Mr. Denman.

1813. *March* 1, *Lincoln.* — Mr. Marriott congratulates
Mr. Denman on a high panegyric from Mr. Justice Gibbs
(Sir Vicary Gibbs), at Derby, in the case of *Rex* v. *Mason
and others*, 'A gentleman (meaning thereby the said Mr.
Denman) whose accuracy of mind I am perfectly acquainted
with.'

1815. *Spring Circuit.*—Mr. Denman is congratulated on
being attended by his wife to Northampton, and condoled
with on her departure thence.—Fine (as usual), one guinea.

It is in the course of the spring assizes at Lincoln, on
March 12, 1811, that the first mention occurs in
Denman's correspondence of Brougham, with whom he
was destined to form so memorable and life-long an
intimacy.

'Mr. Brougham,' he writes to his wife, 'has given
us a better speech to-day than he did in town;
notwithstanding which, his client was found guilty.'

The reference here is to Brougham's defence of

---

[1] This must refer to some occasion on which Vaughan, owing to
pressure of judicial work or to the illness of one of the regular judges,
presided in his place, for Vaughan was not raised to the Bench till 1827,
fifteen years after the date of this entry.

John Drakard, the proprietor of the ' Stamford News,' who was tried at the Lincoln spring assizes of 1811 for an alleged seditious libel contained in an article in that paper reprobating in strong terms the practice of flogging then in force in the army.   Brougham, whose circuit was the northern, had been specially retained for the defence, and the speech he made, which will be found reported in his collected speeches, was a most forcible and admirable one.   The other speech, referred to as having been made in town, was his defence of Messrs. Hunt, the proprietors of the ' Examiner,' against whom a criminal information had been filed for copying into that paper the article from the ' Stamford News.'   The London speech, notwithstanding a very strong adverse charge from Lord Ellenborough, was successful, the Messrs. Hunt having been acquitted. The Lincoln speech, though truly characterized by Denman as better than the other, failed owing, no doubt, to the strong local prejudices and inferior intelligence of the provincial jury to which it was addressed.

Denman was himself somewhat disappointed, and his friends were still more so, at his not having been retained for the defence in this case.   Merivale, writing to him later in the same year, makes a passing allusion to this feeling.

I never felt joy at an event turning out contrary to my political inclinations but once, and that was on a late occasion at Lincoln.   I need not explain myself further.   In general, I heartily wish for the getting off of all political libellers, except such as have not sense enough to see the absurdity of going 200 miles out of their way to look for a defender.

In the latter part of 1811 Merivale had a dangerous illness (typhus fever), which kept him long a prisoner to his bed, at Cockwood, near Exeter, the residence of his father-in-law, Dr. Drury, the late head-master of Harrow.[2] After his recovery (November 22, 1811), he writes to Denman in a strain which pleasantly shows the deep affection subsisting between these old friends :

My mother had a letter the other day from a friend who had seen you at Lincoln [no doubt at the October Quarter Sessions], and gave an account of your being in a state of wretched despondency owing to the danger of a friend whose name she heard was Merivale. She proceeds to compliment both, and says it is no longer a matter of wonder to her that I am so very accomplished and amiable, seeing that I have such a companion and friend as you.

Yours ever most affectionately,
J. H. MERIVALE.

Herman is in coat and breeches, very proud of being taken for Tom.[3]

In the year 1812 Denman's uncle, Dr. Joseph Denman, died, aged 82, leaving to his nephew a reversionary interest in the bulk of his property, including the house and grounds of Stony Middleton and an estate near Lynn, in Norfolk.

Mrs. Baillie, in her memoir, tells an anecdote in connection with the later years of Dr. Joseph Denman's life which deserves insertion here, as there can be little doubt that the fact it relates made a strong impression

---

[2] Dr. Drury retired from the head-mastership and was succeeded by Dr. Butler in 1805.

[3] Present Under-Secretary of State for India, and present Lord Denman.

on the future Chief Justice, and led to his being very cautious in relying, in serious charges, on mere circumstantial evidence, however apparently conclusive.

'An uncle of his,' writes Mrs. Baillie, 'upon whose death he had reason to expect some property, had agreed to divide with him a pipe of wine, and the present Chief Justice, being then young and without much occupation, had undertaken to superintend the bottling of the wine himself. While thus employed, one of his children [the present Admiral Denman], a little boy of three or four years old, who was playing near him, threw down one of the bottles which had just been filled, and broke it to pieces. In gathering up the fragments, his father perceived a sediment of white powder, and, upon minutely observing the other bottles, some of them filled and others prepared to be so, a similar powder was found in them. They were consequently sent for examination to a chemist, when it was discovered that this powder was *sugar of lead*, these bottles having been previously filled with a mixture of this kind, and most unpardonably sent in this state to be used for other purposes.

'The horror with which this discovery was made could be equalled only by thankfulness for the escape, in which, indeed, the hand of Providence seems to have interfered in a manner the most direct and remarkable, choosing for its instrument a little child, and this child the uncle's god-son, christened after him by the name of Joseph.

'But for this discovery, the catastrophe must have been dreadful! Dreadful enough even without legal condemnation; but I have heard the Chief Justice say that he thought in almost every court of law the proofs of guilt would have been considered as sufficient, all the circumstances being taken into consideration. For, in addition to those already mentioned, it would have been proved that the uncle at that very time was preparing another will, considerably detrimental to the nephew's interests, of which intention the nephew was aware ; and it would also have been proved that the very bottles in which this sediment had been found had been intended solely for the uncle's use, the other portion of the wine having been bottled previously, and already placed in the nephew's cellar.

' As the person assisting him in the bottling had perceived their appearance upon the breaking of the bottle, concealment could then hardly have been practicable, had it been desired.'

The great war did not come to a close without leaving its impress of near and familiar sorrow on Denman's household. A brother of his wife's, Lieutenant Charles Vevers, as bold and dashing a young naval officer as ever paced a quarter-deck, was shot dead on the last day of August 1813, at the terrible storming of San Sebastian, a service on which, with characteristic gallantry, he had volunteered. Denman, who was very much attached to this brother-in-law, had been with his wife and her sister Ann at Leamington when the first intelligence reached England. He at once hastened up to London to learn fuller particulars, whence he wrote as follows to his wife :

Oh, my dearest love, how can I address you on this melancholy occasion, or how pretend to offer you that consolation which I so much need for myself? Notwithstanding all the preparations which his known danger gave, and all the melancholy forebodings with which I pursued my journey, still I could hardly persuade myself that my eyes were not deceiving me when at last I saw the fatal truth in the paper. Gallant and daring as he was, his exposure was but too certain. His fellow sufferers and our fellow mourners are numerous, indeed; but to your gentle and feeling heart this is but an aggravation of sorrow. But we must derive some comfort from reflecting that his death has been most glorious, and that his life was not worn away by the painful and lingering disorders produced by fatigue and wounds. But, indeed, I have no talent for consolation. I can weep with you, but I cannot pretend to tell you that your tears ought not to flow. Never did they more deservedly fall or embalm a memory more justly beloved. But I well know, when the first edge of affliction is taken off, you will exert yourself for the sake of all, and you and dear Ann will be a mutual support to each other. I must fear lest my confidence that no particulars could have been yet received may have betrayed her into a situation more painful than in any case it must have been, for the first shock of such intelligence in a public room would be overpowering. I believe Fetzer [newsagent near Queen's Square], from motives of humanity, did not send the ‘ Gazette,’ which would otherwise have reached us sooner. I found it was known in the neighbourhood as soon as I arrived. Of course I have been nowhere and done nothing; but I shall return the moment I can wash my hands of the business that brought me to London. I have made up my mind to return with you, and postpone my journey into the country [for the Michaelmas sessions] till the latest possible moment. I wish I could flatter myself that the dreadful blow will not affect your health.

I have nothing more to say, and yet am loath to conclude: it seems like another parting at this heart-rending moment. God bless and sustain you, and under all trials assure yourself of the warmest and tenderest affection of your faithful and adoring husband.　Adieu !

The following letter, written in the spring of next year from circuit, will show the usual tenderness of his family affections, the steady increase of his practice, and the effect produced on him by the wonderful events on the Continent that led to and immediately preceded the abdication of Napoleon, which took place the day before this letter was written, but was, of course, not then known in England.

Coventry : April 7, 1814.

My dearest Love—The best thing in our long separation is that it gives such full time for the mother and child to recover health, spirits, and good looks, with the pleasing anticipation of finding you both all I could possibly wish on my return.[4]　I consent with a sigh, and bid a protracted farewell to all the objects of my dearest affections.　My delay must now extend to April 26 or 27.[5]　Too long a time I fear to detain Tom [present Lord Denman, then nine] from school; but we must contrive to manufacture another short holiday for him after my return.　I have been thinking with delight of the joy he must have experienced this morning in returning home, and I feel confident that you will have the satisfaction of seeing him in all respects much improved.　Give my most affectionate love to him, with many thanks for his well-written letter.　Perhaps he will be able to write to me a longer letter from home.　If it is not quite so well written I will not quarrel with it.　Tell Doc [Theodosia, Hon. Mrs. Wright, then eight] that I am also

---

[4] His third surviving son, the Hon. Richard Denman, had been born late in the preceding year.

[5] This was before the legal terms were fixed, and when they varied with the incidence of Easter, an inconvenient practice, which caused great irregularity in the commencement of the circuits.

much obliged by her letter, and very glad to hear they all get out and walk so frequently.

The intelligence from France is indeed most glorious; we are half wild with it, and look forward to a long peace and happy times. The conduct of the Allies exhibits such a union of military greatness and royal magnanimity as the history of the world cannot parallel; and it is a proud thought that the single-handed and almost desperate resistance of England to the tyranny of Bonaparte has led to these immense results.

There is some difficulty in descending from such subjects to the common concerns of life; yet it will give you some pleasure to be able to tell my father that the present circuit has been by far the most satisfactory to me of any, and that I feel myself every day more rooted in business. My only hope of getting to London before the sessions depended on my having no business at Warwick, but some briefs for that place have already come in.—Ever yours.

It has been already noticed that one of Denman's earlier retainers at the bar was connected with the election of Lord Cochrane for Westminster, in 1807. On the trial of this celebrated person (afterwards Earl of Dundonald) in 1814, before Lord Ellenborough, for assisting in the well-known Stock Exchange fraud concocted by De Berenger,[6] Denman was counsel, not indeed for Lord Cochrane, but for some of the subordinate agents in the alleged conspiracy.

'My son,' writes Dr. Denman in his diary for July 1814, ' was concerned for the defence of those who may not improperly be called the minor criminals. His

---

[6] The confederates, having previously operated to an enormous extent in the funds, in order to procure a rise in the market got up a sham express of the death of Bonaparte. De Berenger was the real culprit.

speech on the occasion was short, but it was reputable, and gained him character additional to that which he had before established.'

The conduct of Lord Ellenborough on this trial of a strong political opponent is one of the blots on his judicial memory.   He would not hear of an adjournment, though, not being a felony, the case easily admitted of it, but kept the worn-out jury up till near four o'clock in the morning.   His summing up was more like the speech of an advocate than the charge of a judge; and his sentence on Lord Cochrane, when convicted—1,000*l.* fine, a year's imprisonment, and to stand an hour in the pillory—was savagely severe, even for those days.

The pillory part of the sentence was afterwards remitted, from fear of the populace.   Lord Cochrane made his escape from prison long before the year expired; while the 1,000*l.* fine was paid by a penny contribution raised by his political admirers.

Lord Cochrane, in consequence of this sentence, was expelled the House, and his name erased from the list of Knights of the Bath; but he was almost immediately after re-elected for Westminster without opposition, and long subsequently, after a brilliant career of naval exploits in all parts of the world, his banner of Knight of the Bath was set up again.   He died in 1860, when past four score years of age, and was buried with honour in Westminster Abbey.

In the Long Vacation of this year, when the Continent for the first time since the peace of Amiens was thrown open to the curiosity of the English, a general rush took place to France, and Denman, like so many others of his countrymen, made a trip with his wife and part of his family to Paris. He has described in a couple of letters to his friend Merivale the impressions made by his rapid tour, and, as so small a portion of his correspondence during this earlier period has been preserved, it may be worth while to make a few extracts. In the first communication he writes :

It was on August 19, 1814, that *Louis de Lachâtre des Princes de Deck* recommended to the attention of all French residents *M. Denman allant en France, accompagné de son épouse, quatre enfants, deux servantes et un domestique,*[7] and on the same day that party arrived at Brighton, where they submitted to the pillage of an evening, and set sail the next morning for the coast of France. The voyage was only too prosperous, as it brought us to the Quay at two o'clock in the morning, when we climbed up a broken pier by torchlight, surrounded by as picturesque a group of civil, obliging, and ruffian-like soldiers and sailors as were ever assembled by the pencil of Salvator. We are now at the Hôtel de Paris, standing in the middle of the Grande Rue, opposite a *place* full of booths erected for the fair which is to be held here to-morrow, and which likewise serves for the assembling of the numerous soldiery that fill the town, parading in drunken parties, and singing gay songs to the most dismal tunes, and with the most abominable voices.

The Grande Rue terminates with a fort standing on a bold and beautiful point of the western cliff—a monstrous high, ancient, and picturesque collection of flinty turrets ; but not more precipitous than the roofs of the ordinary houses, or the ladies' gigantic upright bonnets crowned with huge bunches of artificial flowers, made to look as if they had been plucked in the morning and were faded in the evening.

---

[7] 'M. Denman, travelling in France, accompanied by his wife, four children, and three servants, two female and one male.'

The soldiers here are in general young men of eighteen : the officers look like gentlemen. Whether they are quite reconciled to peace and the new state of things I know not; but the first sentry-box on the pier is inscribed with recent chalk 'Vive l'Empereur! Vive N.!'

They (the soldiers) have taken possession of so many houses that we are deprived of all chance of a private lodging here, and shall proceed with all practicable speed to Rouen, where a most friendly introduction from Butler [Charles Butler, the great conveyancer] to the principal banker there will replenish a purse already exhausted, and perhaps provide us with a comfortable shelter. If we fail in this we shall proceed to Paris, where, at any rate, my wife and I shall be for a short time.

Then follows, at the close of the letter, a rather interesting reference to the celebrated Francis Horner, a member, like himself, of the Midland Circuit. From some unknown cause an ill-feeling had, as already mentioned, for some time existed between Denman and Horner on circuit. It is pleasant to read what follows :

I ought not to conclude my letter without mentioning that our voyage put an end to my old seven years' grudge against Horner, who was also a passenger, and took an early opportunity of showing some civility to Joe [Denman's second son, now the admiral, then about six years old]. Forgive my weakness, but how can one sea-sick person persevere in dignified resentment to another ?

Horner, whose health was even then very delicate, died less than three years afterwards of consumption, at Pisa. His premature death called forth from the House of Commons a public and formal expression of regret, of which Mackintosh has recorded that

Never was so much honour paid in any age or nation to intrinsic claims alone. A Howard introduced, and an English House of Commons adopted, the proposition of thus honouring the memory of a man of thirty-eight, the son of a shopkeeper, who never filled an office or had the power of obliging a living creature, and whose grand title to this distinction was the belief in his virtue.[8]

The next letter, written immediately after returning to London, conveys Denman's general impressions as to the actual and probable future political and social state of France, which, read by the light of subsequent history, are not altogether without interest.

You see [he writes in allusion to the shortness of his stay— only about six weeks] this was taking a bird's eye view of things, but I flatter myself I may safely assure you that Bonaparte will not return. I mixed very much with the people, conversed with everybody [he spoke French with fluency], and dined at the tables d'hôte, and though the Emperor is adored by the military and regarded by all ranks with pride and admiration, and though I really believe that if a wish could restore him he would reign to-morrow, yet there is that kind of exhaustion pervading the French people that makes all efforts in his favour hopeless, and in the meantime gives full effect to possession in the king, and acquiescence on the part of his subjects. With such a people the fact of enjoyment is everything. It goes for a great deal in Bonaparte's case, and his reign is now called the *ancien régime.*

He has, indeed, many claims, military glory, internal improvement of everything—the monuments of art, and, above all, the embellishment of Paris. How this last object has been carried on to the astonishing extent we see, by a man constantly engaged in such wars, is perfectly inconceivable.

<hr>

[8] Life of Mackintosh,' vol. ii. p. 340.

You will think I am infected with the admiration felt for this extraordinary man by his late subjects, who, however, admit his obstinacy, his mistakes, his contempt for the blood of his fellow creatures, while, nevertheless, they extol him as a demi-god, scout the idea of his cowardice, talk of his expected suicide as a *bétise*, contend that Paris was sold, and his *beaux* plans for its defence defeated only by Marmont's treachery and Joseph's drunkenness, and own their highest obligation to him for their present exemption from civil war.

The speculation as to his future destiny is the most curious possible : it happens that all France can boast of is connected with his name, and that all the inconveniences arising from his mighty projects only began to be felt in the time of his successors, who have the further disadvantage of appearing to be forced on the nation by his old rival, England. Notwithstanding all this, I feel pretty confident the Bourbons will stand their ground.

Denman's fondness for theatrical representations has already been mentioned : it was indulged to the full during his short stay in France.

' You know me well enough,' he writes, ' to be sure that I half lived in the theatres. We were fortunate at Rouen in the occasional visit of Madlle. Duchesnois, the first tragic actress of the Théâtre Français, and in the world, I believe, whom I saw as Gertrude, Queen of Denmark, Adelaide, in Gaston, and in a new Bourbon play called the ' Retour d'Ulysse '[9] containing the line,

> .   .   .   . bénissent l'heureux jour
> Qui rend, après vingt ans, un père à leur amour,[10]

which was rapturously applauded, and lastly, in ' Les Horaces ' of Corneille. These exhibitions increased my regret that Kean

[9] Return of Ulysses.

[10] Bless the happy day which restores, after the lapse of twenty years, a father to their love.

[who had made his great debut as Shylock at Drury Lane on February 26 of this same year] did not visit France : they are perfection, and in his way exactly. Paris was deserted by Duchesnois, Talma, and all its first performers, but I saw Racine's 'Iphigenie' respectably acted, followed by his 'Plaideurs,' the representation of which was inimitable. The French little farces (Vaudevilles) are exquisite; the music of the French opera is fine, its singing delectable, its dancing beyond all praise.

We saw the 'Triumph of Trajan,' composed expressly to compliment Bonaparte, and introducing the famous column on the scene, now acted for the first time since the Restoration. It was a great opportunity for Parisian discontent to display itself, but nothing occurred.

You know the statue was deposed from the said column. I saw it, with its legs hacked by the Cossacks, in the foundry where it was cast : it is about twice my height, extremely beautiful, composed, dignified, imperial. The column itself, though finely executed in detail, I do not think a fine thing in its effect : it is extremely crowded with figures, and the pedestal is a contemptible mass of trophies, caps, and regimentals, worthy of Monmouth Street.

Excuse haste, prosing, and nonsense; but I would not delay giving you some account of what we had seen. I am indignant at the Drury Lane managers, who, instead of giving Kean a fair respite, are doing their utmost to weary the public of him by serving him up as a single dish at a time when London has scarcely an audience, and those who are likely to attend would prefer Elliston and dogs or lions to the highest efforts of genius. I mean to attend his first appearance to-morrow.

We are all well. My brother-in-law brought Tom [the present lord] from school to meet us on our arrival : he is going on very desirably. All join in every good wish with, dear Merry,

Yours most affectionately,
THOMAS DENMAN.

The year following this excursion (1815), Denman, through the interest of his kind and steady friend the third and famous Lord Holland (the Lord Holland of Hallam, Rogers, Sydney Smith, and Macaulay) was appointed Deputy Recorder of Nottingham, an office which he retained till he resigned it on becoming representative of the borough in 1820.

The Circuit duly recorded and imposed a fine on this promotion, as appears by the following entry in the circuit book :

1816. *March* 15.—Mr. Denman congratulated by the whole circuit on his appointment to the office of Deputy Recorder of Nottingham.—Fine one guinea.

In the latter part of the same year he lost his admirable and excellent father. Dr. Denman died at his then residence in Mount Street, Grosvenor Square, on November 26, 1815, in the eighty-third year of his age. He had retained his health, vigour, and active habits to the last. During his latest visit to Derbyshire, when past fourscore, he had on one occasion walked more than seven miles out and home with his eldest grandson, the present Lord Denman. On another occasion during the same visit, after having been out all the morning with the harriers, he rode on a coach horse, the only means of conveyance at the moment available, to attend an urgent case of mid-wifery at a distance of ten miles from the place (Stoke Hall) where he was staying.

His death, when it came, was quite unexpected. 'There had been no previous confinement,' writes his daughter,

Mrs. Baillie : ' scarcely even the slightest indisposition. Not a moment was allowed for preparation ; but his whole life was a preparation for this awful change. I cannot go on,' she adds, ' without mentioning his virtues and his talents : his excellent understanding, his spotless integrity, his persevering industry, his warm affections, his peculiar readiness to sacrifice every selfish and personal indulgence, with his extreme liberality of every kind towards others.'

There is no exaggeration in this tribute of a daughter's affection : few men have ever lived who deserved and enjoyed a more widely-diffused reputation for virtue and ability than Dr. Thomas Denman.[11]

---

[11] Dr. Denman's 'Treatise on Midwifery' is still of repute in the profession as a standard work : his lectures were very able, and several practitioners who subsequently rose to eminence were among his pupils. He had paid attention to that terrible malady, cancer, and was one of the most zealous promoters of the scheme (since carried out) for establishing a cancer hospital. He induced the beautiful Duchess of Devonshire, whom he attended in her confinements, to nurse her own children, and for a time made that practice fashionable among the higher classes in England.

CHAPTER VI.

DEFENCE OF BRANDRETH AND OTHERS FOR HIGH TREASON.

A.D. 1816, 1817.   ÆT. 37, 38.

Denman's practice on circuit and sessions very considerable in 1816,
1817—Defence of Luddite prisoners in 1816—Circuit Book entries—
Condition of the operatives in Nottinghamshire and the Midland
Counties during and after the close of the Great War — Byron's
testimony to the condition of English operatives in the House of
Lords, February 27, 1812—Distress of the people increased after the
termination of the war—Heavy taxation—No reform, either social or
political—Poor laws—Corn laws—Eldon, Sidmouth, and Castlereagh
—Effect of the great French Revolution on the propertied classes and
the proletariate in England—The year 1817—Famine price of bread—
Stagnation of trade—General want of employment—Distress in Nottinghamshire and the neighbouring counties—Rising under Jeremiah
Brandreth, '*the Nottingham Captain*'—Brandreth's address to his
followers, June 8, 1817—Plan of operations—Night march of the
rioters, June 9, 1817—Brandreth shoots Mrs. Hepworth's servant – Terror
inspired—Arms seized—The yeomanry assemble—Insurgents disperse
at dawn—The leaders captured—Special Commission at Derby, October
14, to try the rioters on a charge of high treason—Denman retained
for the defence of Brandreth, Turner, and Ludlam—Facts clearly
proved—Only question whether they constituted the offence of high
treason by 'levying war against the king'—Argument on this point
in speech for Brandreth—Brandreth convicted of high treason—
Denman, in speaking for Ludlam and Turner, dwells on the strange
power of Brandreth over his fellow men : quotes Byron's description
of Conrad in the 'Corsair'—Conviction and sentence of the three
prisoners—Their execution, November 7, 1817—Graciousness of his
Royal Highness the Prince Regent—Letter from Denman to Merivale
of September 10, 1817—Miss Austen's ' Emma '—Bland and Hodgson
—Ride from Leamington to Dunsbourne (Dr. Baillie's)—Studying the

law of high treason at Fontainebleau—More facts as to Brandreth—
In prison before trial—'No more Derbyshire ribs'—Oliver, the
government spy—What shall we do with our boys?

THE time was now approaching when Denman was to
emerge from the comparative obscurity of mere
provincial reputation, and obtain a wider and more
general recognition of his abilities.

In the summer assizes of 1816 he was extensively
retained for the defence of various Luddite prisoners,
charged with machine-breaking and rioting.   The
exertions thus imposed on him, in addition to his
ordinary circuit work, which had now become considerable, were pretty severe.   To his brother-in-law,
the Rev. R. W. Vevers, he writes on September 4
of the circuit then recently concluded as the 'most
fatiguing and harassing that has ever befallen me.'   It
was also the most profitable he had ever had, and he
had about the same time been able to send to his wife,
who was then with her children at Margate, the welcome intelligence that 'on balancing his banker's
accounts, he found them favourable beyond all expectation.'

That he acquitted himself with great ability in defence of his unfortunate clients is sufficiently attested
by the quaint records in the Circuit Book, which contains the following entries relating to the period now
referred to :

Summer Assizes, 1816.—Mr. Denman congratulated on a
puff from the judge : ' One comfort is, your defence cannot be
in better hands.'—One guinea.

Mr. Reynolds congratulates Mr. Denman on a gross puff

from the judge at Warwick: 'The learned and eloquent counsel, who has defended his client most ably.'

Derby. — The Attorney-General [i.e. of the circuit] presents Mr. Denman for the horrible and merited applause which he received in court at Nottingham.

Before proceeding to relate the facts of the case, which in the next year, 1817, had so much to do with raising the forensic reputation of Denman, a word or two is necessary as to the nature and causes of these Luddite outbreaks. The operatives of Nottingham-shire and the adjacent midland counties had for some years been in a state of chronic discontent—breaking out from time to time into spasmodic acts of violence. It may be remembered that Byron, in 1812, a few days before the publication of 'Childe Harold,'[1] had made his maiden speech in the House of Lords, on a Nottingham Frame-breaking Bill, by which, with the usual policy of those times, it was attempted to repress increasing discontent by increasing severity. The young peer produced considerable effect by his solemn declaration—the declaration of a man of genius who saw vividly into the real truth of things, and on this occasion spoke what he thought—'I have traversed the seat of war in the Peninsula, I have been in some of the most oppressed provinces of Turkey, but never under the most despotic of infidel governments have I beheld such squalid wretchedness as I have seen, since my return, in the heart of a Christian country.' The misery which Byron thus described in 1812, in-stead of diminishing, went on increasing. The Dra-

---

[1] On February 27, 1812.

conian laws, whose policy he denounced, had, as he prophesied would be the case, wholly failed in their object. Nothing was done to improve the social conditions in which these excesses of desperate and famishing men had their origin, and in a few years the discontent and the danger increased to a still more alarming point.

There probably never was a period of our history in which there was so much wretchedness and consequent disaffection among the English lower classes as in the four or five years that immediately followed the close of the Great War. The glory and the excitement of the conflict were over, and the country was left to sustain as it could the enormous burdens imposed by the gigantic struggle. Taxation had never been so oppressive. No Factory Laws had interposed their humane regulations between the avarice of Capital and the sufferings of Labour. The administration of the Poor Laws, giving a positive premium to improvident marriages and numerous families, and making of the poor serfs of the parish, if not of the glebe, was utterly destroying the independence, and materially interfering with the free labour, of the peasantry. The Corn Laws, aided in their malign operation by the occurrence of one or two deficient harvests, kept bread up almost to a famine price. The voice of complaint in the House of Commons could only make itself feebly heard ; for the House of Commons, under the rotten-borough system, was itself under the paramount influence of the land-owning and capitalist classes. Under Lord Liverpool's administration, the grim triumvirate of

Eldon, Sidmouth, and Castlereagh were resolute in repressing all change. Repressive laws, bayonets, and the gallows, were the only remedies they would admit of for popular discontents.

The principles of the French Revolution, which had been carried by the arms of Napoleon over every part of the Continent, shaking thrones, subverting feudalism, radically changing the laws of property and inheritance, had gained no effectual foothold in England, protected from their influence by her 'inviolate' isolation, and her obstinate and successful resistance to the great conqueror. Here the principal effects produced by the great and terrible convulsion had been to animate the possessors of property with a resolute determination to resist all change, and to stir up the proletariate to occasional acts of hopeless insurrection, in the vain quest rather of political Utopias than of real political and social reforms. The working classes were then without the knowledge or the organization they have since acquired. They obeyed only the promptings of a blind despair: the wildest schemes were advocated, the most violent and hopeless enterprises resorted to.

The year 1817 was signalized by several of these attempts at insurrection.[2] It was a period of great and terrible distress. The summer of the preceding year had been one of the worst ever known in England: the rains had been incessant, the harvest was a complete failure, wheat stood rotting in the fields as late as the middle of November. In the next winter, spring,

---

[2] Including among others the insane attempt of the Watsons on Tower Hill.

and summer the price of bread was as high as it had been during the worst years of the war: the profits of trade had been greatly reduced, the demand for our manufactures had diminished, numbers of operatives were thrown out of employment—the sufferings of the poor had reached a climax.

In no part of the country was the distress greater than in Nottinghamshire and the neighbouring counties; and in this district, during the summer of 1817, the people broke out into various acts of armed insurrection.

Among these, one of the most conspicuous was that headed by Jeremiah Brandreth, popularly known in those parts as the 'Nottinghamshire Captain.' It presents a melancholy picture of the ignorance and the desperation of the operatives of those days.

On Sunday, June 8, 1817, at the village of Penkridge, in Nottinghamshire, Brandreth, having convened a meeting of his followers at a public house called the White Horse, proceeded to unfold to them his plan of insurrection. A general rising, he assured them, had been organized with a view of bringing about by armed force a change of government. The party headed by himself was to commence operations on the next night, Monday, June 9. They were to provide themselves with fire-arms by requisitions on the various householders resident in the district, and, when thus supplied with weapons, were to march on through the night to a place of general rendezvous in Nottingham Forest, where they were to be joined by other bands of insurgents from various parts of the

Midland Counties. Brandreth addressed his followers sternly and briefly, repeating at the close of his remarks the homely lines of some rustic Tyrtaeus which embodied the pith of his rugged harangue.[8]

On the Monday night, as arranged, the insurgents began their march : arms were obtained by threats and violence from several householders too terrified for resistance. A Mrs. Hepworth, more courageous than the rest, withstood the demand, barring her front doors and windows at the approach of the tumultuary force : Brandreth ran round to the rear of the premises, and, firing through the back kitchen window, killed an unfortunate man-servant on the spot. The ruthless act answered its immediate purpose : arms were given there and elsewhere without further resistance, and the insurgents marched on through the night towards Nottingham. Meanwhile the authorities had been alarmed. The yeomary were assembled, and when morning dawned on the straggling and desperate band they saw themselves confronted by a force which made resistance hopeless. They dispersed rapidly, without risking an encounter, strewing the ground with the weapons they had so lawlessly obtained.

The leaders of the abortive enterprise, who were speedily captured, were tried for high treason, before a Special Commission, which was opened at Derby, on

---

[8] According to the recollections of the witnesses the lines ran thus :

> Every man his skill must try,
> He must turn out and not deny :
> No bloody soldier must he dread,
> He must turn out and fight for bread ;
> The time is come, you plainly see,
> When Government opposed must be.

October 14, in the same year, under the presidency of Chief Baron Richards. The offence with which they were charged was 'levying war against the king.' Copley, who had greatly distinguished himself on the trial for high treason of the Watsons in the early part of the year, led for the Crown; Denman (Mr. Serjeant Cross with him) was retained for the defence of the principal prisoners—Brandreth, Turner and Ludlam.

The facts were clearly proved, there was no question as to the identity of the prisoners—the case was really a hopeless one for the defence. All that could be done was to contend that the facts proved did not sustain the charge of high treason by *levying war against the king*, but only amounted to an *aggravated riot*.

Denman's argument on this point in the speech for Brandreth was powerful, and ably supported by reference to all those venerable authorities,[4] by virtue of which, in charges of high treason, the accused, in Erskine's phrase, 'stands covered all over with the panoply of the law.'

One of his principal topics was the total and ridiculous inadequacy of the proved means to the alleged object.

The question [he said] is, has war been levied and raised? The charge is the levying war against the king,

---

[4]   'The old laws of England—they
        Whose reverend heads with age are grey
        Children of a wiser day!

from the masque of 'Anarchy,' written in Italy by Shelley in 1819 on hearing the tidings of the Manchester Massacre. Shelley had doubtless read Denman's speeches in defence of the Luddites.

and I deny that this is a levying of war against the king.
Something positive, distinct, and defined is absolutely necessary to distinguish a treason from a riot, and I put 'it to
every one of you whether that is not the impression on your
own minds.   What did these men mean?   What did they
do?   Oh, they meant to overturn the Government.   What
measures did they propose, what steps did they take to effec-
tuate that atrocious purpose?   Did they intend, or in
reasonable language, had they anything like a practicable
contemplation of subverting the Government by levying war
against His Majesty—the mightiest monarch on the face of
the earth—with these few miserable men as their army, with
even their neighbours against them, with more than overpowering resistance at every house to which they came, with
the exception of a few, and particularly that where the
unfortunate occurrence took place of which you have so often
heard.   They were defeated almost without opposition, and
at once put down without a blow.

The advocate put it clearly to the jury that what he
pressed for was not an absolute acquittal, but only an
acquittal on the charge of *treason by levying war
against the king.*

I am not [he said] asking impunity at your hands.
God knows the unfortunate men brought here to-day are
liable to punishment, even when you shall have dismissed
them.   God knows, if the evidence affecting this unhappy
man on other charges besides that of treason be taken to be
true, there is but little fear he will escape with impunity.
Too many laws have been violated, too many feelings have
been wounded, to suppose that this matter should be passed
lightly over.   I think it is not to be expected, and I tell you so
fairly, feeling as I do that this is a public duty I am performing.   I tell you fairly that I do not wish to see these
persons escape with impunity.   I think they ought to be
punished, that they ought to be made sensible of their crime,

and that others ought to be warned by their example. But do not let it be by a strained construction of positive law, which cannot be effected without violating the security of all the king's subjects and the stability of our free constitution.

Notwithstanding the efforts of his counsel, Brandreth, under the direction of the presiding Judge (Chief Baron Richards) that armed insurrection for the purpose of effecting a change of government amounted in ' construction ' of law to a levying of war against the king, was convicted of high treason.

In his speeches for the other two principal prisoners, Turner and Ludlam, Denman endeavoured to find an additional topic of defence in the commanding and overbearing influence of Brandreth (undoubtedly a man of extraordinary powers), which, as he contended, hardly left the responsibility of free agents to those who were acting under his orders and were the mere puppets of his iron will.

In his speech for Turner,[5] the advocate drew a striking picture of the insurgent leader:

Gentlemen, you have seen that man, you were present in court when he was arraigned; you were present in court during his trial, you were present in court when he received his verdict of guilty. I will ask you whether you ever saw a more extraordinary man, a man more evidently gifted by nature with the talent of swaying the minds of the common people with that sort of instinctive influence which even in his humble station there is no resisting—the influence of great courage, of uncommon decision, of unrelenting firmness; the influence of an eye like no eye that I ever beheld before, of a countenance and figure formed for

----

[5] Vol. i. p. 509 of Gurney's verbatim report of the Trials of Brandreth, Turner and Ludlam for High Treason. 2 vols. Butterworth, 1819.

activity, enterprise, and command. Even the dark, strange beard he wore, and his singular costume, seemed to accord with his wild and daring character. The witnesses had seen him but once before, in the night, several months ago, and never paused for a second look—they recognised him in a moment. Like the captain of a band of pirates, or the head of a troop of banditti, he was obviously one of those persons who have in all ages exercised the most absolute control over people in their condition, and to whose natural superiority their moral and physical forces have ever yielded implicit homage. He was their leader—a stranger in the midst of them- -sent over from Nottingham or some other place to delude these miserable men. You heard the tales—the wretched tales he told of a rising in one place and a rising in another; whether he believed them or not, we know that they were entirely false, but they proceeded from him alone, and such are the means by which a few starving villagers were urged to commit all these outrages for bread. It is not wonderful, gentleman, that they had neither intellect nor strength of mind to question his authority, when you saw even the witnesses in the box, who unwillingly attended him in his desperate expedition, speak of him as the 'Captain' in terms of involuntary deference and respect. It was he who directed this wild career of mischief; it was he who stepped forward when a daring act was to be done; it was he who gave the tone and spirit to them all; nor would they have stirred a step without his influence and command.

In his speech for Ludlam, instead of repeating his own description of the 'Nottinghamshire Captain,' he quoted from Byron's 'Corsair' the splendid and well-known lines which depict the personal appearance of Conrad, and reveal the secret of his influence over his followers,[6] ' a passage,' said the speaker ' which will

---

[6] With these he mingles not but to command,
Few are his words, but keen his eye and hand,

perfectly bring before you the character, and even the appearance of Brandreth—the commanding qualities of his powerful but uncultivated mind, and the nature of his influence over those he seduced to outrage.'[7]

Turner and Ludlam, like Brandreth, under a similar direction from the presiding judge, were both convicted of high treason, and all the three were respectively sentenced to be hanged, beheaded, and quartered.

The sentence was pronounced on October 25, 1817, and on November 7, as the grim record runs, 'Jeremiah Brandreth, William Turner, and Isaac Ludlam the elder, were drawn on a hurdle to a platform erected in front of the county gaol of Derby, where they were hanged till they were dead; when they were cut down and their heads were severed from their bodies; His Royal Highness the Prince Regent, in the name and on the behalf of His Majesty, having graciously remitted the remainder of the sentence, the quartering.'

Although Denman failed in procuring an acquittal, which, indeed, on the clearly proved facts of the case, under the ruling of the Court, and in the alarmed temper of the times, would have been a practical impossibility, yet the spirit, the manliness, and the high tone of his speeches for the defence had attracted con-

His name appals the fiercest of his crew,
And tints each swarthy cheek with ashen hue;
Still sways their souls with that commanding art
That dazzles, leads, yet chills the vulgar heart.
What is that spell that thus his lawless train
Confess and envy, yet oppose in vain;
What should it be that thus their faith can bind ?—
The power, the nerve, the magic of the mind.

[7] Vol. ii. Brandreth, Turner, and Ludlam trials, pp. 235, 236.

siderable attention, impressing the Bench and the Bar with a conviction of his ability, and the public with a sentiment not only of admiration for his eloquence, but of confidence in the firmness of his character and the strength and ardour of his constitutional convictions. He was henceforth regarded as a man marked out for future eminence.

The following passages from a letter to Merivale, written in the Long Vacation that immediately preceded this celebrated trial, will show how laboriously Denman prepared himself for his important task. It gives also some particulars, not devoid of interest, as to his literary tastes and as to the then status of two of his old college friends, Hodgson and Bland, while it supplies still further information as to the singular man who headed the Nottingham rising, and whom Denman had just been retained to defend.

Stoke Albany: September 10, 1817.[8]

My dear Merivale,—I felt myself a very shabby fellow for not at once accepting your challenge, and sending you a letter of three sheets from Leamington [where Denman had been spending part of the Long Vacation], nor do I well know what has prevented me except downright idleness. The books, however, that you recommended never fell in my way, nor were they, indeed, at all accessible. 'Lalla Rookh' was the only new work I could lay hold of, unless 'Emma' (by the author of 'Pride and Prejudice') deserves the name—a very silly book I think.[9] Who wrote 'l'Esprit de la

---

[8] It was here that Lord Denman died in 1854 : it was at this time in the occupation of his brother-in-law, the Rev. R. W. Vevers, the then incumbent of the parish.

[9] A judgment that will shock those who, not without reason, regard 'Emma' as the masterpiece of Miss Austen, but in an ardent and ambitious

Ligue.'[10]   By great good luck I found it and was delighted. Bland I saw often.[11]   He seems to be going on very comfortably, and is in good spirits and as entertaining as ever. Hodgson was with him one day, the picture of health, and with a stock of learning (according to Bland) increased by his solitary life in the High Peak to a superhuman extent.[12] Tom [13] is become a very decent companion : we rode a journey of sixty miles, from Leamington in Gloucestershire, on a visit to the Baillie's, who live in one of the most beautiful wooded valleys in the world.[14]

To-morrow I go to London on my way to Fontainebleau. My particular reason for making this journey is that I may have complete leisure to pursue without distraction my studies on the subject of High Treason. Of this I knew ten days ago as much as I do of the practice of the Court of Chancery, but since it will be my duty about a month hence to defend some of the persons who are to take their trials in Derbyshire for that offence, it is my duty to be able at least to talk a language intelligible to those who know something on the subject. I shall cram Hale and Hawkins (' Pleas of the Crown '), Gibbs, Wetherell, and Copley, with unremitting assiduity.[15] The fees to be taxed on this occasion will not make any man's fortune, as every man among them is as destitute of money as common sense, and the great ringleader of them all has actually for many years been receiving parish relief. His name is Brandreth : much is said of the

young advocate not an unnatural judgment.   The defender of Brandreth was hardly likely to take much interest in the irrepressible gossip of Miss Bates, or the imaginary ailments of Mr. Woodhouse.

[10] Anquetil.

[11] Bland was now married and settled on a curacy at Kenilworth.

[12] Hodgson had become Vicar of Bakewell, where he was now living with his first wife, a sister of Mrs. Bland.

[13] The present Lord Denman, then in his thirteenth year.

[14] Dunsbourne, near Cirencester, purchased by Dr. Baillie, now owned by his son, Mr. W. H. Baillie.

[15] Sir Vicary Gibbs, Sir Charles Wetherell, and Mr. Copley had greatly distinguished themselves in the trial of the Watsons for High Treason (1817).

stern and inflexible patriotism of his character. When visited in prison by a gor-bellied magistrate he poured out upon his figure a volley of abuse and mockery, and, when solemnly warned that what he had done was very likely to prove fatal to him, he replied, with great indifference, 'I need not care whether I live or die, for there are no " Derbyshire ribs" now.' Perhaps you may be as much puzzled as I was to find out the force of this reason for despising life : it turned out, on enquiry, that his livelihood had depended on making hose of a particular description bearing that name, and for which, in the change of fashion, there had ceased to be any demand. There is great reason to believe that the respectable Mr. Oliver [16] is at the bottom of the whole business, and you will do me more service than I can describe if you will tell me any pretty stories you can collect from Herodotus to Froissart—from Froissart to the 'Causes Célèbres,' and from the 'Causes Célèbres' to the last Newgate Calendar, touching the credibility and honour of spies. At any rate, I will not excuse you from writing me a long letter to London in a fortnight, when I shall return from the land of violets.

I hope Mrs. Merivale is quite well, your family going on happily, and all your boys flourishing. Have you at all considered what to do with them? It is but yesterday that they were born, but in a still shorter time they must be disposed of. I used at one time to think partially of trade in some of its branches, but am frightened by the fate of ' Derbyshire Ribs.'

[16] A noted Government spy and informer of these bad times, specially skilled in 'getting up' insurrections. In the summer of 1817 Sir F. Burdett had specially brought the conduct of this infamous person under the notice of the House of Commons, and accused Government of employing him as an agent to seduce the ignorant and unwary into seditious practices and then betray them.

CHAPTER VII.

PARLIAMENT—M.P. FOR WAREHAM AND NOTTINGHAM.

A.D. 1818 TO 1820.   ÆT. 39 TO 41.

Denman, in 1818, returned to Parliament for the close borough of Wareham—Letter to his brother-in-law, Vevers, August 21, 1818—His political stand-point—A constitutional Whig, opposed to Burdett and the Radicals—Denman takes his seat January 14, 1819—The Whig opposition in 1819—Denman's earlier career in the House of Commons less brilliant than was expected—Causes of this—Parliamentary distinction not his first object—Doubtful whether he ever could have become a leading debater in the House of Commons—His talents and character better adapted for the House of Lords—Denman's course as a member of the House of Commons honourable, useful, and enlightened—His own estimate of his House of Commons career from 1819 to 1826—The first session of 1819—Legal reforms advocated by Denman—Opposes allowance of 10,000*l.* a year to the Duke of York for taking care of the King his father—Speech on Foreign Enlistment Bill—The Holy Alliance characterised—The recess—Condition of the people in 1819—Meetings for Radical reform of Parliament—The Manchester Massacre, August 19, 1819—Meetings called to protest against it—Lord Fitzwilliam, for presiding at one, dismissed from the Lord Lieutenancy of the West Riding—Second session of 1819—The Six Acts—Denman's opposition to—Denounces the Manchester Massacre—Speech against the Seditious Meetings Bill—Against the Blasphemous Libels Bill—Close of the session of the Six Acts—Death of George III. and accession of George IV., Jan. 20, 1820—The Cato Street conspiracy—Dissolution of Parliament—Denman invited to stand for Nottingham—Returned after a close contest—Expenses of the election—Denman's means a good deal crippled by them—His difficulty in getting money together—Letter to his wife from Warwick, April 10, 1820—Dr. Parr at Hatton and in Warwick for the Assizes—The Blands at Kenilworth—Michael Angelo Taylor—Messrs. Parkes's smoke-consuming apparatus—Last sessions as Deputy-Recorder of Nottingham—Political feeling there after the election.

THE reputation he had acquired by his defence of the Nottinghamshire insurgents, and a just confidence in his own abilities, led Denman, at the general election of 1818, to aspire to a seat in the House of Commons. After a previous unsuccessful attempt at Nottingham, he was returned with Mr. Calcraft for the close borough of Wareham, in Dorsetshire, by the joint influence and at the joint expense of the Duke of Devonshire and the Marquis of Lansdowne, two great Whig potentates, who were desirous of securing so able and efficient a recruit for the ranks of the Liberal party.

The following passage from a letter written by Denman, soon after his election, to his brother-in-law, the Rev. R. W. Vevers, then on a visit to Lord Chesterfield at Bradby Hall,[1] will show clearly enough his political position as a nominee of the two Whig leaders:

I agree with you in thinking that an exposure of Sir Francis Burdett's conduct and principles [Burdett was then the leader of the ultra-Liberals] might be useful to the good cause of Whiggism; but I am quite convinced by my own experience at Nottingham that, on that subject above all others, whenever passion is excited, there is an end to reason. Sir Francis Burdett's popularity is personal in a remarkable degree. A Whiggish attack on him would have more effect in making the Whigs suspected than in undeceiving a single partizan.

I flatter myself that the party is gaining the best possible strength—the influence of public opinion; but this can only

---

[1] Vevers married a sister (illegitimate) of the sixth Lord Chesterfield— long Master of the Buckhounds—who afterwards gave him the living of Cubley, near Ashdowne, in Derbyshire.

be secured by a greater deference to the principles of Reform and Retrenchment than perhaps any party, as such, would yet be willing to pay. The more I see of the men I am associated with, the better I like them, and the more I am satisfied that these men are patriotic and generous, with as little alloy of selfishness as can be consistently with the currency of the metal. Among the real leaders I do not think there is one whose ambitious sentiments are not closely connected with the wish and intention to serve the public in the best possible manner.

Denman first took his seat as member for Wareham on January 14, 1819.

The death of Horner in 1817, and still more that of Romilly in November 1818, had somewhat enfeebled the Whig Opposition, which was now nominally led by Tierney, supported by Mackintosh, but which really owed the greater portion of its influence with the country to the energy and genius of Henry Brougham. There was a favourable opening for a young politician of high ability, and a good deal was expected of the new member for Wareham.

It cannot be concealed that Denman's earlier career in the House of Commons, though useful, manly, honourable and dignified, did not quite equal in brilliancy the anticipations of the chiefs of his party, or the high-raised hopes of his friends.

A main reason for this no doubt was that Parliamentary distinction was never his primary object, and accordingly never called forth the full exercise of all his powers. In a letter written to his mother, who, on the occasion of his first attempt at Nottingham, had expressed some alarm at the probable effects on his professional practice of a premature entrance into the House, he explained his views on the subject with his usual sincerity and distinctness. ' Do not,' he writes, ' suffer anyone to suppose that I am sacrificing my profession to politics : *my family being always my first object, my profession is and always will be my second.*'

This partly, no doubt, accounts for the fact of his want of prëeminent success in the House of Commons, but it does not, perhaps, entirely account for it. It may be doubted whether, even if he had devoted himself more exclusively to politics, his success would have been of the highest order. He wanted some of the qualifications, natural or acquired, for a House of Commons leader. He had not the indomitable energy, the active combativeness, the restless and unsleeping vigilance, the vast and varied information, which made of Henry Brougham in his prime a Parliamentary power of the first magnitude. The judgment seat and the House of Lords were the proper fields of distinction for Denman. In the House of Lords, especially, his high character, his unswerving consistency, and his dignified eloquence ultimately won for him a position which formed a marked contrast to that occupied by his old friend—the brilliant and versatile ex-Chancellor— during the long twilight of his political decline.

But though Denman's career in the House of Commons was neither so brilliant nor so successful as his reputation before he entered it had led many to expect, yet it is only when tried by the very highest standard that it can be pronounced to have fallen short of the mark. His general views on all the leading

questions of the day were enlightened ; his attachment
to constitutional liberty was ardent ; his sense of public
duty was high and pure ; his courage in supporting the
truth and the right was firm and unflinching. He never
lost an opportunity of promoting the amendment of the
law, or of mitigating the severity of our then sanguinary
criminal code ; the abolition of death punishment in
cases of forgery was mainly his work ; he was forward
and fearless in denouncing all instances of jobbery and
corruption in high places ; every species of oppression
at home and abroad, especially the crowning iniquity
of the African Slave Trade, ever found in him an active
and unsparing foe.

In a paper which he has left behind him relating to
the events of 1820, and the immediately subsequent
years—a paper from which copious extracts will be
made in the following pages—he has thus placed on
record his own estimate of his Parliamentary career
from 1819 to 1826. They are the words of one not
given to self-praise, nor too easily satisfied with his own
performances. ' I fairly own,' he writes in 1828, ' that
I look back on my Parliamentary career with no small
satisfaction. I have never wished to recall a sentiment
I uttered, or to change a vote I gave. I did my best
for the interests of freedom, justice, and truth in every
part of the world. For every species of reform,
Parliamentary, legal, and economical, I constantly lifted
up my voice ; to every corruption and abuse I declared
the enmity I felt. In all debates on the question of
slavery I took that side which must mitigate its horrors
and ultimately accomplish its abolition. With a strong

sense of the just deference due to the party, I sometimes differed from them, especially on Irish questions and the necessity at particular periods for what, by a strange perversion of language, are called strong measures—rashness, violence, the substitution of arbitrary power for law being, in my opinion, at once proofs of weakness and acts of weakness. My constituents and I were strictly united in general opinion, but I offended many among them by constantly supporting the principles of Free Trade, in spite of their partiality for restrictions of sundry kinds. Though my language was sometimes reckoned too strong, and my course too indiscriminating, I have reason to think that on the whole credit was given me for honesty of intention ; and in the House of Commons I had the good fortune to make many friendships of the highest value.'

In the first session of 1819 he was not an infrequent speaker. His contributions to the progress of Law Reform, though neither comprehensive nor important, were all in the right direction. On the 4th of February he supported a motion of Michael Angelo Taylor for giving the benefit of a general gaol delivery and commission of assize and nisi prius to Westmoreland, Cumberland, Durham, Northumberland, and Newcastle-on-Tyne ;[2] on the 10th of the same month he spoke in favour of the Attorney-General, Sir Samuel Shepherd's, Bill for abolishing the antiquated abuses of appeals of murder, and wager of battle on writs of right ;[3] and on the 28th of April he himself brought in a bill

---

[2] Hansard, Parl. Deb. vol. xxxix. p. 294, 295.
[3] Hansard, Parl. Deb. vol. xxxix. p. 417, 418.

for facilitating the despatch of business in the Court of King's Bench by allowing one of the judges to sit in Term for hearing causes, while the rest were sitting in Banco ; by enabling sentence to be passed in many cases at the assizes, instead of, as hitherto, in Term ; and by allowing the Court to sit on the 30th of January, the 'martyrdom' of Charles the First notwithstanding.[4]

On the 25th of February, 1819, he spoke at some length, and with considerable force, against the resolution introduced by Lord Castlereagh, to pay 10,000*l.* a year out of the Civil List to the Duke of York to meet the expenses incurred by him as custodian of His Majesty's person.   On this occasion he declaimed against the hardship and injustice of calling upon the people, at a time when they were overwhelmed with the difficulties brought upon them by the late war, ' to submit to an increase of their burdens for the purpose of inducing a son to perform the most sacred of all duties to an aged parent. While Parliament (he reminded the House) was discussing grants of thousands to royal dukes, the questions out of doors were, " How many more paupers must be consigned to our workhouses ? " " How much more of misery and crime must exist ? " " In what degree must we add to the contamination of our crowded gaols ? " ' [5]

---

[4] Hansard, Parl. Deb. vol. xxxix. p. 1481.

[5] Hansard, Parl. Deb. vol. xxxix. p. 667 to 776. It was on this occasion that Scarlett made a famous speech, ' one of the ablest,' says Brougham, ' that any professional man ever made '—a great success, but fated to be almost his last (' Memoirs,' vol. iii. p. 471 in Appendix). ' He sate down amid loud and general cheers ' (Hansard, Parl. Deb. vol. xxxix. p. 599 to 605).

On the 3rd of June he made a spirited speech in support of Sir Robert Wilson, who had moved the rejection of the Foreign Enlistment Act, introduced by the Attorney-General, the real object of which was to prevent British subjects from assisting the Spanish colonies of South America in their struggle for independence.[6]   He declared that

there was not a man in the country with the heart of an Englishman that did not ardently pray for the success of the Spanish Independents; and he denounced the government of Ferdinand as ' the worst government in the world.'

If this Bill [he said] had originated from any communication on the part of the Spanish Government, he thought the House called upon to regard it with the gravest suspicion; but if it proceeded from a higher than its ostensible quarter, if it came recommended by that imperial combination (the Holy Alliance) which had arrogated to itself the right of disposing of the fates of kingdoms and empires, and which had undertaken to regulate Europe, and to maintain what it chose to term her tranquillity, it was, in his opinion, still more objectionable.

During the Parliamentary recess of this year the people, who were still suffering from aggravated distress, held meetings in various parts of the country, under Hunt and other popular leaders, in favour of root-and-branch measures—*radical* measures, as they about this time began to be called—of Parliamentary Reform —Universal Suffrage, Annual Parliaments, and Vote by Ballot.   The condition of England was such as to

---

[6] It was in the course of this debate, but on an earlier night, May 19, that Mackintosh made one of the ablest of his speeches in Parliament (see ' Lord Dalling's Historical Characters : Mackintosh,' part ii. sec. v.). It is very imperfectly reported in Hansard. Denman's speech is in Hansard, Parl. Deb. vol. xl. p. 876 to 884.

fill thoughtful minds with the greatest disquietude. ' My views of the state of England,' wrote Lord Grey about this time to Henry Brougham,[7] ' are more and more gloomy.   Everything is tending, and has for some time been tending, to a complete separation between the higher and lower orders of society, a state of things which can only end in the destruction of liberty, or in a convulsion which may too probably produce the same result.'   The Government, blind to the real signs of the times, were determined to put down the growing spirit of disaffection by sheer force.

On August 19, 1819, took place the memorable transaction known in history as the ' Manchester massacre,' when a great assembly in St. Peter's Field, near Manchester, having met, in the exercise of a clear constitutional right, to petition for Parliamentary Reform, was violently dispersed by the yeomanry, many of the people being trampled down and wounded, and several killed.

This unjustifiable act of violence produced the strongest feeling of indignation throughout the country, and various public meetings were held, more especially in the north of England, to protest against the action of the Government.   For presiding at one of the most important of these meetings—that held in the great county of York—Earl Fitzwilliam, on the 23rd of October, was summarily dismissed from the Lord Lieutenancy of the West Riding.   It was on this occasion that Brougham, writing to Lord Grey,[8] said

[7] ' Lord Brougham's Memoirs,' vol. ii. p. 342: letter from Lord Grey of August 25, 1819.

[8] Ibid. vol. ii. p. 340 : letter to Lord Grey of October 24.

deliberately of the Tory Administration, ' I have little doubt that they seriously and desperately intend to change the Government into one less free.'

On November 23 a short but important session of Parliament was held for the purpose of passing the Government measures of repression, generally known as the Six Acts—Acts for the seizure of arms, for the suppression of secret military training, for the punishment of blasphemous and seditious libels, for the putting down of seditious meetings, for increasing the stamp duty on newspapers.

To one and all of these restrictive measures Denman offered a firm and constitutional resistance. His tone was elevated and lofty, manly and spirited; but although, on one or two occasions, he sat down amid general cheers from the Opposition, there is nothing in his speeches, as reported, which makes an approach to the highest order of eloquence.

His opinion on the legality of the Manchester meeting, and the illegality of its suppression, was given clearly and decisively in the debate on the Address :—

He conceived that the meeting was perfectly legal, and that it was improperly dispersed. It was a most momentous subject—a subject that would never be exhausted until the House granted a full enquiry. All that he would now say was, that he could never concur in the Address until he should be convinced of the necessity of the measures to which it referred, and until the greatest evil of which the people of England ever had to complain—not merely the establishment of military despotism, but, which was more alarming, an attempt to maintain that military despotism by force as consistent with the law of England—had been thoroughly investigated.[9]

This was on November 26 : on the 30th he went fully into the facts and law of the case in a speech which called forth the general applause of the House, and which concluded as follows :—

The people assembled at Manchester were ignorant of the nature of the warrant against Hunt ; and yet many of them were cut down and maimed for impeding, or being supposed to impede, its execution. Such conduct could not, he contended, be regarded as consistent with the law of England, or with the law of any civilized nation upon the earth, and therefore the circumstances connected with it imperiously called for enquiry. This enquiry was the more necessary in consequence of the measures proposed by the noble lord, to none of which, as an Englishman anxious for the maintenance of his country's rights, could he possibly persuade himself to give his assent.[10]

In committee on the various bills he was active and persevering in his opposition. On December 8, upon the clause of the ' Seditious Meetings Bill ' indemnifying magistrates in case of killing or maiming in dispersing such meetings, he exclaimed, ' Unless everything cruel and despotic is to be raked into this measure, unless a contradiction is to be given in it to every principle of law and justice, unless complete power is to be placed in the hands of magistrates over life, limb, and liberty, without responsibility, this clause, I am confident, cannot pass.'[11] But pass it did, like all the other unjustifiable clauses of these unjusti-

<hr>

[9] Hansard, Parl. Deb. vol. xli. p. 313, 314.
[10] Hansard, Parl. Deb. vol. xli. p. 550 to 553.
[11] Hansard, Parl. Deb. vol. xli. p. 867.

fiable and oppressive laws.   The last protest he made was on December 23, against the 'Blasphemous Libels Bill.'

His great objection [he said] to the measure was the total absence of all necessity for entertaining it.   This was a period of alarm.   But the liberty of the Press was not to be looked upon as fit only for seasons of calm, as a fair-weather friend to be discarded in a storm.   He might say of it what had been said of literature in general, that it adorned prosperity—'secundas res ornat'—and that it was our security in times of danger—'in rebus adversis perfugium et solatium præbet.'   He had said on a former night that the restrictive measures now adopted would drive the people to desperation unless more attention were shown to their feelings.   In defending their liberties, he, for one, would never consent to lower that proud tone which was held in the best times, fearing, as he did, that if the shackles at present intended for them were once imposed, the effect of lowering that tone would be to perpetuate them.[12]

The Session of the Six Acts was closed just before Christmas, ministers having succeeded in passing all their bills without any substantial alteration.

Soon after the commencement of the ensuing year, on January 29, 1820, George III. died, in the 82nd year of his age, and the new reign of George IV. had hardly begun when the desperate enterprise led by Thistlewood, and generally known as the Cato Street Conspiracy, was discovered and defeated.   The conspirators had arranged that on February 23, at a cabinet dinner to be given by Lord Harrowby, in Grosvenor Square, they were first to massacre all the ministers then and there assembled, and next to stir up

---

[12] Hansard, Parl. Deb. vol. xli. p. 1516 to 1524.

insurrection throughout London, by proclaiming in different parts of the metropolis the downfall of the Government. The plot was discovered in time; the police acted adroitly, and, on the evening of February 23, the conspirators were surprised, and after some resistance seized, in the loft where they used to assemble, in Cato Street, Edgware Road, just as they were on the point of setting forth on their mad and murderous enterprise. They were speedily tried, convicted, and sentenced—Thistlewood and four others of the leaders being beheaded.

The Tories, of course, all exclaimed that this wild and wicked attempt proved the policy and necessity of the Six Acts; the Whigs, with more reason, argued that it only showed the tendency of extreme measures of coercion to drive the people to despair.

A dissolution of Parliament had taken place as of course on the demise of the Crown, and Denman, in the general election that ensued, became, for the first time, member for Nottingham.

'My success in Parliament,' he writes, in the autobiographical fragment already alluded to, ' had not been such as to induce the party to bring me in a second time as representative for a close borough.' Tierney, as official leader of the Opposition, in anticipation of the old king's death, had spoken to him with a view to his providing himself with a seat, and at Northampton, while on the spring circuit, he was invited by a numerous and influential deputation to become a candidate for Nottingham, an invitation which he at once accepted.

The contest proved to be close and severe. Denman and his colleague, Mr. Birch, were returned, at the close of the twelfth day's poll, by a majority of 33, with the singular circumstance that precisely the same number of votes were given for the two candidates in each interest—1891 to 1858.

The expense was, of course, considerable. The agreement between the candidates had been that each should contribute 1,000*l.*,[18] and their friends in the town 1,000*l.* more; beyond the 3,000*l.* thus provided for, the two candidates were to be jointly responsible. The actual cost, as almost always happens, greatly outran the estimate. 'I was soon,' writes Denman, in the paper already quoted from, 'some hundreds of pounds out of pocket, beyond my stipulated 1,000*l.* ; and, though very handsome things were done respecting the subscription, Earl Fitzwilliam, to whom I was then an entire stranger, giving 500*l.*, Lord Sondes 500*l.*, Lord Lansdowne 100*l.*, Lord Yarborough 100*l.*, &c., yet my affairs received a very severe shock.' The apprehensions, therefore, of his friends as to the imprudence of the step in a financial point of view had not been unfounded; but, as events soon proved, the object was well worth the sacrifice.

The following letter to his wife, written from War-

---

[18] 'I had great difficulty,' Denman writes in the MS. already referred to, 'in scraping my money together; fees due, rents in arrear, the little I had in the funds, only 300*l.* or 400*l.* : my excellent brother-in-law, Dr. Baillie, lent me 500*l.*; Reader, who had at Northampton strongly advised me to become a candidate, 400*l.*, &c., &c.' This seems to show either that Denman had not greatly benefited in a pecuniary sense by the deaths of his uncle and father, or that what he had so inherited had to a great extent gone in payment of debts previously incurred.

wick shortly after his success at Nottingham, gives a fair notion of his life on circuit after he had risen to a leading position at the bar, and a seat in the House of Commons.

Warwick: April 10, 1820.

My dearest Love,—Our labours draw to a conclusion. There are not more than four or five cases remaining for trial, in one of which I have been long retained—a horrible murder of a farmer's wife by a maidservant who had robbed her. But for this important matter I should long ago have withdrawn from the trifling concerns that have been lingering on through the week. Now for my private history. On *Sunday* I dined at Hatton (near Warwick) with Dr. Parr [14]—a most good-humoured, animated, and instructive conversation. *Monday* and *Tuesday* with the few remaining barristers, who, by good fortune, are gentlemanly men, and form a very pleasant party. *Wednesday* at Mr. John Parkes's, a most excellent and friendly family; Dr. Parr was there, and in the highest spirits. *Thursday* at Mr. Greathead's,[15] where we had music, good pictures, literary talk, and first-rate wine. *Friday* at the Judges, and in the evening drank tea at Parkes the elder's, where Parr was again the delight of the assembly. Yesterday (*Saturday*) I was engaged to dine with the Blands, at Kenilworth,[16] but I was prevented by my late attendance in Court; so I am going over to pay them a visit this morning, and afterwards dine again at Hatton (Dr. Parr's). There is still more gaiety in store, for Mr. Parkes is to entertain Michael Angelo Taylor to-morrow, and I am expected.

[14] Dr. Samuel Parr, born 1747, died 1825, æt. 78.

[15] Of Guy's Cliff, near Warwick. His heiress in 1822 married the Honourable Charles Percy, son of the Earl of Beverley, brother of the late, and uncle of the present, Duke of Northumberland.

[16] Bland died at Kenilworth, in embarrassed circumstances, in 1825. Denman, with characteristic generosity, headed a subscription got up for the widow, with a contribution of 100*l.*, which, at the time, he could but ill spare.

You will ask who the Parkes's are?   Answer: Great manufacturers in worsted, who have recently discovered a method for making fires consume the whole of their own smoke.   They employ a steam-engine, and have three large furnaces in their factory, the smoke of which escapes through one chimney, but is so entirely destroyed in its passage that the mouth of the chimney is surrounded with as clear an atmosphere as can be found on the top of Mont Blanc. Conceive the advantages of this invention in great towns, choked as they are with breweries, soaperies, &c.   They want a patent for it, and I hope we shall get them one.   Taylor was chairman of a committee in the last Parliament for discussing a method of effecting this object, and is coming to witness its complete success here on Tuesday.

I hope to leave Warwick, and shall hold my last sessions at Nottingham as Deputy-Recorder on Thursday.[17]   Our adversaries are extremely ill-tempered, and have been acting a most despicable part since the election: they talk of petitioning, but we laugh at their threats.

I fear I must not hope to see you before Sunday, but then! oh then! how happy we will be!   Your picture of the boy is beautiful.[18]   God bless you and all the children.   My best thanks and kind love to my mother, whose letter [no doubt of congratulation on his success at Nottingham] is only too short.   The carriage is at the door for Kenilworth.   Ever most faithfully and affectionately yours.

[17] Denman resigned the Deputy-Recordership on becoming member for the b rough.

[18] The Honourable Mr. Justice Denman, born 1819.

CHAPTER VIII.

THE QUEEN'S ARRIVAL—DENMAN HER SOLICITOR-GENERAL.

A.D. 1820.   ÆT. 41.

Trial of Queen Caroline—Denman's MS. narrative of the year 1820—
Drawn up in 1821—How dealt with—Antecedents of the Queen—
Lives separate from her husband since 1796—His scandalous profligacy
—She leaves England in 1814 and resides abroad till 1820—Her con-
duct while abroad—Milan Commission in 1818—Its secret report, 1819
—The Queen's name ordered to be omitted from the Liturgy, Feb. 11,
1820—The Queen determines to come to England—This determination
supported by Wood—Opposed by Brougham—Antagonism between
Brougham and Wood—Denman takes a middle line—His chivalrous feeling for the Queen—Feeling of the people for the Queen and against the
King—Commencement of MS. narrative—Denman appointed Solicitor-
General to the Queen, Brougham being her Attorney-General—Ought
the Queen to come to England?—Arguments in favour of her coming
— Alderman Wood—Denman's opinion of him—Brougham's nickname
for him, 'Absolute Wisdom '—Line of the Whig Opposition—Tierney's
alternative policy—Scheme of a divorce—Sir John Leach—Denman's
opinion of the Whig policy—Tierney's interview with Denman as to
his acceptance of office from the Queen—Possibility of the King's
taking a fancy to the Queen—'Fat, fair and fifty '—Interview of
Brougham and Denman with Lord Eldon respecting professional rank
—'The serpent more subtle than all the beasts of the field '—
Brougham and Denman called to the Bench of Lincoln's Inn—Sir F.
Burdett tried at Leicester, March, 20, 1820, for seditious libel—Makes
his own speech and is convicted—Denman moves for a new trial—
Mr. Justice Bayley's judgment in *Rex* v. *Burdett*—The Queen leaves
Italy and arrives at Geneva—Alderman Wood goes to Geneva to meet
her—Queen at St. Omer's—Brougham goes to meet her—She leaves
him there and sets out for London, where she arrives June 6—Denman
in Brougham's absence, acts as her chief law officer—Brougham

arrives—Denman summoned to meet the Queen at Alderman Wood's
house—Her progress through the streets—Alderman Wood by her
side—The Queen in sight—The Queen's bearing, dress and appearance
—'That beast Wood'—The Queen's delusion as to the King's feeling
for her—Denman's first reception by the Queen—Brougham imparts
his apprehensions to Denman—Denman's testimony as to Brougham's
zeal for his client—The Queen's suspicions of Brougham—The charges
against the Queen opened in the House of Commons—Brougham's
incomparable first speech—Queen's suspicions of Brougham not removed—Social position of the Queen—Are the ladies to call upon
her?—Mrs. Brougham and Mrs. Denman do not call—Denman's reflections on this—Remarks by the present writer—High spirit of the
Queen—'I will be crowned'—Addresses to the Queen—Her reception
of the Lord Mayor and Common Council—Her popularity with the
London mob.

THE TRIAL of Queen Caroline was one of the most important events of Lord Denman's life, and he has left
behind him in manuscript a narrative drawn up in the
year 1821, of what he then considered most worthy of
being recorded in connection with it.   Had this narrative been composed at a later date, or with a view to
present publication, it would probably have omitted
some particulars which have now ceased to be either
interesting or important ; and would almost certainly
have included others, some mention of which, though
then unnecessary, has, after the lapse of more than half
a century, become absolutely indispensable to a right
understanding of the course of the proceedings, and of
the part taken in them by Denman himself.   It would
be neither just to its writer, nor fair to the reader, to
print this fragment simply as it stands : the plan
adopted will be to give textually by far the greater
portion of it, omitting nothing that is material, and
supplying from time to time such few additional items
of information as may seem requisite for presenting a

clear view of Denman's exertions in the progress of this celebrated cause.[1]

Caroline of Brunswick, it may be as well to remind the reader at the outset, was in the fifty-third year of her age when these proceedings commenced.[2] In 1796, after a single year of cohabitation, she had lived apart from her husband, whose whole life and conduct, ever since the first day of their unfortunate union, had been, and down to the period now under consideration had continued to be, one unbroken course of bare-faced and notorious profligacy.

In August 1814, the Princess had left England for the Continent (almost as soon as the Continent was open), and had resided there, principally in various parts of Italy, but occasionally making excursions as far as Egypt and the Holy Land, till the death of George III., at the commencement of the year 1820, made her titular Queen of England.

Her own conduct, during her six years' residence abroad, even if it had not provably overstepped the line which separates levity from guilt, had been, at all events, reckless and compromising to the extremest verge of imprudence.

In 1818, at the suggestion of Sir John Leach, then Vice-Chancellor of England (a favourite of the Regent and a rival of Lord Eldon, whose high office he coveted), there was issued, with the sanction of the then Cabinet,

---

[1] The additional matter will of course be carefully and clearly distinguished from the text of the fragment.

[2] Caroline Amelia of Brunswick; born, May 17, 1768; married, April 8, 1795; separated, April 30, 1796; died, August 7, 1821, in her fifty-fourth year.

a Secret Commission to investigate and report on the alleged irregularities of the Princess. This Commission, called, from the principal place of its sittings, the Milan Commission, submitted to the Cabinet a secret report, which charged Caroline with several acts of flagrant and scandalous immorality, especially with having carried on an adulterous intercourse with her Italian chamberlain, Bergami.

The first result of this damaging secret report was soon to be made public. On February 11, 1820, within a fortnight after the accession of George IV., the name of the Queen, as Caroline had then become, was by solemn Order in Council directed to be omitted from the Liturgy. This public insult, the crowning sequence to innumerable acts of petty persecution during the long years of her continental residence, seems to have finally determined the Queen to brave all risks, and return at once to England, to clear her character and claim her rights.

This determination was strongly supported (if not originally suggested) by that party among her advisers whose leader was the famous Alderman Wood (father of the late Chancellor, Lord Hatherley), and was as strongly discountenanced by Brougham, who had for some time been her principal legal adviser, and who, as subsequent events proved, had formed a much sounder judgment than her more hot-headed supporters as to the course best suited to her real interests.

In reading Denman's personal narrative, this species of antagonism between Brougham and Wood must not be lost sight of : it explains a good deal of the jealousy and suspicion which the Queen appears throughout to have entertained with regard to her principal legal adviser.

Denman, who knew far less than Brougham of the Queen's antecedent conduct, and whose chivalrous temper led him principally to regard her as 'the most wronged and insulted of womankind,' occupied a sort of middle position between Brougham and Wood ; but he was occasionally more inclined than his less enthusiastic leader to take part with what may be called the extreme left of the Queen's adherents.

As to the great body of the People, they, with the rough instinct of English generosity, inflamed in this instance by dislike and distrust of the Government, sided heartily with the weaker party, who, even if she had been culpably imprudent, nay, it might be criminal in her conduct, had at all events been most atrociously ill-treated by the husband who was now hunting her down to her destruction. As Lord Brougham has well expressed it in his 'Autobiography,' ' the strength of the Queen's case lay in the general demurrer which all men, both in and out of Parliament, made, viz., admit everything to be true which is alleged against the Queen, yet, after the treatment she has received ever since she first came to England, her husband had no right to the relief prayed by him, or the punishment sought against her.' [3]

With these few words of preliminary explanation we proceed to cite verbatim from the autobiographical

---

[3] 'Brougham's Memoirs,' vol. ii. pp. 385, 386.

fragment, which is headed ' The year 1820,' and commences thus :

THE YEAR 1820.

I am not quite sure whether it was not at the close of the preceding year (1819) that Brougham told me a general retaining fee would be left at my chambers for Her Royal Highness the Princess of Wales. It was brought in a mysterious manner by a clerk from Coutts', who, I believe, knew nothing of the contents of the packet.

A short time after the king's death, Brougham happened to attend a consultation at my chambers in the great case of the *King* v. *Parkyns, Waithman and others,* for obstructing the election of the Lord Mayor. At the close of the conference he stayed behind and talked to me about our royal client, then Queen of England. He asked me if I would accept the office of Solicitor-General to Her Majesty, and I instantly agreed to do so. He sent off Sicard to Her Majesty, who then doubted whether she would come to England, but soon sent back warrants appointing Brougham and myself her law officers.

Brougham was strongly of opinion that she would continue abroad. In the course of the preceding summer negotiations had commenced between him and the ministers of the Prince Regent, though without direct authority from the Princess, for a complete separation, including her foreign residence. He justly observed that that project, however practicable while she was a subject, became infinitely more difficult on her accession to the royal title, and as it was known that her conduct had undergone an investigation by the Milan Commissioners, any surrender of her rights would have been regarded as a confession of her guilt. It would have been hard to call on the overburdened people to pay a magnificent allowance to one who, by submitting to her own degradation, would have appeared to sanction the truth of slanderous reports industriously circulated against her, and there is a good deal of probability in the supposition that if she had acquiesced in such an arrangement, the House of Commons would not have agreed to carry it into effect. With the people at large she would certainly have lost all credit, and might have found herself placed wholly at the mercy of a mean-spirited and vindictive husband.

I have reason to believe that such views actuated the conduct of Alderman Wood—a man whose intellect has been much underrated in consequence of Brougham's attack on him after the Queen's arrival.[4]   He unquestionably possessed uncommon perseverance and activity, no small share of natural sagacity, and much acquaintance with the character of the English people.

Tierney's game [as leader of the Whig Opposition] was, if I may so express it, one of alternative policy; either the Queen is insulted, or the King betrayed. If she is innocent ministers are deserving of severe censure for bringing her into suspicion and disrepute; if she is guilty it is due to the King and the State to insist on a divorce. He rather preferred the latter position, as personally most agreeable to the King, and even when the People had so loudly declared for the view of the subject implied in the former he could not resolve to take complete advantage of the popular feeling and opinion. His constant object seemed to be to induce a belief in the King's mind that he and his party would be able to effect that divorce which his actual ministers hesitated to propose. This scheme might have been assisted by Sir John Leach, the Vice-Chancellor, the great promoter of the Milan Commission, who was on good terms with many leading members of the Opposition (though he had deserted that party) and would probably have been glad to bring them into power. He was known to be on bad terms with Lord Castlereagh, and certainly wished to displace and

---

[4] In the course of the speech alluded to Brougham excited the merriment of the House and the country by suggesting that the initials A. W (Alderman Wood) might stand also for *Absolute Wisdom*, which thenceforth became a popular nickname of the Alderman.

succeed the Chancellor [Lord Eldon] who disliked and despised him.

I have always thought that the Whigs, by accepting office on condition of carrying the measure of divorce, would have undone themselves for ever with the public, and even in the present [5] unprosperous state of their affairs, I think them fortunate in having escaped that snare. But the general feeling had not then declared itself, and Tierney was watching for an opportunity to turn out the Ministry by appearing more ready than they had shown themselves to comply with the wishes of the King.

He [Tierney] sent for me when I was leaving London for the spring circuit, to discuss my coming into the next Parliament. After mentioning various places where an impression might be made, he said he hoped the report he had heard of my accepting a law appointment from the Queen was untrue. I immediately avowed it, saying that I had received a retainer from Her Majesty (when Princess of Wales) some time before; that I could not refuse to act for her in the great cause that was expected, and that I thought it impossible, when it was offered me, to refuse the rank which it is in the power of the Queen of England to confer on a barrister, without betraying a degree of indifference to her interests which would justly induce her advisers to exclude me from the defence. He said that there was indeed no great chance of the Whigs coming into power, but if they did the King might perhaps object to adopt the Queen's Solicitor-General for his. My answer was that if that should happen I could only lament it. I remember his adding, with a laugh, that the King might possibly take some strange turn, and consider that as a recommendation, and we agreed that as the Queen was advanced in years and reported to be grown very fat [6] it was not impossible that her husband might fall violently in love with her. Upon the whole,

----

[5] Written in 1821.

[6] The King's taste in women was popularly described by the well-known alliteration ' fat, fair and fifty.'

Tierney seemed satisfied that I could not have declined the appointment.

On returning to London [after his election for Nottingham, as related in the preceding chapter] I found Brougham still in expectation that the Queen would not come to England, though she appeared to be on the move. Her Majesty had sent duplicates of our appointments, and it now became necessary to take decisive steps. We had both written to the Chancellor, requesting precedency at the bar, and had thus given him an opportunity of promoting us in the manner usual with regard to attorneys and solicitors general to the Queen. He took no notice of these applications, and thus compelled us to announce our new situation. We produced our warrants to his lordship in the common room at Lincoln's Inn : he expressed his doubts whether they ought not to be stamped. We put forward the usual practice of giving to the Queen's officers the rank of King's Counsel. He courteously denied that this was a matter of right, referring to the case of Serjeant Vaughan, who was some years Solicitor-General to Queen Charlotte without being made King's Serjeant. The precedent had probably been established by his lordship from a prudent foresight of the difficulty that now arose. His conversation was extremely skilful. Brougham said to me, when walking away, ' Do you observe how much more subtle the serpent is than all the beasts of the field ? '

We went to Somerset House the next day to get our warrants stamped, and called upon the several judges to notify what had happened. Doubts were entertained by the Benchers whether we should be called to the bench [of Lincoln's Inn]; some of the shabby politicians were for excluding us, but Sir William Grant [Master of the Rolls] moved for our call, which was then unanimous.

The first case moved by me in my new station was that of Sir Francis Burdett, convicted of a [political] libel at Leicester (March 20, 1820.) The whole of the proceedings are of course well known to lawyers. I have never had a doubt that the conviction was against law; that if I had acted for him as counsel at the trial, in the usual manner, he would have been acquitted; and that the information itself was erroneous for uncertainty. He himself addressed the jury, less ably than could have been expected, and without knowing how to avail himself, as any lawyer would, of the technical defects in the proof. It is one of the most mortifying circumstances of my professional life, not only to have had unrighteous sentences pronounced against my clients, when charged with political offences, but to hear the judges lay down principles destructive to constitutional freedom, and at variance with the very elements of justice. On this occasion Mr. Justice Bayley acted a noble part, and gave reasons for differing from the rest of the court, which remained without an answer. He incurred thereby the lasting hatred of tyrants and sycophants—the most un-equivocal of all proofs of fidelity and honesty in a judge.[7]

Whether the Queen would come to England was still very doubtful. She had, indeed, left Italy and gone to Geneva, but was reported there to have said that she had no intention of coming to England. I imagine that Her Majesty's wish was that Brougham should go out to her there, in which case she would probably have renewed the negotiations of the preceding year, and perhaps have for ever broken all rela-tions with a country which could possess few charms for her. Her daughter dead, her husband alienated, the higher ranks deterred by his known displeasure from paying her any outward tokens of respect, the minds of all persons filled with suspicions of her conduct, and with disgust at the infamous stories in circulation—how could it be desirable for her to establish herself in England?

The Alderman, however, had resolved that the Queen should come to this country, and was probably confirmed in

---

[7] Afterwards Mr. Baron Bayley; created a baronet on his retirement from the Bench in 1834, after twenty-six years of eminent judicial service. The case of *The King* v. *Burdett* is reported in 4. *Barnewall and Alderson*, p. 95 et sqq.

his resolution by observing Brougham's cordial disinclination to that proceeding. He often spoke to me on the subject, consulted me as to the proper course to be pursued, and on my answering him in general terms, saying that Her Majesty must decide from her knowledge of her own conduct whether she would face her enemies or not, he desired me to give an opinion in writing that she ought to come. This proposal I declined, on the current lawyers' plea, that no written opinion can be given except on a written case, *but added, that from all I heard and knew, it would be desirable that she should come.* One night he walked late with me from the House of Commons, and told me he was determined to go for her at Geneva. In a day or two he was gone.

Brougham still flattered himself that negotiations might succeed in preventing her from landing in this country ; but this was in truth entirely hopeless after her arrival in the French territory, and most manifestly so when she was at St. Omer's, within a few leagues of England. [She reached St. Omer's on the 1st of June.] If it had been questionable whether her continued residence in Italy would not have endangered her honour, her station, and her safety, her sudden retreat after so great an advance would have been an utter abandonment of them all. Brougham still had hopes : the terms he was authorized to propose (50,000*l.* a year, and all the rights of a Queen Consort, especially as regarded money and patronage, on consenting to live abroad)[8] were indeed magnificent, if the Queen was guilty. Relying on them, on his personal influence and unbounded talents, he formed the determination to accompany Lord Hutchinson, the emissary of the Cabinet, to Boulogne.

It is not necessary to follow the personal narrative in the details that immediately follow this : suffice it to say that Brougham's negotiation, as appears from his memoirs,[9] completely failed. The terms offered were

---

[8] ' Brougham's Memoirs,' vol. ii. p 356. .   [9] Vol. ii. p. 357–366.

indignantly rejected, and the Queen, in spite of his remonstrances, and without any notice to him, on June 4, in company with Alderman Wood and Lady Ann Hamilton, left St. Omer's for London, where she arrived on the 6th. Brougham, in his very natural indignation at this proceeding, hastily wrote a strong letter to Denman, intimating the probability of his ceasing to be her chief legal adviser, and containing the expression, ' I suppose she will have Wood for her Attorney-General.' The personal narrative then proceeds as follows :

I received that letter on the day of Brougham's return to London (June 6), and communicated its contents to John Williams,[10] who was delighted with the prospect of my becoming Attorney-General to the Queen, and himself her Solicitor. I went to the House of Commons expecting to hear Lord Castlereagh's denunciation of Her Majesty, fully believing myself to be at that time her only law-officer, and perfectly resolved to discharge all the duties attached to that character. Lord Castlereagh threatened that a message from His Majesty (the message communicating the papers connected with the Milan enquiry, sealed up, as the custom is, in a green bag—hence called the Green Bag Papers) would forthwith be brought down to the House. Brougham had not then appeared since his arrival from the Continent, but he entered the House while Lord Castlereagh was speaking. On behalf of the Queen I thought it right to put a question as to the course intended. Brougham then observed to some persons near him that the ministerial threat prevented him from resigning.

By this time the Queen had arrived in London ; a summons, written by Lady Ann Hamilton, was brought to

____

[10] Of Counsel for the Queen ; raised to the bench, 1834 ; died, after thirteen years' judicial service, in 1847, æt. 70.

me at the House by a low person (an election agent of Wood's), who was so drunk when he brought it that the officers in attendance turned him forcibly out of the lobby. In obedience to the command, I instantly went to the Alderman's house in South Audley Street, and having, with the utmost difficulty, got admission through the multitude, I there awaited the royal personage to whose service I was bound.

Her progress was slow through the countless populace, her travelling equipage mean and miserable ; her attendants appeared ill-calculated to conciliate good-will in this country. Hardly a well-dressed person was to be seen in the crowd. Two or three men on horseback assumed a rather more respectable appearance ; but one of these was my bankrupt cousin John Holloway ; another, a sheriff's broker well-known in courts of justice. I need not relate that the Alderman was seated in the carriage by Her Majesty's side,[11] and Lady Ann Hamilton sat opposite. It was an open barouche of shabby appearance. Six or seven carriages followed ; on the box of one was a man with a turban, in another Hieronymo and Carlo Forti, with immense mustachios. The press of people, the cheers, the acclamations, beggared all description. They were long in sight before they reached the door, and long after they reached it before any of them could dismount and ascend the steps. From

---

[11] ' The King was reported to have expressed anger at this, exclaiming, "That beast Wood sate by the Queen's side." I told the Queen of this report, and her answer was rather remarkable ; she said, ' That was very kind in the King." The pertinacity with which she cherished hopes of a reconciliation continued to the very last. Within a short period of his death she spoke to me of the King's feelings towards her. She mentioned that at no great distance from the time of her marriage the King had entertained the present [seventh] Duke of Bedford and his wife, and that after paying high compliments to that lady, he pronounced her just like the Princess of Wales. She looked at me with uncommon earnestness, and used, I think, these very words: "I know that man well ; mark what I say, We shall be good friends again before we die." (Note by Lord Denman, A.D. 1821.)

the drawing-room window I had ample opportunity to survey at leisure Her Majesty and the whole cavalcade.

What a melancholy contrast to regal state! Nothing ever gave me a deeper impression of sadness than the aspect of this forlorn-looking court, though the enthusiastic shouts of the people and the courage that shone in the fixed eye of the Queen somewhat roused my spirits, and made me feel proud of my royal mistress. She was dressed in mourning for the late king, with a ruff on the model of Queen Elizabeth's; her step was assured, her bearing firm and graceful; and when, after a short delay, she, at the Alderman's desire, went forth on the balcony and saluted the people, nothing could be more noble or attractive than her manner, look, and gestures.

She received me with some general compliments, and then began to converse on her own affairs, complaining that the conduct of ministers had made it necessary for her to come to England. Speaking with the greatest animation, she often asked, ' If they wished me to stay abroad, why not leave me there in peace? No woman of character could submit to the insults they have offered.' Then, having enumerated a variety of circumstances that appeared to leave her no alternative, she often repeated, like the burden of a song, ' And so here I am.' She was extremely exasperated against Brougham, and when I said that he would be ready to obey her commands, she said very coldly that she should be glad to see him, but her opinion of him was much altered—she even spoke of his betraying her. I obtained permission to bring him after Her Majesty's dinner, and went to him at his house in Hill Street, Berkeley Square, in the immediate neighbourhood.

Here, in the most solemn and alarming manner, he laid open to me all his apprehensions on the subject of the Queen's case. He had received from various quarters the most sinister reports, and that with too much credulity. I shall never forget the tone and manner with which he said to me, at the close of a long series of awkward statements,

'So now we are in for it, Mr. Denman.' I complained a little of having been kept so much in the dark about these suspicions, but he observed that it would have done no good to have communicated them to me. We had, indeed, small inclination to look back; all our thoughts were directed to the future.

Let me here state, once for all, that from this moment I am sure that Brougham thought of nothing but serving and saving his client. I, who saw him more nearly than any man, can bear witness that from the period in question his whole powers were devoted to her safety and welfare. He felt that the battle must be fought, and resolved to fight it manfully, and 'to the utterance.'

Nothing remarkable passed on our return to Her Majesty, except that she suffered Brougham to leave the room first, and detained me some moments with an observation on him. She said, 'He is afraid.' She was certainly right, but his fears were on her account, not on his own.

Brougham lost no time in commencing the struggle. On the next day (June 7), the Green Bag having been previously communicated to both Houses, and a select committee of fifteen peers having been appointed in the Lords to enquire into and report on its contents, Lord Castlereagh moved for the appointment of a similiar committee in the Lower House. This was opposed by Brougham in a memorable speech, in which he at once entered into the whole case, and produced such an effect on the House that the appointment of a select committee of the Commons had to be deferred, and was finally abandoned. It was in this speech that he made the house merry by his remarks on 'Absolute Wisdom.' The personal narrative thus describes the effects of Brougham's masterly advocacy:

The Green Bag having come down, the general nature of the charges was opened, and Brougham made his incomparable speech, so terrifying to the country gentlemen. Half a dozen of them, one after the other, rose to implore the noble lord (Lord Castlereagh) not to press the matter further; not from any feeling for the unhappy Queen, not from any sense of attachment to the despicable King, but because they thought their property might be compromised by the proceeding. They spoke and acted just in the same spirit as when an agricultural tax is to be repealed, or the price of corn raised by Act of Parliament. This timid, selfish, and purse-proud race, who love and cherish a ministry in proportion to its weakness, because their own importance is increased in the same ratio, just went far enough to condemn themselves and the ministers in the course that was taken (viz. deferring the appointment of the committee), without daring to act decisively on the principles of justice and sound policy, and crush the proceedings altogether.

On the night of Brougham's great speech, I called at Wood's house about an hour after midnight to make my report of it, but the Queen had retired to rest. On the next day, feeling the great importance of preserving a good understanding between the Queen and her Attorney-General, I made the most favourable report in my power of his mighty exertion on the preceding evening. Her answer was delivered with great coolness, ' I saw he would make a good speech;' but her indifference proceeded less perhaps in this instance from any resentment towards Brougham than from a general sense of the inutility of speeches, which often betrayed itself.

The Queen's unfortunate distrust of Brougham broke out in various ways. She knew his value, but I am certain that his resignation would have been satisfactory to her. All her immediate attendants contributed to foment her jealousy of him,—the Alderman, Lady Ann Hamilton, and shortly after Dr. Parr.

Brougham could not but be sensible how much of her

confidence he had forfeited, and the effect on his conduct was attended with mischievous consequences, the worst of which was the want of countenance and attention from the Whig ladies of quality.   If he had sent Mrs. Brougham to pay her respects on Her Majesty's arrival, many of these ladies, with whom he was living upon terms of the greatest intimacy, would have followed her example, particularly the Countess of Jersey, whose popularity in the fashionable world was unbounded.   A report was spread that she had confidentially asked Brougham for his advice, and that he exhorted her to abstain from calling.   The truth of this is unknown to me, but it is certain that when the newspapers inserted Lady Jersey's name and that of Lady Fitzwilliam among the visitors at the Queen's miserable residence in Portman Street [Lady Ann Hamilton's, to which she had removed from South Audley Street] the statement received a formal contradiction.

My wife was extremely anxious to call, but I begged her to wait till Mrs. Brougham should do so, *dreading that such scenes of vice and debauchery would be proved as would overwhelm with shame any woman who had formed any acquaintance with the criminal.*

I have often regretted this weakness, but whoever considers the abominable slanders that were then freely circulating in society, and remembers that Brougham had infinitely better means than myself of appreciating their truth, will not perhaps entirely condemn it.   Besides, I had not been honoured by the Queen's previous notice, and Mrs. Denman filled no rank in society, and mingled very little with the world.   At the same time her view of the case now appears to me perfectly right, and my own erroneous.   The visit would have been a homage due to the rank of my royal mistress, and would have been justified by it and by my official relation to her, as long as the charges were unproved, even if they could have been established afterwards, while its being withholden bore the appearance of a knowledge on the part of her legal defenders that her conduct had been disgraceful, and thus to a certain degree assisted the evidence against her.

The above passage appears hardly just either to Brougham or to Denman himself. As far as Brougham is concerned, it seems not fair to suppose that his conduct in this matter was mainly or at all influenced by the Queen's obvious distrust or dislike towards himself. It was not because the Queen distrusted or disliked him that Brougham hesitated at this stage of the proceedings to commit his wife or the ladies of the Whig nobility to a distinct espousal of the Queen's cause. The words above printed in italics seem to supply quite a sufficient reason for the line taken at this period both by Brougham and by Denman. Neither could then know what might or might not be proved against the Queen. It must further be observed, as Denman indeed intimates, and as Brougham in his 'Autobiography' has expressly stated, that the latter was acquainted with circumstances unknown to the Queen's other advisers, ' of great indiscretions on her part, though entirely unconnected with the charges now made against her.'   The knowledge of these circumstances no doubt influenced Brougham's conduct and demeanour in the earlier part of the proceedings, and greatly accounted for the Queen's distrust.

In this state of destitution [the personal narrative proceeds], without more than half a dozen ladies of rank and character having even left their cards at her door, it was marvellous to contrast the Queen's daily life with the royal spirit that sustained her. Tindal[12] will never forget the look and

---

[12] Of Counsel for the Queen; Solicitor-General, 1826; Chief Justice of Common Pleas, 1829; died, 1846.

gesture with which she said to us, in her miserable back drawing-room in Portman Street, ' I will be crowned.' Her popularity meanwhile continued to increase. The season of addresses set in. The Lord Mayor and Common Council filled Oxford Street with their long string of carriages, and were received with grace and dignity by the woman who occupied the highest rank in Europe in two mean drawing-rooms of an inferior ready-furnished house. When that body had retired, she greeted the populace assembled in that narrow street from a little railed balcony, on which Alderman Wood spread a shabby rug to distract the impertinent gaze of those who stood directly beneath. Frequently in the course of a day she was called to the window by the crowd and appeared. When she took an airing it was in a hired chariot and pair, driven by a post-boy, with Lady Ann Hamilton by her side within, and William Austen [13] and the black seated on the dicky. Popularity, indeed, was secured, but I have always thought that more of it, and of a better sort, might have been acquired by a very different line of conduct.

[13] Child of a father of same name, a sailmaker in Deptford dockyard; adopted by Caroline in 1802. Brougham, however, says that the William Austen of 1820 was not the son of the sailmaker, but of Prince William Louis of Prussia, by one of Caroline's attendants in Germany: this lad, he states, had been substituted for the Deptford child a few years before 1820. ('Brougham's Memoirs,' vol. ii. p. 425.)

CHAPTER IX.

THE QUEEN'S TRIAL—EARLIER STAGES.

A.D. 1820.   ÆT. 41.

Amicable arrangements attempted—Conference between Wellington and
Castlereagh for the King, and Brougham and Denman for the Queen—
First meeting on June 14—Conference broken off on the 19th—
Description of the interview in the personal narrative—Attempts at
mediation by House of Commons—Wilberforce's motion June 22—
Denman s speech, ' All that are desolate and oppressed '—Castlereagh
avows that the striking the name out of the Liturgy was the King's
own act—Hence the Queen's resolution to make no terms—Wood (and
Denman too) opposed to her leaving England—Hesitation of the Queen
—Brougham prepares answer accepting, Denman one rejecting, the
House of Commons' address—How the Queen receives the House of
Commons deputation—The address rejected—The Queen's answer to the
address read in the House of Commons—Curious scene—Denman's view
of the conduct at this crisis of ministers and the majority—The country
gentlemen—Attempts at arrangement having failed the enquiry goes
on—Petition at Bar of Lords to suspend proceedings of Secret Com-
mittee till arrival of witnesses, June 26—Denman's quotation : ' Some
cogging, cozening slave,' &c.—Bill of Pains and Penalties introduced,
July 5—Resolved that the trial should commence on August 17—
Counsel for the Queen—Wilde brought into the case by Wood—
Feeling against him at first—Denman's testimony to his usefulness
and ability—Pause in proceedings from July 10 to August 17—
Brougham and Denman on circuit—Denman's exertions and fatigue—
Defends Major Cartwright—Presides at Nottingham election dinner
—Return to London—The Queen at Brandenburgh House—Her dis-
trust of Brougham as strong as ever—Parr discourses on the propriety
of discarding Brougham—'If my head is on Temple Bar it will be
Brougham's doing'—Proceedings resumed on August 17—Counsel
heard against the principle of the bill—Denman's speech on the 18th
—Its strong expressions of loyalty to the Queen—Denman's account of
the effect of his speech against the principle of the bill—The Queen's

compliment, 'My God, what a beautiful speech!'—A most unbecoming familiarity—The Attorney-General (Giffard) opens for the Crown, August 19—Examination of witnesses from August 21 to September 7—Cross-examination of Majocchi and Louise Demont—The Solicitor-General (Copley) sums up—Further proceedings adjourned till October 3—The Queen's agitation at first sight of Majocchi—Her general demeanour at the trial—Denman, during the break in the proceedings, runs down to Cheltenham—His triumphal entry—The parson's windows broken—Denman appeases the mob—His letter to Merivale of September 24—Expresses surprise that the unanswered evidence against the Queen has not had more effect on the country—Certificate at Cheltenham to a foreign servant that he was not Majocchi.

WHILE the secret committee of the Lords were engaged in examining the Green Bag papers, various attempts at an amicable arrangement were unsuccessfully made. One of the earliest of these was the conference between the Duke of Wellington and Lord Castlereagh as representing the King, and Brougham and Denman as representing the Queen. The points to be discussed were; 1. The future residence of the Queen abroad; 2. The title to be assumed by her; 3. The nature of the patronage she was to exercise in England; 4. The income to be assigned to her for her life.

The first meeting of this conference took place on June 14: on the 19th the negotiations were finally broken off, the Queen wholly rejecting the conditions proposed with reference to the first point, viz. her foreign residence.

The circumstances connected with this meeting are thus related in the personal narrative:

We were received by Lord Castlereagh in his parlour, after he had entertained a party of foreign ambassadors. He was covered with diamonds, stars, and ribands; the Duke of Wellington was equally splendid. We two meagre lawyers must have formed an amusing foil to the eye of a painter, but Lord Castlereagh answered our apologies about inferior rank by assuring us that it was their wish to meet us as men of business, rather than persons of high station and formality. He assumed an air of agreeable frankness, and contrived to place himself in a position which cut me off, as the left wing, from Brougham's main body. My leader showed great address in introducing the subject of the Liturgy, which had not at that time been brought forward in a manner at all proportionate to its importance. Speaking of some expedient to reconcile Her Majesty to a stipulation that she would reside on the Continent, to which he merely said that she had no *insuperable objection* (though, in fact, this was the basis of our negotiation), he suggested in a sort of hurried whisper that the restoration of her name to the Liturgy might answer that purpose. Lord Castlereagh promptly replied, 'You might as easily move Carlton House.'

The conference having come to nothing, the House of Commons, on June 22, passed a resolution, on the motion of Wilberforce, declaring their opinion that, when such considerable advances had been made towards an adjustment, Her Majesty, by yielding to the wishes of the House, and forbearing to press further the propositions on which a material difference still remained, would not be understood as shrinking from enquiry, but only as proving her desire to acquiesce in the opinion of Parliament.

In the debate that ensued on this motion of Wilberforce's, Denman made a powerful and impressive speech, in the course of which he pronounced a few memorable words, the sudden coinage of high-wrought emotion, which were soon current throughout all ranks of society. In reply to the suggestion that, though all particular mention of the Queen's name was omitted from the Liturgy, she might yet be considered as being comprised in the general prayer for the royal family, he said, in a tone of the deepest and most solemn pathos, that 'if Her Majesty was included in any general prayer, it was the prayer *for all that are desolate and oppressed.*'

The personal narrative relates as follows the debate on Wilberforce's motion, the presentation of the House of Commons address, and its rejection by the Queen.

This important motion was introduced by Wilberforce in an excellent and most conciliatory speech, but in the course of the debate Lord Castlereagh avowed that Her Majesty's name had been deliberately excluded from the Liturgy with the intention of fixing a stigma upon her (he spoke of it as an act done by the King himself in his closet). This expression was conveyed to her by I know not whom, most probably by Wood, who privately told me of his great aversion to her quitting the country on any terms whatever, and Lady Ann Hamilton wrote me a letter, which was received by me during the debate, strongly announcing the Queen's determination not to enter into any further stipulation after such an avowal. Her Majesty had hesitated and continued to hesitate extremely, but was, I firmly believe, decided by the circumstance now alluded to. Without feeling confident that the advice of the House of Commons would have been followed if the minister had abstained from that ill-timed insult, I can distinctly declare that it was the decisive weight that actually turned the balance.

Many well-wishers of the Queen thought her rejection of the proffered mediation unwise. Wood's view of the matter was this, ' If she leaves the country she confesses guilt; she will be hooted by the people to the shore; and I, for one, will not vote her a farthing of the public money.' I think he was right, an acceptance of the offer would have been to withdraw herself from the protection of the People, and place herself at the mercy of the King and the ministry, i.e. of a majority of the House of Commons.

The interval of two or three days that passed between this vote and the Saturday when the address was to be presented was full of irresolution and anxiety. Her Majesty frequently asked advice. Her own feeling appeared to be unfavourable to any terms of compromise; but so much was there of uncertainty to the very last, that when Brougham and I attended a little before the appointed hour, we entertained opposite opinions as to the course that would probably be chosen by her. We found the Queen, however, determined to decline the mediation. She had prepared a written answer to that effect, composed, I believe, by a Miss Grimani, who was much with her. It did not appear to us quite proper in point of style, and each of us produced one which we had prepared according to our respective calculations—Brougham's acquiescing, mine rejecting. From these two we framed that which was delivered, and which I was in the act of writing out when the deputation arrived.

Nothing could exceed the stateliness of manner with which Her Majesty received these leading members of the House of Commons (Wilberforce, Banks, Wortley, M.P. for Yorkshire, Sir T. Acland, for Devonshire). Wilberforce complained afterwards of the coldness she displayed. In our great wigs and gowns, Brougham stood on her right, I on her left, and he read the answer. After they had kissed her hand, kneeling, they immediately withdrew, not without some apprehension of violence from the vast crowd assembled in the streets. As we got into our carriage we were eagerly asked what answer Her Majesty had given, and warmly greeted with acclamations when her refusal was made known.

It was Saturday, but the House met to receive Her Majesty's answer to the address. The scene was rather ludicrous, for Wilberforce could not be found, and Mr.

Stuart Wortley, who had seconded the motion and was one of the deputation, proceeded to read it to the House standing at the bar. Before he had finished Wilberforce came in, and stationed himself behind his shoulder, occasionally correcting both the language and his emphasis. Both were evidently displeased. The message was heard in dead silence, and an adjournment immediately followed.

Never shall I forget the apparent mortification of these baffled mediators: the wound inflicted on their own self-sufficiency they avenged by indulging the bitterest personal resentment against the Queen. Instead of admiring her courage and constancy, instead of pausing to consider how far her conduct on this occasion could be reconciled with the supposition of conscious guilt, they found no consolation for their personal disappointment but in anticipating her destruction and disgrace. Their address had in effect proposed to recognise her innocence, on condition of her waiving her claim to have her name inserted in the Liturgy; but when she had given the strongest proof that she prized her honour and her character above all earthly considerations, they instantly took the Green Bag for gospel and were delighted at the prospect of crushing her with its contents. Never shall I forget the sort of hurried canvass that took place, and the animation with which honourable members encouraged one another to conspire the ruin of the most injured and insulted of womankind. 'I am for proceeding *now*, are not you for going on with the business?' I never witnessed a scene more disgusting, or less honourable to human nature.

In these observations I do not make the slightest allusion to Wilberforce himself, who acted throughout with views the most honourable and benevolent, and was unquestionably much concerned at the failure of his attempt. I speak of the country gentlemen who had on the former occasion *implored* Lord Castlereagh out of tenderness to their land and beeves, to spare the menaced constitution of the country, yet now were ready to hand it over to the King and his ministers, its worst enemies, to gratify the splenetic cravings of their wounded pride. But I have ever thought that Wilberforce may be justly reproached, in common with these persons, for not making one effort more to rescue the People and the King from the danger and the shame of that disgusting enquiry which now, like a pestilential vapour, impended over the country.

His conduct in the subsequent session satisfied me that he was afterwards convinced of the mistake he had committed in proposing to address *the Queen*. An honest House of Commons would have addressed *the King*, with a firm, but earnest prayer that he would rescind the Order in Council for expunging the Queen's name from the Liturgy. That impolitic and unchristian act was as clearly illegal as anything can be for which no specific remedy is provided by law. The construction of the Act of Uniformity admitted of no reasonable doubt, and the propriety of the Order in Council was in no debate defended by any single member of either House of Parliament, except the ministers themselves. In the circumstances in which Her Majesty was placed, it was iniquitous and cruel to expect that she should be a consenting party to the sacrifice of any right; but the legality of the proceeding adopted by the King's ministers being at least extremely questionable, while its impolicy and injustice could not be doubted, and were universally condemned, the Representatives of the People had a clear duty to perform. Of their disposition to perform that duty Wilberforce probably formed a just estimate, and abstained accordingly from bringing the proposal before them; but I think it was due to his own character to record those sentiments which must have been entertained on the subject by every impartial man.

This is one of the numerous occasions on which the present ministers (1821) have found strength and security in the excess of their misconduct. They proclaimed their own responsibility for this Order in Council in that tone of pompous formality which led everyone to suppose that it was in truth the King's personal act. Lord Castlereagh, in fact, in the debate on Wilberforce's motion, had spoken of it as an act done 'by the King himself in his closet.' The country gentlemen accordingly felt that a vote of censure on the proceeding would have been a personal declaration of war against the King, and not one of them chose to incur such a hazard. Thus an express law was violated, an outrageous wrong was done to the first subject of the realm, then under accusation, and the King's Ministers allowed him to commit himself personally in a matter in which his own feelings were notoriously wound up to the highest pitch ; and, for all these reasons, the House of Commons takes no step. The law remains violated, an unconstitutional and odious precedent is established, the individual injury remains unredressed, the outraged feelings of the People vent themselves in angry murmurs, which find a response in every bosom except those of their representatives, because no member of Parliament chooses to question the personal act of the King.

Things were now approaching a crisis. At the bar of the House of Lords, on June 26, an endeavour was made to induce the Secret Committee to suspend proceedings till after the arrival of the witnesses whose written depositions were contained in the Green Bag. Denman urged the delay with great energy and ability, and it was in the course of his speech on this occasion that he so hugely delighted Lord Eldon, by applying to his rival Leach, the great promoter of the Milan Commission, the celebrated quotation from ' Othello ' :

> Some busy and insinuating rogue,
> Some cogging, cozening slave to get some office,
> Must have devised this slander.

The application failed, and the disgusting enquiry took its course. On July 4 the Lords' Committee reported that the charges against the Queen ought to become the subject of a solemn enquiry, and on the 5th a Bill of Pains and Penalties, founded on this report, was introduced by Lord Liverpool. The preamble of this bill recited that the Queen had carried on a criminal intercourse with Bergami, and proposed to enact that she should be therefore degraded from the title and station of Queen, and that the marriage should be annulled. What was usually called the Queen's trial was, in form, an examination before the House of Lords of the truth of the recitals set forth in the preamble of the Bill of Pains and Penalties.

On July 6 counsel were heard on the mode and time of proceeding on the Bill, and on the 10th it was resolved that the trial (in the sense above indicated) should commence on August 17.

In addition to Brougham, Denman, Williams and Tindal, there were at this time also retained as counsel for the Queen, Dr. Lushington[1] and Mr. Wilde.[2] Mr. Vizard continued to be her attorney. The retainer of Wilde was at first very distasteful to Denman, and rendered Brougham outrageous. Wilde had originally practised as an attorney, had been lately engaged as counsel for Wood in some mining transactions, and did not at that time stand high in the esteem of the profession. He had been brought into the case by Wood's influence with the Queen, without a word of communi-

---

[1] Right Hon. Stephen Lushington. Born 1782; called to bar, 1806; Judge of High Court of Admiralty, 1838; retired, 1867; died, æt. 91, in January 1873.

[2] Born 1782; called to bar, 1817: Solicitor-General, 1840; Attorney-General, 1841; Chief Justice of Common Pleas, 1846; Chancellor (Lord Truro), 1850 to 1852; died, 1855, æt. 73.

cation with her law officers.   Notwithstanding this unfavourable introduction, Wilde's talent and energy soon made themselves appreciated.   'We were no sooner acquainted with him,' says Denman, 'than our prejudices vanished.   He thought of nothing but success, and contributed most largely towards it. Extremely able and acute, generally very judicious, always active and persevering in the highest degree, his habits as an attorney qualified him for many things to which counsel are incompetent.'   From this point we will again follow for a time the text of the personal narrative :

Our circuits now took us from London, and we left the Queen to the care of Dr. Lushington, and occasionally of Wilde, who did not travel the whole round.   The circuits were important objects to Brougham and myself, who now first went as leaders from the rank given us by Her Majesty. Brougham made a wonderful harvest at York, and I kept my ground on my little theatre (the Midland) very fairly. It may seem trifling to advert to the bodily fatigue caused by these various exertions, but I never lost sight of the profession as the principal object of my hopes.   On Tuesday, travelling all night, I went from London to the Northampton assizes : on their termination I returned to London on Wednesday or Thursday.   On the Saturday I had the conduct of an important action at Guildhall, brought by Colonel De Bosset against Sir Thomas Maitland; for oppressively cashiering him at Corfu, in which I had the good fortune to obtain a verdict, with 100*l.* damages.   Vizard (solicitor for the Queen) was the defendant's attorney, and I well remember taking him to my house in Russell Square [3] to luncheon, when, after the labour of the day, in the hottest

[3] Denman had moved from Queen Square to No. 50 Russell Square about two years before this.

weather, I was so dog-tired that I not only sate down to eat, but actually set off on my journey to Lincoln assizes, without either washing or changing my linen. I had flattered myself with a comfortable bed on the road, but found all engaged, and was obliged to travel all night and sleep in the carriage as I could.

The circuit was laborious, and concluded (for me) with my making a two hours' speech for the defendants in the silly prosecution against Major Cartwright and others for their foolish mock election of a 'legislatorial attorney' for Birmingham. The next day I was obliged to go across the country to a dinner given in honour of our election at Nottingham, where, arriving a few minutes before the appointed hour, I found that both Lord Holland and Birch declined the chair, and was under the necessity of taking it at a moment's notice. The party consisted of near 500, and the exertions attending the office of President were great and entirely new to me. These circumstances very naturally explain the attack of jaundice which was visible and confirmed when I came to London.

On returning to London Denman hastened to pay his respects to the Queen, who had then moved to Brandenburgh House, Hammersmith, which he describes as 'rather pleasantly seated on the Thames, but a strange, dilapidated, half-furnished foreign-looking mansion.' He was personally extremely well received, but he found the Queen's distrust and dislike of Brougham if possible even increased. On Sunday, August 13, only four days before the commencement of the trial, in compliance with an anxious summons from Dr. Parr, he went to Brandenburgh House, when the Doctor entered into an earnest discourse with him on the propriety of dismissing Brougham! 'The Queen also,' he says, 'walking with me in the garden, complained of Brougham.

" If he had come over to me at Geneva," she exclaimed, " I should have been spared all this trouble ;" and Lady Ann Hamilton,' he adds, ' told me that one of the very few occasions upon which the Queen was entirely overwhelmed by her feelings was the visit of the Usher of the Black Rod, announcing that the Bill of Pains and Penalties was brought in.   She walked about the room in extreme agitation, repeatedly exclaiming, " *If my head is upon Temple Bar, it will be Brougham's doing.*" ' It is needless to point out how pitiably unjust this was to the man who had from the first dissuaded her from coming to England, and to whose splendid exertions, after she had once taken that step, the defeat of her enemies was mainly owing.

The day of trial—Thursday, August 17—was now at hand.   On that day, and on the 18th, counsel were heard against the principle of the Bill, in other words, against its being read a second time.   On the 18th Denman delivered a very powerful speech against the second reading, remarkable for the boldness of its attacks on the real prosecutor, the King, and concluding with the following emphatic declaration, which made him extremely popular with the Queen's supporters out-of-doors.'

I beg to say, my Lords, that whatever may be enacted— whatever may be done by the exertions of any individual, by the perversion of truth or by the perjury of witnesses, whatever may be the consequences which may follow, and whatever she may suffer—I will for one never withdraw from her those sentiments of dutiful homage and respect which I owe to her rank, to her situation, to her superior mind, to her great and royal heart ; nor, my Lords, will I ever pay to any one who may usurp Her Majesty's station that respect and duty which belong alone to her whom the laws of God and man have made the consort of his present Majesty and the Queen of these kingdoms.

Denman, in the personal narrative, thus speaks of the effects of his speech against the second reading :

I had the satisfaction of learning that my speech against the second reading of the bill had acted forcibly on many of the peers.   The Queen entered the House on that occasion while I was speaking, and remained to the conclusion. She came afterwards and found me alone in her apartment, where she greeted me with this compliment, 'My God, what a beautiful speech!'   I was reposing, much fatigued, on one of the sofas, and had thrown my wig on the other.   When she entered, I expressed great distress at having taken so great a liberty with her room, and she answered me laughing, with an allusion to what I had been saying about the preamble of the bill, 'Indeed, it is a most unbecoming familiarity.'

It having been decided that the Bill should be proceeded with, the Attorney-General, Sir R. Giffard, on August 19, commenced opening the case for the Crown.

On August 21 the examination of witnesses began, and lasted till September 7, including those two great master-pieces of forensic skill—the cross-examinations of Theodore Majocchi by Brougham, and of Louise Demont, by Williams.

On September 7 Copley (then Solicitor-General) summed up the case for the Crown with consummate ability, after which, on September 9, it was resolved that the Bill should stand adjourned till October 3, in order, as Ministers stated, to give the Queen's advisers time to prepare their defence; as their opponents surmised, to let the unanswered and un-contradicted evidence for the Crown produce a prejudice against the Queen throughout the country.

To enter into any details of the detestable proceeding [writes Denman in the personal narrative] would be to open an endless volume. All the world knows all about it. Our royal client was in a state of considerable agitation at first, which is the only account to be given of her strange exclamation at the apparition of Theodore Majocchi. [When this witness was introduced the Queen exclaimed 'Theodore! no, no!' and rising from her seat, abruptly quitted the House, followed by Lady Ann Hamilton]. She was copiously bled that night, and when she took her seat the following day in the House of Lords I never saw a human being so interesting. Her face was pale, her eyelids a little sunken, her eyes fixed on the ground, with no expression of alarm or consciousness, but with an appearance of decent distress at being made the object of such revolting calumnies, and a noble disdain of her infamous accusers. We did not think it proper for her to give her attendance during the whole investigation, but advised her to be absent except when required for any particular reasons.

In the middle of the proceedings we had a three weeks holiday [from September 9 to October 3, as already stated] and I went and washed away my jaundice at Cheltenham. My entrance into that town was a striking proof of the state of public feeling. My carriage having been waylaid for many hours, and my name being discovered, I know not how, long after it was dark the people took out the horses, drew the carriage near a mile, and surrounded the house with loud shouts of 'Queen! Queen!' with which I had been so often surfeited in Portman Street. Ill as I was I had serious thoughts of leaving the place again on the instant, but at length resolved to muster up voice and spirits for a speech at the window, and finding myself opposite to a brilliant star, I told the multitude that the Queen could no more be plucked from her throne than that beautiful star from the heavens. They were in great good humour with me, and at my earnest solicitation left me alone, but betook themselves to breaking some of my neighbour's windows, particularly the parson's, who had very imprudently refused them permission to ring the bells on my arrival. One of the magistrates called to request my interference to prevent further violence, and going among the mob I prevailed upon them to disperse and spare the few of his windows that remained unbroken.

The following passages from a letter written by Denman while at Cheltenham to his old friend Merivale may be inserted here :

Cheltenham: September 24, 1820.

My dear Merivale,—It is neither my wife's fault nor mine that I have not written to you sooner; the entire occupation of the mornings in engagements, and of the evenings in prepense idleness, has prevented it. Before I left London the jaundice had worn itself from pure gold to counterfeit silver, and Baillie has sent me here to wash away the last remains of gilt. I love the place, and find the waters most beneficial. We ride every day, and hear Miss Stephens sing in the ' Comedy of Errors ' to-night. Mackintosh is here, and Dwarris.[4] Lushington has come over from Malvern, and Cradock, of Jesus, has been—just the sort of society that was required under existing circumstances.

You heard of our triumphant entry—the most unexpected tribute to the innocency and honour of my royal mistress— and how the mob proceeded to break the parson's windows because he would not suffer the bells to be rung for me. That ungracious divine, however, has not mentioned in his

---

[4] Afterwards Sir Fortunatus Dwarris, one of the Masters of the Court of Queen's Bench.

newspaper account that I made a most earnest speech to the populace, deprecating their attack on his house; and afterwards, by the desire of the only magistrate who could be found, went to that house, and, by mingling with the crowd, prevailed on them to disperse quietly. Egotism is always excusable, if not laudable, in letters, but at this present crisis I have some mercy upon you, for on that subject (as Miss Demont expresses it) '*Je ne taris point.*'

Tell me, if you have the means of observing, the state of the public mind in your part of the country on the one subject. I frankly own I am surprised, after the scandalous and unsuffered-to-be-contradicted-or-commented-on evidence, to see how warmly public opinion in this part of the world still espouses our cause. Not that I think the evidence of the odious unjust serving men ought to be taken as making out a case against us; but it is singular to see that the old *calumniando semper aliquid hæret* seems to be actually reversed on this occasion.

Denman, in the personal narrative, relates one or two further incidents of his visit to Cheltenham, which place in the strongest light the popularity of the Queen and the hatred of the people for the 'unjust serving men' who had borne witness against her.

The Queen's extraordinary popularity was made manifest in a thousand ways. Respectable persons, strangers to me, met me in the walks and the streets, called me by my name, pressed my hand, wished me success, and called for blessings on Her Majesty. There was one very ridiculous occurrence. A German servant called with a publican, entreating me to give him a certificate that he was not Majocchi, having been grossly ill-used and insulted, and his wife driven from her lodgings, by reason of the suspicion that he was that detestable traitor. I gave the most explicit negative to the report, but he could hardly be satisfied without the certificate, which would evidently have availed him nothing.

CHAPTER X.

THE QUEEN'S TRIAL CONTINUED AND CONCLUDED.

A.D. 1820.   ÆT. 41.

Proceedings in the Lords after the resumption on October 3—Brougham's
great speech—The peroration—Its effect on Erskine—Brougham's
conduct of the case criticised—Speech of John Williams—Witnesses
called for the Queen—Copley's cross-examinations—Exultation of
ministers—Witnesses for the Queen kept back by Government—
Denman at Holland House, preparing his speech on summing up the
evidence—Dr. Parr's suggestions—Octavia and Nero—The 'honest
chambermaid's Greek '—' Oh dear, Mr. Denman, don't be squeamish '
—Denman's great speech, October 24 and 25—Unfortunate reference at
close, ' Go and sin no more '—Parallel between Octavia and Caroline of
Brunswick not happy—The Greek quotation a mistake—*Not* intended
by Denman to apply to the King—The King convinced it *was*—The
King nicknamed Nero—Carlton House ' Nérot's Hotel '—Great general
merits of the speech—Graceful compliment to Brougham, ' We kept
together in our chivalry '—The famous apostrophe to the Duke of
Clarence, afterwards William IV., ' Come forth, thou slanderer ! '—-
Great personal advantages of Denman as an orator—His speeches, at
the time, preferred to Brougham's—The Attorney-General's reply—
Unexpectedly good—The debates on second reading—Lord Grey's
speech the best—Divisions on second and third reading—Majority for
third reading only nine—Result communicated to the Queen—' Regina
in spite of them '—Denman kisses the Queen's hand—Lord Liverpool
withdraws the bill—Final close of the proceedings—Denman's general
estimate as to the conduct of the case—Exultation in the country at
the abandonment of the bill—Freedom of the City voted to Brougham,
Denman, and Lushington.

AFTER completing the account of Denman's stay at
Cheltenham, the personal narrative thus proceeds to
relate the progress of the Queen's trial, from its

rcsumption on October 3, till its final close on November 10.

The House of Lords resumed its sittings on October 3, and was on that day addressed by Brougham in one of the most powerful orations that ever proceeded from human lips. His arguments, his observations, his tones, his attitude, his eye, left an impression on my mind which is scarcely ever renewed without exciting strong emotion. The peroration was sublime,[1] 'Spare the Altar, which must stagger with the shock that rends its kindred Throne.' Erskine rushed out of the House in tears.

The defect of the speech was a want of due care in the comments on the prosecutor's case. If he had taken pains to demonstrate the falsehood of a large part of the evidence, and contrast the proof with the opening, we might have had a fair excuse for claiming an acquittal on the failure of all the charges against us. But this would have been suspicious and difficult, after pausing three weeks on the case, and when it was known that we had sent for witnesses from so many different quarters. Of all the scandalous per-

---

[1] 'My Lords, I pray you to pause. I do earnestly beseech you to take heed! You are standing on the brink of a precipice. It will go forth your judgment if it goes against the Queen, but it will be the only judgment you ever pronounced which, instead of reaching its object, will return and bound back against those who gave it. Save the country, my Lords, from the horrors of this catastrophe; save yourselves from this peril; rescue that country of which you are the ornaments, but in which you can flourish no longer when severed from the people than the blossom when cut off from the roots and the stem of the tree. Save that country that you may continue to adorn it; save the Crown, which is in jeopardy, the Aristocracy, which is shaken; save the Altar, which must stagger from the shock that rends its kindred Throne. You have said, my Lords, you have willed, the Church and the King have willed, that the Queen should be deprived of its solemn service. She has instead of that solemnity the heartfelt prayers of the People. She wants no prayers of mine. But I do here pour forth my humble supplications at the throne of mercy, that that mercy may be poured down upon this people in a larger measure than the merits of their rulers may have deserved, and that your hearts may be turned to justice.'

versions of justice of which we had so much reason to complain, the most revolting was the prohibition to enter upon our defence the moment the case against us was closed, unless we undertook to proceed with our witnesses immediately. The Chancellor had the hardihood to assert that his asking Brougham whether he intended to call witnesses before he permitted him to begin his defence was in conformity with the practice of all courts : this is directly contrary to the truth, and I thought that Brougham ought to have refused to answer. Every counsel has a right to enter upon the defence of his client the moment the accusation is brought to an end, and to make up his mind, from observing the effect he produces on his judges, whether he will call any witnesses or not. The case against the Queen was permitted to circulate through the world and sink deep in every mind during the three weeks of adjournment, without contradiction or comment; and with willing hearts and an easy faith the result was an impression which no negative testimony could have the least chance of removing.

Williams followed Brougham, and it is but justice to say of him that he was most anxious to be excused from speaking. It was unfortunate that his mode of treating the subject brought him so much into direct comparison with such a model, but it was indispensable that the evidence should be more minutely sifted than it had been, and he argued that part of the case closely, powerfully, and ingeniously.

Our witnesses were called, and their evidence is known to the world : the tricks of our adversaries are not known. What I said in my speech of the low character of their manœuvres was literally true. Copley's cross-examinations were forcible and skilful ; that of Flynn restored a lost cause. The ministers (impartial judges !) could hardly restrain their joy. Lord Sidmouth said they were 20 per cent. better than they had been the day before.

Without entering into minute particulars, I must give one sample of the conduct of the ministers, who not only set on foot the accusation and sate as judges 'on the accused, but had the control of all the means of obtaining witnesses or securing their absence.   One John Adams was said to have been the only British seaman on board the famous polacca. It was reported that he had seen the Queen and Bergami in an unequivocal situation : the 'Courier' newspaper insinuated that she had caused him to be assassinated to prevent his appearing as a witness.   This very man happened to arrive at Bristol in the king's ship to which he belonged, pending the proceedings.   Alderman Wood, being informed of this, and that the ship was immediately ordered to Portsmouth, employed a friend at the latter place to take Adams' deposition; it was entirely favourable.   Wood instantly wrote to his friend to send Adams to London, but before the letter arrived the man had been ordered away.

During a great part of the proceedings, Lord and Lady Holland had most kindly insisted on my passing the Sundays and parts of the Saturday and Monday at Holland House, where I luxuriated in an admirable library, and the best company in the world; at the same time recruiting my health in good air and delicious gardens.   I generally occupied Mr. Fox's chamber, and was as happy as a man can be.

While we were calling our witnesses, and I was at Holland House on Sundays and at home in the evenings, anxiously sifting the minutes of evidence, Dr. Parr was my frequent correspondent, pointing out illustrations of many parts of our case from history and classical literature.   He earnestly besought me to look into Bayle, and weave into my summing-up allusions to Judith, Julia, and Octavia.   The two first seemed to me inapplicable; the third flashed upon me like lightning.   In a moment I resolved to make the unhappy wife of Nero my heroine, and indeed, the parallel was perfect. I was deeply smitten, too, with the honest chambermaid's Greek, but, trembling as to the effect it might produce, I wrote back to ask Parr whether I could venture to bring it forward.   He, in reply, at first suggested a method of periphrasis, but, at length, recurring to it in the postscript to a long letter, he burst out, ' Oh dear, Mr. Denman, I am for the word itself—don't be squeamish.'

My speech was as successful with a view to my own reputation as my friends could desire. I hope, too, that it was of some use to the Queen, though the unfortunate turn that was, not quite unjustly, given to the parable of the woman taken in adultery has given me some of the bitterest moments of my life. Not that the subject was unfit to be touched, for it could not fail to have some effect on persons possessing religious feelings; but it ought not to have formed the concluding sentence, and might have been more guardedly introduced, and more dexterously softened off. It came into my head after ten hours' speaking,[2] at four, when the House had uniformly adjourned with the utmost punctuality, and at a moment when the feelings of that assembly were wrought up to the very highest pitch. These circumstances account in some degree for an indiscretion which nothing can fully justify.

The passage here alluded to is at the very close of Denman's address, and is thus reported in Hansard:

He who the sword of Heaven would bear
Should be as holy as severe,

and if your lordships have been furnished with weapons and powers which scarcely, I had almost said, Omniscience possesses, for coming at the secret, I think you will feel that some duty is imposed on you of endeavouring to imitate at the same moment the justice, the beneficence, and the wisdom of that Divine authority, who, even when guilt was detected, and vice revealed, said, ' If no one come forward to condemn thee, neither will I condemn thee: *Go, and sin no more.*'

It must be admitted that this was unfortunate.

Neither can it be denied that the parallel between Octavia and Caroline of Brunswick—between the pure,

---

[2] On two successive days, October 24 and 25

innocent girl bride of Nero, one of the saddest and most touching figures in ancient story, and the mature, bold, coarse, and immodest, even if not vicious, Queen of George IV.—though worked out with considerable ingenuity, was, to say the least of it, in very questionable taste.

The quotation, too, of the ' honest chambermaid's Greek,'[3] ' the scathing sarcasm which,' in the eloquent words of Mr. Merivale, ' clings like the shirt of Nessus to the name of Tigellinus,'[4] was a temptation which it would, on all accounts, have been better to have resisted. As this quotation stands in Hansard's report of the speech, it is clear from the context that it was intended to apply, not in any way to the King himself, but to witnesses like Majocchi, and Sacchi, and Rastelli—discarded menials, who came forward with perjured evidence to betray their former mistress.

The King, however, as will be seen hereafter, suspected that it was meant for himself (nor, indeed, is it at all certain that Parr might not have so intended it), and his resentment, naturally enough, was deadly, and for many years unappeasable. Denman would have done much better not to have given way to the suggestion of the officious and overrated old pedant.

[3] Bayle, article ' Octavia,' cites the parallel passages from Tacitus and Xiphilin ; Tacitus Ann. xiv., c. 60, Xiphilin p. 176; and see also Dion lii. 13. Neither the Latin nor the Greek can be quoted with decency. Tigellinus was presiding at the examination in which the female attendants of Octavia were being tortured to prove their mistress guilty of adultery with a slave. The imputation cast upon Tigellinus by the ' honest chambermaid ' was of a nameless impurity, which made him peculiar for infamy even in the infamous court of Nero.

[4] Merivale, ' History of the Romans under the Empire,' chap liii., vol. vi. p. 339, edition in 8 vols. of 1865.

For the moment, however, the town was delighted with the parallel between Caroline and Octavia; the King was everywhere talked of as Nero, and Moore (then in Paris, on account of his Bermuda money difficulties), records in his diary that the dandies of the day thought it witty to speak of Carlton House as ' *Nérot's Hotel.*'[5]

The speech, in spite of these occasional lapses from good taste, was in an eminent degree bold, vigorous, and manly. It is pervaded throughout by a deep sense of earnestness, a profound conviction of the truth and justice of his client's cause. The high tone of generous and vehement indignation never for a moment flags, and the comments on the evidence, minute, searching, and ingenious, are masterly in the extreme.

It contains, just before the close, a graceful and generous tribute of praise to the magnificent exertions of Brougham ; an expression of friendship and admiration which at the time was much and deservedly applauded.

Before I conclude, I must be permitted to say that during the whole of this proceeding (though, personally, I have every reason to thank the House for its kindness and indulgence) the highest gratification resulting to my mind has been that I have been joined with my learned friend on this great occasion. We have fought elsewhere the battles of morality, Christianity, and civilized society, throughout the world ; and, in the language of the dying warrior, I may say

> In this glorious and well-foughten field
> We kept together in our chivalry.

While he has been achieving an immortal victory, an illustrious triumph, and protecting innocence and truth by the adamantine shield of his prodigious eloquence, it has been

---

[5] Moore's diary, under date Nov. 6, 1820.

my lot to discharge only a few random arrows at the defeated
champions of this disgraceful cause. The House will believe
me when I say that I witnessed the display of his surprising
powers with no other feelings than a sincere gratification that
the triumph was complete—with admiration and delight that
the victory of the Queen was accomplished.' [6]

Another passage which especially commended itself
to the popular sentiment was the famous apostrophe
' *Come forth, thou slanderer,*' addressed to the Duke of
Clarence, afterwards William IV., who, though his own
life had been notoriously profligate, affected to be
deeply shocked at the immoralities of his sister-in-law,
and was known to be a most industrious circulator of
all sorts of scandal against her. ' Thou slanderer'
was a sobriquet which for some time clung as closely
to the king's brother as that of ' Nero' to the King,
though William, as it afterwards appeared, had
what George wanted—the royal magnanimity to
forgive. The passage is worth citing, as a fair specimen of the style of speaking which made Denman in
those days one of the most popular men in England.[7]

I know that rumours are abroad of the most vague, but,
at the same time, of the most injurious character; I have
heard them even at the very moment we were defending Her
Majesty against charges which, compared with these rumours,
are clear, comprehensible, and tangible. We have heard and

[6] From Nightingale's report of the trial (3 vols. 8vo. 1820) vol. iii.
p. 291, 292. The report in Hansard is much tamer and less spirited.

[7] Here again the citation is from Nightingale, vol. iii. p. 289, 290.
The report in Hansard is very inferior, and it even omits the words
' Come forth, thou slanderer,' which were most certainly spoken, and
were in all mouths at the time. The present writer has often heard
them from his own father, who was present during Denman's speech.
The Duke of Clarence was in the House at the time.

hear daily, with alarm, that there are persons, and these not of the lowest condition, not confined to individuals connected with the public Press—not even excluded from this august assembly—who are industriously circulating the most odious and atrocious calumnies against Her Majesty.[8] Can this thing be?—and yet can we live in the world in these times, and not know it to be a fact? We know that if a juryman on such an occasion should be found to possess, or affect to possess, any knowledge on the subject of enquiry, we should have a right to call him to the bar as a witness. 'Come forward,' we might say, 'and let us confront you with our evidence; let us see whether no explanation can be given of the fact you assert, and no refutation effectually applied.' But to any man who could even be suspected of so base a practice as whispering calumnies to judges—distilling leprous venom into the ears of jurors—the Queen might well exclaim, '*Come forth, thou slanderer, and let me see thy face!* If thou would'st equal the respectability even of an Italian witness, come forth and depose in open court! As thou art, thou art worse than an Italian assassin! because, while I am boldly and manfully meeting my accusers, thou art planting a dagger unseen in my bosom, and converting thy poisoned stiletto into the semblance of the sword of justice!' I would fain say, my Lords, that it is utterly impossible that this can be true; but I cannot say it, because the fact stares me in the face. I read it even in the public papers; and had I not known of its existence in the high places of the earth I should have held it impossible that anyone with the heart of a man, or with the honour of a peer, should so debase his soul and degrade his honour. I would charge him as a judge, I would impeach him as a judge; and if it were possible for the Blood Royal of England to descend to a course so disgraceful, I should fearlessly assert that it was far more just that such conduct should deprive him of his right of

---

[8] The imputations were atrocious; amongst them was one that George III. had been induced to take his daughter-in-law's part by the vilest and most impure of motives.

succession, than that all the facts alleged against Her Majesty, even if true to the last letter of the charge, should warrant your Lordships in passing this bill of degradation and divorce.

In reading this and similar passages the great personal advantages of the speaker must not be forgotten, especially the commanding range and power of his voice. In all that the Greeks comprised under the term of action (ὑπόκρισις), in voice, in expression of eye and face, in gesture and in attitude, in all the histrionic part of oratory—that part of it which is physical and perishable—Denman possessed qualifications that have very rarely been surpassed. On this occasion, it was remembered by some who were present that at the words ' Come forth, thou slanderer,' &c., he raised his voice to the full measure of its magnificent compass, till the old roof rang again, and a thrill of irrepressible emotion pervaded every heart in the densely crowded assembly.

The speech at the moment undoubtedly took the taste of the general public even more than the carefully prepared oratory of Brougham,[9] though of *that* some passages now endure for all time among the master-pieces of eloquence, while *this*, more carelessly thrown off and never adequately revised, is now almost completely forgotten.

On the whole, Denman might well say of his speech

---

[9] This view was not confined to the outside public : some of the Peers were of the same opinion. Lord Fitzwilliam, no bad judge, told Dr. Maltby (Bishop of Durham), in the hearing of the present Lord Denman, when a young man, that he considered Denman, on the Queen's trial, to have even surpassed Brougham.

that 'it was as successful with a view to his own reputation as his friends could desire.'

It is time to return to the personal narrative. It
continues:

The Attorney-General's reply was unexpectedly good, much
superior to the Solicitor's, and to all the Attorney-General
had done before. It was remarkable, indeed, as an almost
unexampled recovery from extreme depression.

The debates of the Lords began on November 1, and I
attended them almost incessantly. Lord Grey's speech, however, admitted to be by far the best that was delivered, I
unluckily missed, having gone at that time with Brougham
to Brandenburgh House to persuade the Queen to come again
to the House of Lords, which she had too completely discontinued. She was seized with some strange caprice, and
we were told that she could not see us, because she had had
a bad night and was still asleep. We waited above an hour,
but her sleep outlasted us. Brougham said, as we got into
the carriage to return, that he saw her peeping at us through
the window of a room adjoining her bed-chamber.

The question for the second reading was carried on November 6, by a majority of 28 (contents 123, non-contents
95). Then the preamble was debated for a day or two:
then, on November 10, came the question upon the third
reading, which was carried by a majority of only 9 (contents
108, non-contents 99). With a throbbing heart I listened
to the votes, which were given by *appel nominal*, beginning
with the youngest baron. The Duke of Richmond's vote
was perhaps the most gallant; the Earl of Portsmouth's the
most amusing, for the poor idiot had voted on the other side
on the second reading, and was nearly prompted to do the
same on the third, when Lord Kenyon, who acted as teller
against the Bill from the gallery, eagerly prevented the interference.

The moment the numbers were known, Brougham summoned me into the contiguous chamber, where the Queen

was, to prepare an immediate petition to be heard by counsel against the Bill's passing. It was hastily drawn up, and Her Majesty, being desired to sign it, uttered those memorable words, after pausing a moment on ' Caroline '—' Regina in spite of them.' Brougham and all her counsel were in the room, and then all left it but myself, to desire some lord to present the petition. I remained behind with Her Majesty and her chamberlain, Mr. Keppel Craven.

At this moment I was seized with an impulse that I could not resist, and believing that the seal was finally affixed to the sentence of degradation of the House of Lords, I went up to the Queen, and requested a favour I had never enjoyed or solicited before, that of being permitted to kiss her hand. She held it out to me with great emotion and a profusion of tears.

Some tumult was now heard in the passage, and the strange tidings were made known that Lord Liverpool had withdrawn the Bill.[10]   All the rest of our party then returned to the Queen, and in another room Lady Charlotte Lindsay, who had watched the proceedings with excessive anxiety, threw herself into my arms in a paroxysm of delight. The same feelings of enthusiastic joy were almost instantaneously awakened in every part of London. The Queen, after a short delay, ascended her state carriage, and weeping, and in silence, proceeded to Brandenburgh House.

Thus closes Lord Denman's personal narrative of the principal events in this memorable trial. He adds a few observations upon the management and conduct

---

[10] Lord Liverpool, greatly to the disgust of Lord Eldon ('Twiss's Life, vol. ii. p. 398) had intimated his intention to take this step in a cabinet held the evening before (November 9). The smallness of the majority on the third reading decided him. In the House of Lords he stated ' that in the present state of the country, with the division of sentiment, so evenly balanced, just arrived at by their lordships, ministers had come to the determination not to proceed further with the Bill.'

of the case, which do not greatly differ from those to be found in Lord Brougham's recently published 'Autobiography.'[11]   His general conclusion on the matter is thus stated :—' Upon the whole, I really do not think, on a calm revision of the proceedings, that our course could either have been more judicious, according to the state of things at the time, or more fortunate in the result '—a judgment in which those most competent to pronounce an opinion will generally be found to acquiesce.

The exultation of the country at the break-down of the prosecution was in proportion to the depth and intensity of its previous anxiety.   Illuminations and public rejoicings were general over the whole face of the land.   The city of London passed a vote of thanks to Brougham, Denman, and Lushington, and resolved that the freedom of the city should be presented to them in commemoration of their splendid and successful exertions.[12]

Denman was justly proud of the distinction thus conferred on him. In his reply to the Common Council address on his elevation to the Chief Justiceship, hereafter cited,[13] he said in reference to it :

The honour of being enrolled among the freemen of London was enhanced by every circumstance that could make it most

[11] ' Memoirs,' vol. ii. chap. xvii.

[12] Mrs. Denman, in her diary for December 8, notes this, and adds that the box containing the freedom was to be ' heart of oak, of the value of 100 guineas.'   The vote was passed on December 7, 1820 ; the actual presentation did not take place till June 7, 1821.

[13] Chapter xxii. post.

honourable. It was shared with illustrious colleagues ; and, on the most trying occasion, bore testimony, not only to individual conduct, but to a principle of unquestionable truth and immense importance—*the connection between the rights and liberties of every subject, and the fearless discharge of the duties of an advocate.*

CHAPTER XI.

THE QUEEN'S DEATH.

A.D. 1821.   ÆT. 42.

Personal narrative continued—Difficulty of the Queen's social position increased by the abandonment of the Bill—Coarse libels of the ministerial press, the 'Courier' and the 'John Bull'—The Queen's name not restored to the Liturgy—Ought the Queen to accept a provision from Parliament?—Opposite views of Brougham and Denman—Message to House of Commons declining a provision—She afterwards changes her mind and applies for one—Allowance of 50,000l. a year and a residence, February 1, 1821—The Queen gives entertainments—Lord and Lady Hood—Bohemianism of the Queen—The King implacable—Petty spite of the Court—The 'George' and the 'Angel'—The Queen's popularity declines—She keeps low company—Brandenburgh House—Her resolution to be crowned in Westminster Abbey opposed by all her advisers—Her repulse at the Abbey on the Coronation Day, July 19—This hastened her end—Denman visits her shortly after—Her wild excitement—She is taken ill at Drury Lane Theatre—Grows rapidly worse—On Thursday, August 2, makes her will—On Saturday, the 4th, pronounced to be better—Brougham and Denman leave town for circuit—On Monday, the 6th, Baillie called in—On Tuesday, the 7th, the Queen dies—Brougham leaves circuit to attend the funeral—Sir Robert Wilson's dismissal—The King at Holyhead on his Irish progress—Castlereagh to Eldon on the Queen's death—The funeral procession through London—Revolting scenes—Brougham at Harwich—Lowering of the coffin from the pier—Byron's 'Irish Avatar'—Byron's high opinion of Denman—Denman at Hastings in Long Vacation of 1821—Letters thence to Merivale—Queen's death a relief—Posthumous malice of 'John Bull'—The Queen's last moments—Never mentions Bergami—Her will—How Denman came to leave her for circuit—Denman's indignation at the conduct of Government regarding the funeral and the dismissal of Sir Robert Wilson—Further extracts from letters to Merivale from Hastings—*Dolce far niente* after two years' hard labour—Scott's edition of Swift—'Blessed are the

book-makers'—Kean—Joanna Baillie's 'De Montfort'—Colman's joke,
' Jane ' and ' fustian '—Kean as Shylock—Elliston in the ' Liar '—Lady
Essex and Mrs. Damer at Hastings.

FROM the abandonment of the Bill of Pains and
Penalties, the autobiographical fragment continues
the narrative of Queen Caroline's career, and of Denman's official connexion with her, till both were closed
by her death in August 1821.

The defeat of the Bill in some respects increased the
difficulties of Her Majesty's situation, for it gave rise to the
necessity for her mingling in that society which had theretofore
avoided her, and been avoided by her. Several ladies connected with the Whig nobility now, for the first time, left
their names at Brandenburgh House, or rather it should be
said they did so at the close of the evidence, and before the
second reading, on the ground that the evidence had failed.

It cannot be denied that this was a bold measure, for
whether the imputations were true or false, the newspaper
reports had unfortunately associated the name of the Queen
with ideas the most immoral and revolting.

The battery of libels had played freely on our cause from
the moment of Her Majesty's accession to her royal state.
It was renewed on her landing, and continued with incessant
activity. The daily ministerial press seemed to have done
its duty with sufficient zeal, but the spirit of persecution
could not be satisfied without a new vehicle of abuse and
slander against the Queen. The Sunday paper ' The John
Bull ' was expressly established for this single purpose, and at
once made good its pretensions to high protection by giving
to the public that part of the contents of the Green Bag
which the collectors of it themselves had been ashamed to
produce. During the trial the ' Courier ' had kept up a
running comment on the proofs offered for the Queen,
constantly insinuating the falsehood of any favourable fact
and a wilful suppression of truth by the witnesses. But

the 'John Bull' was the climax and consummation of all villany.

Lord Liverpool having promised, or rather threatened, that the Queen should be restored to all her rights if the measure of accusation failed, we had reason to expect that her name would be forthwith restored to the Liturgy, and the whole public loudly called for that act of justice, which the unmanly hatred of the baffled persecutor still obstinately refused. The Parliament, of course, acquiesced in the known wishes of the King. The extent of Her Majesty's establishment and provision was even left doubtful.

I went with Brougham to Brandenburgh House for the express purpose of considering what steps should be taken in the delicate matter of negotiating for a revenue. Brougham had cherished the wild hope that the people of England would raise a revenue for the Queen by public subscription, and actually advised her, not merely to decline, if offered, but positively to declare, before any offer was even made, that she would not accept a provision recommended in the ordinary way by the King to Parliament. She was anxious, on the other hand, for conciliation, and proposed to address a very civil letter to the King on the subject. They were discussing these opposite views, when she suddenly called to me, 'What do you say, Mr. Denman?' I proposed a middle course, condemning the imprudence of rejecting a bounty not yet proffered, but to which she was strictly entitled; and at the same time thinking that any language which could be construed as humbling herself before such a husband would involve too great a sacrifice of her advantage. I am confident my advice was good, though Burdett, as he afterwards told me, thought her want of real power made her own scheme the best, and Brougham prevailed. He delivered her message to the House of Commons on the same day, to the annoyance and astonishment of our friends, and the cordial joy of the ministers.

She ought to have acted consistently with his bold counsel. But scarcely had Brougham left London for the northern circuit than she told Wood that she meant to write to Lord Liverpool, to ask for an income. He remonstrated and begged that I might be first consulted : she agreed. This was on a Saturday. I went to pay my respects as usual on the Sunday, between one and two, and Lushington arrived soon after, when she told us, laughing and delighted, that she had sent a message to Lord Liverpool on the subject. This inconsistency of conduct and apparent avidity for money was in no small degree injurious to her cause in the public mind.

An allowance of 50,000*l.* a year having been granted to her (on Feb. 1, 1821), the Duke of Cambridge's house in South Audley Street was purchased for her, and called 'The Queen's House.' She gave some splendid dinners and evening concerts, went sometimes to the play, where she was not too well received, and once to the opera, where she was shamefully insulted by young noblemen and aspirants after place. Lady Ann Hamilton was rather ungraciously dismissed from personal attendance, though placed in the highest office in Her Majesty's household as Mistress of the Robes, and Lady Hood came into waiting. Lord Hood also resided in the house. It became evident, however, that there was something in her manners and disposition ill calculated to preserve her popularity with the serious and sober people among whom she dwelt. Dress parties were a restraint upon her : at one of them she unceremoniously made me sit on a sofa by her side, and told me how little she approved of being ' stuck up ' among fine people. She said, ' The fact is, I have lived so long among Turks, Jews, and infidels, that I am not fit for good company.' This appears to have been her natural turn of mind, and was, of course, encouraged by her foreign residence and her wandering habits. How different might all have been had she given her hand to an honourable and feeling husband.

On her husband's part no symptom of forgiveness or generosity betrayed itself :—

> Forgiveness to the injured does belong,
> But those ne'er pardon who have done the wrong.

His resentment showed itself in acts of paltry littleness. When, for instance, the Queen gave a party, her royal consort took means to spoil it, by giving another on the same night, and so depriving her of her expected guests. She alluded to this in conversing with me at one of her parties which was thus deserted, with some humour, and comparing it to the patronage given to different inns, 'Some go to the " *George*," ' she said, ' and some to the " *Angel*." '

The warm feelings excited by the Queen's danger had now subsided ; some disgust was given by her acceptance of the money ; she had lost the charm of novelty ; numerous disappointments must have taken place in quarters where her patronage had been promised or expected ; and 'John Bull' and the other papers still continued to throw dirt with no small effect. The Queen, though possessing a suitable residence in London, still lived principally at Brandenburgh House, inviting very little English company, and entertaining a succession of Italians who appeared to be of no high order. In a word, her popularity was daily declining, when the fatal event of the Coronation gave it the last blow. Her attendance was, I believe, recommended by nobody. Lord Hood had remonstrated against it, though when her resolution was taken he became whimsically angry with those who opposed it. Lord Archibald Hamilton endeavoured to point out the difficulties, and ascertain her intentions. I had the misfortune to fall under her heavy displeasure ; Brougham, I think, stayed away. Hopeless as it was, we had still, however, some expectation that she had either formed a scheme of action, or that some happy idea would strike her at the moment of need.

This expectation proved unfounded : the attempt to enter the Abbey was a miserable and ignominious failure. ' At the decisive moment,' says Brougham, ' she flinched, I verily believe for the first time in her life.'[1]

----

[1] 'Brougham's Memoirs,' vol. ii. p. 422.

On one of the hottest days ever remembered in this country (July 19, 1821), she stood for a length of time in a burning sun, vainly soliciting, sometimes even demanding, admittance, first at one entrance, then at another. The doors of the Abbey were inexorably shut against her, no demonstration of any sort was made by the crowd in her favour; and she had to return home, worn out with fatigue, fevered with exertion and broken down with shame and vexation. There can be no doubt that this misjudged act and its consequences hastened her end.

I went to Brandenburgh House [proceeds the personal narrative] a few evenings after, and found her with a large party, dancing, laughing, and romping, with spirits frightfully overstrained. A few nights after, she was taken ill at Drury Lane Theatre: she grew daily worse, and on the Wednesday (August 1) I found Dr. Holland full of apprehensions. It was determined that Brougham should be sent for (he had been absent during his eldest child's illness, which terminated fatally), and that the propriety of making her will should be suggested. I think it was on Thursday that this was first mentioned. We all attended to pay our duty, and were received with the most unselfish kindness. The Queen was lying on a sofa-bed without curtains; she sate up in it, her head bound with a silk handkerchief, the face flushed, the eye remarkably bright. She spoke cheerfully, though sensible of her danger, and conferred with Lushington alone. He remained some time, taking her instructions, and I shall never forget the feeling with which I heard from him that she desired to be buried in Brunswick, and her tomb to bear no other inscription than that simple one —' Caroline, the injured Queen of England.' [2]

---

[2] Brougham says it was ' the *murdered* Queen of England.' Denman's is the correct version.

During the greater part of Friday (August 3), we wandered listlessly over the apartments and gardens, in restless uncertainty as to the result of Her Majesty's illness.   Lady Ann Hamilton was in constant attendance, as were Lord and Lady Hood, though the Queen had dispensed with the attendance of them all, and the Hoods had actually made preparations for leaving the house, when she was seized with her fatal disorder.   She had taken the Reverend John Page Wood,[3] the alderman's son, into favour, appointed his wife to some office about her person, and became excessively fond of their young child.   Brougham always thought this *engouement* for young children an instinct that belonged to her character, which might explain many of her proceedings.   The little Victorine, the daughter of Bergami, was early a favourite, and became one of the objects of her testamentary bounty.[4]

On the Saturday (August 4), all the physicians took a flattering view of the Queen's situation, and thought there was no danger.   Brougham set off on his circuit about noon with this impression ; I started for mine the same evening, and though, on taking Brandenburgh House on my way, I found the state of things less satisfactory, I proceeded on my journey with decided expectations that the Queen would recover.

Her state unhappily grew worse.   On the Monday morning (August 6), Baillie arrived from Dorsetshire, and saw no cause for excessive alarm : the internal obstruction appeared to be removed.   He told me afterwards that he could not account for her death, which happened on the next day, Tuesday, August 7.   No death could be more courageous or more amiable.

Brougham and I had agreed that in case of Her Majesty's

---

[3] The Rev. Sir John Page Wood, 2nd Baronet, d. 1866.

[4] Victorine lived in Italy after the Queen's death, and was respectably married to an Italian Count. William Austen, the Queen's earliest child-favourite, also received a considerable legacy. He also went to Italy, and lived near Victorine, but he turned out a good-for-nothing person, became deranged, and died in a lunatic asylum. 'Brougham's Memoirs,' vol. ii. p. 425.

disorder becoming fatal, we could not be expected to leave the circuit in order to attend the funeral ceremony; but his long and intimate connection with the Queen, and the advice of his friends, very properly induced him to alter his resolution.

I shall not describe the revolting scenes, which I did not witness, but cannot refrain from recording my sense of the cruel injustice that stripped Sir Robert Wilson of his military rank, for no crime or offence, on account of clandestine and detected falsehoods, when his conduct entitled him to the highest praise for gallantry and humanity.[5]

The King, who had started on his memorable Irish progress not long after the commencement of the Queen's illness, was at Holyhead when the news of her death reached him. Lord Castlereagh, who was then in attendance, writing from Holyhead to Lord Eldon, on August 9, speaks of the Queen's death ' as an occasion which cannot be regarded in any other light than the greatest of all possible deliverances, both to His Majesty and the country.'[6]

The funeral procession left Brandenburgh House on August 14, in a dense downpour of rain that lasted for hours. The Ministry had determined that the hearse should not pass through the City on its way to Harwich; the Queen's friends had determined that it should. The soldiers fired on the funeral procession to turn it out of Piccadilly, one of the bullets striking the carriage in which Brougham and Sir Robert Wilson were seated. Ultimately the body was carried through the City

---

[5] His real offence was his having attended the Queen's funeral: the ostensible one, wholly false, was his having attended a seditious meeting in connexion with it. 'Brougham's Memoirs,' vol. ii. p. 417.

[6] Twiss's 'Memoirs of Lord Eldon,' vol. ii. p. 432.

amid a shameful scene of squalid disorder and confusion.

Brougham went down to Harwich, and was present at the embarkation (on August 16). 'The multitudes,' he says, 'assembled from all parts of the country, were immense, and the pier crowded with them; the sea was covered with boats of every size and kind, and the colours of the vessels were half-mast high, as on days of mourning. The crimson coffin slowly descended from the pier, and the barge that conveyed it bore the flag of England floating over Caroline of Brunswick, " the *murdered* Queen of England," the inscription directed by herself, and the justice of which was acknowledged by thousands, who had indignantly seen the indecent haste of the funeral procession from London, and felt their share in a kind of national remorse, as well as commiseration for all that had passed.'[7]

The great English poet, from his self-chosen exile in Italy,[8] gave voice to the feeling of the time, in that tremendous philippic 'The Irish Avatar,' whose opening stanza concentrated in a few scathing words the pity

[7] 'Brougham's Memoirs,' vol. ii. p. 428. The inscription was '*injured* Queen,' not 'murdered Queen.' A plate, with the inscription engraved, was fixed on the coffin while it rested for the night in Colchester Church, but was afterwards taken off again, by order of Government, before the embarkation at Harwich (see Hansard, Parl. Deb. N.S. vol. vi. p. 923 to 977, Debate on Queen's funeral.)

[8] Byron had always a high sense of Denman's ability and a certain interest in his career. In an unpublished letter to Hodgson, of October 22, 1820, from Ravenna, he writes, 'Your friend Denman has been making a figure. I am glad of it: he had all the auguries of a superior man about him before I left the country.'

and the scorn which were then striving for mastery in
the indignant heart of the English people :

> Ere the daughter of Brunswick is cold in her grave,
>   While her ashes still float to their home o'er the tide,
> Lo! George the triumphant speeds o'er the wave
>   To the long-cherished Isle which he loved like his—*Bride!*

Denman, after the conclusion of his circuit, went
down to pass the Long Vacation at Hastings. A few
extracts from letters written by him while there to his
friend Merivale furnish some further particulars as to
the Queen's last days, and also serve to show what
his feelings were at the time with regard to the sad
and shameful events that attended and followed on
her funeral.

Under date September 4, 1821, he writes :

' It would be the height of hypocrisy to deny that the sad
death of the unhappy Queen has brought, as you supposed, no
small relief to my mind. Her situation in point of society was
deplorable, and seemed to admit of no improvement, so complete was the triumph of calumny and base servility. ' John
Bull,' more malignant since her death than even in her lifetime, intimates that worse charges than those brought forward
last year were suppressed out of tenderness to the Queen's
station, and that those stigmatised as her persecutors have
been in truth the best of her friends. Is it possible for malice
to go further ?

On September 12, from the same place to the same
correspondent, he writes as follows in reference to the
Queen's last hours :

Lord Hood mentioned that the phrase ascribed to her in
the papers was in fact often in her mouth, *Je pourrai souffrir
des douleurs physiques, mais je quitterai la vie sans regret.*

Wilde stated that he was with her to the last, and that for
the last two hours she was delirious, and talked incessantly.
It is a fact of great importance that *the name of Bergami
never passed her lips.* Lady Hood has sent my wife a
beautiful lock of her hair. We first thought her disorder serious
on the Thursday night, and the next morning, finding the
physicians much alarmed, I set about acting as her first legal
adviser (Brougham being out of town with his wife on the
loss of their child); brought down Lushington and Wilde,
and had the will drawn up in the best manner the time
allowed. Brougham joined us while this was going on. On
the Saturday morning the doctors were surprised that the
Queen was alive without material amendment, but said that
every hour's existence promised everything for her final
recovery. Brougham set off for the circuit at 4 P.M., I at
midnight, after hearing the result of a medical consultation,
which scarcely seemed to leave a doubt of her recovery. It
was not without a long deliberation that I resolved to go,
although there could not be a doubt it was right. I daresay
the least token of attention from the Queen would have
detained me, but as she neither named me as an executor,
nor expressed any wish to see me after the will was attested,
I was perfectly free to take the only step that was proper.

In the course of the same letter Denman gives vent
to very natural feelings of indignation at the gross
brutality of the funeral outrages :

The conduct of ministers is incredible. The low spite of
prohibiting the corpse from passing through the City, *Ne
gemitus quidem populi Romani liber foret,* is worthy of the
heads and hearts that conceived and executed it. Doubtless
the husband of Octavia must rejoice at the blood and filth
that have polluted her funeral procession. I am glad the
People resisted and gained their point.

In a later letter he thus adverts to the infamous
treatment of Sir Robert Wilson :

My mind has been on the whole fairly tranquil, but the removal of Sir Robert Wilson is beyond endurance. It is clear they had no case when the step was taken, or they would have been too happy to prove one before a court-martial; but I doubt not, if pressed, they will get up one. The attempt to reduce an honourable man to ruin and beggary, without confronting him with an accuser, or apprizing him of the charge, is the introduction of a political Inquisition into the Army. Did you observe that the papers on the two different sides exchanged blunders—the 'Courier' promising to tell particulars and the 'Times' pledging Wilson to make a statement. I wrote to him to remonstrate with all my might against making any defence to surmises, and am clearly of opinion that nothing beyond demanding a court-martial in the first instance ought to have been done by him. The subscription does not seem to go on as could be wished; but I trust there is a well-founded confidence of raising enough when the rich come to town. I tendered twice as much as I was put down for.

Denman liked Hastings extremely, and protracted his stay there till towards the close of October. The following further extracts from letters written thence to Merivale will show how he passed his well-earned holiday :

We are all well, enjoying a fine coast and delicious climate, in a country which almost rivals your own Devonshire in beauty, and abounds besides with most interesting reminiscences. The vacation is really delightful, a double vacation after two years of labour, and what labour! What a contrast between this day in 1821 and in 1820 [when the Lords resumed their sitting]. I bathe, ride three hours a day, with my wife, some of the children, and Phillips [9] alternately, and,

---

[9] Mr. Samuel March Phillips, author of the well-known 'Treatise on Evidence,' afterwards permanent Under-Secretary for the Home Department.

lodging on the Marine Parade, lead a life of perfect idleness.

Walter Scott's edition of Swift is my present companion, and I have hardly an idea of earthly happiness beyond an idle summer passed among the volumes full of notes, anecdotes, and illustrations, that are devoted by zealous editors to the complete works of authors of real original genius. 'Waverley' and 'Old Mortality' are admirable in their way, but to my taste at this moment above all things 'blessed are the bookmakers.' I speak it in the sincerity of gratitude.

Edmund Kean is here; he enquired kindly after you. At his request Joanna Baillie has altered the catastrophe of 'De Montfort' from hanging to suicide; and he is now studying the part with sanguine hopes. My impression of the superior power and beauty of the play is even strengthened by this return to it; but what will Drury Lane do without the possibility of giving him a sister? Colman[10] was requested to alter the conclusion, and said that for want of *Jane* (name of De Montfort's sister in the drama) they must resort to *fustian*.

A little later he writes :

The day is a most happy one. We are preparing (a party of seven) to see Kean act Shylock and Elliston in the 'Liar' —very good-natured to the native troop. The judgment of Kean coincides too much with yours, and, indeed, with my own, though not with my wishes, concerning 'Alberic';[11] but there really is a great deal of very spirited writing in it, and the incident of the banquet, immediately followed by a restoration of Roman liberty, would form a striking denouement.

As usual at a watering-place, we find that we might have a most agreeable society if we stayed on—your admiration,

<hr>

[10] The famous wit, George Colman the younger.
[11] One of Joanna Baillie's plays.

Lady Essex, Mrs. Damer and others. To say the truth, I
am quite content that this discovery was not made before.
We have been able to live to ourselves in a degree you
would have thought impossible. It is with something like
melancholy that I see the termination of this delightful
holiday so near.

CHAPTER XII.

FROM DEATH OF QUEEN TO DEATH OF CANNING—DENMAN, COMMON SERJEANT.

A.D. 1821 TO 1827.   ÆT. 42 TO 48.

Personal narrative of Denman's career from the Queen's death to that of
Canning (1821-1827)—Professional rank of Brougham and Denman
after the Queen's death—Circuit resolution—John Williams M.P. for
Lincoln, 1822—Attacks by Denman and Williams on Lord Eldon and
Chancery abuses—Denman elected Common Serjeant, March 1822—
Bolland his competitor—Respective number of votes—Entry and fine
in Circuit Book—First sittings in April 1822—Trial for blasphemy
and sedition of Humphrey Boyle, shopkeeper of R. Carlile, prosecuted
by the *Constitutional Association*—A difficult task for Denman—Status
of the defendant—Character of the libel—Denman's conduct of the
trial—Refuses to stop the defendant in his speech to the jury—Leaves
to the jury the meaning of the libel, and the question whether the
publisher was aware of its contents and tendency—Sentence, eighteen
months' imprisonment—Thought severe by many—Comments of the
Press—Reasonable Liberals not dissatisfied—Denman's performance
of the duties of Common Serjeant—His expedition in trying
prisoners—Dislike to technical objections—Testimony to the excellence
of Old Bailey juries—Advocates reforms in criminal law procedure—
Article in the 'Edinburgh Review' for 1824 on the 'Law of Evidence'
—Suggestions from time to time to Home Office regarding law
amendment—Emoluments of office of Common Serjeant—Its effect
on professional practice—Influence of forensic and judicial engagements
on parliamentary success—Denman, for financial reasons, not a candidate at the general election of 1826—A new era in 1827—The Canning
administration—Split in the Whig party—Brougham and Lord Lansdowne favourable to Canning—Lord Grey joins Duke of Wellington
in strong opposition to him—Position of the leading lawyers—Copley's

THE personal narrative, from which such copious extracts have already been made, is followed by another, written in 1828, and containing a brief record of the principal events of Denman's public and professional life from the death of the Queen, in 1821, to the formation, in 1827, of Canning's administration.   It commences as follows :—

The question now arose whether the silk gowns lost by Her Majesty's death would be renewed by the King.   Brougham and myself both determined to make no application to the Chancellor, having requested promotion of him in general terms before her appointment of us was known.   The members of · the Midland Circuit who were my seniors insisted on my keeping the lead in all causes in which we had been already retained together ; [1] but in the spring of 1822 we went the circuit without any rank.   That period was marked by two events.

The representation of the city of Lincoln became suddenly vacant while the assizes were being held there.   I had the opportunity of taking steps which secured the return of my friend, John Williams, at a very moderate expense.   In Parliament his vigorous attacks on the abuses of the Court of Chancery and on Lord Eldon were followed by great

---

[1] On August 9, 1821, at a special circuit court held at Nottingham, in consequence of the Queen's death, it was unanimously resolved 'that it is the wish of the circuit that Mr. Denman should retain during the present circuit the rank and precedence to which he was entitled as Solicitor-General to her late majesty.' (Entry in Midland Circuit Book).

results, and will probably be, however late, the cause of a real reform in that monstrous jurisdiction.[2]

The next event was my own election to the office of Common Serjeant, then likely to be vacated by Newman Knollys, Esq., who soon after succeeded Sir John Sylvester as Recorder.   At Warwick, several leading members of the Common Council applied to me to stand for the appointment. I complied, and, coming to London, found a most formidable competitor in Bolland,[3] one of the most blameless and honourable men living, possessed of very competent talents and much curious learning (especially in early English literature), but rather deficient in nerve and promptitude in business.   Though his political opinions were by no means of a Tory cast, his opposition to me gave the contest a decided party character, and for the moment few excited greater or more general interest.

Though I had resolved to enter into no personal canvass for a judicial situation (in which Bolland was induced to follow my example), I often attended my committee, and stimulated them to the utmost exertions, both for their own honour and mine.   Both sides were confident of success, but on the day of ballot my number of votes was exactly half of the whole body (262); Bolland's inferior by twelve [the respective numbers were—for Denman 131, for Bolland 119]. To his great honour, his defeat, though an unexpected and severe blow after his long connection with the City with a view to that very object [he had been for eighteen years, since 1804, one of the four City pleaders], never interrupted the pleasant terms on which we had lived.

Denman's circuit of course took speedy cognizance of this appointment : the entry relating to it runs thus :

[2] This anticipation has to a great degree been fulfilled.   Denman does not mention his own exertions in the same cause : they will be noticed in the next chapter.

[3] Sir William Bolland. Born, 1772; called to bar, 1801; City Pleader, 1804; raised to bench as a Baron of the Exchequer, 1829; resigned, 1839; died, 1840, æt. 68.

Lincoln : July 23, 1822.—The whole circuit congratulates Mr. Denman on his elevation to the high office of Common Serjeant, and the Common Serjeant being allowed to fix his own fine, prayed to be amerced a turtle only.

Proposed by Mr. Adams that the circuit do meet Mr. Common Serjeant's fine by a good dinner.

Seconded by Mr. Phillips ; agreed *nem. diss.*

Proposed and agreed that that dinner should be at Warwick, and that the wine treasurer be instructed to provide all necessary on that occasion.

Proposed that the judges be invited to that dinner.

The personal narrative proceeds :

My judicial duties began in April. From my experience at Nottingham (as Deputy-Recorder) I found myself quite at home in the common run of criminal trials, but on the very first day of my sitting I had a most peculiarly difficult task. I, the champion of the liberty of the Press, the denouncer in Parliament of the self-styled Constitutional Association,[4] which assumed a larger prerogative than the Crown itself in punishing libels, I, the censor of judges who had acted with undue severity on similar occasions, was called to preside at the trial of a libeller prosecuted by that very Association.

The delinquent was sincere, extremely well-behaved, and not without talent : he was found guilty and sentenced to imprisonment for the long period of eighteen months.

Some of my ardent political friends murmured, but I have never repented of what I then did. On the contrary, I acted on my own principles, and took the line by which I have ever since abided in cases of libel.

The defendant was one of Carlile's shopmen.[5] He refused to tell his name, which I believe was Humphrey Boyle. He was, therefore, indicted by some clumsy circumlocution, and

[4] In the session of 1821. See next chapter.

[5] Richard Carlile, notorious in those days as a publisher of revolutionary and atheistic tracts.

to prevent any inconvenient doubt of his identity, I kept him in Court the whole time, and contrary to the then usual practice at the Old Bailey, passed sentence upon him at once, instead of leaving him to the Recorder at the close.

His libel was of the very worst description, a resumé of every offensive passage, both on religion and politics, that had appeared in the periodical work styled 'The Republican.' The fact of selling was clearly proved.

The defence was written, very long, full of attacks on the Bible, as justifications of the argument in that part of the libel. Mr. Adolphus,[6] who prosecuted for the Association, requested me to prevent his going on ; but I declined to interfere. I did, indeed, remonstrate with the defendant, but I left him to his own discretion in taking care of his own interest. Mr. Justice Best (Lord Wynford) had so interfered, but I had presented the petition to Parliament which complained of him for so doing.[7] His interruption was by imposing a fine for what the defendant had said. Lord Chief Justice Abbott (Lord Tenterden) had also stopped some one in his defence. I peremptorily refused.

In summing up the case to the jury, I left it wholly to them to pronounce on the meaning of the libel,[8] and his address left them no doubt on this subject. I then told them that they must also be satisfied that the publisher was aware of the contents and mischievous tendency of the libel ;[9]

---

[6] The celebrated criminal barrister ; author of the continuation of Smollett's 'History of England,' father of the late accomplished John Leycester Adolphus.

[7] In Session of 1821. Petition of Thomas Davison, Feb. 23, 1821, chap. xiii.

[8] 'Mr. Fox's Libel Act has, in my opinion, been virtually repealed whenever the Judge has directed the jury that the prosecuted paper is in point of law a libel. The words of the statute, which have been supposed to require him to do so, only leaves it to his discretion, "as in other criminal cases." Much less can they excuse the vehement inflammatory terms in which this supposed point of law has been often denounced from the bench.' (Note by Lord Denman.)

[9] 'I can never accede to the doctrine that the publisher is criminally answerable for a paper of the contents of which he was utterly ignorant,

but on this point also his speech was conclusive against him.

The sentence (18 months) was thought severe by some;[10] but it was much lighter than any which had then lately been passed on persons convicted of blasphemous libels, even when unconnected with incentives to sedition and violence. Two aldermen sate on the bench that evening—Brown, who was excessively shocked both by the publication and by the line of defence, and whom I could hardly prevent from interfering to stop the speaker; and Thorpe, well known for opinions as completely liberal as his disposition was humane. The former proposed two years, the latter, one; the middle course was adopted.

Those of the newspapers which censured my conduct founded their comments on some very imperfect reports of what had passed, despatching a trial of several hours in a few lines, and giving no idea of the real character of the libel. But I had the satisfaction of hearing that disinterested persons who were present found no fault. Dr. Birkbeck told me this respecting some friends of his, entertaining the most liberal sentiments on political matters; and Mr. Richard Taylor informed me that when the defendant himself was urged to petition Parliament, because he had not been fairly tried, he refused to do so, declaring that no man could possibly have had a fairer trial.

notwithstanding the authority of Lord Mansfield, or of any other judge. The sentences upon Johnson and Cuthill for selling some books of Gilbert Wakefield (A.D. 1797) always have appeared to me disgraceful to Lord Eldon, then Attorney-General, as well as to the Court of King's Bench. It is to me incomprehensible that a jury should be charged to find such persons guilty on an indictment which states that they "with mischievous intentions, maliciously published."' (Note by Lord Denman.) See the defence of Cuthill in Lord Erskine's speeches.

[10] Brougham, in writing to Lord Grey on Denman's elevation to the Chief Justiceship, says, 'I remember Lambton, Cutler, Fergusson, and others of our friends in the House of Commons, were quite indignant at Denman's sentence, and cried, "All lawyers are alike. Who would have expected this!" The fact is,' adds Brougham, 'judges *must* go by the law.'—Letter of November 5, 1832, 'Memoirs,' vol. iii. p. 222, 223.

In performing the judicial duties of Common Serjeant, I have some reason to believe that, with this single exception, so peculiar in itself and remarkable in all its circumstances, I have escaped all serious animadversion.

Not only so. Lord Denman's performance of the duties of Common Serjeant during the eight years he filled that office was deservedly the subject of high and general approbation. He displayed on the Old Bailey bench those eminent judicial qualities which afterwards distinguished him as Chief Justice of England— towards the accused, firmness tempered with lenity, the strictest impartiality, and a determination to have every case tried on its merits; towards the Bar, a dignified courtesy of demeanour, and a total abstinence from those interruptions and interlocutory comments from the Bench which tend to irritate the temper of counsel, and seriously to retard the despatch of business.

The magistrates, from the time of my appointment, though extremely distasteful to the majority of them, treated me with the greatest kindness and liberality; and I believe they were not a little pleased with the saving of time which was effected by my method of trying prisoners. That economy has always appeared to me an important judicial duty, not only as affecting the numerous bodies of witnesses, whose long attendance is so severe a penalty upon them, but as securing from the jury the willing sacrifice of time, and the adequate consideration of those cases in which reasonable doubts arise; for nothing tends more to discourage the free employment of the understanding than undiscriminating pressure on cases of unequal difficulty, or the habitual exaggeration of trifles. Strongly convinced that no encouragement is so productive of crime as impunity, I have adopted the habit of yielding reluctantly to technical objections. Even when they have appeared well founded, I have nevertheless preferred submitting the facts to the jury, and reserving the law for the judges, to a hasty proclamation of the inadequacy of the law by directing an immediate acquittal.

It is a grateful task to bear testimony to the excellent conduct of juries at the Old Bailey Sessions. I do not remember a single *conviction* that appeared to me unjust. Some *acquittals* have startled me; but often very good reasons, which had not occurred to me at the trial, have been suggested afterwards, and I have often thought that their mistakes might be traced to their feeling too much deference for certain vulgar scraps of judicial phraseology which have come to be considered as principles of law.

Various reforms of the administration of criminal law have presented themselves to my mind while presiding at the Old Bailey. In 1824 I laid many of them before the public in the 'Edinburgh Review,' where I wrote a critique on Bentham's ' Traité des preuves judiciaires ' (' Treatise on Judicial Proofs ') edited by Dumont.[11] I have been in the constant habit of communicating my ideas on these points from time to time to the Secretary of State, as well before and since as during the time when that office was filled by Lord Lansdowne. Many alterations which I have thought desirable have been accomplished; and I have given all the assistance in my power, both in and out of Parliament, to the amendments brought forward in my time.

The salary attached to the office of Common Serjeant was 1,000*l.* ; the fees on city business varied from 150*l.* to near 400*l.* by the year. The addition thus made to my income could not be unacceptable with so large a family, and the rank was professionally valuable, more especially on circuit. In London I kept always a respectable portion of business, and (while Queen's Solicitor-General) had been occasionally forced by my silk gown into the lead; but the old stagers

---

[11] This able article is noticed and largely quoted from in Chapter xiv.

kept their place, and Brougham was naturally selected to lead for cases of importance when those were retained on the other side. My judicial occupation, too, took me also away from court, and parliamentary duties often engrossed my attention and exhausted my powers.

In Parliament the same distraction prevented me from making so good an impression as perhaps I might. Once or twice, particularly one night when I went down and spoke for Lord Althorp's motion for repealing the Foreign Enlistment Act, I was conscious of the feebleness of my efforts, and received a disagreeable hint from a quarter not to be trifled with. For when I first rose afterwards, in support of Mr. Brownlow's motion of censure against Lord Wellesley's Government in Ireland for their proceedings against those who were called the Orange conspirators of 1822, the newspaper reporters made a decided attempt to prevent my being heard. I was, however, in a very good state of nerves, full of the subject, and strongly impressed with its importance : the formidable opposition was silenced, and I got through with some *éclat*.

Then follows the passage, already given elsewhere, (pp. 121, 122, *ante*) containing Lord Denman's general estimate of his Parliamentary career from 1819 to 1826. The narrative afterwards continues :

At the general election in 1826 I found my funds utterly unable to maintain any contest at Nottingham ; and though Birch and myself were too well esteemed, and the Whig party there too well established, to fear any opposition from Tory candidates, yet my finances would not have been equal even to an undisputed election, and besides, I thought it better to withdraw from Parliament and give more time to my profession. My line was decided ; I resigned in favour of Lord Rancliffe, and declined a borough for which Brougham procured the promise from the Duke of Norfolk.

Things went with me rather better from the increased

attention I was now able to afford to business, but 1827 was
a new era. The old Tory Government was broken up (by
Lord Liverpool's disabling attack of paralysis on February 17,
1827), and (in April, 1827) Canning, supported by several
of the Whigs, formed a new one. Brougham, from the
northern circuit, conveyed to him, on the political death of
Lord Liverpool [his natural death did not occur till December,
1828], his favourable sentiments, and thus encouraged his
separation from his former colleagues. But there was a wide
and important rent in the Whig party too. Lord Grey stood
aloof [from rooted distrust and dislike of Canning, proceeding,
Brougham says in his ' Memoirs,' ' on the old Fox feelings
towards him '],[12] and at length supported Wellington in a
decided and even factious opposition.[13] Lord Lansdowne was
reluctant, though friendly : Canning insisted on being joined
by two of his (Lord Lansdowne's) immediate friends, and the
two members for Calne—Abercrombie and Macdonald—took
office, the former becoming Judge Advocate, the latter a
commissioner at the India Board.

The lawyers were oddly shifted about. Copley [afterwards
Lord Lyndhurst, then Master of the Rolls], as member for
the University of Cambridge, had made a strong speech against
Catholic emancipation in March [on Sir F. Burdett's annual
motion, which was this year defeated only by four]. Canning
[who had got up from a sick bed at Brighton to be present
at the debate] attacked him with ferocity and contempt,
exposing both the impudence and baseness of his conduct
with virulence. Everybody pitied the Master of the Rolls,
and thought him lucky in having obtained that situation,
from which he could never expect to emerge. His speech

---

[12] ' Brougham's Memoirs,' vol. ii. p. 481.

[13] See Hookham Frere's epigram : Canning *loquitur :*

> I was destroyed by Wellington and Grey.
> They both succeeded ; each has had his day.
> Both tried to govern, each in his own way ;
> And both repent of it—as well they may.

(' Works of J. Hookham Frere,' by Sir B. and W. Frere, 1871.)

was bad—politically, morally, and intellectually. Yet this very man was made Chancellor by Canning in the very next month [Canning became Prime Minister in April].

Sir Charles Wetherell refused to keep the Attorney-Generalship under a popularly affected minister. Scarlett,[14] then the leading Whig lawyer, was applied to. He asked my advice before Lord Lansdowne enlisted, and while the Whigs hung back. I told him that if Lord Lansdowne refused to join, while the body of the party were ready to act with Canning, he was bound to accept the tendered office. He said to me—it was at Guildhall—' I wish you would write me a letter to that effect.' Before I sate down to dinner I complied with his desire, urging the importance of the crisis, and the great advantage Liberal principles of government were gaining. A few days after he showed me a letter from Lord Fitzwilliam, who had brought him into Parliament for Peterborough. His lordship's mind was by no means made up, and he afterwards joined Grey in opposition, but at this period he advised Scarlett to accept office, and agreed in the reasoning of my letter. I must, however, add that the counsel was followed before the condition was performed : for he became Attorney-General before Lord Lansdowne either accepted or refused the union with the new Prime Minister. Tindal consented to be passed over, and continued Solicitor-General under Scarlett, under Wetherell again in a few months, and again under Scarlett when the latter returned to office in 1829.

At this point the personal narrative comes somewhat abruptly to a close, a matter much to be regretted both by the reader and by the present writer.

It may be as well to transcribe the letter above alluded to as written by Denman to Scarlett at his

---

[14] James Scarlett, the most successful advocate of his time ; born 1769; called to the bar, 1791 ; King's Counsel, 1816 ; Attorney-General, 1827 ; again, 1829–30 ; Chief Baron of Exchequer, 1834 ; and then created Lord Abinger ; died on Norfolk circuit of apoplexy, A.D. 1844, æt. 75.

request. It shows very clearly the feeling entertained by its writer towards the Canning administration :

Dear Scarlett,—On the interesting subject of our short conversation, I feel a strong impulse to add a few words on paper, though perhaps I have already signified my opinion better by word of mouth, because I am convinced that so critical a moment for the country has not occurred in our time. It seems to me that liberal principles of government are on the very confines of life and death; unlooked for and surprising advantages on the one hand, certain destruction on the other.

Such in my judgment is the question whether Canning's ministry maintains itself or falls. Among all persons who share our general opinions the same feeling is warm, unanimous, and decided. Of course there is an anxious wish that the negotiation with Lord Lansdowne may have the effect of uniting the Whigs with Canning in office.

What possible bar can prevent this union? Surely no public views, for there is not a single political question for which we have contended which would not be materially advanced by it. The difficulties I hear talked of cannot be the real ones, for they really amount to nothing; but, if the delicate sense of honour which belongs to Lord Lansdowne may have betrayed him into the fault of creating differences where none really exist, the extreme regret of his friends would be nothing to what he would have prepared for himself when he witnesses the state of things to which his refusal would reduce the country.

If, as I have heard it reported, so very important a step has been taken, from whatever laudable motives, against the general views of the Whig party, I now deliberately repeat the opinion I declared to you two hours ago, that you would be fully justified in accepting office under Canning; and, if your doing so could give stability to his government, I do not think you would be justified in refusing it.

Yours very sincerely,
T. DENMAN.

For Canning personally Denman had a high admiration. In a letter written to his friend Merivale shortly after Canning's death [15] he says, ' the loss of Canning is to me a very sad and afflicting circumstance ; few men ever possessed more titles to admiration.   I always felt a personal liking towards him, and his unexpected, sad, and rapid decay is truly melancholy.'

It was not only as a brilliant scholar, orator, and statesman that Denman admired Canning ; there can be little doubt that he was also considerably influenced in his favour by the manly part taken by him, in strong contrast with all the rest of the Liverpool ministry, throughout the whole business of the Queen.

[15] Which took place August 8, 1827.

CHAPTER XIII.

DENMAN IN HOUSE OF COMMONS FROM 1821 TO 1826.

A.D. 1821 TO 1826.   ÆT. 42 TO 47.

General estimate of Denman's Parliamentary career for this period—*Session of* 1821—Presents petition from Thomas Davison, fined 100*l.* for contempt, by Mr. Justice Best, on his trial for blasphemy, February 23, 1821—Speech on Mr. Lennard's motion for repeal of Seditious Meetings and Blasphemous Libel Acts, May 8, 1821—On Sir F. Burdett's motion for enquiry into the Manchester Massacre of 1819, May 15, 1821—On Sir J. Mackintosh's bill for abolishing death punishment in cases of forgery, June 4, 1821—Observations on the proceedings of the Constitutional Association, July 3, 1821. *Session of* 1822—Speech on the proceedings at the Queen's funeral, March 6, 1822—On Lord John Russell's motion on the state of the Representation of the People, April 25, 1822—Against renewal of Aliens' Regulation Act, June 5, 1822—On same subject, July 19, 1822. *Session of* 1823—Speech on petition from Richard Carlile, fined and imprisoned for blasphemous libel, May 8, 1823—On motion of Mr. John Williams for enquiry into delays in Court of Chancery, June 5, 1823—Instances of delay cited by Denman in his speech. *Session of* 1824—Speech on Mr. George Lamb's motion for leave to bring in a Bill for allowing counsel to prisoners charged with felony, April 6, 1824—Against farther renewal of Aliens' Regulation Act, April 12, 1824—Speech on petition of James Silk Buckingham, May 25, 1824—On trial and capital conviction of Missionary Smith at Demerara, June 11, 1824—On Government bill for the suppression of insurrection in Ireland, June 14, 1824. *Session of* 1825—Passage in King's speech as to the Catholic Association, February 2, 1825—Denman's speech in debate on the Address, February 4, 1825—Speech on Government bill for suppressing unlawful societies in Ireland, February 10, 1825—Attack on Lord Eldon as the chief opponent of Catholic Emancipation—Speech on petition against re-enacting the Combination Laws, May 4, 1825—Speech on Chief Justices' and Judges' Salaries Bill, May 16, 1825—Denman's views in 1825 on the position and status of Puisne Judges—Income of Lord Ellenborough while Chief Justice of King's Bench—Sums realised by Chief Justice Eyre by sale of offices in Common Pleas—Salaries of Chief Justices and Judges as fixed by Act of 1825, and as subsequently reduced by Acts of 1832 and 1851—Speech on proposed increase of allowances to the Duchess of Kent and the Duke of Cumberland, May 27, 1825—Quarantine Laws—Dr. Baillie s opinion, June 3, 1825— Speech on Sir F. Burdett s motion for producing the evidence taken before the Chancery Commissioners, June 7, 1825—Damaging attack on Lord Eldon as Chancellor. *Session of* 1826—Denman's observations in debate on Address on the omission of all reference to the Corn Laws in the King's speech—His statement of the distress among the operatives, February 2, 1826—Speech on introducing to the House the case of certain slaves hanged in Jamaica in 1823, 1824—Denman's motion —Canning's speech and amendment — Denman's reply — Canning consents to modify his amendment, March 1, 1826—Speech on Prisoner's Counsel Bill, April 25, 1826—Last speech of Denman in this Parliament on Brougham's motion for enquiry into the state of Colonial Slavery, May 19, 1826—Parliament prorogued prior to dissolution, May 31, 1826.

DENMAN'S own appreciation of his services as a member of the House of Commons, from his entering it in 1819 to his temporary retirement from it in 1826, has already been given in the personal narrative of 1828. It is proposed here to fill up the outline by stating the principal occasions on which he addressed the House during the period intervening between the close of the Queen's trial and the dissolution of Parliament in May 1826, giving extracts from the more important of his speeches.

On the whole, it will probably be found that his own estimate of his Parliamentary career for this period is entirely borne out by the facts. His voice was never silent when right and liberty were to be upheld ; he was a bold denouncer of all oppression and wrong, a firm and enlightened advocate of all useful reforms ; but he relied too much on his ready powers of elocution, and his great personal advantages as an orator.[1] He did not prepare himself with sufficient care and study, and his speeches accordingly, though usually vigorous and occasionally eloquent, were deficient in that display of matured knowledge and statesmanlike wisdom which can only be the result of previous research and careful thought, and without which no permanent or prominent fame as a speaker is to be acquired in the House of Commons.   For the same reason they were not distinguished by that happiness of diction—that curiosa felicitas—those pointed epigrams or 'burning words,' which sparkled in the graceful orations of Canning or lit up like lightning flashes the stormy denunciations of Brougham; and which, however apparently spontaneous, were, as is now well known, the fruit in both cases of the extremest labour, the most unsparing effort, and the most consummate art.

One of the earliest occasions on which Denman addressed the House in the session of 1821 may be mentioned as illustrating the spirit in which justice was administered in those bad times.

On February 23, he presented a petition from one Thomas Davison, tried for blasphemous libel before Mr. Justice Best (afterwards Lord Wynford), in October 1820, at Guildhall, stating that Davison, while making his defence, had been three times fined by the

---

[1] Lord Leveson Gower, when, after Denman's re-election for Nottingham in 1830, he congratulated the House on the re-appearance of 'that well-graced actor,' expressed, probably with more justice than good-nature, the estimate of Denman's speaking then current in the House.

learned judge : first 20*l.* for stating to the jury that no counsel at the bar would honestly defend him, and afterwards twice in 40*l.* (making 100*l.* in the whole) for reiterating to the jury the substance of the libel he was tried for.[2]

The Attorney-General having stated in reply (as the fact was) that the Court in Banco had decided that the imposition of such fines, regarded as fines for contempt of Court, was not illegal, the House divided on the question of receiving the petition, when the ayes were 37 and the noes 64, so it was rejected without being read.[3]

On Mr. Lennard's motion (May 8, 1821), for the repeal of the Seditious Meeting and Blasphemous and Seditious Libel Acts, Denman spoke at some length, urging that both bills (they were two of the famous Six Acts), were an innovation on the Constitution, and that there never existed any necessity for their enactment. 'The act against popular meetings,' he said, 'had established a fatal precedent : it had severed the People from the Throne, it had destroyed feelings and associations which ought to be most sedulously cherished.' 'As to blasphemous libel,' he said, 'with regard to what is or is not blasphemy scarcely any two men could be found to agree : different persons formed widely different opinions on the subject,

---

[2] This is the case Denman refers to in his personal narrative, when giving an account of the first trial that took place before himself in 1822—that of Carlile's shopman, Humphrey Boyle, for blasphemous libel. Denman was accustomed to say that Best was the worst judge by far he had ever known on the Bench.

[3] Hansard, Parl. Deb. N.S. vol. iv. p. 918–933.

and no human mind had attempted to define it precisely.'[4]

On May 15, 1821, Sir Francis Burdett brought
forward his motion for an enquiry by a committee of
the whole House into the Manchester massacre of
August 19, 1819, prefacing his motion by a speech of
admirable and touching eloquence, which was received
with loud cheers from both sides of the House.[5]

Denman rose late, amid repeated cries for adjournment, and his speech, as reported, hardly rises to the
' height of that great argument.'

In the course of it

he charged the Government with having given to the
magistrates the instructions on which they had acted that
day, for he could not think it possible that they would otherwise have departed from the usual course pursued by
magistrates in this country on similar occasions; nor could
he otherwise account for the premature, precipitate, and
unfeeling satisfaction expressed by His Majesty's ministers
in that odious letter of Lord Sidmouth's, when all they
knew of the case was that the blood of the people had been
shed.

The reference here is to the then famous, or rather
infamous, letter of August 21, 1819, in which Lord
Sidmouth expressed to the magistrates, by command
of His Majesty, ' the great satisfaction the King derived
from their prompt, decisive, and efficient measures for
the preservation of the public tranquillity.'

---

[4] Hansard, Parl. Deb. N.S. vol. v. p. 564-568.   Mr. Lennard's motion
was, of course, defeated by an overwhelming majority.

[5] It was in the course of this speech that he so well applied to the
 massacre the line

     ' Immortale odium, et non sanabile vulnus.'

As to this letter, Sir F. Burdett had exclaimed, 'Great God! was it not monstrous to declare that a King of England could have derived great satisfaction from the perpetration of these horrid crimes; " great satisfaction " indeed, at the slaying of his subjects— " great satisfaction " on hearing of the instantaneous massacre of a large number of his people, cut down without distinction of age or sex.'

Denman in his speech went on to say:

It was not for the purpose of ascertaining how many persons were actually received into the Infirmary; it was not for the sake of proving the number of sabre wounds inflicted; it was not with the view even of affording relief to the unhappy sufferers—but it was to vindicate the laws and constitution of England from the wrong they had sustained that his honourable friend (Sir F. Burdett) pressed for enquiry. His honourable friend had been charged with want of candour in not bringing forward his motion before—but how could he have done so. Last session [that of 1820] a strong interest was newly awakened in another matter of importance [the Queen's trial]. When enquiry was then pressed, it was urged that enquiry could not be conveniently pursued in that House; that the forms of the House were not adapted to the examination of witnesses, and that it never proceeded with an enquiry on evidence without involving itself in discredit. And at what period was it that this argument was urged? At the very time when those who urged it were willing to subject an injured woman to such enquiry! It was when they were sweeping the hotels of Germany and Italy of pimps and panderers to swear their foul and perjured calumnies against the character of a lone and defenceless woman! It was when they had determined, through such an ordeal, to drag the Queen of this country to that fate from which she had been rescued by the people of England.[6]

6 Hansard, Parl. Deb. N.S. vol. v. p. 762-766. Denman was a little too

The debate was adjourned at 3 o'clock in the morning; the division on the adjourned debate took place at 2.45 the next morning, when Sir F. Burdett's motion was rejected by a majority of 124, the numbers being 255 against 111.

On June 4, 1821, Denman earnestly supported Sir James Mackintosh's bill for the abolition of death punishment in cases of forgery, except of Bank of England and country notes and bills, saying, with reference to the exceptions

that he took all he could obtain and took it thankfully, regretting at the same time that he could not procure the whole of what he desired. If [he added] after reading the evidence any sort of doubt was entertained as to the expediency of altering the law, or should that sort of blindness to practical truths which could only be accounted for by a superstitious veneration for anything that had long existed, still prevail, he would point to the fact that the bankers of London came forward and stated that they did not like to prosecute while the culprit was liable to be visited with the punishment of death. When men of such respectability stated this, the question in his mind was decided. To permit the law to remain in its present state was, under such circumstances, an encouragement to forgers.[7]

So incontrovertible were the arguments for a change in the law, that on the third reading the bill was carried against Government by a majority of 6—ayes 117, noes 111. But this alarming step in criminal law reform was speedily retraced, for on the question

fond of referring to the Queen's trial, as Cicero was to his having saved Rome from Catiline.

[7] Hansard, Parl. Deb. N.S. vol. v. p. 1109.

'that the bill do pass,' Lord Castlereagh succeeded in getting it rejected by precisely the same majority of six that had previously carried the third reading, the numbers being 115 for and 121 against.

A Society called the 'Constitutional Association' had been formed under the Tory reign of terror of 1819–20, for the avowed purpose of prosecuting, with the resources of joint-stock funds, the writers and publishers of blasphemous and seditious publications. Denman, who was convinced that far more harm than good was done by the probably well-meant efforts of these zealots, took occasion, on July 3, 1821, on a motion for returns as to the proceedings of this Society, of stating that which to his mind was a principal objection to this and all similar associations, viz.

that they could not exist without becoming a seminary for spies and informers. He dwelt also on the illegality of a society possessing large funds, and established not for the punishment but for the ruin of such booksellers as fell under their lash. The power thus placed in the hands of individuals was most enormous, and the number of bills presented by the association, and already thrown out by grand juries, was alone enough to excite grave suspicion.[8]

In the following session, on March 6, 1822, Mr. Bennett brought before the House the scandalous scenes connected with the Queen's funeral, in a motion affirming 'that the respect and solemnity which, by ancient custom, had been observed at the funerals of the

---

[8] Hansard, Parl. Deb. N.S. vol. v. p. 1493. It was this society that prosecuted Humphrey Boyle, on the first occasion of Denman's presiding as Common Serjeant—a circumstance to which he refers in his personal narrative.

Queens of England, had been at the funeral of her late majesty Queen Caroline unnecessarily and indecorously violated.' This was an occasion which, it might have been supposed, would have called Denman's powers as an orator into full exertion. It was not so. His speech was short and singularly deficient in the vigour and the pathos that he frequently displayed on matters far less interesting. The only passage that produced any effect on the House was that in which, adverting to the alteration in the line of procession, he observed :

It was true Her Majesty directed that her funeral should be conducted with as little pomp as possible, but could she be supposed by that clause in her will to decline that spontaneous homage of the heart which the inhabitants of London were prepared to pay her remains on the direct road through the City. The assembled people on this occasion could not be called a mob ; they were composed of the respectable portion of society among the middle and lower classes. Why refuse them the gratification of their wish to see the funeral procession of her whom, when alive, they respected and honoured. The act was ill-judged and cruel.[9]

On April 25, Lord John Russell made his celebrated motion ' that the present state of the Representation of the People requires the most serious consideration of the House,' a motion which he introduced in an able and elaborate speech, which conclusively fixed his reputation as a rising statesman.

Denman spoke without adequate preparation, and with comparatively little effect.

The moral evil of the existing system, even apart

[9] Hansard, Parl. Deb. N.S. vol. vi. p. 967.

from its political effects, was one of his great arguments for a change.

It was [he declared] a most pernicious evil, both in a moral and political point of view, to see a species of consecration given, as it was under the existing system, to sacrifice of principle, dereliction of character, and venal barter of opinions. That House [he said] had become the influenced organ of every act of Government, without the confidence of the public, and even without the respect of Government itself.

The justice of these observations was proved by the division list. The House rejected Lord John Russell's motion by a majority of 105, the numbers being 164 for, and 269 against it.[10]

On June 5, 1822, Mr. Secretary Peel having moved the renewal of the Aliens' Regulation Bill, the motion was opposed in a most eloquent and admirable speech by Sir James Mackintosh, who characterised it ' as vesting in Government a direct and absolute power of banishing from the home of their choice, from the conduct of their affairs, perhaps from the seat of their fortunes, some 25,000 persons, and this on the bare assurance of a Secretary of State that he would only exercise this absolute power in cases where it might be necessary and expedient.'

On this occasion Denman, who always felt and expressed himself very strongly on this and kindred subjects, made a vigorous and spirited speech.

He declared he would give the bill in every stage his unqualified opposition. No proof, he said, had been

---

[10] Hansard, Parl. Deb. N.S. vol. vi. ; see the debate under date.

given of its necessity : that rested on the mere statement of the right honourable secretary (Mr. Peel).

The right honourable gentleman had spoken as if he
alone were to be the responsible administrator of the measure ;
but, in fact, he must in its administration entirely depend on
others, and this was one great and necessary evil of a
measure executed by a secret power, called into action by
secret spies, and, in the whole of its progress worked by
clandestine machinery. The right honourable gentleman
has made a strong appeal to the House to entrust him on
his own responsibility with the working of this bill. To such
an appeal I am compelled to reply that it is a strong
objection to the fitness of any man for office that he commences his career by wishing to be invested with such a
power.

After contrasting, with some degree of humiliation,
' the hospitable securities of Magna Charta ' with the
' fatal ' provisions of the bill before the House, and
avowing his preference for the old law to the new, he
continued thus :

And is it in the eighth year of peace in this country, ' the
eldest born of freedom,' that a minister of the Crown should
call, on his own responsibility, for the re-enactment of this
most obnoxious and dangerous law. It is with pain and
mortification that I have heard the declarations that have
accompanied the support of this measure. With what other
feeling could the denizen of a free country hear the struggles
of freemen in other parts of the world compared to the
machinations of conspirators against lawful authorities whom
they are bound to obey? Thus the struggles for liberty in
Spain, the efforts in Portugal, the successes of what are
called the revolted colonies in America are alike denomin-
ated the intrigues of conspirators; and the House was told
that some of them who had been engaged in them had been

received, or rather suffered to reside, in England, with an oblivion of their crimes. Of what crimes?—the unforgiven crime of having fought for the liberties of their country! I hope the voice and spirit of the country will be raised against so odious a measure! Let the People of England never forget that though in the present case it is only called for to oppress persecuted and unprotected foreigners, the example may be hereafter adduced to bring about the application of the same machinery for the destruction of their own liberties also.[11]

On July 19, when the bill came up for the third reading, Denman renewed his hopeless but honourable opposition, on this occasion dwelling principally on the topic that no precedent was to be found in our ancient laws for the possession or exercise of such a power by the Crown.   He urged that

In none of the old law books or digests was the slightest intimation to be found of aliens being expellable from the country at a moment's warning at the mere caprice of a minister of the Crown. Mr. Fox strenuously denied that such a power existed in the Crown; Mr. Pitt never asserted it, and Mr. Burke admitted that it was to be only conceded under circumstances of extreme necessity. Not a single statute relating to aliens made the slightest mention of this supposed prerogative of the Crown. The Proclamations were regarded by Lord Coke as against the law of the land; and his objection to them derived additional confirmation from Magna Charta. Either Magna Charta ought to be repealed, or this act ought not to be passed. Where is the necessity for the bill? Arbitrary power may always be talked of as desirable, but it is not because it is convenient that it therefore ought to be granted. He saw nothing to apprehend from what had been called the ruining of empires.

---

[11] Hansard, Parl. Deb. N.S. vol. vii., under date, June 5, 1822.

That South America should be separated from Spain was not an event pregnant with very formidable consequences. From the downfall of the Bastille, of the Inquisition, and of the principles which supported these establishments, he augured nothing but advantage to the world. He should vote against the present measure because he thought it most injurious both to the honour and interests of England.[12]

In the session of 1823 Denman was as usual a frequent speaker.

On May 8, Hume presented a petition from Richard Carlile, the publisher, complaining of interruption in his defence, and of the severity of the sentence passed on him — 3 years' imprisonment and 1,500*l*. fine.

In introducing the petition Hume stated that Carlile, previous to the distresses of 1816, had been a respectable mechanic; he then became a hawker of pamphlets, afterwards a publisher of irreligious books the sale of which, after his prosecution by the Constitutional Association, had been increased from about 300 to more than 13,000 copies. After his recent sentence, Carlile continued the sale by means of his wife, his sister, and other agents, who had all been successively imprisoned, notwithstanding which the sale went on increasingly.

Denman, in the course of his speech on the subject, observed

that the proceedings in the case before the House proved that *irreligion could also produce its martyrs*. Such were the effects of the reaction which the operation of the joint-stock purse of the so-called ' Constitutional Association ' had produced. He understood that the funds of that purse were

<hr>

[12] Hansard, Parl. Deb. N.S. vol. vii. pp. 1723, 1724.

exhausted, never, he hoped, to be replenished. As to the punishment, he considered it excessive, and trusted Government would interfere and modify it.[13]

On June 4, Mr. (afterwards Sir) John Williams, who had been elected for Lincoln the year before, brought before the House the subject of the arrears of business in the Court of Chancery, and the causes thereof, in the first of a series of motions, subsequently renewed from session to session, and which, though uniformly defeated by large ministerial majorities, produced a great effect on the public, and ultimately led to the efforts which have since been made, with the best intentions and considerable success, to diminish the cost, to simplify the procedure, and accelerate the movement of litigation in the Courts of Equity.

Denman, who spoke on the second night of the debate (June 5), mentioned several recent instances of delay, the statement of which produced a great effect on the House.

The first to which he adverted was the case of *Ware* v. *Horwood*. It had been in the court for nine years; had stood at the head of the paper two years and a half ago; but had been constantly postponed, till the infant for whose benefit the suit had been instituted some twenty years before died of a broken heart, on account of having been kept out of his property, a fund of 10,000*l.*, locked up in court pending the decision of Lord Eldon.

The solicitor engaged in the suit thereupon wrote privately to Lord Eldon, stating these facts, and adding:

---

[13] Hansard, Parl. Deb. N.S. vol. ix. pp. 114–116.

'I have to contend against the bitter feelings of his relations.' On this, Lord Eldon, struck with compunction when too late, sent for the solicitor to his private apartments, and at once noted down the minutes of his decree, which he might just as well have done two years and a half before—' before,' said Denman, ' the person for whose benefit it had been intended, and in whose favour it was drawn up, had perished in despair of obtaining it.' [14]

' Really,' exclaimed the speaker, ' after so frightful a history of the consequences of delay as this, and after seeing the ghostlike forms of the suitors that are daily hovering about the Court of Chancery, miserable, heart-wearied, heart-broken, their hopes blasted, and their fortunes squandered, the admirable description by the poet Spenser would appear no exaggeration,' and then he cited, with great effect, the well-known passage beginning with

> Full little knowest thou who hast not tried
> What Hell it is in suing long to bide,

and ending

> To fret thy soul with crosses and with cares,
> To eat thy heart with comfortless despairs,
> To fawn, to crouch, to write, to ride, to run,
> To spend, to give, to want, to be undone.

The next case cited by Denman was that of *Collis* v. *Nott*, which he stated thus:

This was a question whether a surety paying off a bond, and not taking over an assignment, could claim as a specialty

---

[14] Mr. Horace Twiss, who, in his admirable ' Life of Lord Eldon,' vol. iii. chap. lxiii. ed. 1844, has said all that can be said in defence of his lordship, virtually gives up the case of *Ware* v. *Horwood* (see p. 339).

or as a simple contract creditor. The Master decided for the specialty, and, in 1817, the case was argued before the Chancellor, by the late Sir Samuel Romilly. In last Hilary Term (January 1823), six years afterwards, when the Chancellor was pressed for a decision, he had entirely forgotten it (hear). The case was then re-argued at considerable expense to the parties, and is still undecided.[15]

A third case, the name of which is not given, was thus stated by Denman:

There was another case, which he had heard of in the course of the day, and which illustrated some of the effects which might be expected to arise from this system of delay. It was that of an application by certain parties to be admitted as creditors on a bankrupt's estate.

The Lord Chancellor, as he was often in the habit of doing, took the opinion of two of the learned judges [of the Common Law Courts] on the point of law. In the interim the money was paid into the hands of a banker. The judges gave their opinions promptly, that, in law, the parties were entitled to be admitted as creditors. No judgment was, however, given by the Lord Chancellor, and the matter remained over till the banker who held the dividends failed.

His lordship then allowed the parties to rank as creditors on the estate of the second bankruptcy (that of the banker); but, still doubting on the point of law raised in the first instance, he consulted two other learned judges, who both gave it as their opinion (to the same effect as the two before consulted) that the parties had the right to rank as creditors.

[15] Mr. Horace Twiss, admitting that in this case the delay, if it had rested wholly with the Chancellor, 'would have been incapable of justification on his part,' endeavours to shift the blame on the parties, who, as he says, ' *seems to have been the case,*' had failed to remind the Chancellor, once at least in the interval, that his decision was expected! Vol. iii. chap. lxiii. pp. 336, 337, ed. 1844. ' *Non tali auxilio!* '

In the meantime, the dividends under the second bankruptcy were paid into the hands of another banker, to await the decision in Chancery. That decision was still delayed, notwithstanding that four of the judges had pronounced an unanimous opinion on the law of the case. At length the second banker, the holder of the dividend, became himself a bankrupt; and thus were the original parties to the suit deprived even of this shadow of a shade, and cut off from all reasonable hope of ever recovering any portion of their money.[16]

Notwithstanding the powerful effect produced by the speeches of Williams and Denman, the ministerial phalanx mustered in their usual overwhelming force, and the motion—which was simply for enquiry into the arrears of the Court of Chancery and the causes thereof—was rejected by a majority of 85—ayes, 89; noes, 174.[17]

In the session of 1824 (on April 6), Denman spoke on Mr. George Lamb's motion for leave to bring in a Bill allowing persons prosecuted for *felony* to be defended by counsel, as in cases of misdemeanour.

This was a subject on which he thought strongly, and ought to have spoken effectively, but he failed to do so, owing to want of due preparation. In one part of his speech, indeed, a thing most unusual with him, he is

---

[16] Mr. Horace Twiss's answer to this case is—1st. That the periods of time which intervened between the first reference and the first failure, and between the second reference and the second failure, are not stated; 2nd. That it was the fault of the parties themselves not to have invested the money in government securities instead of depositing it with bankers.' The first answer is merely evasive; the second only shows that the parties were not blameless; it does not at all show that the Chancellor was not in fault. Twiss's 'Life of Lord Eldon,' vol. iii. chap. lxiii. pp. 335, 336, ed. 1844.

[17] See for the debate, Hansard, Parl. Deb. N.S. vol. ix. pp. 700-794. Denman's speech is reported at pp. 743-747.

reported as having hesitated for some seconds, for which he apologized to the House by saying that he had only been in town a few hours and was altogether unprepared for the discussion: he had risen rather from his anxiety to bear testimony on the subject as a witness, than to address to the House the arguments which ought to be urged on it.[18]

It must seem scarcely credible to those who are acquainted with the inimitable and unanswerable articles with which Sydney Smith, in the 'Edinburgh Review,' was at that time enlightening the public mind on this most palpable and gross abuse in our then criminal system that the motion should have been rejected by a majority of 30—ayes, 50 ; noes, 80—and that the absurd anomaly should have lived on for twelve years longer, not having been finally extirpated till the year 1836.

On April 12, Denman recovered all his spirit and energy in denouncing the renewal of the Aliens Bill.

After inveighing bitterly against the French Bourbons for having invaded Spain, ' under the most base, hypocritical, and atrocious of false pretences,' he proceeded thus :

I know it is thought inconvenient to express myself with this degree of freedom on the conduct of foreign Governments. Lectures have been read of late to some of my honourable friends upon diplomatic etiquette and political decorum in debate. If it were only to speak of these foreign powers as of kings and emperors ruling within their own states,

---

[18] Hansard, Parl. Deb. N.S. vol. xi. pp. 181–219. Denman's speech is reported pp. 214–218.

and administering their own governments, I should be the
last man to countenance or in any way to pander to the base
and vulgar spirit of detraction, which is only opposed to
those enjoying high station from envy of the advantages to
be derived from it. But this is not so—it is a question of
intervention by these foreign powers with other states, with
the rights and liberties of all other peoples as well as of the
people of their own states. And this House is the only place
where the conduct of these princes can be called in question.
This is the sole assembly in which the aggression, and bloodshed, and violence of the invaders of Spain can be adequately
denounced. And how are mankind to be the better, supposing
those who object to the strictures of the British Parliament
should succeed in silencing them.

In another part of his speech he said :

My honourable friends have been taunted as to their views
and motives in their opposition to this bill. For my own
part, I can conscientiously say that I have had nothing at
heart in it but the honour and interests of England. It
appears to me that this is a power which it is not necessary
for the Government to possess; which it has not heretofore
possessed ; from the very want of which the country has
grown and flourished beyond any other; a power which no
great statesman could wish to have, but rather be glad to
get rid of, not at the expiration of two years only, but as
soon as the House would allow him to lay it down, as a weight
of grievous and inconvenient responsibility.

The majority against Lord John Russell's amendment
was 50—ayes, 43 ; noes, 93—Lord John and Denman
being tellers of the minority. Denman then moved
that the bill should be renewed for one year only, not
for two years ; but this was negatived by a majority of
sixty-four.[19]

[19] Hansard, Parl. Deb. N.S. vol. xi. pp. 370-383.

On May 25, Mr. Lambton (afterwards Earl of Durham) presented, and prefaced by a most able speech, a petition from James Silk Buckingham, complaining of his expulsion from India, early in 1823, by Mr. John Adams, senior member of council, and acting Governor-General (between the departure of the Marquis of Hastings and the arrival of Lord Amherst), for publishing in the 'Calcutta Journal,' of which he was editor and proprietor, some severe strictures on the appointment of Dr. Bryce, the head of the Presbyterian Church in India, to the office of Superintendent of Stationery.

Denman on this occasion made a vigorous speech, concluding thus:

The honourable chairman of the Court of Directors (Mr. Astell) had talked of the repeated warnings which Mr. Buckingham had received, as if they were the distant rumblings of thunders that were to throw a man on his knees to pray Heaven to avert from him the menacing storm. But why was the storm to fall as it did? Surely Mr. Adams might have waited a few weeks, until the arrival of the new governor. But the whole proceeding, from beginning to end, showed the nature of that system, which, from the top to the bottom, required unsparing revision and correction. It was the bounden duty of Parliament to take care that the Press in India enjoyed that degree of liberty which might safely be granted to it; and, above all, to deprive the Government in that country of the power of deportation towards any individual who might happen to displease them by the manliness and independence of his conduct.[20]

On June 1, 1824, commenced the animated and important debate, continued and concluded on June 11,

---

[20] Hansard, Parl. Deb. N.S. vol. xi. pp. 858–890. Denman's speech is reported pp. 883–887.

on the trial and capital conviction of missionary Smith, at Demerara, on a charge of having incited, and attempted to conceal, an insurrection of the slave population. Denman spoke late on the concluding night of the debate, immediately after Canning, in vehement condemnation of the proceedings of the court-martial by which Smith had been tried and condemned to be hanged — a sentence he only escaped by dying of dysentery in the horrible dungeon in which he had been confined in that tropical climate, preparatory to his murder on the scaffold.

Denman's speech was not deficient in energy or power, but it will not bear comparison with certain others delivered on that occasion, especially with that masterpiece of denunciatory eloquence which was one of the greatest oratorical achievements of Henry Brougham.

As to these proceedings [he said] he need not go further in their condemnation than the defender of them, his learned friend [Scarlett] had done, who only condemned them in the beginning, the middle, and the end (hear, hear). He was, he continued, no fanatic; he subscribed to no Missionary Society; and he had no other feeling on the subject than that it would be wise to let West Indian subjects alone for the present, if only the people in Demerara would let them. Yet with all these feelings he had read the evidence with utter astonishment. He had looked through page after page for proof of Mr. Smith's guilt, but had found none; and looking fairly and honestly at the whole case, he thought the man had been most foully and unjustly treated, nay, that the very circumstances put forward in proof of his guilt established his innocence.[21]

---

[21] Hansard, Parl. Deb. N.S. vol. xi. Denman's speech is reported pp. 1287–1294.

On June 14, the Ministry brought in their bill for the suppression of insurrection in Ireland, the nature of which may be judged from the statement that it contained a clause providing that in the disturbed districts any person found in a public-house, whether licensed or not, between 9 P.M. and 6 A.M. at any season of the year should be liable to transportation.[22]

In the debate that ensued Denman spoke briefly, but well. He said:

The evidence gave them a little insight into the causes of the discontent in Ireland. From that evidence it appeared that the high rents and tithes exacted from the miserable inhabitants were among the principal causes of those discontents which this bill was intended to suppress. He perfectly agreed with an honourable member that the renewal of the Insurrection Act was well calculated to counteract all the moral effect which might otherwise be expected from the improvement of the police, the magistracy, and the nightly patrol and watch, as well as the advantages which might be expected from the introduction into Ireland of a better system of education. These were all moral causes which would operate for the improvement of Ireland, if the baneful influence of this act did not prevent their activity. Was this the way to tranquillize a country, by bringing all under the act of accusation, and accounting as guilty all who were not able to prove their innocence? These were powers which ought not to be granted to any set of men. The Government which wished to receive such powers showed that it did not know how to govern a great country on the

---

[22] It was with reference to this act that Moore wrote his famous parody—

> I've found out a gift for my Erin,
>   A gift that must surely content her,
> Fond pledge of a love so endearing,
>   Five million of bullets I've sent her.

principles of a free constitution. Under no circumstances could he give his consent to the passing of such an act as this.

The second reading, however, passed by a majority of nearly 5 to 1—the ayes being 112 and the noes only 23.[23]

When, on June 21, the bill came up for a third reading, Denman, calling attention to the fact that the words ' without lawful excuse ' did not form part of the clause visiting with transportation persons found in public-houses between 9 P.M. and 6 A.M., proposed to alter or strike out the clause. His efforts, however, were wholly nugatory, and the measure passed as it was originally framed.

The King's speech at the opening of the session of 1825 contained the following paragraph with reference to the state of Ireland and the proceedings of the Catholic Association :

Industry and commercial enterprise are extending themselves in that part of the United Kingdom. It is, therefore, the more to be regretted that associations should exist in Ireland which have adopted proceedings irreconcileable with the spirit of the constitution, and calculated, by exciting alarm and by exasperating animosities, to endanger the peace of society, and to retard the course of national improvement.

On February 4, Denman spoke in the debate on the Address, chiefly with reference to the state of Ireland and to the Catholic Association.

By the declaration of His Majesty's Government it was evident that they were determined, if they could not put down

---

[23] Hansard, Parl. Deb. N.S. vol. xi. pp. 1336, 1337.

the Catholic Association in any other way, to put it down by coercion, by the sword, by an army of 20,000 men—and that at the very moment when they were complaining of the Association as being contrary to the spirit of the British Constitution.

What was it that the Catholic Association had done? They had united for the purpose of defending themselves against an undue administration of the laws (cries of *Hear, hear*). He repeated it—the undue administration of justice in that country. He maintained that there was an unfair administration of justice to the Roman Catholics of Ireland. What was the situation of that large and respectable body at present? After having had their hopes excited from year to year—after having suffered such a variety of misery that the oldest men could only call to mind the register of their hopes and their disappointments—was it, he asked, too much to suppose that they had a right to combine in their own defence?

The Catholic Association had claims on the people of England, inasmuch as it spoke the sense and represented the feelings of six millions of their fellow subjects. Their cause was one which it was the duty of that House to take into its most serious consideration; it was a question which His Majesty's ministers were bound to bring forward in such a manner as to ensure the object sought to be attained. It was singular that in this great country, surrounded as we were by danger, and opposed as we were by more despotic powers, we should omit to conciliate so large a portion of our fellow subjects by giving them that equality of rights and privileges to which they were so justly entitled. In a little time it would hardly be believed that such disqualifications could have existed. Their removal could not be long delayed, but the misery that might fill up the interval could not be regarded without horror by any one anxious for the welfare of England and Ireland.[24]

---

[24] Hansard, Parl. Deb. N.S. vol. xii. pp. 112–115.

On February 1, Mr. Goulburn introduced the Irish measures of the Government, in moving for leave to bring in a ' bill to amend certain acts relating to unlawful societies in Ireland,' the object being the suppression of the Catholic Association.

The debate that followed lasted for four nights, and was characterized by great animation and eloquence on the part of the leading Liberals—Brougham, Mackintosh, Tierney, and Burdett having especially distinguished themselves.

Denman rose late on the first night of the debate, and his speech was able and spirited.

The result [he said] of this bill, if it were successful, would be to drive those, who now met openly and without disguise, into clubs and cabals and secret associations, which former bills had been in vain enacted to put down. It was time that the British Parliament should seek to discover some other remedy for the evils of Ireland than the augmentation of penal statutes. There was a remedy that had never yet been tried, but which was plain and compendious. Redress the people's grievances; emancipate the Catholics from the trammels of bad laws—remove the cause, and the effect will follow ; with the grievance will depart the evil, and then Parliament will have acted not only with justice and wisdom, but in obedience to the united recommendations of the wisest statesmen of modern times.

Adverting to the hostility of the Church and of Lord Eldon to the removal of Catholic disabilities, Denman expressed himself as follows :

The Catholics know they must expect the great weight of the Established Church against them. The Church forms a compact and extensive body, which doubtless presents a front

of dangerous hostility; and it must not be denied that there
exists a similar deep-rooted enmity in another very high power
in the state—I mean the Lord Chancellor—an eminent and
illustrious man, remarkable for the pertinacity and ability
with which he has succeeded in securing to himself for twenty-
five years the honours and emoluments of the highest offices
in the state—a man who has law in his voice, and fortune in
his hand—who, in opposing the schemes of liberal policy,
whether at home or abroad, must undoubtedly be considered
as a most formidable opponent. Why, let me ask, does a
statesman of enlarged and liberal views [Canning] permit
such an influence to exist? Why does not the eminent
lawyer himself either yield to the flow of Liberal opinions
which has of late poured into the Cabinet, or else retire, as
so many of his predecessors have done when their sentiments
were manifestly incompatible with the retention of official
station? I am astonished that a statesman so pre-eminently
gifted as the right honourable gentleman [Canning] can
consent to compromise his great position by accommodating
his sentiments on subjects of almost vital importance to the
prejudices of such a person as the noble lord.[25]

At the conclusion of his address Denman declared
that he gave 'his direct negative to what he conscientiously believed to be the most unjust, the most unfair,
the most mischievous, and the most destructive measure
that had ever been proposed in Parliament.'[26]

The measure not inaptly thus characterized passed,
notwithstanding the strenuous exertions of the Opposition, by a majority of 155, the ayes being 278, and the
noes only 123.

On May 4, 1825, Denman, in presenting a petition

<hr>

[25] The secret was that Eldon, as Canning well knew, had the ear and
the support of the King in opposition to the Catholic claims.

[26] Hansard, Parl. Deb. N.S. vol. xii. pp. 262-275.

from certain mechanics of Walsall, praying that the House would not re-enact the Combination Laws, took occasion to observe that in his opinion the statutory provisions created by the Combination Acts, which had been repealed, were unnecessary for the punishment of the offence of combination where it was so conducted as to call for punishment. He thought the common law of England was quite sufficient to punish any substantive offence committed by the workmen against their employers; and was of opinion that the Combination Acts had been very properly repealed, as they produced no good, and gave rise to much evil. It was far better to leave the matter to the old common law, since legislation appeared totally useless.[27]

On May 16, 1825, Government introduced a measure abolishing the perquisites accruing to the Chief Justices of the Common Law Courts from the sale of offices, requiring all fees now paid to the judges in addition to their nominal salaries to be paid into the Exchequer, and in lieu of such fees and perquisites fixing on a liberal scale the salaries and retiring pensions of the Chief Justices and Judges.

The discussion which ensued is not without interest to the members of the legal profession.[28]

Denman, entirely agreeing in the abolition of all fees and perquisites arising from the sale of offices, and in making an adequate compensation by way of fixed salary to the Chief Justices for the loss thence accruing to them, dissented from the amount of salary (6,000*l.* a

[27] Hansard, Parl. Deb. N.S. vol. xiii. pp. 364, 365, 372.
[28] Hansard, Parl. Deb. N.S. vol. xiii. pp. 611–643.

year) originally proposed by Government for the Puisne Judges.

He thought 4,000*l.* a year sufficient. He had never [he said] heard of any gentleman at the bar who had refused an elevation to the Bench on the ground of inadequate emolument. It was not mere emolument that made men desirous to obtain the situation, but the dignity and elevation of the office, and, besides that, the certainty of its continuance for life. He could not see that the judges would be bettered in the public estimation by the proposed addition of income. It was impossible, by any increase of salary, that they could ever be raised to an equality with the great. At present they might be said to be at the head of people of middling fortune, which was better than being at the foot of the higher order; and, though some aristocratic gentlemen in that House had treated their usual place of residence with so much contempt as to profess they did not know where Russell Square was, he thought they were much more respected in that quarter than they would be if they were to intrude themselves among the fashionable inhabitants of Grosvenor Square, where, he must confess, he apprehended the proposed increase of salary would not screen them from feeling themselves awkwardly circumstanced.

In another part of his speech he had said :

If the Government wish to consult the real dignity of the Bench, let them at once make it known that the puisne judges need no longer expect to be raised to a higher situation on the bench ; that they are not to be made peers of, or, to speak in the language of another House, relating to another profession, that they are never to be, in consequence of their obsequiousness, translated ; but that they must look to their elevated situations as their permanent and honourable position for the remainder of their lives.[29]

[29] Denman's speech is reported at pp. 618-621 of Hansard, Parl. Deb. N.S. vol. xiii.

In the course of this discussion the Attorney-General (Copley) stated that Lord Ellenborough, during the whole period he was Chief Justice of the King's Bench, had been in receipt of 16,000*l.* a year—9,000*l.* the pecuniary emoluments of his own office, and 7,000*l.* the annual value of the chief clerkship, an absolutely sinecure office, which he ultimately gave to his son, the late Lord Ellenborough, who held it till the day of his own death.[30]

Sir John Copley also stated that Chief Justice Eyre, during the time he held the office of Chief Justice of the Common Pleas, had received no less a sum than 30,000*l.* for the offices he had disposed of.

Ultimately the proposed increase in the salaries of the puisne judges was reduced from 6,000*l.* to 5,500*l.* a year, and with this alteration the Government measures became law, as the 6 Geo. IV., c. 82, 83, 84.

By these acts the salaries and retiring pensions of the chief justices and judges of the common law courts were thus fixed :

	Salary	Pension
Chief Justice of the King's Bench	10,000*l.*	4,000*l.*
Chief Justice of the Common Pleas	8,000*l.*	3,750*l.*
Chief Baron of Exchequer	7,000*l.*	3,750*l.*
Puisne Judges, each	5,500*l.*	3,500*l.*

The salaries of the puisne judges were, after the appointment of three new judges in 1830, reduced to

---

[30] When on one occasion the late Lord Ellenborough was asked by a member of some committee whether he thought this sinecure salary might not be diminished, his lordship gravely replied, 'No ; reduction of salary must proceed on the ground of diminution of duty. Now, as nothing ever has been done in that office it is impossible that less could be done in it in future.'

5,000*l*. (by Act 2 and 3 Will. IV. c. 116), and those of the Chief Justice of the King's Bench and Common Pleas respectively to 8,000*l*., instead of 10,000*l*., and 7,000*l*., instead of 8,000*l*. (by the Act of 14 and 15 Vic. c. 41), at which amounts they now stand.

On May 27, the Chancellor of the Exchequer proposed an increased allowance of 6,000*l*. a year to the Duchess of Kent for the education of her daughter Victoria (her present Majesty), then 6 years old ; and also a similar annual sum to the Duke of Cumberland for the education of his son (now **ex-King** of Hanover.)

Denman said :

He thought the cases of the Duke of Cumberland and the Duchess of Kent were totally dissimilar. In the latter case only 6,000*l*. a year was to be granted to the Duchess for the support and suitable education of the Heiress Presumptive to the Crown. Of the moderation of this grant no one could entertain the least doubt. But he could not see why the Duke of Cumberland should now, because he had a son born to him six years ago, take 6,000*l*. a year from the people in addition to the 19,000*l*. a year he already took from them, and the whole of which he spent abroad.

Both resolutions passed. That for the Duchess of Kent, who had only 6,000*l*. a year before, making 12,000*l*. with the new grant, was carried *nem. con.* ; on the other the House divided, but it passed by a majority of 15— ayes, 79 ; noes, 64.[31]

On a question which arose with regard to the Quarantine Laws, on June 3, 1825, Denman cited to

<hr>

[31] Hansard, Parl. Deb. N.S. vol. xiii. pp. 918, 919.

the House the opinion of his late brother-in-law Dr. Baillie, among whose papers, he said, he had found one showing that he had examined the subject with great care, and had arrived at the conclusion that it would be unsafe to remove the existing precautions against infection.[32]

On June 7, 1825, Sir Francis Burdett having moved 'that the evidence taken before the Commissioners appointed in 1824 to enquire into and report upon the practice and procedure of the Court of Chancery be laid before the House,' Denman spoke in support of the motion, and in the course of his speech made a very damaging attack on Lord Eldon as Chancellor.

There was, he knew, a great deal of tenderness manifested towards the individual who presided in the Court of Chancery. This proved nothing more than the extent of his influence. No man wished less than he did to give that noble and learned lord offence; but he could not help alluding to him when he heard honourable gentlemen argue the question on the ground that no personal fault could be found with the learned person who was the head of the Court of Chancery. He did not mean to assert that there *was* personal fault, but there might be personal fault: all that was a matter which he felt ought to be well considered.

One fact alone would show the manner in which the business of the court was conducted. At the beginning of last Michaelmas term forty-five causes were set down in the paper to be heard during the term, and on the last day of term they still remained on the paper. Not one of those causes had been touched; and he begged the House to recollect that every one of the parties connected with each cause had to pay 1*l.* for their being set down alone, exclusive of

[32] Hansard, Parl. Deb. N.S. vol. xiii. p. 1038.

incidental expenses. If, for instance, as often happened, there were ten parties plaintiffs and twenty parties defendants in a cause, each of them had to pay 1*l.*, or, in the case supposed, a total of 30*l. for the privilege of not being heard.*

He threw out these observations without meaning anything disrespectful to that learned person. At the same time, God knew, he wished to pay him no unnecessary compliment; on the contrary, he would speak his mind boldly and fearlessly. He wished to show that the system, though bad, was not wholly to blame; and, if so, those at the head of the Court ought not to escape all censure on account of certain alleged defects in its organisation. *The Lord Chancellor had been for five-and-twenty years a constant witness of all the evils resulting from the system, and it was not a little surprising that he had, in all that time, made no attempt whatever to remedy its defects; on the contrary, he had uniformly opposed, with all his power, every effort which had been made to remove them.*[33]

The King's speech at the opening of the session of 1826, having, while announcing certain concessions in other respects to the principles of free trade, made no mention of any intention to deal with the Corn Laws, Denman, who spoke on the debate on the address on February 2, thus expressed the disappointment he felt at this omission :

While the principles of free trade were to be acted upon with regard to many articles which administered to the comfort and luxury of the rich, was it dealing fairly by the poor man to withhold the same benefit from him, and to uphold by restrictive laws the price of the chief article of his subsistence? This could not continue without bringing misery and desolation among thousands and hundreds of thousands.

[33] Hansard, Parl. Deb. N.S. vol. xiii. pp. 1074-1077.

There was an amount of distress among the People of which ministers were by no means aware.   In a multitude of occupations the best workmen in full employment could not earn more than six, seven, or eight shillings a week.   How was a man to support and clothe himself out of this wretched pittance.   Foreign manufacturers were now allowed to compete with us in our markets at home, while we were shut out from the possibility of entering into competition with them abroad, by the high price which the landowners exacted from the poor man for his bread.   He did not quarrel with the principle of free trade; he only complained of its partial operation.   He did not blame ministers for repealing prohibitory duties; but he contended that, while free trade was properly allowed in minor articles, it should be extended to the most important of all—bread.[34]

On March 1, 1826, Denman brought before the notice of the House the case of several slaves who had been tried, sentenced, and hanged in Jamacia, in the years 1823 and 1824, on a charge of intended insurrection, upon evidence the most untrustworthy, with scarcely any forms of law, and with the most indecent precipitation.   He moved:

That the House deem it their duty to express, in the strongest terms the sorrow and indignation with which they contemplate the perversion of law and violation of justice displayed in these trials; that they deeply lament the precipitation with which sentences of death, wholly unwarranted by proof, were in several instances carried into execution; and they cannot refrain from declaring their conviction of the necessity of an immediate and effectual reform in the administration of the criminal laws affecting slaves in the island of Jamaica.

Denman's speech was principally confined to a

<hr>

[34] Hansard, Parl. Deb. N.S. vol. xiv. pp. 87–89.

narrative of the facts, which were, indeed, of a nature that required little more than simple statement to produce a profound impression on any assembly of men whose feelings of justice and humanity had not been deadened by living in slave-holding communities. At the close he said:

Under such circumstances he might be asked what was his remedy? He was free to confess he knew but of one—one just in principle, effective in practice, and simple in operation—*the absolute extinction of slavery* (hear, hear, hear).

Mr. Canning, after a dexterous and plausible speech, suggested for the adoption of the House the following motion in lieu of that proposed by Denman, viz:

That this House sees in the proceedings which have been brought under its consideration with respect to the late trial of slaves at Jamaica further proof of the evils inseparably attendant on a state of slavery, and derives therefrom increased conviction of the propriety of the resolutions of May 16, 1823 [in favour of ameliorating the condition of the slave population in the colonies, so as gradually to prepare them for freedom]; *but that, however desirable it is that the law under which the late trials took place should be amended, it does not appear to this House expedient or safe to impeach sentences passed by competent tribunals upon persons brought to trial according to law, and convicted by juries impannelled and sworn to give a verdict according to the evidence laid before them.*

The words italicised, and the cold cautious tone of Canning's speech, stirred Denman to indignation, and he made a vehement and powerful reply, in the course of which he said:

We are told that the *system* of the law ought to bear all the blame. Is it to be endured that public functionaries should thus carry unjust sentences into execution in such a precipitate manner, and the House should do nothing more than coolly say that all the blame rested with the system? Is the House prepared to say that it never would enquire into any judicial proceedings in which, although the essence of justice had been violated, the forms had been complied with? If so, he must protest against a doctrine so utterly unconstitutional. Whatever forms had been observed in the case of these eight slaves, the substance of justice had been denied to them, and eight men were consigned to death who ought not to have suffered. It was proved that four of them were convicted on the evidence of a perjured rogue and robber, and that one was executed after the Governor was aware of the infamy of the witness.

Notwithstanding the atrocious nature of the case, Denman's motion was rejected by a majority of 40, the ayes being 63 and the noes 103.

Afterwards, on the suggestion of Brougham, Canning consented to alter his amendment by omitting that portion of it above printed in italics, and thus modified it passed *nem. con.*[35]

On April 25, 1826, Mr. George Lamb renewed the motion he had made two years before for leave to bring in a Bill enabling persons prosecuted for Felony to make their defence by counsel.

Denman's speech in favour of the motion concluded with the following query:

He would just add, suppose any one of the honourable gentlemen present were put upon his trial for felony—and it should be remembered that the chances against that event were not so utterly improbable as might be imagined, for human nature is frail, and the highest in station might yet

[35] Hansard, Parl. Deb. N.S. vol. xiv. pp. 1007–1074.

be levelled with the lowest—if such an event should happen, would he not wish for counsel to defend him ? and if he felt the necessity of having legal assistance in his own case, why should he withhold that advantage from others.[36]

The motion was lost by a majority of 69, the ayes being only 36 and the noes 105 !

The last occasion on which Denman addressed the House in the then Parliament was on May 19, 1826, on Brougham's motion for an enquiry into the state of slavery in the West Indian colonies. He rose amid loud calls for a division, and, after persevering for some time, was at length prevented by the impatience of the House from proceeding further.[37]

Thus, his last exertion in the House of Commons during this period of his parliamentary life was an effort, however unsuccessful, to mitigate the sufferings of the slave population in the West Indies—a cause which he never abandoned, and to which, as will be seen hereafter, he devoted all the energies of his maturer powers, after his elevation to the House of Lords.

Parliament was prorogued, immediately previous to its dissolution, on May 31, 1826. Denman, for reasons already explained in the personal narrative, did not seek re-election in the new House of Commons.

---

[36] Hansard, Parl. Deb. N.S. vol. xv. pp. 590-633. Sydney Smith, in one of his inimitable articles in the ' Edinburgh Review ' on this subject, suggested that some honourable member—' we ask but one '—should be patriotic enough to commit some act which would unfortunately necessitate his appearance in the dock as a felon, in order that he might feel himself, and prove to the world at large the inconvenience of being deprived, under such circumstances, of counsel's assistance.

[37] Hansard, Parl. Deb. N.S. vol. xv. pp. 1352-1356.

CHAPTER XIV.

DENMAN'S EXERTIONS OTHERWISE THAN IN PARLIAMENT
FOR THE AMENDMENT OF THE LAW.

A.D. 1824 TO 1828. ÆT. 45 TO 49.

Denman's article in the 'Edinburgh Review' for March 1824, on Law
Reform—Defects of the English law of evidence pointed out—Exclusion of testimony on the ground of interest—Exclusion of prosecutor's
evidence as to genuineness of signature in cases of forgery—Interest
ought never to exclude testimony—Query as to the case of parties—
Protected cases: 1. Case of Catholic priest and confessing penitent. 2.
Legal adviser and client. 3. Husband and wife—Remarks as to testimony of Husband and Wife—Present state of English law (1873) as to
testimony of husband and wife—As to confidential communications
between Client and Legal adviser—Denman's criticism of defects then
(1824) existing in our criminal law procedure—Question as to the
superiority, or the reverse, of the French system of interrogating the
prisoner over the English system of non-interrogation—Denman's objections to the French system as it affects both the prisoner and the tribunal
—Balance of advantages and disadvantages pretty even—Passage from
the article relating to the slow progress, but ultimate triumph, of the
criminal law reforms of Romilly and Mackintosh—Peel's criminal
law codification of 1823, abolishing death punishment in above 100
cases—Encouragement to law reformers to persevere—In 1828, in consequence of Brougham's great speech of February 7, a commission
appointed to enquire into and report upon the proceedings in actions
at law—Denman's answers to questions submitted by the Commissioners
suggesting various measures of legal reform, all of which have since
been carried out—Denman also publishes a pamphlet on Law Reform
under the title of 'Considerations submitted to the Commissioners, &c.,'
urging, *inter alia*, that *no* evidence should be excluded on the ground
of interest, and suggesting a preliminary settlement of issues, and disposal, at that stage, of all merely formal objections—Means of proof
to be interchangeably exhibited by both parties before trial—Advantages of the proposed system illustrated by Denman in his pamphlet—

DENMAN was always interested in, and took an active part in promoting, the Amendment of the Law, both civil and criminal. His exertions in Parliament for this purpose have already been mentioned, but they by no means comprise all his efforts for the accomplishment of this important object.

In 1824 he contributed to the ' Edinburgh Review ' a very able paper on Bentham's ' Treatise on Judicial Proof,'[1] which had the effect of awakening public attention to several of the defects then existing in the English law of evidence and procedure—defects which he himself, as a legislator, did much in subsequent years to remove.

From this article some passages remarkable for a spirit of enlightened liberality very uncommon with English lawyers in those days, with whom it was the fashion to regard our Law of Evidence as the peculiar glory of our judicial system, may here be inserted. Admitting that in all systems of legal procedure some *rules of evidence* must be laid down, he thus proceeds :

But we are far from intending here to express unqualified admiration for that particular set of rules which has been adopted, and seems so highly favoured in English courts of law. On the contrary, we rise from an examination of Mr. Phillip's treatise on that subject—the latest, the ablest, and

---

[1] 'Edinburgh Review,' March 1824. Art. viii. pp. 169–207. ' Traité des Preuves judiciaires. Ouvrage extrait des manuscrits de M. Jérémie Bentham, Jurisconsulte anglais, par Ét. Dumont, etc. 2 vols, Paris, 1823.

the most approved [2]—not more delighted by the fulness and
precision of the learned author's collections, than we are
often surprised by the reasonings and conclusions which he
has undertaken to record. The clearness of his arrangement
throws, in fact, too clear a light on the confusion of the
numberless dicta which he has been obliged to transcribe
from notes taken at Nisi Prius. The exclusion of testimony
in many cases of minute *interest*, while in others it is freely
admitted in spite of the most important temptation to deviate
from the truth, exhibits a contradiction hard to be conceived.
In other cases the absolute rejection of light, because there
is a possibility of its leading astray, is difficult to be explained on rational grounds. Take as an example the case
of forgery. Unless the crime has been committed in the
presence of witnesses it can only be *proved* (in the proper
sense of the word) by the individual whose name is said to
have been forged. Yet that person is the only one whom
the law of England prohibits from proving the fact. The
trial proceeds in the presence of the person whose name is
said to have been forged, who alone knows the fact, and has
no motive for misrepresenting it. His statement would at
once convict the prisoner if guilty, or, if innocent, relieve
him from the charge ; and he is condemned to sit by, hearing
the case imperfectly pieced out by the opinions and surmises
of other persons, on the speculative question whether or not
the handwriting is his. And this speculation, incapable
under any circumstances of satisfying a reasonable mind,
decides upon the life of a fellow-citizen, in a system which
habitually boasts of requiring always the very best evidence
which the nature of the case can admit.[3]

Even where there is a real interest in the event of the
suit, Mr. Bentham advises that the witness should be exa-

---

[2] This was written in 1824, very many years before Mr. Pitt Taylor's
masterly and enlightened work on the subject had thrown all other
treatises on evidence entirely into the shade.

[3] This absurd and anomalous exclusion of evidence has long since been
done away with.

mined, and that the jury, making all rational allowances, should determine upon the extent to which his wishes may affect the credibility of his deposition.[4] We think him perfectly right; and are nearly prepared to carry this principle so far as to call upon the contending *parties* to testify to facts within their knowledge. The degree of hesitation that we feel arises chiefly from our inexperience as to the practice.[5]

Mr. Bentham truly observes that if all the exclusions that may be selected from the different codes were found co-existing in one it would be scarcely possible that an admissible witness to any fact whatever could be produced under that system. He is a warm advocate for throwing down all such exclusions—with one exception. He would protect the confidence between a Catholic priest and a confessing penitent. On the whole, we are much disposed to agree with him; but we would introduce two other exceptions in addition.

Denman then proceeds to state his opinion in opposition to Bentham's. 1. That all confidential communications made by a client to his legal adviser ought to be sacred. 2. That married persons should be disqualified as witnesses for or against each other.

This latter disqualification [he says] we should propose not entirely on account of that dread entertained by the English law of conjugal feuds, though these are frequently of the most deadly character; but the reason given in the case of the priest applies, for the confidence between married persons makes their whole conversation an unreserved confession, and they also could never be contradicted but by

---

[4] Exclusion of testimony on the ground of interest was abolished by the Act of 1843, commonly called Lord Denman's Act, 6 and 7 Vic. c. 85.

[5] This further extension of the principle was, with Lord Denman's entire approval, carried out by the Legislature in 1851, by the 14 and 15 Vic. c. 99, generally known as Lord Brougham's Act; see post.

the accused, while external circumstances might be fabricated with the utmost facility to give apparent confirmation to false charges. But our stronger reason is, that the passions must be too much alive, where the husband and wife contend in a court of justice, to give any chance of fair play to the truth. It must be expected as an unavoidable consequence of the connection by which they are bound that their feelings, either of affection or hatred, must be strong enough to bear down the abstract regard for veracity, even in judicial depositions.

Notwithstanding the views thus urged (and which have often been urged by others), a considerable approach has in later times been made in the English Law of Evidence towards freedom from judicial restriction on the evidence of husband and wife. As the law now stands (and in the humble opinion of the present writer it might be advantageously still further extended), husbands and wives of parties to the record in *civil* suits, but *not* the husbands and wives of defendants in *criminal* proceedings, are now competent and *compellable* to testify, but are still privileged from disclosing any communication made to them during the marriage.[6]

With respect to confidential communications between the client and his legal adviser, these are still, and as it would appear rightly, protected from disclosure, subject to the limitation that the privilege is that of the client, not of the legal adviser : if the client does not object to the disclosure the legal adviser cannot do so.

[6] Evidence Amendment Act of 1853, 16 and 17 Vic. c. 83, and see 'Taylor on Evidence,' § 1219 at p. 1171 of the edition of 1868. The admissibility of husband and wife to testify has been extended also to suits for Divorce and Dissolution of Marriage.

The latter portion of the article deals more particularly with *criminal* procedure. It condemns the practice, then too frequent among judges, of endeavouring to induce prisoners to withdraw pleas of guilty and take the chances of a trial ; ridicules the over-scrupulous refinements by which the confessions of prisoners were, and still are, frequently rejected as inadmissible, acknowledges and laments as a grave defect in our criminal jurisprudence the absence of a Public Prosecutor, and exposes with great vigour the absurd anomaly (not put an end to till 1836) which, while allowing counsel to defend prisoners charged with *treason* and *misdemeanour*, denied the same privilege to prisoners charged with *felony*.

On another, and a very vexed question of criminal procedure, Denman records his entire dissent from the views propounded by Bentham, who advocates the French system of interrogating and cross-questioning a prisoner, as a far better process of arriving at the truth than the English system, by which, on the one hand, no questions are allowed to be put to the prisoner at all, while on the other he is not allowed to open his lips to give evidence on his own behalf.

Denman's objections to the French system are two-fold—it is unfair to the prisoner, and it is compromising to the dignity of the court.

As to its bearing on the prisoner, he says :

If the nerves stood always firm, and the mind remained untroubled when a man is brought before a magistrate, charged with a crime, and if, moreover, we could be sure that he knew all the proofs on which suspicion is founded, we might find it difficult to contend against the arguments of Bentham. But, if the contrary of all this is manifestly the most probable; if the mere fact of being accused is, in itself, an overwhelming calamity to an innocent man—and the more so in proportion to his abhorrence of the crime—we must pause before we agree in the propriety of exacting any explanations from him. How open to misconstruction will be his language, his gestures, his very looks! How easy to attribute to feelings of shame the glow of indignation, and confound the agony of undeserved reproach with remorse or fear! All the explanations which can be offered may possibly be inadequate, and then they recoil on the accused; or they may even excite new suspicions, from coincidences merely accidental, which may also possibly defy explanation.

Upon the other part of the question, the tendency of the practice to impair the dignity of the tribunal, he observes as follows :

This keen encounter of wits between judge and culprit, these unseemly bickerings between two persons so widely removed from each other, have a direct tendency to degrade the dignity of justice, because they always disturb its calmness and serenity. It is easy to see which side will have the best of the argument. The master of thirty legions had no such advantages as he at whose mercy the life of his antagonist is. The base and vulgar, indeed, will be seen cheering on the stronger party, to the confusion and dismay of the weaker, and the worshippers of Power always adore it most fervently in its excesses ; but every generous and feeling mind listens with silent indignation, and retires from the debate with diminished respect for the law, and a diminished sense of his own security.

These are weighty objections forcibly urged, and in some points, perhaps, not capable of an entirely satisfactory answer.

It is a somewhat remarkable circumstance that in this controversy the French and English jurists seem respectively to give the preference to the procedure prevailing in the rival country. Bentham argues in favour of the French system, Dumont with equal energy in favour of the English; and so it continues to the present day, many eminent French jurists regarding the English abstinence from interrogating, above all from cross-examining, a prisoner as a great improvement upon the course prevailing among themselves; while several of the most distinguished and enlightened of our own jurists, among whom it may be sufficient to name Mr. Fitzjames Stephen, seem inclined, with all its admitted defects, to give the preference to the French practice over our own.

The present writer inclines to the opinion that on the whole the balance is probably in favour of the French procedure as an engine for discovering the truth (*the primary object*), but that this advantage is not attained to so great an extent as to counterbalance the loss of judicial dignity, and the consequent diminution of public respect and sympathy for the administration of justice, which would seem to be the unavoidable results, even under the most favourable conditions, of the practice prevailing across the Channel.

The advantages of neither system, in short, appear sufficiently preponderating to induce either nation to change its own procedure for that adopted by the other.

The mention of the great name of Romilly in connexion with the criminal code of England introduces the following passage, which is full of interest and encouragement for those who are engaged in that arduous, and still very imperfectly accomplished work —the Amendment of the Law.

The moderate improvements first suggested by Romilly in 1809, wisely calculated as they were to relieve the administration of justice from an odium which did not fairly belong to it, and so to secure its calm and impartial execution, procured for him the usual calumnies and sarcasms. He was not only held up as a vain and wrong-headed speculator, eager to destroy our venerable institutions by setting wild theories in the place of experience, but denounced as a Jacobin, a lover of strife, an hypocritical pretender to humanity, a promoter of crime, an enemy to the establishments which form the safeguard of society.[7] His projects were assailed by the whole tribe of ministerial lawyers in Parliament, from the Lord High Chancellor, down to the meanest candidate for a Welsh judgeship. The twelve judges of England stepped down from their pedestals, and through Lord Ellenborough, then Chief Justice of England, favoured the House of Lords, for the first time, with an unasked opinion respecting a matter, not of Law, but of Legislation, protesting against any abridgment of their powers of life and death. The motion was annually renewed, but supported by minorities, in point of number, contemptible, *and one single measure of mitigation was alone effected in the lifetime of the author of the reform—the abolition of death punishment for the offence of stealing from the person.*

Since his death, Sir James Mackintosh has pursued the subject in a manner worthy of his cause, his predecessor, and himself; and, having succeeded in obtaining, in 1819, an enquiry before a select committee, he has since procured the abolition of capital punishment in a variety of cases.

[7] The 'Quarterly Review' for July 1816 (p. 574) had this passage:— 'We have our professors of humanity, *like Robespierre*, who proposed the abolition of capital punishments.' (Note by Reviewer).

But this is not all. Several statutes, exempting from capital punishment about *an hundred* felonies, were introduced during the last session (1823) into the House of Commons by Mr. Peel, the Secretary of State for the Home Department; and they passed without a dissentient voice—without a whisper of dissatisfaction, except from the friends and disciples of Sir Samuel, who contended that something more ought to be done. The bills were carried to the Lords, and passed through all their stages unanimously, without even a debate, though Lord Eldon at that time presided over the deliberations of that assembly. The royal assent was given, without any difficulty, to measures which had been represented as so mischievous and alarming within about fourteen years from the date of their first suggestion.

And such is the ordinary routine. Common sense requires an obvious improvement: an Opposition member brings it forward, and is overpowered by sarcasms, invectives, and majorities. But public opinion decides at once in its favour, and gradually diminishes the majority, in each succeeding year, till the scale is turned, and independent men of all parties become anxious to see the alteration effected. Suddenly the minister proposes the reprobated project as a government measure, and converts, while he laughs at, his former adherents.

Mr. Peel's five acts in the session of 1823 for effecting Sir Samuel Romilly's proposals have not been so celebrated as they deserve, because they still leave one great reformation unaccomplished. We allude to the abolition of capital punishment in the case of forgery; for in parliamentary tactics it is well understood that those who fight for principles must complain as if nothing was done while there still remains anything to do. The concessions, however, which have been made with respect to the other felonies must gradually lead to the same result in the case of forgery also [but not finally till 1837]; and we must not be deterred from glorying in the victories actually achieved in the cause of justice and humanity merely because they might have been more perfect and satisfactory.

To record such triumphs is to excite public men to similar exertions for the future, by the certain prospect that sooner or later, in their lifetime or after their death, through evil report and good report, public opinion will finally award the palm of victory to truth.

This very admirable paper, written with the knowledge of a lawyer, and in the style of a man of letters, did infinite service to the cause of Law Reform by enlisting an active public sympathy on its side.

Apart from his exertions in the House, which were noticed in the last chapter, Denman's next important contribution to the progress of law amendment was in 1828, when he had ceased for a time to be a member of the legislature.

In that year, in consequence of the great effect produced on the House and in the country by Brougham's celebrated speech (on February 7, 1828) for an address to the Crown relative to the state of the Law,[8]

[8] This was one of Brougham's greatest oratorical achievements: he spoke for nearly six hours, travelling over the whole vast field of the administration of the law. The conclusion of his speech ranks among the masterpieces of English eloquence. One passage in it is particularly celebrated—that in which, after adverting to the boast of Augustus, ' that he found Rome of brick, and left it of marble,' he continues—' But how much nobler will be our Sovereign's boast when he shall have it to say, that he found Law dear, and left it cheap; found it a sealed book, and left it a living letter; found it the patrimony of the rich, left it the inheritance of the poor; found it the two-edged sword of craft and oppression, left it the staff of honesty and the shield of innocence.' Thirty-five years have passed since these memorable words were spoken, and the great aspiration is still far from being accomplished; but in those thirty-five years so much progress has been made that the Law Reformers of to-day may well be encouraged to proceed hopefully with their great work, moving on unweariedly—' without haste, but without rest.'

a Commission was appointed to enquire into and report
on the proceedings in Actions at Law.

In his answers, sent in on November 14, 1828, to
certain queries circulated by the Commissioners, Denman gave a great deal of valuable evidence, in the
course of which he strongly recommended many legal
reforms, the whole of which have since been carried
out,—such as the abolition of the Welsh judicature ; an
increase in the number of the Common Law Judges ; [9]
the assimilation of practice and procedure in the three
Courts of Common Law ; the throwing open of the
Court of Common Pleas to the whole bar ; the abolition
of legal fictions, the simplification of pleadings and
forms of action ; the practice of allowing the defendant's counsel to sum up the evidence, leaving to the
plaintiff's counsel, if he chooses to exercise it, the right
of the general reply.[10]

But he did not limit himself to simply answering the
questions thus put to him. He also made public his
general views on some important points connected with
the amendment of the law (not directly adverted to
in the paper circulated by the Commissioners) in a
pamphlet entitled ' Considerations respectfully submitted
to the Commissioners now sitting to enquire into proceedings in Actions at Law.'

In this publication, besides a strongly expressed
and ably reasoned view (a view since embodied in an
act of the legislature by Denman's own instrumen-

---

[9] By 11 Geo. IV. and 1 Wm. IV. c. 70, passed July 23, 1830.

[10] All these reforms have since been carried out : those last-mentioned
by the Common Law Procedure Acts of 1852 and 1854.

tality),[11] to the effect that no evidence whatever should be absolutely rejected on the ground of incompetency from interest, he also made several valuable suggestions regarding the *preliminary Settlement of Issues*, which appear well worthy of attention even by the Law Reformers of to-day. Under this impression, and as the pamphlet has been long out of print, the following passages from it relating to this matter are here reproduced :

After the action is commenced, measures should be at once taken for affording to the litigants a pause for consideration, and opportunities for adjustment. The way ought to be cleared for a fair trial of the real point at issue, if tried it must be. A judge at chambers, or some similar authority, should bring the parties together, and require from both reasonable admissions, which ought to be preserved and handed forward for subsequent use in the progress of the cause.

In this preliminary stage the description of the litigants might be definitively settled. Not one moment of the precious hours devoted to public justice ought to be wasted in enquiring whether the parties to the suit have given themselves a true description. Such enquiries are now of frequent occurrence : they sometimes defeat substantial justice, and plaintiffs are compelled to pay their debtor's costs, exceeding, in some cases, the amount of the debt, because their witness, at the moment of trial, has forgotten the names composing the firm under which they trade.[12]

The written instruments on which claims are founded, and by which they may be answered, should be produced to the party whose signature they bear. ' If the handwriting is yours, and the day of payment past, pay the money forthwith,

---

[11] The Act of 1843, 6 and 7 Vic. c. 85, known as Lord Denman's Act.

[12] This has been remedied in a great measure of late years by granting increased facilities of amendment at the trial.

or show a sufficient excuse, otherwise judgment and execution.[13] The same kind of language to the plaintiff, when the burden of proof is shifted back to him, as by the production of a receipt, &c.   In such cases a formal procedure and lengthened pleadings are but a pedantic mockery—judges and juries an unwieldly machinery for securing that delay of justice which is so often synonymous with its denial.

Many suits would thus terminate before they were well begun, by being early proved desperate or irresistible, and that to the great advantage of the parties.   A long pedigree might be put *hors de combat* in a moment by a single parish register.   If the dispute turned solely on the construction of a deed or will, the decision of this preliminary judicature would either at once extinguish groundless hopes, or, if the party chose to persevere, a case might be drawn up for the Court without the expense and delay of a trial.   So, if it were made apparent, from a statement of demands, that long mutual accounts must be unravelled, a power might be given of immediate reference to an arbitrator or an auditor.

In this, the proper opportunity for explanations, they ought to be frankly given or rigorously exacted, and the suppression of known and material facts not only be deemed disreputable, but punished with costs.

But when the cause must go on to trial, the same machinery might be employed to sweep away extrinsic circumstances, and bring the plain question of fact alone to the cognizance of the jury.   Thus, in actions on penal statutes, or against magistrates or public officers, questions whether the suit is brought at a proper period, in the proper place, after the proper notice, &c., might be settled at this preliminary stage. In cases depending on written documents, as actions of covenant and the like, actions or prosecutions for libel or for perjury, the parties should agree at this preliminary stage on the identical paper that gives birth to the contest.

---

[13] This principle has been to some extent adopted in the Bills of Exchange Act of 1865, 18 and 19 Vic. c. 67.

To prevent future mistakes or surprise, it should be fully inspected by both parties, or those representing them, verified by the signature of both, and of the judge, and intrusted to impartial hands (the officer of the court for instance) to be produced at the trial. This would save the time of the public, often shamefully wasted in minute examinations, and would often prevent the discomfiture of justice.[14]

These are valuable and weighty observations. Each litigant ought, before proceeding to a final trial, to know exactly the case on which his adversary relies (as in the French and other continental systems), all objections of mere form and technicality (if allowed to be made at all) should be disposed of in the first instance, leaving nothing to be adjudicated upon in the last resort but serious and substantial questions of fact, going to the real merits of the case—the very right and truth of the cause, for the decision of which the litigants have invoked the assistance of the Court.

The above were the principal *public* contributions made by Denman to the cause of Law Amendment during the period now under review ; but, besides these, · he was also in the habit, as he has stated in the personal narrative, of communicating from time to time to the

[14] Settlement of issues has been the rule in the Indian Presidency Courts since 1862. The present writer, having had a seven years' judicial experience of the system in Bombay, is greatly in favour of it, as tending to check vexatious litigation, and cause cases to be finally tried on their merits only. It involves, perhaps, rather more active personal intervention between the litigant parties than is consistent with the habitudes of English judges, and has also a tendency, unless strictly watched, to become costly ; but on the whole, and with proper supervision, it is an excellent system, and might be advantageously introduced into English jurisprudence.

Home Office all such suggestions for the improvement of legal procedure as struck him while practising at the Bar or presiding over a criminal court as Common Serjeant. As will appear hereafter, he continued this laudable practice after he became Lord Chief Justice of England, and if these private and secret exertions be added to those which were public and avowed, it may be doubted whether any jurist of his day and generation did more to help on the progress of Law Reform than Lord Denman.

CHAPTER XV.

FAMILY AND SOCIAL LIFE, HOLLAND HOUSE, ETC.

A.D. 1821 TO 1828.

Denman's social position from 1821 to 1828—Residence in Russell Square
—His family complete in 1823—Excursion into Scotland with
Brougham in 1823—Hospitable reception by the Scotch Liberals—Lord
Rosslyn and Duke of Hamilton—The Glasgow Banquet—High spirits
of Brougham and Denman—How Brougham made the Scotch post-
horses go—Death of Dr. Baillie in 1823—His high character and
great professional sagacity—His diagnosis in Horner's case—The key
and the thong—Promotion to the Bench of Gaselee, 1824—His
eccentricities—The Mr. Justice Stareleigh of 'Pickwick'—'Rise up, Sir
Stephen'—Circuit entries—Going special to Cambridge—Fall in hunting—Marriage of Denman's eldest daughter to Ichabod Charles
Wright, Esq., 1825—Letter from Denman to Mrs. Baillie (September
24, 1825) as to the intended marriage, &c.—Denman's position in
London society, Holland House, &c.—Friendship with Sir J. Mackintosh—Note from Mackintosh as to Burke's passage about Hyder Al
hanging like a cloud over the Carnatic—From same as to the context
of the Greek quotation in Denman's speech for the Queen—From
same as to further diminution of capital punishments—'Capital'
anecdote from the Old Bailey, 1826—Sydney Smith—Rogers—Moore
—Campbell—Moore: 'a headless note'—A 'Reginal dinner'—Why
Mr. Errington was not called on Queen's trial to prove King's marriage
with Mrs. Fitzherbert—Brougham's correction of Moore's statement—
Thomas Campbell—His rhyming invitation to Denman to eat calve's
head on January 30, 1829——Denman's rhyming reply—Mrs. Denman
makes her son promise to dine with her on next January 30—The
humble memorial of 'Henry Brougham, labourer,' to Mrs. Denman—
Mrs. Denman's reply—Inaugural discourse in 1828 at City of London
Literary and Scientific Institution—Extracts from, and remarks on its
high character as a composition.

THE last few chapters have been devoted almost exclusively to Denman's public and political career. It may be as well now to refer briefly to his social position, and domestic relations during the period intervening between the death of the Queen and his obtaining the long withheld honour of a silk gown.

His residence ever since his first entrance into Parliament had been, and till his elevation to the peerage continued to be, at No. 50 Russell Square, where the last of his children Caroline Amelia (now the Hon. Mrs. Beresford) was born to him in 1823.

His family now consisted of eleven—five sons and six daughters, and as the three elder boys were sent successively to Eton the expenses of their education must have made a considerable demand on his resources.

In the summer of the year 1823 he joined his intimate friend Henry Brougham, already the foremost political man of his time, in a visit to Scotland, where Brougham and Denman had been invited to a great public dinner at Glasgow. The journey was a very agreeable one. They met at Brougham Hall, and in their progress northward were received with all that cordial hospitality for which the sister country has ever been celebrated.

Among the members of the Scotch aristocracy who welcomed them as guests were Lord Rosslyn, at Dysart, and the Duke of Hamilton, at Hamilton Palace, where Denman was particularly charmed by the singing of the Duchess (a daughter of Beckford of Fonthill) in 'Auld Robin Gray.'

The expedition wound up with the political banquet

at Glasgow, which was a great success. The number of
the guests exceeded five hundred, and the after-dinner
speaking, as might be expected where Brougham and
Denman were among the performers, was of an order
of excellence very much above the average.

This was the first and only time that Denman ever
crossed the border : he enjoyed himself immensely, and
both he and Brougham were in the highest flow of
spirits. The present Lord Denman, then a youth of
about 18, who accompanied his father, has vividly
impressed on his memory the artifice with which
Brougham contrived to get a maximum of speed out
of the Scottish post-horses. ' *Those* horses can't go,' he
used to cry, as he stepped into the chaise, in his most
sarcastic of tones—those tones which none who may
have chanced to hear him when he was in his prime
can ever forget. This roused the national spirit of the
Scotch post-boys, and away they went at a gallop, to
show the southron the mistake he had made in ' talking
scorn ' of their cattle.

It was soon after his return from this Scotch tour
that Denman lost his distinguished brother-in-law,
Dr. Baillie.

Dr. Baillie died of overwork. For some years,
indeed, before his death he had ceased to practise
except as a consulting physician ; but, even in this
capacity, owing to the universality of his reputation,
the demands on his time and the wear and tear of his
faculties, mental and physical, were excessive and continuous. At last he gave up practice altogether ; but
it was too late. His constitution was irretrievably

undermined, and only a short interval separated his retirement from his death.

As a physician Dr. Baillie has probably never been surpassed, especially in the almost unerring tact and sagacity with which he was able to divine the true nature of disease from its symptoms. As a man he was simply admirable in all the relations of life. He left a considerable fortune behind him, and twice refused a baronetcy.[1] Some time after his death the principal members of the medical profession, honouring themselves in doing honour to his memory, placed his bust in Westminster Abbey, with an inscription which records, in terms of high but not unmerited eulogy, his consummate science, his varied accomplishments, and his many virtues.[2]

In the summer of 1824, much to Denman's satisfaction, and to some extent, it would seem, in consequence of his exertions, the meritorious legal veteran, Stephen Gaselee, was raised to the Bench.[3]

---

[1] His son, William Henry Baillie, Esq., of Dunsbourne, near Cirencester, is his present representative.

[2] Brougham, in the second volume of his 'Memoirs,' relates a striking instance of Dr. Baillie's skill in diagnosis in the case of Horner, who died at Pisa in 1817. Baillie, when he last saw Horner, pronounced that he was suffering from one or both of two maladies, each so rare that in his whole practice he had scarcely met with a case of either. When the body was opened it was found that both the indicated maladies had conduced to Horner's death. Brougham aptly compares this to the skill of the connoisseur in 'Don Quixote,' who, having pronounced that the wine in a certain cask tasted both of leather and iron, was justified by the discovery at the bottom of the cask of an iron key with a leather thong attached to it.

[3] Sir Stephen Gaselee, born 1762; called to the Bar, 1793; King's Counsel, 1819; Judge of Common Pleas, July 1, 1824; resigned, Hilary Term, 1837; died 1839, æt. 77. If Denman at this time had any influence

This excellent and learned lawyer combined with high character and great professional knowledge a considerable amount of personal eccentricity.

His extremely short stature,[4] and comically pompous manner, were an endless source of amusement to the Bar. Denman, writing to his wife on July 2, 1824, after saying 'my efforts have been crowned with success, and Gaselee is the new judge,' adds, ' you would have been amused by his swelling pomp when he walked out of court after the announcement: it was like the swelling of a balloon.'

Dickens has immortalised, and scarcely caricatured, some of Mr. Justice Gaselee's oddities of manner on the Bench under the punning sobriquet of Mr. Justice *Stareleigh*, the presiding judge in the famous cause of *Bardell* v. *Pickwick*.

In the Spring Assizes of 1824, Denman went down on a special retainer to Cambridge to defend a fellow of his old college, St. John's, the Rev. Thomas Jephson, from a false but formidable charge of misdemeanour. The defendant was very properly acquitted, and the

over the Chancellor it could only have been the influence of fear, arising from the Parliamentary attacks of himself and Williams; but Denman was the last man in the world to make use of such an influence as this. The statement in Denman's letter as to his share in Gaselee's appointment cannot be explained by the present writer.

[4] So short was he that when knighted by George IV. on his being made a Judge, the King, so runs the story, who had already once in the usual form directed him to rise, thinking he was still on his knees, repeated the injunction, ' Rise up, Sir Stephen,' an injunction with which poor Sir Stephen, who had already risen to the fulness of his stature, was, of course, unable to comply. There is too much reason to fear that this venerable jest is of far older date than either George IV. or Mr. Justice Gaselee, but if not originally invented for the latter, it was at least currently applied to him.

ability with which Denman conducted the defence was generally admitted to have been of the highest order.

In the Circuit Book the following entry relates to this occurrence :

1824. *March* 17. *Derby.*—Mr. Denman is congratulated on going special to Cambridge. Fine (the usual one), 5*l.* 5*s.*

As no similar entry relating to Denman is to be found in the Circuit Book, it may be inferred that this was the only occasion, previous at least to his Attorney-Generalship, on which he ' went special.'

It may be as well here to add a shortly subsequent entry relating to a different subject—a fall from his horse on what is believed to have been the only occasion of his having yielded to his brother-in-law's persuasions and joined the hunting-field. The Rev. R. J. Vevers rode to hounds like a Leicestershire man. Denman, who, though a fair enough horseman on a turnpike road, had never cultivated the science of going across country, came to grief at his first fence, with the results described in the following entry :

1825. *March* 23. *Leicester.*—Mr. Denman is congratulated on falling so softly from his horse in hunting, or trying to hunt, in the neighbourhood of Lincoln, as only to become covered with mud and lose half his pantaloons.

In 1825, Theodosia, Denman's eldest daughter (so named after her mother), then in her 19th year, made the first marriage that took place in a family in which, out of six daughters, not one ultimately remained single.

Her husband was Ichabod Charles Wright, Esq., a

gentleman and a scholar, of good fortune and high literary culture, the best, probably, of all the English metrical translators of Dante, and inferior to few if any as a translator of Homer.[5] Denman, writing from London, thus communicates the intelligence to his widowed sister, Mrs. Baillie, in a letter that gives several pleasant particulars of the courtship, of the future bridegroom, and of his family:

50 Russell Square: Sept. 14, 1825.

My dear Sister—My mother's absence from town at the time of my return to it is a double grievance, for it both prevents me from telling her my news with my own lips, and also deprives me of the best of all possible amanuenses in imparting it to others. Of course you anticipate something of no light consequence, and not without good reason. I fancy you already guess right. Doe [Theodosia] is going to be married. She has engaged the affections of a Mr. Wright, eldest son of a Nottingham banker, of the very highest character, himself a partner in the bank, an amiable and excellent young man. He is an Etonian and an Oxonian, at this time fellow of Magdalen College. He has ten sisters— five uncommonly well married, the others young and single— and two brothers. He is just twenty-nine, rather well-looking.

The intimacy took place at Mr. Smith Wright's, who married Lady Sitwell. An old Scotch woman is the housekeeper there, who surprised us by inquiring after you, having known you many years ago, when she was in the service of Mrs. Cullen. My wife said something to her in praise of Doe, when she replied, 'She cannot be better than *somebody else*, and I daresay they will be very happy.'

His parents and family received us all the other day with

---

[5] Mr. Wright died in 1871, in the seventy-fourth year of his age; his widow, the Honourable Mrs. Wright, survives.

the greatest cordiality, and are delighted with the future. They are going to be at Buxton during the next fortnight, and my wife, with the three eldest girls and Margaret,[6] mean to remain there during that time. They will then pay a visit to Mappert, the father's place near Nottingham, and come slowly to London, where I imagine all things will be speedily concluded; but they must first get a house in the country.

This house in the country is the only circumstance I regret, but I submit to it patiently on account of Doe's decided preference for a country life; in all other respects I can conceive no union to promise more happiness. My contribution of fortune must of course be very moderate indeed, but he has enough for respectability and comfort. I have known the family well, though not intimately, for many years, and always thought the mother and daughters particularly amiable. I left them yesterday at Newstead Abbey, on the road to Buxton. Doe looks perfectly and quietly happy. Mamma has not quite recovered from the first confusion that follows such a surprise. Remember me kindly to those of your party that I have the good fortune to know, and believe me, my dear sister,

Your most truly affectionate brother,

T. DENMAN.

Denman's position in London society had not remained unaffected by the fame and popularity he had acquired in the Queen's trial. Many of the most distinguished personages of the Liberal party sought his acquaintance, especially the members of that brilliant society of statesmen, poets, wits, and politicians who then gave celebrity to Holland House.

With Mackintosh, one of the principal ornaments of

---

[6] Now respectively the Hon. Mrs. Wright, Hon. Mrs. Hodgson, Hon. Lady Baynes, Hon. Mrs. E. Cropper.

that famous circle, his friendship was of earlier date.
He had for some time worked with him in Parliament
at the reform of the criminal law, and had assisted him,
after Romilly's death, in at length forcing upon Lord
Liverpool's Government the important measures introduced by Peel in 1823, which abolished the punishment
of death in nearly one hundred cases where it had
previously existed.

Among the few stray notes from Mackintosh which
have casually been preserved among the Denman
papers, one or two are characteristic. In the beginning
of 1827, Denman had been staying with him for a few
days at Ampthill Park in Bedfordshire, a seat of Lord
Holland's, where Sir James was for some years a
resident, and during his stay a question, it seems, had
arisen as to the originality of Burke's celebrated description of Hyder Ali and his tumultuary host hanging
like a cloud over the plains of the Carnatic. Mackintosh
writes :

I experienced as much gratification from your visit, and
feel as much thankfulness for it, as I could do from that of
any human being.[7]

The passage about the cloud is this :—*Annibalem
quoque ex acie redeuntem dixisse ferunt, tandem eam nubem
quæ sedere in jugis montium solita sit, dedisse procellam
cum imbre.* This is a compliment to Fabius, expressed with
lively familiarity. Livy and Burke looked at the same
object with quite different feelings. A couplet of ' Hudibras '
might give a hint to the imagination of Milton; but this
accident, of which he might be unconscious, could not make

---

[7] This is thoroughly in Mackintosh's vein of hyberbolic, but perfectly
sincere, laudation of all persons and things that he thought excellent.

him an imitator.   This, I am aware, is an extreme case, which would be an objection to it as a proof, but not as an illustration.

The above is itself a good illustration of the learning, the earnestness about elegant trifles, the *strenua inertia* which made Mackintosh so charming as a talker and a correspondent, but which too often diverted him from the more practical objects of every-day life.

In another note, of the same year, Sir James expresses his wish to have his memory refreshed as to Denman's much talked of Greek quotation on the Queen's trial.

I will come to you [he writes] on Wednesday if you will let me, as I am at present engaged to go to Holland House on Thursday. I have a great desire to examine the quotation of 1820, and the words which introduced it, which my illness at the time prevented me from storing in my memory as I should otherwise have done, with all that fell from the speaker. Being without books I wish you would help me when I see you, that I may be the better prepared to do the duties of friendship against the ungenerous and the lukewarm, for I apply the word 'against' to the latter also, who are not worth distinguishing from the former.

Sir James's object, no doubt, was to co-operate with other friends of Denman's in proving that the quotation did not necessarily involve, and was not intended to convey, that personal imputation against the King as to which so much will shortly have to be stated.

In another note, written in the course of the next year, from Clapham, Mackintosh consulted Denman on the subject which both had so much at heart, the still further abolition of capital punishment in certain cases not touched by Peel's codification of 1823.

I find myself [he writes] called on by your City determination as to forgery, &c., to make one more attempt at capital punishment, which I spoke to you about two or three months ago. Before you begin your circuit I should like to have some conversation with you, particularly on these points. 1. Would it be best to confine myself to forgery, on which alone the City petitions. 2. Or should I move to limit the punishment of death to a few crimes [which he specifies, adding]—The practical change would be in forgery, stealing in the house, house-breaking in the day time, and sheep-stealing. 3. Can you point out a barrister who could and would draw the bill, which Peel's codification would render much easier. My reason for rather wishing a general measure is that it must, with me, be somewhat of a testamentary nature.

All these changes have long since been carried out, the abolition of death punishment for forgery mainly owing to the exertions of Denman himself.

In a note of Denman's to his wife, written in 1826, from the Old Bailey, where he was at the time presiding as Common Serjeant, there is a passage which curiously illustrates in what a state, notwithstanding several previous reforms, our criminal law then was.

I have got to *capital* offences now, and as the wisdom of the law still makes it capital to steal in a dwelling-house when anybody is there, the life of the prisoner is, on the *face of the indictment*, placed in jeopardy on numerous occasions ; but the circumstance, though stated in the indictment, is in fact never proved. On enquiring into the reason for thus charging in the indictment a graver crime than is intended to be established in proof, I find that there is a *higher fee for drawing an indictment for a capital offence !*   Capital ! !

Among those of the Holland House circle with whom Denman in these years had become more or less intimate were Sydney Smith, Rogers, Moore, and Campbell.

With Sydney Smith he was always on very cordial terms, and with Rogers he formed a friendship which continued unabated till death.

Moore he saw frequently in general society, and occasionally at his own house.[8]   A note from the poet at the earlier period of their acquaintanceship, accepting an invitation to dine and sleep in Russell Square, commences thus :

As you will not call me ' dear Moore,' and I could not venture to set a Common Serjeant the fashion, we must needs go on in this *headless* manner.

On a later occasion, Moore records in his diary that Denman had driven him down to dine with Mackintosh at Clapham ; and under date December 20, 1824, there is the following entry :

Dined at Denman's—the party a most *Reginal* one ; himself, Brougham, and Williams, with old Charles Butler to dilute.   Very agreeable.   Brougham seemed to lay great stress on the marriage of the King with Mrs. Fitzherbert, and the forfeiture of the crown thereby.   On Charles Butler saying he wondered this was not thought of on the Queen's trial, Brougham said it *was* thought of : the only witness to the marriage, however (I forget his name), was dead.

[8] Mr. Justice Denman informs the present writer that he perfectly recollects Moore's frequently singing in the evening at his father's, during a Summer Vacation (about 1826), when they had a house near Hammersmith.

Brougham, in his 'Memoirs' (vol ii. p. 410), corrects Moore's statement as to the death of the sole witness. That witness, Mr. Errington, the uncle of Mrs. Fitzherbert, was alive at the time of the Queen's trial; but the matter was not gone into because, as Brougham explains, the abandonment of the Bill of Pains and Penalties rendered it unnecessary to resort to so extreme a measure of recrimination as the impeachment on this ground of the King's title to the crown.

With Campbell Denman was for many years on terms of frank and cordial intercourse. He was not only an enthusiastic admirer of the poet's genius, but he heartily sympathized with the boldness and vigour of his political sentiments, which went to the utmost verge of the 'eleutheromaniac' Liberalism of those days.

The following jeu d'esprit, preserved among the Denman papers, may find a place here, not, certainly, on account of its literary merits, which, as regards both poet and lawyer, are of anything but a high order, but rather as proving that the passion for the 'Good Old Cause' was at least as strong in the Common Serjeant at 50 as it had been in the Cambridge student at 20.

Campbell's lines are headed thus: 'Song of Invitation from T. Campbell to Common Serjeant Denman to dine with him on January 30, 1829, in commemoration of the Blessed Death of Charles I.'

Tune: Will ye go the Ewe Buchts, Marion.

Will you come and dine with me, Denman,
  Will you eat calve's head with me;
You're a *long-headed* lawyer, but then, man,
  A *Roundhead* I know you to be.

> There is many a speaker and penman
>   In the cause of ' sweet Libertie '
> That speaks well and writes well, my Denman !
>   But none that can match with thee.
>
> So come, and with port wine and sherry
>   To the downfall of 'Tyrannie,'
> On the 30th of January,
>   We'll toast with a three times three.
>
> That the noddles of Tyrants demolished,
>   May be made the footballs of the free,
> And all taxes and pensions abolished,
>   Except a small pension for me.
>
> So come and dine with me, Denman,
>   And eat calve's head with me,
> You're a long-headed lawyer, but then, man,
>   A Roundhead I know you to be.

Seymour Street West: Jan. 14, 1829.

Denman's impromptu answer runs as follows, rather, it must be confessed, with an occasional limp in its paces.

> I will dine with thee, Tom Campbell,
>   Thou poet of ' Libertie,'
> And greet, with glass and gambol
>   The 30th of Januarie.
>
> Let English patriots cherish
>   Their great anniversary,
> For when tyrants justly perish,
>   'Tis the birthday of Liberty.
>
> *We* [9] may rail at force and wrong,
>   *We* may plead for equal laws,
> But the magic power of *Song*
>   Is the salt of the Good Old Cause.
>
> While the Western World is clearing
>   In the brightness of Freedom's ray,
> And her light old France is cheering,
>   Though cursed by a Bourbon's sway,
>
> While Hope e'en yet is striving
>   To heal the woes of Spain,
> And Athens assumes, reviving,
>   Her myrtle crown again,

[9] *I.e.* the lawyers.

> On the soil where it best is planted,
>   Let us circle Freedom's tree,
> And new songs in her praise be chanted
>   By the bard of 'Libertie.'

It is not improbable that the presence of the Common Serjeant at the banquet to which the above invitation refers may have caused some little scandal among the straiter sect of the political and professional world. At all events, his mother, ever sedulous for the complete stainlessness of her son's reputation, appears to have taken alarm, and exacted from him a promise that on the next anniversary of the Martyr's death he would consider himself as 'specially retained' to dine with her.

As the next January 30 approached, a rumour of Denman's intended absence from the anniversary banquet having got about, Brougham was deputed to petition Mrs. Denman that her son might on that day have permission to appear among them. He executed his task in that quaint, formal style of legal banter by dint of which he had so often set the mess of the Northern Circuit in a roar—a feat not very difficult to accomplish on any circuit mess when once the bottle has had its due circulation.

It runs thus:

The humble memorial of Henry Brougham, of Hill Street, in the county of Middlesex, labourer, sheweth

That Saturday next, the 30th of this month, being the anniversary of the execution of Charles Stuart, heretofore unlawfully exercising the office of king of this country, your memorialists and other good and loyal subjects of his present Majesty rightfully governing these realms intend to keep the same holy.

That unless T. Denman shall have full liberty to be present on the said occasion, not only will the said celebration be imperfect, but divers hazards will be encountered, from the which his attendance will mainly tend to guard the persons assisting thereat :

That he may help to prevent them from confounding the past with the present times, and thereby conceiving rancour against the rulers of these present days :

That he will be ready to act in his capacity of magistrate, and upon perceiving any tendency to a breach of the peace, by sallying forth for purposes of decapitation and so forth, he will bind over the persons so disposed to be of good behaviour towards all kings and others :

That he will exercise a careful superintendence over the upper extremity of the calf then and there made manifest, and upon perceiving it to bear, or to have maliciously been made to bear, any resemblance to the ' portraiture of His Sacred Majesty,' that he will decently cover over the same, or deface it, or peradventure summarily deal with it, by himself swallowing the greater portion thereof :

That he will vigilantly obstruct all tendency to compare the future prospects of the French reigning family with the past history of the Scotch family now no more, and in general will exercise a wholesome severity in repressing disrespect towards all kings fled.

For these reasons, and out of a regard to the interests of royalty, your memorialist humbly prays that the said T. Denman may have leave to attend on the occasion aforesaid, and your memorialist will ever pray.

H. Brougham.

Tuesday, January 26, 1830.

The venerable old lady, however, was resolute, and returned under her own hand the following answer to the ' Humble Memorial ' :

T. Denman, in the month of January, 1829, promised that he would dine with his mother on January 30, 1830, and she cannot dispense with his engagement, more especially as it has been the endeavour of her life, ever since she became a mother, to root in the hearts of her children a never-failing love of truth.   Moreover she feels assured that Mr. Brougham would be sorry to deprive her of this long-promised visit, knowing, as he does, how few opportunities she has of seeing her son, and that she is now in her eighty-third year.

Welbeck Street: January 27, 1830.

The pursuit of this trifle to its close has led to a slight departure from the regular order of time, and the narrative must now revert to the year 1828.   In the spring of that year Denman, who, amid all the pressure of public and professional engagements, never in any degree lost his interest in and devotion to literature, found time to prepare and deliver a very admirable ' Inaugural Discourse,' on the opening of the City of London Literary and Scientific Institution.

As this ' discourse ' is almost the only piece of prose writing in which Denman has done full justice to his really great powers of composition, room must be made for a few of its more striking passages.

After speaking generally of some of the leading characteristics of English literature, he proceeds thus :

Two peculiar circumstances occur to my mind as happy auguries of the enduring and increasing grandeur of English literature.

The first is our community of language with the United States. Our own colonies, however distant and extensive, seem but to echo back our voice ; but the inheritance of our language by the great North American Commonwealth, an independent, a powerful, and a rival nation; the attachment to our habits of thinking and speaking on the part of one of the most civilised of countries, if civilisation depends on the diffusion of knowledge, and the protection of equal laws; the identity of education between our sons and the multiplying millions of those boundless regions; the filial but formidable competition with which the offspring has awakened the admiration and must stimulate the energies of her parent; all these things hold forth the auspicious promise of stability to the literature common to both countries, as well as of peace, liberty, and happiness to the Old World and the New.

The other circumstance to which I advert is the regular succession by which our literature has maintained its state from an early period quite down to the present time. Its current, even at this point so remote from its source, has betrayed no symptom of exhaustion, no danger of being swallowed up in the barren sands of the desert. Its unimpaired stream is still wonderful for depth and breadth, for clearness and power. Some flats indeed, some shoals, may be here and there detected, but so rare and partial as scarcely to arrest our notice, and never to disturb our faith. To prove by an appeal to living genius how well the glory of former ages has been sustained in this would be a pleasing but an endless task. Our sanguine hopes, however, for the future are well justified by the contemplation of the past, which shows Burke still in possession of the same commanding eminence attained by Bacon, and can trace the family of our poets through an unbroken pedigree from Byron back to Shakespeare.

At the sound of that great name I pause but for a moment. A few simple facts record the praise of Shakespeare: the insatiable demand for his works, the swarming theatres which find them ever new and delightful, the pride with which real histrionic genius aims at embodying his conceptions, while it disdains to receive its task from any meaner hand. His power is manifested in tears and smiles, in agony and rapture, on its first display to the sensibility of youth;

in the tranquil delight, on its hundredth repetition, of reflecting age; in the permanency imparted to our language by
the richness, the strength, the ever-varying graces of his
style; in the gentle yet generous spirit, the sympathy with
all the kindly affections, the high feelings of magnanimity
and honour, by which he has produced a lasting effect on the
character of Englishmen.

After many illustrations, well chosen and happily
expressed, of the great advantage to be derived by men
of every profession and calling from the cultivation of
a literary taste, the speaker concludes his address in
the following eloquent words:

Would that these weighty considerations had been urged
by a more powerful advocate. They are a theme for talents
of the highest order, acting freely in perfect leisure, undisturbed and undivided. He who, without any of these, has
now rather invited your own reflection to the noblest subject
than discoursed upon it, could not, however, decline the task
which a too partial kindness assigned him. This was forbidden, not only by his sympathy with your feelings, but by
the sentiments of esteem and confidence which he has long
cherished towards his respected friends, the promoters of your
Institution, and by his attachment to that illustrious city to
which he is proud to belong. For nothing can so effectually
contribute to the prosperity and honour of London as the
emulous advancement of her sons in the career of science and
literature. He trusts that his zeal may in some degree
supply what is wanting in ability; and he can offer at least
his testimony as a witness, speaking from experience and
observation, to the value of literary pursuits as a means of
happiness. They are in truth, in the language of that lesson
imbibed in his early years, 'the nourishment of youth, the
delight of age, the ornament of prosperous life, the refuge
and consolation of adversity, the companions of our weary
travels, of our rural solitudes, of our sleepless nights.' These

words were uttered near two thousand years ago by the great statesman and orator of Rome, who in those characters performed but a fleeting service to his own country, while, as a philosopher and a man of letters, he has conferred benefits on all mankind which must be felt while the world endures.

It is not often that the strength, grace, and harmony of which English prose is susceptible in the hands of a master, have been better illustrated than in the above passage, each sentence in which was no doubt the product of careful study and diligent labour, while the general effect of the whole, as is the case with all true art, is an air of simplicity, nature, and freedom.

CHAPTER XVI.

KING'S COUNSEL AT LAST.

A.D. 1828.   ÆT. 49.

Rank of King's Counsel vexatiously withheld from Denman—Effect on his practice and professional emoluments—Denman, twenty-two years after his call to the Bar still only a stuff-gown—His speech at Fishmongers' Hall in 1827, referring to this exclusion—Denman, in 1828, first learns the real cause of his exclusion, viz. the King's belief that the Greek quotation conveyed an odious personal imputation against himself—On this, Denman, as a gentleman, becomes eager to disabuse the King's mind—Applies, but without effect, to Lord Lyndhurst—Then to the Duke of Wellington, at that time Prime Minister—The Duke proposes to speak to the King: 'I'll do it; you may rely on me, I'll do it'—Denman's memorial to the King, of July 24, 1828—The Duke presents it to the King—Result of the Duke's application—Meeting, in Downing Street, of the Duke, Lyndhurst, and Denman, on December 1, 1828—King's observations on the memorial—Patent of Precedence granted as from July 24—Denman's gratitude to the Duke of Wellington—Letter from Denman to the Duke (meant to be shown to the King), December 2, 1828—General satisfaction felt at Denman's at length attaining the long withheld professional rank—Congratulatory letters from Lord Holland and Spring Rice (Lord Monteagle)—From Abercromby and Lord Rosslyn; from Lord Nugent; from William Smith, of Norwich; from Denman's old personal friends, Francis Hodgson and William Empson; from his mother.

WHILE he stood thus high in social and popular estimation, Denman's professional practice had in some degree suffered through the obstinate refusal at head-quarters to give him the rank of King's Counsel.

His talents peculiarly fitted him for the lead, but according to the well-known etiquette of the English

Bar he could not, in the conduct of causes, take precedence of those whose rank was the same as his own, while their call to the Bar was of earlier date. Yet amongst the men thus excluded from acting under him were several whom it was highly important, especially in cases involving nice questions of law and pleading, to have retained as junior counsel, men of great legal learning and sound judgment, though immeasurably inferior to Denman in capacity for addressing a jury or cross-examining a witness.

Clients were accordingly placed in a difficult alternative, and to escape from it frequently were forced to retain for the conduct of their causes King's Counsel whose talents were certainly not superior to Denman's, but whose professional rank enabled them to take the lead of those veteran adepts in the minutiæ of law and practice whose aid was so indispensable in the more difficult and lucrative class of cases.

This state of things had lasted for a length of time which was generally felt to be excessive and exceptional. In the year 1828, after twenty-two years of practice, Denman, with all his admitted powers, high reputation, and great experience was still only a member of the outer Bar—a 'stuff gown,' as it is called in the language of Westminster Hall, not a 'silk gown,' or King's Counsel.

Denman had long felt this unjust exclusion very severely. Soon after the formation of Canning's Ministry, in the summer of 1827, his health having been proposed at a dinner at Fishmongers' Hall by the Warden of the Company, with a high eulogium on his

services as an advocate at the Bar and in his judicial
capacity as Common Serjeant, Denman, in the course of
a very eloquent reply—one of the most spirited efforts
of his oratory that has been preserved—made the
following observations on this exclusion, and on what
he then supposed to be its cause :

If, with the assistance of upright magistrates and excellent
juries, I have had the good fortune to render any useful
service to the public, the opportunity has been derived from
that portion of my life which the advisers of the Crown have
deemed it right to stigmatise. I trust that those with whom
the exclusion originated, and those by whom it is continued,
may reflect on their counsel with as much satisfaction as I
can do on my conduct. But I could not forego the earliest
occasion of vindicating myself and you : you from the charge
of giving countenance to a factious firebrand, and myself
from that of perverting the office of an advocate to objects
equally abominable and absurd. We feel in common that
we are not guilty. (*Loud cheers.*) You felt the difficulty
and the danger of the task imposed upon me—

a noble task,
With which all Europe rang from side to side—

and I will venture to assert that my performance of it
found a faithful echo in every English bosom. I offer, then,
no uncalled-for apology. I utter no unfelt regret; nor will
I enter into any explanation, for what could exceed the injustice of demanding any at the end of seven long years.
(*Loud cheers.*)

On one of the great topics that have long divided the
nation I can offer a little personal experience, having received
a practical lesson on the meaning of the word *exclusion*. I
have been taught to consider myself a proscribed man during
a life which we all pray may be long preserved, and if any
friend of mine now present warmly enters into the feelings,
not of the most agreeable nature, which he may ascribe to

me on that subject, let me in passing entreat him to reflect on those which are likely to agitate the thousands and millions of our fellow-subjects in both islands who, with all their posterity, are doomed to similar proscription on account of the faith of their forefathers.

In my own case, whatever may be said or insinuated against one too highly placed for explanations, God forbid that I should be either arrogant enough or disloyal enough to believe myself the object of personal animosity in such a quarter. The first principles of the Constitution teach me where to look for the responsibility that belongs to all official proceedings, pronouncing my exclusion not to be the act of the Crown, but of those entrusted with the dispensation of its legal patronage.[1] That they have given correct advice I may be allowed to doubt, without playing the judge in my own cause, because the very conduct which is made my crime procured for me the favour of this ancient and loyal city. The freedom of London was presented to me for the zealous discharge of my duty as an advocate in the most important process which this country has beheld for ages. Almost a stranger to every member of the Corporation, I was enrolled among its citizens on the proposal of an honourable friend near me (Mr. Oldham), seconded by the gentleman who now fills the office of Chief Magistrate, and adopted without a division. The resolution of thanks, too flattering to be alluded to by me except in my own defence, may save me from the humiliation of a superfluous profession that I am incapable either of abusing my privilege as an advocate by wantonly wounding the feelings of the meanest, or of shrinking from its plain duties for fear of offending the highest. (*Loud cheers.*)

The voice of the city of London was not heard alone or for a moment : this patriotic company also received me as one of its members, and the Corporation, after a lapse of two years, deliberately placed me on the judgment seat.

---

[1] In the present case, as will soon appear, this was a mere constitutional fiction. The exclusion was the King's own act : neither Eldon nor Lyndhurst dared to say a word to him on the subject of Denman's promotion.

Thank God, I have no apology to make for sacrificing my illustrious and unfortunate client to any hopes of advantage to myself. I own I look back on the past with pride, and if in future I shall be called to a similar conflict, casting aside all regard for personal consequences, I shall again go through it in the same spirit and on the same principles; and, whatever lot may befall me, find consolation in the approbation of my conscience and in the esteem of men like you. (*Loud and enthusiastic cheering, which continued several minutes.*)

In the above speech, Denman, it will have been seen, expressed his determination to attempt no explanation of anything he may have said as advocate for the Queen, his impression then being that the enmity of the King had arisen rather from the general tone of bold denunciation which ran through the whole of his speeches on the Queen's trial, than from any particular insinuation or charge. When, however, early in the summer of 1828, he learned from Lord Lyndhurst (then Chancellor) that the real cause of the King's deep and abiding resentment was his firm conviction that Denman's Greek quotation from Dion Cassius conveyed, and had been intended to convey, a specific personal imputation against the King of being stained with a practice of revolting depravity, the case was changed. Denman, though no lover of the King, had not intended anything of *this* kind, and, as the belief that he *had* touched in some degree his honour as a high-bred gentleman, he became immediately most anxious to have the King's mind disabused on this point, and pressed Lord Lyndhurst to convey to His Majesty a formal written denial of there being any ground for the suspicion that had taken possession of the King's mind. Finding that Lyndhurst, though profuse and plausible in profession, was reluctant and dilatory in act, Denman obtained an interview on the subject with the Duke of Wellington, then Prime Minister, [2] who, though vehemently opposed to Denman in politics, in his usual straightforward and manly manner at once undertook the business and promised to urge it on the King's attention. Denman's note of the interview with the Duke, which took place on July 23, 1828, is thus communicated to his wife:

I am just come from the Duke. He says that there are feelings in the King's mind which it may still take some time to remove; that the Chancellor has really had no opportunity, and has shown a friendly disposition; that I must leave it to them to consider the best mode of doing it, and whether the one or the other should be the proposer; that many feelings as strong had been got over, but pressing the matter unreasonably could only defeat the object, as some feelings last longer than others. He said, however, repeatedly, ' I'll do it,' and with a most marked and animated manner. ' You may rely on me, I'll do it. The King must be made sensible how unreasonable such feelings are. I should like to feel my way a little, but even if I find the subject is not agreeable, I will yet press it, notwithstanding.' I told him that my present object was not to ask for a silk gown, but merely to remove the imputation, which I considered important even as a preliminary towards getting the silk gown, and absolutely necessary for my character. He said he understood me perfectly, that it was a fit thing to be done, and ' You may rely upon me, I'll do it.'

The next day (July 24), Denman drew up and

_____

[2] The Duke had become Prime Minister on January 28, 1828 (after the resignation of the Goderich administration), and continued so till Nov. 15, 1830.

signed a memorial to be presented to the King, disavowing in the strongest terms the imputation attributed to him.

Your memorialist [so runs the document] has heard with extreme sorrow, but with still greater astonishment, that a speech delivered by him in the discharge of his duty as an advocate in October 1820, has been perverted to a sense wholly foreign to his intention, and most abhorrent to his feelings—a passage quoted from a Greek historian for an entirely different purpose having been construed into an insinuation of a revolting nature against your Majesty.

He had the mortification to learn that your Majesty had been led to think him capable of giving utterance to such an insinuation.

Your memorialist sincerely declares that the misfortune of lying under this suspicion is heavier and more intolerable to him than any consequences to himself that can result from it.

He is particularly anxious of assuring your Majesty that from the first moment when he had authentic information that such a stigma had been affixed to his character, he has made every exertion in his power to remove it, having then, and repeatedly since that time, importuned the Lord Chancellor to lay before your Majesty his solemn disavowal of the offence imputed to him.

And he earnestly prays your Majesty to believe his declaration that no such insinuation was ever made by him, that the idea of it never entered his mind, and that he is utterly at a loss to conceive how it ever came to be suspected or could even be thought possible.

This memorial the Duke presented to the King, though not until after some considerable delay, so extremely reluctant was George IV. to enter on the subject, even with his friend and favourite 'Arthur.'

It was not till towards the close of the year that Denman, by the Lord Chancellor's appointment, waited on the Duke to learn the issue of the protracted, delicate, and difficult negotiation. His note of the interview is as follows:

On December 1, 1828, I met the Lord Chancellor by his own appointment at the Duke of Wellington's office in Downing Street. The Duke spoke to this effect: 'Mr. Denman, we have gained this point, but *I never had a tougher job in my life.* His Majesty certainly took great offence at this speech of yours, and had charged both Lord Chancellor Eldon and my Lord Chancellor (Lyndhurst) never on any account to mention your name to him. He has at length, however, permitted the explanation to be made, and has ordered that a patent of precedence be made out for you. His Majesty consented to this about six weeks ago, but he was desirous of stating his feelings with his own hand on your memorial, which he could not then do, and I am to read to you what he has written.' The Duke then read nearly what follows ——

Denman then proceeds to give from memory a surprisingly accurate version of the King's observations, the text of which, however, having been since made public in the recently issued volume (the 5th) of the Duke of Wellington's 'Civil and Political Correspondence,' will be substituted here, in place of Denman's recollections.[3]

The King has read the statements in the annexed memorial.

The King could not believe that the Greek quotation

---

[3] A proof of these observations of the King, and also of Denman's subsequent letter to the Duke, were very courteously communicated for the use of the present Memoir while the fifth volume of the 'Civil and Political Correspondence' was being carried through the press.

referred to had occurred to the mind of the advocate in the eagerness and heat of the argument; nor that it was not intended; nor that it had not been sought for and suggested for the purpose of applying to the person of the Sovereign a gross imputation.[4]

The King, therefore, considered it his duty to command the late Lord Chancellor Eldon and the Lord Chancellor Lyndhurst never to approach the King with the name of the memorialist.

Nevertheless, as the memorialist has distinctly denied, disowned, and disclaimed all intention to apply the quotation in question to the person of the Sovereign, and has expressed his sorrow that the King should have believed he intended so to apply it; and has, moreover, in his memorial, prayed His Majesty to believe that no such insinuation was ever made by him, that the idea of it never entered his mind, the King commands that he may have a patent of precedence from the day of its date [of the memorial that is, viz. July 24, 1828.]

Denman throughout life entertained a deep sense of the manly, disinterested, and zealous exertions of the Duke of Wellington in the conduct of this disagreeable and difficult business. On the day succeeding the interview he wrote to the Duke a letter of acknowledgment (evidently drawn up for the express purpose of being shown to the King), which is here also transcribed from the same volume of the Duke's correspondence to which reference has already been made :

[4] We know from Denman's own account of the mode in which his speech for the Queen was prepared that the King was quite right in supposing that the quotation had been studiously sought for and suggested. IIe was wrong in supposing that *Denman* ever meant to apply it to himself; what *Parr's* intention may have been is a matter more open to question.

My Lord,—At the risk of being thought troublesome, I take the liberty of stating more fully than it was possible to do yesterday at the interview with which you honoured me the sentiments excited in my mind by the communication of His Majesty's pleasure.

I hope that the simple fact of His Majesty's compliance with my request for promotion sufficiently proves that His Majesty is convinced of the truth of what I asserted in my vindication.   But, as this is a point on which no possibility of doubt should be permitted, I beg leave to repeat that assertion in the most solemn manner.

If I had been conscious of the real nature of the offence suspected, instead of asking for rank at the Bar, I should have deemed myself unworthy of being received into society. If I had known that the suspicion was entertained, my first care would have been to endeavour to remove it, nor would I have solicited any favour from the King, nor twice presented myself at His Majesty's court, till effectual measures had been taken for accomplishing that object.

I entreat your Grace to offer my dutiful acknowledgments to His Majesty for permitting an explanation on a subject so painful and delicate, and for granting the application I made to the Lord Chancellor.   I feel grateful, also, for the distinct avowal of the reason for my exclusion which His Majesty has condescended to make, and which has removed much unpleasant feeling from my mind.

To your Grace I cannot too strongly express my sense of obligation.   I am quite confident that you would not have urged any claim on my part with His Majesty without being fully convinced that the assertion made by me was true, and the opportunity of clearing my character from the imputation that rested on it is to me of inestimable value.

With the greatest respect and gratitude,

I have the honour to be, my lord,

Your Grace's most humble servant,

T. DENMAN.

50 Russell Square: December 2, 1828.

The removal of the long-standing royal proscription against Denman was hailed by men of all opinions and classes with sincere and deep-felt satisfaction. As illustrating the estimation and regard then generally entertained for him, it may be as well to transcribe some out of the many letters of congratulation which on this occasion poured in upon him, and which have been preserved among his papers with unusual care.

His old and steady friend Lord Holland writes as follows from Brighton, December 7, 1828.

Dear Denman,—I do, indeed, rejoice most warmly at an act, however tardy, of justice to you. It comes, I fear, a little too late to be of much pecuniary advantage in your profession ; but the sincere satisfaction it gives to so many, and, indeed, to all honest men, must afford you a gratification of a higher order.

It is a proof that your conduct and exertions in every good cause had not been thrown away upon the public. Lady Holland and Mr. Allen partake of my pleasure at this event, and beg to join in my congratulations.

Yours ever,
VASSALL HOLLAND.

Spring Rice (afterwards Lord Monteagle) writes from the same place :

My dear Denman,—I cannot refuse myself the pleasure of one line of congratulation. A tardy act of justice has been done in your case, but one called for loudly by the public and the profession, as well as by your friends. I have been looking out anxiously for the event, and confess I envy the Tory Duke the honour of this, *his* act. Every one I hear speak on the subject is rejoiced, and views the matter in a right light. We have all the world at Brighton. The Hollands, Hallam, Rogers, Dudley, Goderich, Lord Essex,

Duke of Devonshire, Sturges Bourne, Edward Ellice, Lady Lyndhurst, &c., &c.

With compliments to Mrs. Denman,

Believe me ever very truly yours,

SPRING RICE.

Abercromby (afterwards speaker of the reformed Parliament, created on his retirement Lord Dunfermline), and Lord Rosslyn, then a leader of the moderate Whigs, write in the same strain. Abercromby says, 'However I may personally regret that this act of justice was not done to you by your political friends, it yet adds to your victory that it has been wrung, by the urgency of your claims, from one on whom you can have had no hold from sympathy in your public feelings and conduct.' Lord Rosslyn writes, 'I cannot but hail the appointment as of good omen, not only of the times, but of the probability that you may aspire with a reasonable hope to the highest honours to which distinguished and unshaken integrity and brilliant success at the Bar can lead.'

The following highly characteristic communication came from his sincere friend, the gifted, eccentric, and honest Lord Nugent, the genial 'Lord of Lilles:'

Lilles: December 10, 1828.

Dear Denman,—One line of congratulation on the advancement which I saw, for the first time to-day, noticed in my 'Times.' My wife also desires me to join her congratulation, sympathising with the best of you as she does in her love of a *silk gown*, and having, just like you, succeeded in getting one, which I brought with me from Ireland, where, I believe, by law, none but Protestant ladies may wear them —a regulation plainly disadvantageous to trade when well understood.

I am glad on every account that you were not deceived in your Duke. From the beginning I thought that the not allowing you to be proscribed on account of your having once done your duty in preventing a client from being murdered by her husband was an act of justice and good sense which was very likely to tickle his fancy. It almost gives me hopes of seeing him give in to another frolic of the same sort on a larger scale of justice and policy elsewhere. [Catholic Emancipation—in a few weeks the writer's hopes were realized.]

You will have some holidays, short ones, at Christmas : will you come and give us part of the benefit of them? This is the best season for cutting down trees. And the two chestnuts still stand saucy and menacing, as if there were not such a thing existing in the world as a 'fell serjeant,' King's or Commons', to keep them within bounds of decency. When will you come? And will you bring your sailor [his son Joseph, now the Admiral] with you, which will double your welcome.

Yours ever truly,
NUGENT.

Lord Nugent's suggestion (soon to be verified) that the Duke's act of justice to Denman was probably an augury of a still grander act of justice to the Catholics is shared by another correspondent, William Smith, of Norwich, a leading light among the Whigs of those days, who writes (*inter alia*) as follows :

I have been intending every day to express to you the pleasure I felt on learning what the Duke had done for you and for us. It does not seem to me at all fit to be considered as an individual favour, but as a symptom of right feeling awakened on a question where it is of so much importance to us that it should prevail, and as affording a presumption that certain great men mean better than many people give them credit for.

To his more intimate personal friends the event seems, probably from the long and weary expectation which had preceded it, to have been a source of more lively pleasure than any even of his later and greater successes. Hodgson, then living with his first wife at the Vicarage of Bakewell, sent this cordial effusion :

December 8, 1828.

My dear Denman,—It is with feelings of the most unfeigned delight that I have just read in the papers the announcement of the performance of a long-delayed act of justice. If what is said of a high personage be true, his conduct on this occasion enhances the value of the act, and makes it approach to an *amende honourable*. For your friends, although they must indeed feel on this occasion that ' *Worth* makes the man,' &c., yet as *Prunella* has its value too, they cannot but rejoice at its falling on such worthy shoulders. God bless you, my dear Denman, and your wife and children. Mrs. Hodgson cordially joins in the above, and I am

Yours affectionately,
F. HODGSON.

Among Denman's early friends on the Midland Circuit was, as previously mentioned, William Empson, a person of very considerable literary accomplishments, but of health too delicate for the rough work of the Bar, and which compelled him frequently to winter in Italy or in various invalid stations in the south of England. On this occasion he sent his congratulations from Torquay.

December 6, 1828.

My dear D.,—My mother is far from well, and she being asleep on the sofa, I opened Tindal's frank, as the ' Times ' had certified by the mouth of Dr. Birkbeck that the Duke had realized his promise. I had waited for a word from you to avoid possible mistakes. Make me congratulated and -tory duly to your wife. There are few things, indeed, that could have happened in this unlucky planet of ours which would give me half the pleasure. As Hone said of himself on my apologizing for having lampooned him in the 'Edinburgh,' 'it is the first act of justice that has been done to you these six years.' Beloved as you are, there are few single acts by which the Duke could have achieved more Benthamically 'the greatest happiness of the greatest number.'

Ever yours,
W. E.

His aged mother, then residing with her widowed daughter, Mrs. Baillie, in Cavendish Square, thus characteristically expressed her joy at the long deserved and long withheld promotion, and her letter probably caused Denman sincerer pleasure than any other which he received upon this fortunate occasion—the turning-point, as it afterwards proved, of his distinguished professional career.

Cavendish Square: December 3, 1828.

With a heart overflowing with love and gratitude to our Heavenly Father, my dear son, I most heartily congratulate you and yours upon your having at last obtained what you have so long merited. In our repeated disappointments I consoled myself with a sentence which you and I learned in our youth,

> 'Tis not in mortals to command success,
> But we'll do more, Sempronius, we'll deserve it.

That this and every acquisition you may make may prove a permanent blessing to yourself and family will ever be my constant and ardent prayer. If I could move I should fly to you on the wings of love; but as I am stationary, and you all know where to find me, I hope it will not be long before

I have the opportunity of showing some of you how cordially
I sympathize in all your concerns.

Give my kind love to your wife, with many thanks for her
note. If she will take the trouble of providing you with
such a silk gown as is suitable to the occasion, I shall have
great pleasure in paying for it.

Believe me always,
Your affectionate mother,
E. DENMAN.

CHAPTER XVII.

DUKE OF WELLINGTON'S MINISTRY—DENMAN M.P. FOR NOTTINGHAM AGAIN.

A.D. 1828 TO 1830.   ÆT. 49 TO 51.

Lord Goderich resigns—Duke of Wellington succeeds, January 1828—Lord Eldon left out of the new ministry—The reason why—Policy of concession in matters of religious liberty—Repeal of Test and Corporation Acts, 1828—Of Catholic Disabilities, 1829—Denman's delight at Catholic Emancipation—Letter on it to his eldest daughter, Mrs. Wright—The Duke's position—Peel's position—Party rancour—The conversion of Saint Peel—Denman at Holkham in Christmas Vacation of 1829–30—Letter to Mrs. Wright—Coke's anecdotes of Fox—Burke and Windham—Dinner at Lord Petre's, 1790—Fox demolishes the confectionary Bastille—Burke implacable—Windham first opposes, then joins Burke—Finally re-unites with the Whigs—Coke of Holkham in his seventy-eighth year—Routine of life at Holkham House—Its pictures—Sir Joshua's 'Fox'—Denman at Covent Garden with his children, January 1830—Letter to Mrs. Wright—'Ferocious Dubashes'—Fanny Kemble as 'Juliet'—'Cock Robin'—Walk home through the snow—Extract from letter to Mrs. Hodgson—Further criticism on Fanny Kemble's 'Juliet'—Pasta and Mademoiselle Mars as 'Desdemona'—'Othello' at the Théâtre Français—Rogers' account of the struggle between the Classicists and Romanticists at Paris—Letter to Mrs. Wright resumed—Political aspects of the time—Ministry weak—Peel irretrievably damaged—Prospects of law reform—The Whigs—The Ultra-Tories—The old 'House of Mumpsimus'—Lord Wynford and the Duke of Cumberland—Continued ill-feeling of George IV. against Denman—Avoids a personal interview with him as Common Serjeant—Town talk as to this—Brougham's letter on it to Lord Grey, January 10, 1830—Attacks on King in the 'Times'—Shaky position of the Wellington Ministry—Sir J. Scarlett's law reforms—Legal Terms fixed—Welsh Judicature abolished—Three English judges added—Death of George IV.

and accession of William IV., June 26, 1830—French Revolution of July—Its effect on England—Eldon's forebodings—Temper of the country—Dissolution (July 24) and General Election—Denman triumphantly returned for Nottingham—Anecdotes of his canvass—Brougham for Yorkshire—His astonishing canvass—Just exultation at his victory—Denman's letter to Merivale, August 25, 1830—Doubts as to expediency of vote by Ballot, but no doubt that it should be tried if desired as a protection.

AFTER Canning had been 'destroyed by Wellington and Grey'[1] a feeble attempt was made by Lord Goderich to carry on the administration. It soon failed, as all men foresaw it must, and on January 8, 1828, Lord Goderich resigned. The Duke of Wellington was sent for, and, after some delay, succeeded in forming a ministry, with Lyndhurst as Chancellor, and Peel as Secretary of the Home Department and leader of the House of Commons.

Lord Eldon, to his great indignation, had not been consulted as to the new arrangements, nor requested to take part in the ministry, even as President of the Council: the only thing done to propitiate him was the reappointment of Wetherell as Attorney-General in the place of Scarlett.[2]

The reason of the old Chancellor's exclusion soon became apparent. The Duke of Wellington and Mr. Peel were both convinced that some concession to the spirit of the times, especially in matters bearing upon religious liberty, had become imperatively necessary, and the first step taken in pursuance of this reluctant

---

[1] Hookham Frere's epigram.

[2] Wetherell retired soon after the passing of the Catholic Relief Bill, and was succeeded by Scarlett, who continued in office till the formation of the Whig ministry in November 1830.

and tardy conviction was the Government measure for the relief of the Dissenters by the repeal of the Test and Corporation Acts, the third reading of which was finally carried in the House of Lords, by a large majority, before the end of April 1828.

Lord Eldon recounts with pious indignation how the Government, 'to their shame be it said, had got the archbishops and most of the bishops to support this revolutionary bill;'[3] he also records how he himself 'had fought against it like a lion,' though, as he expresses it, 'my talons had been cut off,'[4] by which playful figure he apparently alludes to his desertion by the dignitaries of the Church.

The stout old Tory champion was too keen-sighted not to discern clearly what must inevitably follow on this fatal first step in the path of liberality and justice. 'What they (i.e. the archbishops and bishops) can mean,' he says, 'they best know, for nobody else can tell; and sooner or later, perhaps in this very year— *almost certainly in the next*—this concession to the Dissenters must be followed by a like concession to the Roman Catholics.'[5]

The prophetic foreboding was verified to the letter. Wellington and Peel, having to choose between a civil war in Ireland and the political emancipation of the Catholics, decided on the latter alternative, and when Parliament met, on February 5, 1829, the King's speech, to the amazement and dismay of all staunch

---

[3] Twiss's 'Memoirs of Lord Eldon,' vol. iii. p. 37.
[4] Ibid. p. 44.
[5] Ibid. p. 38.

Protestants, was found to contain a paragraph recommending the Legislature 'to review the laws which impose civil disabilities on His Majesty's Roman Catholic subjects.'

What followed is matter of familiar history, and need only be glanced at here. Lord Eldon, representing the alarmed bigotry of the country (he was entrusted with no less than 900 petitions against the Bill), declared in the House of Lords that, ' If he had a voice which would sound to the remotest corner of the empire, he would re-echo the principle which he most firmly believed, that if ever a Roman Catholic was permitted to form part of the Legislature of this country, or to hold any of the great executive offices of the Government, from that moment the sun of Great Britain would be set.'[6]

Times had so far changed that even in that assembly of peers and prelates the solemn warning was received with an irreverent laugh, and, after infinite debate, and the bitterest display of party animosity both in and out of Parliament, the third reading of the Relief Bill was, on April 10, 1829, carried in the House of Lords by a majority of 213 against 109, and, three days later (April 13), after many hysterical protests of the King to the old ex-Chancellor that he was miserable beyond what words could express, that he was in the state of a man with a pistol presented to his breast, and much other maudlin stuff of the same kind, it finally received the royal assent and became one of the laws of the land.

[6] Twiss's ' Memoirs,' vol. iii. p. 63.

What Denman's feelings on the matter were may be judged of by the following extract from a letter written by him to his eldest daughter, Mrs. Wright, soon after the introduction of the ministerial bill :

I thank you heartily for your congratulations on what I consider the greatest event that has happened for the last hundred years. It gave me the more pleasure because I confidently augured its completion from the Duke's noble conduct towards myself. The redress of a single act of injustice is a jubilee for honest men, and the establishment of general rules for preventing the repetition of acts of injustice is one of the noblest works of legislation. How infinitely more gratifying to redress the wrongs of millions, inflicted by the Legislature itself, deceived by false pretences, and perpetuated by the interested bigotry of ages. The Duke and Mr. Peel will find their reward first in their own consciousness of rectitude (*pulcherrima premia primum Dii moresque dabunt vestri*);[1] but still more perfectly, and more permanently, in witnessing the restored prosperity of Ireland, and the strength and union of the empire consolidated. The situation of Mr. Peel, indeed, is not quite so enviable as that of his illustrious colleague, but it is impossible to doubt that he has taken his present course in the full persuasion that it is both right and necessary. For my own part, I have long suspected that he had undergone a change of sentiment, and has done some violence to his own understanding in the long resistance he has made. But his offence, whatever it may be, has been more than expiated by the torrent of abuse poured out against him by his quondam friends. Never was so fierce an attack made to run down a heretic. The Pope's Bulls of the thirteenth century are nothing to the anti-Pope's anathemas of our time. Such attacks have generally some small admixture of wit and

---

[1] Denman's eldest daughter, being married to a ripe scholar, Latin quotations are often to be found in her father's letters to her : she was herself also a very accomplished person.

playfulness, but in all this infernal *fire-work* I have only seen one squib deserving of the name, *viz.*—the Pope has ordered a new festival in the Calendar—*The Conversion of St. Peel.*

In the Christmas Vacation of 1829–30, Denman spent some days at Holkham, in Norfolk, the seat of the great Whig landowner, Mr. Coke, who, having represented Norfolk in Parliament for considerably more than half a century, was in 1837 elevated to the peerage by Lord Melbourne's Government as Earl of Leicester.[8] Denman describes this visit in a letter to Mrs. Wright, only a portion of which has been preserved. The anecdotes it relates of Fox, Burke, and Windham, have appeared elsewhere, [9] but will bear repetition, and the account it gives of the habits and character of the venerable host, then in his seventy-eighth year, is too interesting to be omitted.

Mr. Coke was extremely intimate with Mr. Fox, both personally and politically, and relates many particulars of his intercourse with him which are worth remembering. You recollect that Burke, after going all possible lengths during the American War, turned violently against his old friends when the French Revolution broke out, and attacked Fox in Parliament with ferocity. Lord Petre, in the hope of reconciling them, made a large dinner (in 1790), which both attended. No traces of disagreement; the most delightful conversation; the ladies remained till 4 o'clock in the morning; a measured declaration of different and even opposite sentiments, but nothing that savoured of hostility. After dinner the confectioner covered the table with a perfect model of the

---

[8] Thomas William Coke, of Holkham, son of Wenman Roberts, who assumed the name of Coke on succeeding to the estates of Thomas Coke, Earl of Leicester, his maternal uncle. Born, 1752; member for Norfolk from 1774 to 1832; created Earl of Leicester, 1837; died 1842, æt. 90.

[9] In Lord John Russell's 'Memoirs of Fox.'

Bastille. Burke was requested to demolish it, but said it would be sacrilege. 'Will not you, Mr. Fox?' said Lord Petre. Here Coke describes Fox saying with all his heart 'That I will,' and rising from his seat, knife in hand, to work he went with his short fat arms till the whole fabric was laid low. When the party separated the two great men were supposed to be on good terms again; but Burke would not be reconciled, and even on his death-bed, eight years after (1797), refused Fox's proffered visit. Even this did not prevent Fox from following him to his grave.

Windham, at the beginning of the Revolution, sided strongly with its friends and well-wishers, and thought Burke mad. He was invited to the same dinner, but (having heard that Burke was to be there and not that Fox was), he declined, because he would not dine at the same table with Burke after he had behaved so ill to Fox in Parliament. He soon afterwards turned short round. 'In this very room,' said Coke, 'Fox produced a letter written by Windham from Paris, (before his defection), expressing his most enthusiastic attachment to the cause of French liberty, and inviting Fox to go to Paris that he might become a member of the Jacobin club. Fox put the letter into the fire, saying it should never appear against Windham. They became friends again, and Windham remained united with the Whigs till his death.'

It is delightful to see Coke so very well, so perfectly un-broken in health and spirits. He gets up pretty early and busies himself about the great concerns of the place, breakfasts about ten, shoots or rides, taking a great deal of exercise, dines at six, goes down to family prayers (which are rather long) about eight, plays whist from nine to ten, and then retires. There does not seem to be a flagging moment through the day. I am confident that his great good humour does much to keep him in such good health. He has no single unpleasant feeling, out of politics, which operate as a blister, drain off every humour that approaches to peccancy, and leave the old man perfectly charitable and happy. His marriage and the birth of his beautiful family, and the company of so

sensible and cheerful a wife,[10] I am sure contribute largely to
the prospect of his going on for many years in the same course
of enjoyment.[11]

The house is full of pictures, valuable both as portraits and
works of art.   Sir Joshua's picture of Fox (the original of ours
and taking in more of the figure) unites both characters.
I am satisfied it is the finest picture Reynolds ever painted, the
colouring, uninjured, of extraordinary depth and brilliancy.
The busts and statues are fine; so is the library, abounding in
precious MSS., many brought from abroad by Lord Leicester,
who built the house, and many in the handwriting of the Chief
Justice Sir Edward Coke, who made the fortune and founded
the family.   You may judge of the moderation and liberality
with which the property is managed by the fact that even
in these times not a single tenant has applied to lower the
rent.

I am afraid of looking back, for I fear this letter is in the
style of some doting old chaplain, and I may yet repent and
keep it back.   Yet I think it will amuse you, and you may
burn it when you please.

A few days later, shortly after his return to town,
Mrs. Wright received another letter from her father,
written from Guildhall, the earlier portion of which
gives a sufficiently lively picture of a pantomime night
spent by Denman at Covent Garden, with some of the
younger members of his family.

Your kind reception [he writes] of my twaddle from Holkham tempts me (being at this moment a looker-on at Guildhall) to write you another letter.   I found all well, except
that your mother was suffering a little from the aguish pains
sometimes brought on by severe cold.   She seems better since
my return, a compliment all good wives should pay good

---

[10] His second wife, daughter of the sixth Earl of Albemarle.
[11] He survived till 1842, being in his 90th year at the time of his
death.

husbands, and the most acceptable of all. Joe's letters[12] gave us great pleasure, but what he wrote to Bessy[13] describing in strong terms the annoyance of rival ships' agents on his landing at Madras—'a set of wretches, called *dubashes*, almost tore me to pieces, till I knocked one down, and the rest became less furious, and I at last made my escape in a palanquin'—really produced no little alarm until I translated the statement into less figurative language.[14] On the same evening, places having been taken for Covent Garden, I joined the party, chaperoning your two elder sisters[15] and your two little brothers.[16] The girls were delighted with the popular actress, Fanny Kemble. Lewis wished that he and she were of the same age, that he might propose to her, but still did not enter deeply into the sorrows of Romeo and Juliet. George declared war against the tragedy, war to the knife, and longed for Cock Robin, which, it must be confessed, is but an indifferent pantomime. What do you think of our Russian hardihood? We missed our carriage (if it was there, which I doubt), and walked home [to Russell Square] at midnight in a thick snow, the girls with nothing on their heads. I sent them off at once to bed and whey, and not the least cold has ensued.'

In a letter written about the same time to his second daughter (afterwards the Honourable Mrs. Hodgson), after relating the adventures of the same evening, he

[12] 'Joe' is the present Admiral, the Hon. Joseph Denman, then serving as a lieutenant in one of His Majesty's ships in the Indian Seas.

[13] Denman's second daughter, Elizabeth, now the Hon. Mrs. Hodgson.

[14] Anglo-Indian readers will remember the horror caused in the House of Commons at the time of the mutinies by the description of the wounded who were carried off by 'ferocious *Dhoolies*'—the Indian word for ambulances.

[15] Fanny and Margaret, then seventeen and fifteen, now the Hon. Lady Baynes and the Hon. Mrs. E. Cropper. Denman calls them 'elder' to distinguish them from the two who were then children, Ann and Caroline.

[16] George, then ten, now the Hon. Mr. Justice Denman; Lewis, then nine, now the Hon. and Rev. Lewis Denman.

adds a few criticisms on Fanny Kemble's acting, and some particulars as to Shakespeare at the Théâtre Français in that early epoch of the struggle between the Romanticists and the Classicists.

I had seen Fanny Kemble two months ago, and thought very highly of her performance. Last night [the pantomime night] I only witnessed the last act, which is not Shakespeare, but a botch of some moon-struck stage-manager—a motley collection of dullness and mock-finery, extravagance and feebleness. The grand alteration is to make Juliet awake while Romeo is still alive—a situation the most tragical that can be imagined—but Miss Kemble certainly produced no great effect in it, and my impression is that she has now reached the highest point of her reputation, and will not carry it higher.[17]

Have you ever seen your favourite Pasta as Desdemona? I am told she makes a strong fight for her life : well, now the same scene is actually exhibited on the French stage! Mdlle. Mars undresses and goes to bed before the audience (after repeating the beautiful passage, 'My mother had a maid, called Barbara,' omitted on our stage), and while she is being smothered, defends herself manfully. Rogers, the poet, was there the first night, and saw the violent struggle between the two parties—the Classic and Romantic. After the play an actor came forward, announcing 'Mesdames et Messieurs, cette tragedie de Shakéspeare!'—prodigious tumult, which lasted many minutes! The silence which was at length obtained proved the success of the Romantic party, for after it the reaction of applause was excessive, and then the actor mended his address, 'Cette tragedie du *grand* Shakéspeare!' This decided the victory, and the tragedy has had an immense run in the theatre, which, in classic hands, had become a desert.

[17] In this anticipation Denman was not far wrong.

In the latter part of the same letter to Mrs. Wright from which an extract has already been made, Denman passes to graver subjects, and thus gives his impressions as to the political aspects of the time :

I think I can tell you on good authority that Wellington is not at this time in the royal favour. The shock of the Catholic affair has not, it seems, passed away, and the reaction is even now producing some bad feeling. The Premier's security consists in the utter impossibility of replacing his ministry, poor as it is, with the exception of himself and Peel, *who is certainly much damaged*. But the Whigs must take part with Wellington if undermined by Court intrigues, and the ultra-Tories are so contemptible in talent that even the vile subserviency by which they would recommend themselves to personal partiality cannot promote them.

I conjecture that Legal Reform will lead to an early explosion in Parliament, for Government means to propose large alterations (including the abolition of the Welsh Judicature). The Chancellor is very likely to stand alone in the House of Lords, with the certain opposition of the old and venerable '*House of Mumpsimus*' — Eldon, Redesdale, Manners—with very uncertain support from Tenterden. In this position, the late Chief Justice Best, now Lord Wynford,[18] with considerable talent and ready eloquence, and the influence of the Duke of Cumberland, whose known adviser he is, may possibly play a part as beneficial to himself as injurious to the ministry and the public. If at such a moment the King should rat, the Cabinet is dissolved.

The House of Commons, also, is most strangely situated,

---

[18] Created 1829. William Draper Best, born 1767; called to Bar, 1789; Serjeant, 1800; Solicitor-General to Prince Regent, 1813; Attorney-General, 1816; Judge of King's Bench, 1818; Chief Justice of Common Pleas, 1824; retired, 1829, and then created Lord Wynford; died 1845, æt. 78. Foss's 'Lives of the Judges,' vol. ix. p. 9.

for though the Sadler[19] party, of themselves are weak, there is so much deterioration in Peel, that Vesey Fitzgerald was to be put forward as a chief; but his health prevented this, and he is almost blind. The ministry, therefore, must rely on the forbearance of Brougham, Huskisson, Lord Palmerston and others, some of whom can be but little depended on.

I must say that the manner in which my name has been mixed up with late proceedings at Windsor has annoyed me a good deal. Whether the King has expressed any personal feelings I know not, but I have a right to the argument against it which arises from the explanation of last year, followed by a patent of precedency, the order for which His Majesty wrote with his own hand on the back of my memorial. Can there be a greater libel than to suppose him still to cherish animosity. Ferocious attacks have been made upon him in the 'Times,' both on this and other grounds, with invidious contrasts between him and his Prime Minister, such as might have been circulated by some of Hugh Capet's partizans before he turned out his master.

The above reference to the 'late proceedings at Windsor' is thus explained.

The Recorder was taken ill in November 1829, and in his absence the duty would have devolved on Denman, as Common Serjeant, of going down to Windsor, and presenting the report of the Old Bailey Sessions to the King in council. The council at which Denman ought thus in due course to have appeared was suddenly put off, and it was generally suspected and reported that this postponement took place to give the Recorder time to recover, and thus save the King the annoyance of a

---

[10] Michael Thomas Sadler, M.P., renowned in those days for anti-Catholic orations and anti-Malthusian treatises, born 1777, died 1835.

personal interview with the Common Serjeant.   In the event the Recorder managed to get down to Brighton in time for the next council, and the dreaded interview was thus avoided.   Brougham, writing to Lord Grey, on January 10, 1830 (about the date of Denman's letter to Mrs. Wright), thus alludes to the circumstance, which, at the time, was a current topic of town talk :

The Recorder [he says] has made a great exertion to relieve his sovereign : ministers were quarrelling with the King in such a way that there is no saying where it might have ended.   It is very absurd not to make Denman a judge, which would be a most perfect and popular appointment, and get rid of their difficulty at once.   But really, if personal exclusions are to be allowed, and personal caprice to weigh, as in Wilson's and Denman's case (I say nothing of my own, because I defy King and ministers to injure me in any manner of way, and it would be well for them, perhaps, if they could say as much of me), and if the King is humoured in these things, we might as well be living in Algiers.[20]

The precarious position of the Wellington administration, and the causes of it, are correctly pointed out in the extracts just given from the last cited letter to Mrs. Wright.   The ministry, in fact, never recovered from the consequences of the great schism in the Tory party which had been brought about by the Catholic Relief Bill, and for many months before its final extinction was kept in existence rather by the forbearance of its former foes than by the support of its former friends.

With regard to the measures of Law Amendment alluded to in the letter—the abolition of the Welsh

---

[20] 'Memoirs,' vol. iii. p. 17 ; see also same volume, pp. 11, 12.

judicature, the increase in the number of English judges from 12 to 15, and the rendering the commencement of the legal terms fixed instead of moveable—they were all carried into effect in 1830, while Sir James Scarlett (who had in the previous year succeeded Wetherell on his resignation) was the Attorney-General of the Tory Government.[21]

Events were close at hand which precipitated the fall of the already tottering Government. The King died on June 26, 1830, and was succeeded by William IV. On July 24 Parliament was dissolved; and on the 27th began the Paris Revolution, which, after three days of street fighting, made Louis-Philippe, by grace of a successful insurrection, Citizen King of the French.

The effect in England of this great popular triumph was indescribable. It fanned to a flame the political and social discontent which had been long smouldering in the heart of the nation. It became obvious that the old aristocratic system of government could no longer be maintained unchanged. The elections, held in the very midst of this excitement, went strongly against the ministerial candidates, and ominous cries for Parliamentary Reform were heard on all sides.

Old Eldon, anxiously watching the signs of the times, writes to his daughter, Lady Bankes, 'It will require a master-head, such as Pitt had, and nobody now has

---

[21] The three new judges rendered necessary by the increase in the numbers of the judicial bench—Pattison, Alderson, and Taunton—were sworn in on November 12, 1830.

in this country, to allay what is brewing here—a storm for changes, especially for Reform in Parliament.'[22]

Denman felt that the time was come for resuming an active part in political life. He resolved to stand for Nottingham, in compliance with a very influential requisition, and was returned with triumphant success.[23]

Mr. Walton in his 'Random Recollections of the Midland Circuit' has given a graphic sketch of Denman's electioneering prowess, and of his popularity at this time, with the people of Nottingham.

The assizes for Nottingham were being held at the very time the election was on, and while in court Denman was informed of the retirement of his opponent [Mr. Bailey]. Speedily divesting himself of his wig and gown, he hurried to the Exchange Rooms in Nottingham's famous market-place, from a window of which building he addressed a multitude, in number many thousands. There is no doubt Denman was always a great favourite with the constituency of Nottingham. On the occasion alluded to, the writer, being in the crowd, was attracted by, and much struck with, the appearance of an old man some eighty years at least, his head bare, and his grey locks hanging down the sides of his face, while, with his hands clasped on his breast, he was gazing intently on Denman, whose nervous eloquence was pouring through the great assemblage of persons with thrilling effect ; and there was that old man, his hands held in the manner I have described, while, with tears streaming down his cheeks, he kept calling out, ' God bless him! God bless him !'[24]

[22] Letter to Lady Bankes, August 19, 1830. Twiss's 'Memoirs, vol. iii. p. 115.

[23] His colleague was General Sir R. C. Fergusson ; their opponent, Mr. T. Bailey, a local wine merchant, only polled 226 votes.

[24] First series, pp. 15, 16. Mr. Walton also describes with much effect an evening meeting of the Nottingham lambs at the 'Durham

It was now that his illustrious friend, Henry Brougham, won the crowning glory of his life, and after a canvass which was itself a miracle of superhuman activity, became one of the members for the great county of York.

Denman, writing to his wife from the midst of his own contest at Nottingham, says, in reference to this great achievement, 'Brougham is making a wonderful progress through Yorkshire—travelling 100 miles and making speeches to 70,000 people a day.'

Brougham himself, in his 'Memoirs,' thus describes his own just exultation at his great victory. 'I may say, without hyperbole, that, when as knight of the shire I was begirt with the sword, it was the proudest moment of my life. My return to Parliament by the greatest and most wealthy constituency in England was the highest compliment ever paid to a public man. I felt that I had earned it by the good I had done, and that I had gained it by no base or unworthy acts.' [25]

Denman, shortly after his return for Nottingham, on August 25, 1830, wrote a letter to his old friend Merivale, containing, among other things, his views, or rather his doubts, as to vote by Ballot, a subject to which recent legislation has given some degree of fresh interest.

Touching the Ballot [he writes] it surely would effect no

Ox,' at which Denman smoked an *Alderman* (long clay) pipe, and at the particular request of his humble friends sang, with vast applause, a song, the burden of which was

> ' " Sessions " and " sizes " are gone and past,
>   And the jolly old judge is gone at last.'

[25] ' Memoirs,' vol. iii. p. 42.

great improvement at Old Sarum; probably none in any place where the number of voters falls short of 300, because in such places concealment would hardly be practicable.

The substantial benefits are expected, I presume, in counties and in borough constituencies really popular; bribery would be avoided in the latter, undue influence in both.

This result, however, appears to me very doubtful.   Bribes would be given for promises, and those promises would generally be kept; the moralist, indeed, asserts the converse, but I believe that, as a rule, they would be kept, from the superior strength of the rude point of honour as a motive to the public spirit of the bribed promiser.

The friends of the ballot assume that bribes would never be offered, on account of the uncertainty.   It requires much more reasoning to convince me of this.   In numerous cases there would practically be no uncertainty, for the great majority would make no secret of their own votes, proudly rejecting all disguise, and feeling it a duty to avow their political course.

Thus the field for speculation might be so narrowed as to convert surmises into confident, often just, opinions on the votes actually given : the same thing may be said of undue influence.

Serious evils of another kind belong to the very nature of ballot—deception, with all its debasing and vicious train. The apparent taking for granted that public duty must give way to private interest, which is not true, would be justly resented in the case of jurymen, magistrates, &c.

The Duke of Newcastle's vengeance, inflicted by guess work, instead of proceeding from knowledge, would involve the painful sensation of seeing your neighbour ejected for *your* vote, which he is *suspected* of having given.   If it is answered that in order to baffle speculation *all* would keep secret their votes, the thing is impossible.   Most men's line would be known from the whole tenor of their lives, unless hypocrisy is to be always at work, and the good cause would lose the benefit of being countenanced by respected and enlightened men.

These objections have passed through my mind : all may receive a satisfactory answer in some clever and comprehensive argument which may have been published. Having as yet met with nothing of the kind I am only *feeling my way*. Meanwhile, it seems to me that the public mind is running away with a strong opinion respecting a very complex and difficult subject without due discussion, and looking to only one of its numerous bearings, as to which I strongly suspect that everything is assumed.

If there is such an argument as I have alluded to, I should be much obliged by your sending it. Has Herman [26] made up his mind on it ? I am really open to conviction ; and, moreover, though unconvinced, if the great mass of the tenantry and artizans of England call for the Ballot as a protection against oppressive interference, *no theoretical doubts ought to prevent them from having the experiment tried.*

[26] Merivale's eldest son, the present Permanent Under-Secretary for India. Mr. Herman Merivale had taken his first class in Classics at Oxford in 1827, and the Chancellor's prize for the English Essay in 1830; he was called to the Bar on November 16, 1832.

CHAPTER XVIII.

LORD GREY'S MINISTRY—SIR THOMAS DENMAN, ATTORNEY-GENERAL.

A.D. 1830 TO 1831.   ÆT. 51 TO 52.

Opening of the New Parliament, November 2, 1830—Brougham's notice of motion on Parliamentary Reform for November 16—The Duke of Wellington's declaration in the House of Lords against any reform in Parliament, November 2, 1830—Denman's first speech in the new Parliament, in debate on the Address, November 3—His reference to and condemnation of the Duke's declaration—Effect of the Duke's declaration—Panic in London—The police maltreated and the Duke himself mobbed—The King and Queen prevented from going to the Lord Mayor's banquet—Lord Macaulay's description of the panic—Denman's speech on November 8, condemning the attacks on the police, and the outrage to the Duke—Peel's compliment to Denman on his speech—Denman's letter to Mrs. Wright of November 12, 1830 —He is of the 'young party'—Believes the Duke's position to be untenable—Had expected him to take up Parliamentary Reform as he had Catholic Emancipation—The Duke of Wellington resigns on November 16—Earl Grey's Ministry formed—Brougham, Chancellor —Denman, Attorney-General—Magnanimity of William IV. and its effects on Denman—His reference to it in the House of Commons— Denman's re-election for Nottingham—The Duke of Newcastle, in the House of Lords, complains of his speech on being re-elected— Brougham explains, and the Duke takes nothing by his motion— Denman's appointment as Attorney-General highly popular—Letter of congratulation from W. W. Pepys—Denman resigns the office of Common Serjeant—Thanks of the City for the manner in which he had discharged it—Testimony to the same effect of the Old Bailey Bar—Denman's opinion expressed in Parliament as to vote by Ballot, November 22, 1830—As to Lord (then Mr.) Campbell's bill for registration of deeds, December 16, 1830—Defence of Brougham from an attack by Sugden, and eulogies on him—Denman at close of 1830 and beginning of 1831 conducts the prosecution against the agrarian rioters, tried before the Special Commissions at Winchester and Salisbury—His humane and able conduct of the prosecution—Interest of the King in the proceedings—Correspondence thereon between Denman and the King through Sir Herbert Taylor—Sense of House of Commons as to value of Denman's exertions shown on Hunt's motion for an amnesty to all the convicts—Denman's speech on that motion, February 13, 1831—Denman's prosecutions, *ex officio*, against Carlile and Cobbett for stirring up the peasantry to insurrection—Passages selected for prosecution in Carlile's case ; in Cobbett's case—Carlile tried on January 10, 1831—Convicted and severely sentenced—Cobbett's trial postponed till July 1831—Cobbett's able speech in his own defence—'The lank and merciless Whigs,' &c.—The jury cannot agree and Cobbett is discharged—Denman, in consequence of this trial, in bad odour with the advanced Liberals—This was the last of Denman's *ex officio* prosecutions, though frequently afterwards pressed to prosecute at the instance of the King—Letter from Lord Grey on the subject, May 4, 1831—Mr. (afterwards Sir) Fowell Buxton's resolutions of April 15, 1831, for the abolition of Slavery—Denman's speech in favour of them—Letter from the venerable William Wilberforce introducing his son Samuel to Denman.

THE new Parliament opened on November 2, 1830, and on that very evening Brougham, in the House of Commons, gave notice that on that day fortnight (November 16) he would bring on the question of Parliamentary Reform, while in the House of Lords the Duke of Wellington, seizing the earliest opportunity of setting himself completely in opposition to the daily strengthening tide of popular sentiment, made the celebrated declaration that the House of Commons needed no reform at all, and that the Government would neither propose nor consent to any.

It may be worth while to reproduce from Hansard the text of this momentous expression of deliberate opinion and fixed resolve.

The Duke declared

That the legislative and representative system possessed

the full and entire confidence of the country—deservedly possessed that confidence ; that if, at the present moment, he had imposed upon him the duty of forming a legislature for a country like this, in possession of great property of various descriptions, he did not mean to assert that he could form such a legislature as they possessed now, for the nature of man was incapable of reaching such excellence at once, but his great endeavour would be to form some description of legislature which should produce the same results.

Under these circumstances he was not prepared to bring forward any measure of the description alluded to by the noble lord (Earl Grey). He was not only not prepared to bring forward any measure of this nature, but he would at once declare that, as far as he was concerned, as long as he held any station in the country, he should always feel it his duty to resist such measures when proposed by others.[1]

Denman, who had expected and (with his high esteem for the Duke) had hoped that Wellington, yielding to the manifestly expressed feeling of the country, would have taken up Parliamentary Reform as he had previously taken up Catholic Emancipation, was deeply disappointed and grieved at this declaration.

On November 3, the first occasion on which he addressed the new Parliament, he said, in reference to this subject :

It was matter of deep regret that a noble person at the head of the Government, who might be said to direct the destinies of Europe, had within twenty-four hours, and within 100 yards from that spot, declared that no proposal for Reform should be listened to : not only would the Government not bring forward a plan of Reform, as had

[1] Hansard, Parl. Deb., third series, vol. i., House of Lords, February 2, 1830.

been fondly expected, but no plan was to be listened to, no amendment of the constitution was to be suffered.

It would have been perfectly easy for Government to have conciliated the people of England by saying to them, 'We know that you have grievances and sufferings and abuses: we will provide an effectual remedy for these abuses, to these sufferings we are not indifferent.' But no, all was defiance, all was menace. 'We will put down sedition!' said His Majesty's ministers; but they would not put a word into the speech regarding the redress of the people's grievances in respect to that unconstitutional and intolerable abuse in the Representation of the People which made it stink in the nostrils of the country. The people mocked at it when they were told that they were represented in the Commons House of Parliament. The people had expected that the King's Government itself would come forward with some measure, and if the Government would not do it they looked to the House of Commons; and if that House would not do what it was their bounden duty to do, *the People would look to it themselves.*[2]

The effect on the People of the Duke's declaration of war was electric. The excitement in London and throughout the country became intense. The Duke himself was mobbed when going to consult his lawyers in Lincoln's Inn; Peel's new police force became the object of brutal attacks on the part of the populace; the King and Queen, who were to have gone in state to dine with the Lord Mayor on November 9, postponed their visit, by the advice of the Cabinet, owing to the apprehension entertained by ministers of a popular outbreak.

Lord Macaulay, in one of his brilliant Reform Bill

---

[2] Hansard, Parl. Deb., third series, vol. i. pp. 169–173.

speeches of the ensuing summer, thus paints, in a few vigorous and masterly strokes, the effect of the Duke's declaration and the panic of the time:

Early in last session the first minister of the Crown declared that he would consent to no reform; that he thought our representative system, just as it stood, the masterpiece of human wisdom; that if he had to make it anew he would make it just such as it was, with all its represented ruins and all its unrepresented cities. What followed? Everything was tumult and panic. The funds fell, the streets were insecure, men's hearts failed them through fear. Such was the state of the public mind that it was not thought safe for the Sovereign to pass from his palace to the Guildhall of his capital.[3]

It was in the thick of this panic and excitement, on November 8, the night preceding that of the City banquet, that Denman, for the second time this session, addressed the House. In the course of his speech, while vehemently denouncing the step taken by ministers in preventing the royal visit to the City as a measure founded on false alarms, and as needlessly inflicting a deep slur on the loyalty of the country, he at the same time took occasion to express, in manly and vigorous language, his abhorrence of the recent brutal treatment of the police, and of the violence and insult of which the Duke had lately been the object, and which he characterised ' as a cowardly outrage on the greatest man of the age, whose extraordinary military services in the cause of the country ought to have

[3] From the speech of July 5, 1831, on the second reading of the Reform Bill. Edition of speeches revised by Lord Macaulay himself.

shielded him from all personal attack on account of his political opinions.'[4]

Peel, who, in the spring of this year (May 3, 1830), had become Sir Robert by the decease of his father, while defending the postponement of the King's visit to the City, as a measure of absolutely necessary precaution, seized the opportunity of paying a high compliment to Denman on the tone he had taken in referring to the mob attacks on the Duke and on the police; 'a tone, however,' said the Home Secretary, 'which has not surprised me, knowing as I do, in common with every other person, the high and honourable character of that learned gentleman. They are sentiments that may draw down on him some unpopularity among the low and vulgar, but they are the sentiments of all respectable and good citizens in the state.'

On November 12, Denman wrote the following letter to his eldest daughter, Mrs. Wright, who had apparently expressed some alarm at the manifestations of the popular feeling. It shows clearly that Denman had at one time anticipated that Wellington and Peel would take the same line on the Reform of Parliament as they had before taken on the Relief of the Catholics:

I am entirely of the young party, and feel no alarm at all for the fate of the country. Never did the popular part of the Constitution exercise such a powerful influence. Our seasonable railing has rendered war in the Netherlands impossible, and our interference has kept the London

4 Hansard, Parl. Deb., third series, vol. i. p. 294.

populace in order, in spite of the most untoward and unjustifiable disappointment. Either measure would have thrown Parliament into the hands of the ministry, which would have taken all to themselves, in the case either of foreign war or insurrection—the former the hot-bed of all jobbery, the latter immediately producing arbitrary invasions of the Constitution.

The Duke's intemperate declaration against Reform stakes his power on that question. We expect to beat him on it, and he is said to be making prudent preparations for a change of position. When he astonished his hearers by that declaration (volunteered, but in vain, for the purpose of conciliating his Newcastle [5] enemies), the Duke of Richmond, alluding to the letter to Dr. Curtis,[6] said, 'these ministers will introduce Parliamentary reform in a fortnight.' I really believe they will endeavour to keep their places, though beaten on that great point. Such a state of things requires the utmost moderation on our part, and I only fear that Brougham will be too moderate on Tuesday (the 16th). Our debate is to last two, three, possibly four nights; both parties are confident of success. If we prevail, the question will be placed where I thought the Duke would have placed it at the opening of the session ; but with his own hostility to Reform publicly avowed, with the ridicule of retracting his opinion, and the odium of having rolled the King in the mire of his own great unpopularity, it seems quite impossible that things should go on thus.

I fully expected the Duke would have followed his own example on the Catholic question, and have compelled the Whigs to support his proposition for Reform. But he has now driven them to war, and has compelled them to turn out himself and all his incapable followers. However these party speculations may terminate, my hopes rest on the

[5] The then Duke of Newcastle was one of the leaders of the ultra-Tories.

[6] Written just on the eve of Catholic Emancipation, repudiating all notion of it.

intelligence and patriotism of the People, to which scarcely anyone does justice. So do not be in pain about public affairs, but take care of yourself.

The debate anticipated in this letter never took place. Unwilling to encounter Brougham's motion, fixed for the 16th, the Duke took the opportunity of giving in his resignation on the morning of that day, in consequence of an adverse vote of the previous evening, on an amendment of Sir Henry Parnell to Mr. Goulburn's motion for going into committee on the Civil List.[7]

Earl Grey was at once sent for, and before November 22 he had succeeded in forming the first Reform Administration.

Henry Brougham gave up the lead of the House of Commons, and one of the highest political positions ever held by an Englishman, ' a political position greater than any that could be bestowed by King or ministry,' to become Chancellor in the new administration.[8]

Denman, with the general approval of the public, and without any objection on the part of the King, was appointed Attorney-General (November 19).

The high-mindedness of William IV., in entirely overlooking the strong language that Denman on the Queen's trial had employed towards the Duke of Clarence, produced a strong effect of liking, respect, and

[7] Sir H. Parnell's amendment was for the appointment of a select committee to examine and report on the accounts connected with the Civil List. The numbers were 233 to 204; a majority of 29 against the ministry.

[8] 'Memoirs,' vol. iii. p. 81, where he enumerates his sacrifices for the party, and their subsequent gross ingratitude.

gratitude in the new Attorney-General towards the 'Sailor King.'

A few months after his appointment, having been coarsely rebuked in the House by Mr. Attwood as not having yet abandoned the habit in which he was once too prone to indulge, 'of uttering libels in that House,' Denman said:

An honourable gentleman opposite has alluded to me and some former transactions of my life. I do not envy the honourable gentleman any state of feeling that could prompt such allusions. I have no apology to make, and I never have made any apology for what I did, and was compelled to do, on behalf of the illustrious but unfortunate client whose interests were entrusted to me.

But since this unhappy subject has been invidiously obtruded on the notice of the House, I will not shrink from declaring that an illustrious personage, to whom it would be unparliamentary more particularly to allude, has given a more signal instance of magnanimity than history has ever recorded of any sovereign since the time of Henry V., when that high-minded and chivalrous monarch presented the sword and balance to the Chief Justice who had personally offended him.

The sword and balance were yet to be given by the royal 'Slanderer,' to the daring advocate who, in the fearless discharge of duty, had so designated him.

Denman was re-elected for Nottingham as a matter of mere form and without the shadow of an opposition, but in the course of his address to the electors he had made some remarks on the famous question of the Duke of Newcastle, then in everybody's mouth, regarding his borough of Newark, 'Have I not the right to do what I like with my own?' which induced that sapient wearer of the strawberry leaves to bring, on December 3, 1830, a formal complaint against His Majesty's Attorney-General in the House of Lords.

According to the report in the 'Morning Chronicle,' on which the Duke relied, the Attorney-General had said, 'I shall use my utmost efforts against the borough mongers. And I freely declare to you that the power which has called forth from a certain nobleman the *scandalous and wicked* interrogatory, "Is it not lawful for me to do what I like with my own?" ought to be abolished by the law of the land.'

Brougham having taken upon himself to explain, on Denman's assurance to that effect, that the two italicised epithets had been misreported, the subject dropped with no other result than that of making his grace of Newcastle a more conspicuous object of public dislike and ridicule than he was before. [9]

Denman's appointment as Attorney-General was the most popular that could possibly have been made. His high and honourable character, his engaging social qualities, and the general sense that was entertained of his having long been the victim of injustice and exclusion simply on account of his fearless discharge of duty, all contributed to this.

From among the many letters of congratulation which he received on his promotion, the following, from one of his old Eton and Cambridge friends

[9] Hansard, Parl. Deb., third series, vol. i. p. 750–760, House of Lords.

Pepys, [10] a very moderate Liberal, if a Liberal at all, has been selected for insertion here, as showing that the satisfaction felt at his appointment was by no means confined to the members of his own party:

Gloucester Place: December 1, 1830.

My dear Denman,—I would not obtrude myself during the first hurry of your appointment and re-election, but cannot let the occasion entirely pass away without my congratulations on the accomplishment of what I have always anticipated, I will not say from the very beginning of our acquaintance, for in those early days we did not look so far forward, but from those at least when you and our friend the Chief Justice of the Common Pleas [11] used to meet in my rooms at Cambridge. You see that, having nothing to boast of myself, I am obliged to plume myself upon *cum magnis vixisse*. As most of those with whom I converse are of very different politics to yours, I am the more pleased to find that, from the high estimation of your character, your appointment is generally approved of. This is more than I can say of that of all your friends, of many of whom they (and I, too), are desperately afraid.[12] Let what will happen, believe me,

Ever yours most truly,

W. W. PEPYS.

On becoming Attorney-General Denman, as a matter of course, resigned the office of Common Serjeant, which for eight years he had exercised with distinguished credit to himself, and great benefit to the public.

Immediately on his resignation, the Common Council

---

[10] Not Charles Christopher Pepys, afterwards Lord Cottenham, but William Willes Pepys, elder brother of the future Chancellor.

[11] Sir Nicolas Conyngham Tindal. He had become Chief Justice in the previous year, 1829.

[12] The allusion here is no doubt to Brougham.

of the City of London unanimously resolved that the thanks of the City should be presented to Sir Thomas Denman (for, as usual, he was knighted on becoming Attorney-General) for 'the eminent ability with which he has discharged the office of Common Serjeant, and especially for the zeal, integrity, and humanity with which he has exercised the judicial duties that have devolved upon him since his elevation to that important position.'

As referring to the same subject-matter, though belonging in point of date to a somewhat later period (that of his elevation to the Chief Justiceship), the following passage from an address by the Bar of the Old Bailey may as well be inserted here, expressing as it does in truthful, sincere, and well chosen language the sense of the profession as to Denman's high merits as a criminal judge.

' The manner in which you discharged the important duties of Common Serjeant, characterised as it was by politeness, impartiality, and, so far as was consistent with the public interests, uniform humanity, can never be forgotten by us. *It dignified the judgment seat, it endeared the judge, and filled all with confidence in the pure and learned administration of the law.*'

Shortly before his re-election for Nottingham, Denman, in presenting a petition from his constituents praying for a *thorough* reform of Parliament, including *vote by Ballot*, spoke of that measure as one requiring the fullest consideration, since so very large a portion of the country was favourable to it. 'In his private opinion,' he said, ' he was by no means convinced of its propriety by any arguments he had as yet heard, though he must confess himself quite open to conviction on the subject.'

On December 16, 1830, Mr. (afterwards Lord) Campbell, in a long and very able address, moved for leave to bring in a bill for establishing a general *register* for all *deeds* and instruments affecting real property in England and Wales.

Denman spoke in complimentary terms of the measure, ' proposed as it was by a lawyer of great eminence, and having the support of many of the most learned members of the profession. If the necessary calls on the attention of the Government at the present moment had prevented them from considering it so as to give it their declared support, still the House was greatly obliged to the honourable and learned member for having brought it forward, and he hoped it would be found that the Government could give it their full and cordial support.' [13]

On the same night, Sir Edward Sugden (now Lord St. Leonards), having, in a speech made by him in moving for returns as to the administration of justice in the Court of Chancery, thrown out some disparag-

---

[13] Hansard, Parl. Deb., third series, vol. i. p. 1265. Registration of *deeds*, as Lord Campbell himself came afterwards to admit, is not the true remedy ; the thing wanted, and *which must come*, is registration of *titles*, with an immediate and indefeasible Parliamentary title granted to all present holders of land. The difficulty in the way of this is the interested opposition of the attorneys, the most powerful of all bodies of men in this, the most lawyer-ridden of all countries under the sun. The lawyers are short-sighted in this matter; the vast increase in the number of land transfers, mortgages, &c., would soon render their practice, while less onerous, more lucrative than it is at present.

ing imputations on Brougham for having followed a course theretofore pursued, but, as Sugden contended, wrongly, by the appointment of solicitors instead of barristers to certain lucrative offices in the Court of Chancery, Denman, while defending the appointments, took occasion to pass a generous and sincere eulogium (not quite borne out in the result as to some of its anticipations) upon his illustrious friend then on the woolsack. 'Though he (Brougham) might not,' he said, ' be as practised an equity lawyer as the honourable and learned gentleman, yet he confessed he should feel himself most grievously mistaken if his noble friend did not turn out to be one of the greatest equity judges that ever presided in the Court of Chancery ; if he did not, in a word, equal all the expectations which that House had formed of him, if he did not fulfil all that was hoped from a man to whom no subject was too vast for his comprehension, nor any detail too minute to elude his research.' [14]

It was not long after his appointment as Attorney-General that Denman was called upon to perform the important and disagreeable duty of conducting the Crown prosecutions against the agrarian rioters o Hants, Wilts, and Dorset, who were tried before special commissions held at Winchester and Salisbury at the close of 1830 and the beginning of 1831.

These misguided and ignorant peasants, driven to despair by the pressure of starvation wages, and the cruel operation of the law of settlement, which made

[14] Hansard, Parl. Deb., third series, vol. i. pp. 1286–1288.]

parochial serfs of them, precluding them from carrying their labour into districts where it was scarce and well-remunerated from others in which it was super-abundant and miserably underpaid—had filled the south-western counties with terror in the later autumn of 1830, congregating in mobs, burning ricks, destroying threshing machines, and occasionally plundering farm-houses.

The humane, temperate, yet firm and dignified demeanour of the Attorney-General in the performance of this irksome and anxious duty was deservedly the subject of universal approval. Through Sir Herbert Taylor he submitted from time to time to the King, who was much interested in the matter, full reports of the proceedings, and by the same channel received the frank expression of the royal satisfaction.

Denman was much pleased with these letters, which he carefully preserved. They are all in the handwriting of Sir Herbert Taylor, and bear date respectively January 2, 5, and 10, 1831. It will be sufficient to cite a passage from that of January 5 : they are all in the same complimentary and even friendly strain, and show that the ' Come forth, thou slanderer,' of 1820, had been completely condoned.

I have had the honour of submitting to the King your letters of the 1st and 3rd, and His Majesty is much pleased to learn from the former that the expression of his approbation has proved so satisfactory to yourself and your colleagues. His Majesty is quite sensible, from all he hears, that there has been no relaxation of zeal and attention in the able discharge of your duties, and he feels that a tone has been given by your proceedings which must have a useful and important effect upon the public mind, and may tend more than anything else to check the recurrence of the mischief which has called for the labours of the Special Commission.'

The sense entertained by the House of Commons of the value of Denman's services as Crown prosecutor, and of the judicious lenity of his proceedings, was conclusively shown by the result of ' orator ' Hunt's motion on February 8, 1831, for an address to His Majesty ' praying for a grant of a general pardon and amnesty to the agricultural and other labourers convicted before the late special commissions.'

On a division this motion was rejected by 269 to 2, majority 267, the minority consisting of Hunt and Hume.

In the course of his speech in opposition to this motion, Denman, who was much cheered by both sides of the House, said, ' that though not less than 1,000 persons had been tried before these commissions, yet the honourable member for Preston (Hunt) had only been able to bring forward three cases of which, with all his enquiries among sources not the most favourably disposed towards the prosecution, he could complain as admitting of doubt with respect to the decision come to or the course adopted.'

With reference generally to the proceedings under the commission, Denman said :

He hoped the examples which had been made would correct errors, deter from future outrages, or should such unhappily occur, encourage a manful resistance. He congratulated himself, the House, and the country on this—that much of the evil had already been put down. He congratulated the

House that a great public evil had been boldly faced, that it had been put down without military conflicts, without shedding of blood in the field, as might have been apprehended; without the aid of any extraordinary enactments, but simply by a firm and temperate enforcement of a legal and constitutional authority. This was a subject on which, to the last hour of his life, he should continue to congratulate himself, whenever he reflected on the humble part he had taken in producing the result.[15]

In the course of his investigations the Attorney-General had become aware that the peasantry had been encouraged in their lawless proceedings by certain public writers, notably by the well-known William Cobbett and by Richard Carlile, the atheistic and revolutionary publisher of that day. Indignant at the thought that these writers should escape while the ignorant peasantry suffered, the Attorney-General was induced to file *ex-officio* informations against Carlile and Cobbett.

It may be of some interest, as showing the character of the ultra-political writing of that day, to reproduce the passages selected for prosecution from the respective pamphleteers.

Carlile addressed the 'rioters' thus:

November 27, 1830.

To the Insurgent Agricultural Labourers:

You are much to be admired for everything you are known to have done within the last month. Much as every thoughtful man must lament the waste of property, much as the country must suffer by the burnings of farm produce now going on, were you proved to be the incendiaries

<hr>

[15] Hansard, Parl. Deb., third series, vol. ii. pp. 246–309.

we should defend you by saying that you have more just and moral cause for it than any king or faction that ever made war had for making war. In war all destructions of property are counted lawful upon the ground of that which is called the law of nations. Yours is a state of warfare, and your ground of quarrel is the want of the necessaries of life in the midst of abundance. You see hoards of food, and you are starving. You see a government rioting in every sort of luxury and wasteful expenditure ; and you, ever ready to labour, cannot find one of the comforts of life. Neither your patience nor your silence has obtained from you the least respectful attention from that government. The more tame you have grown, the more you are oppressed and despised, the more you have been trampled upon ; and it is only now that you begin to display your physical as well as your moral strength that your cruel tyrants treat with you and offer terms of pacification. Your demands have been so far moderate and just, and any attempt to stifle them by the threatened severity of the new administration will be so wicked as to justify your resistance even to death and to life for life.

The passage selected for prosecution from Cobbett's 'Register' ran as follows :

December 11, 1830.

But without entering at present into the *motives* of the working people, it is unquestionable that their *acts* have produced good, and great good, too. They have been always told, and they are told now by the very parson that I have quoted above, that their acts of violence, and particularly the burnings, can *do them no good*, but *add to their wants* by destroying the food that they *would have to eat*. Alas ! they know better ! they know that one threshing machine takes wages from ten men ; and they also know that *they* should have none of this food, and that *potatoes and salt* (*their food*) do not burn. Therefore this argument is not worth a straw. Besides, they see and feel *that the good comes*, and comes *instantly*, too. They see that they *do* get some *bread* in consequence of the destruction of part of the corn; and while they see this, you attempt in vain to persuade them that what they have done is *wrong*. And as to one effect, that of *making the parsons reduce their tithes*, it is hailed as a *good* by ninety-nine hundredths even of men of considerable property; while there is not a single man in the country who does not clearly trace the reduction to the acts of the labourers, and especially *to the fires*; for it is the terror of these, and not the bodily force, that has prevailed.

The result of the two prosecutions was very different.

Carlile, who was tried on January 11, 1831, was convicted and sentenced to be imprisoned for two years, to pay a fine of 2,000*l.*, and to find recognizances in 1,000*l.* for two years more—a sentence which even in those times was regarded as sufficiently severe.

Cobbett's trial did not come on till July 1831. By that time the country had gone mad with the great excitement caused by the first rejection of the Reform Bill, and Cobbett, who, with characteristic energy, had thrown himself heart and soul into the movement, had risen to a height of popularity which even he had never before attained. He was loudly applauded on entering the Court to take his trial, still more loudly on concluding his speech, which was full of rough vigour and telling power. In the course of it he did not forget to remind the jury how ' a person never a hundred miles distance from Sir Thomas Denman had compared the late king to Nero, and called the present king a slanderer.' He declared that the Whigs, during their seven months' tenure of office, had, with their Whig Attorney-General, carried on more state prosecutions than the Tories in seven years. He denounced them as ' these Whigs, who have been out of office for five-and-twenty years, these lank Whigs, *lank and merciless as a hungry wolf*, who are now filling their purses with public money,' and who hated him for his honest and constant efforts to cut off useless places and pensions. ' That, gentlemen,' he exclaimed, ' is my true offence ; it is for this that I must be crushed, and to-day, gentlemen, they will crush me unless you stand between me and them.' Finally, he called the Lord Chancellor himself, that Harry Brougham of whom, as he reminded the jury, Mr. Attorney had once said boastfully that ' they kept together in their chivalry,' to prove that ' the said Harry ' had not so very long ago applied to him (Cobbett) for permission to republish in the ' Useful Knowledge Society ' a letter written by him many years before to the Luddites, condemning in strong terms the breaking of machinery.

The jury, who retired at half-past six to consider their verdict, were unable to agree : they were locked up all night, and the next morning, two of their number still holding out resolutely against a conviction, they were discharged.

The Attorney-General, who had incurred considerable odium among the advanced reformers by persisting in this prosecution (a public meeting in condemnation of his proceedings had been convened, under the presidency of Joseph Hume), was only too glad to enter a *nolle prosequi*.[16]

This was the last time that Denman, as Attorney-General, appeared as a public prosecutor *ex-officio* for libel.

The King, who was sensitive on the point, and who during the great excitement of the Reform struggle, especially in its later stages, was, together with the Queen, occasionally made the object of abuse, virulent and coarse to a degree of which these tamer and more decorous times furnish no example, frequently urged the Attorney-General to greater activity.

The following is a specimen of these incentives, applied shortly before the trial of Cobbett, through the medium, in this case, of the Prime Minister :

Downing Street : May 6, 1831.

My dear Sir,—The enclosed publications were sent to me last night by the King, who is greatly annoyed by these and similar productions, which those who wish to alarm him lose no opportunity of bringing under his notice.

That they are libels of a most flagitious nature no one can doubt, and conviction, I conclude, would be certain. The *prudence* of prosecuting is another question, and I wish you would make a report to me of your opinion on the whole matter, with a view to its being laid before the King.

I am, my dear Sir,
Yours very truly,
GREY.

To the Attorney-General.

There will be occasion hereafter to revert to this subject of *ex officio* informations, and to Denman's

---

[16] See 'Annual Register' for 1831, p. 95.

final opinion of their impolicy as submitted to the King in his memorial of May 1832. The order of time has already been too far departed from for the sake of following up the result of the proceedings against Cobbett, and now, leaving the Reform Bill discussions for consideration in the next two chapters, mention must be made of the only other important debate on *general* subjects in which Denman took part in the Parliament of 1830–31, that, viz. on Mr. (afterwards Sir) Fowell Buxton's resolutions of April 15, 1831, regarding Negro Slavery in the West Indian Colonies.

Mr. Fowell Buxton's resolutions were in these terms :

That in the Resolutions of May 16, 1823 (referred to in Chapter XIII.), this House distinctly recognized it to be their solemn duty to take measures for the abolition of Slavery in the British colonies:

That in the eight years which have since elapsed the Colonial Assemblies have not taken any measures to carry the resolutions of this House into effect :

That, deeply impressed with a sense of the inhumanity and injustice of Colonial Slavery, this House will proceed to consider and adopt the best means of effecting its abolition throughout the British dominions.

Denman supported these resolutions in an able and effective speech, at the conclusion of which, referring to an appeal made by Sir Robert Peel to ' the spirit of the House ' to oppose the motion, he said :

That for his part he too appealed, like the right honourable baronet, to the spirit of the House ; not to the spirit of false pride and wounded self-importance ; still less to the spirit of animosity, excited perhaps by other measures, but gratified by opposing this; but to the spirit of justice and mercy, of real and honourable consistency. He would not appeal to the spirit of deference to public opinion, though that ought to be cherished in a representative body; but he laid it on the conscience and honour of every member to bear his part as an Englishman in wiping off the foulest stain that ever rested on the character of the country.[17]

There is a close and intimate connexion between the subject of Slavery and the name of the most celebrated of its antagonists; and before closing the present chapter room must be found for a communication, interesting both from its writer and its subject, which Denman received shortly after his appointment as Attorney-General from the venerable and illustrious William Wilberforce, introducing to Denman's notice his son Samuel, afterwards the celebrated Bishop, first of Oxford, then of Winchester.[18]

It reads thus:

Highwood Hall, Middlesex: January 12, 1831.

My dear Sir,—My son, the Reverend Samuel Wilberforce, a young man of whom I may assure you, without being chargeable with partiality, that he is a young man of very superior qualities both of head and heart, desires me to give him a line of introduction to you concerning a gross abuse of a charity in a parish with which he was recently connected. I assent to his request the more willingly because I thereby enjoy the opportunity of expressing the pleasure with which, though now retired from the public stage, I have witnessed

---

[17] Hansard, Parl. Deb., third series, vol. iii. pp. 1408–1409.

[18] The late Bishop of Winchester was at this time only in his twenty-sixth year. He had taken a distinguished degree at Oxford in the Michaelmas Term of 1826. Checkendon, in Oxfordshire, where the Bishop had been a curate, is believed to be the parish referred to in this letter.

VOL. I.   Z

the just advancement of a man, in your instance, of superior
independence.

Permit me to express my sincere wishes (strengthened by
the regard and esteem I felt both for your father and your
mother) that it may please God to bless you with a long
course of usefulness and comfort, to be followed, permit me
to add, by still more durable and unalloyed happiness in a
better world.   I remain with cordial respect and regard,

My dear Sir, yours sincerely,

W. WILBERFORCE.

The future Bishop improved into friendship the
acquaintance thus commenced with the future Chief
Justice, with whom he was thereafter to take an active
and glorious part in the House of Lords against the
infernal traffic in slaves.

CHAPTER XIX.

THE REFORM BILL—SESSION OF 1831.

A.D. 1831. ÆT. 52.

Original Reform Bill drawn by Denman as Attorney-General—Note to him respecting it from Lord John Russell, February 1831—Denman's duties in connexion with the Bill—His first speech on the Bill in debate on first reading, March 2, 1831—Passage in answer to Lord Leveson Gower—'Men of intelligence and integrity should not stoop at all '—Reference to his own entry into Parliament as member for the close borough of Wareham—Second speech on the Bill in debate on second reading, March 22, 1831—The majority of one for the second reading—Third speech on the Bill on General Gascoigne's motion of April 19, 1831—Majority of nine against Government—Dissolution of April 22, 1831—Denman's letter to Mrs. Wright—The Borough-mongers die hard—General election of 1831—'The Bill, the whole Bill, and nothing but the Bill '—Denman's re-election at Nottingham—No opposition—His letter on it to Lady Denman of April 29—His great popularity at Nottingham—The bill re-introduced into the Commons —Second reading carried on July 7, by a majority of 136—The Bill in Committee for forty sittings—Labours of the Attorney-General— The summer session of 1831—Mrs. Hodgson's recollections of it— Bill passes the Commons by a majority of 109 on September 22, 1831 —Denman's letter to Mrs. Wright describing the debate—Macaulay— Stanley—Croker—Peel—Brougham's Bankruptcy Bill brought down from the House of Lords on September 28—Denman's letter to his wife of April 29—Threatened opposition to the Bankruptcy Bill— Brougham at Windsor—William IV. shows him the royal kitchens— Prospects of Reform—The King, the Queen, the Lords—Discussions on Brougham's Bankruptcy Bill—Strong and harassing opposition of the Tory lawyers—Finally passed on October 18—Denman's friend, Merivale, appointed a Commissioner—The Lords throw out the Reform Bill by a majority of forty-one on October 8, 1831—The great debate in the Lords—Speeches of Brougham and of Lord Grey—Wild commotion through the country—Nottingham—Bristol—Birmingham—Bill

LORD DENMAN'S papers throw no light whatever on
the secret history of the Reform Bill, nor is it likely
they would. He was simply charged as Attorney-
General with the duty of drawing the Bill, under
instructions from the Committee, consisting of Lords
Durham and Duncannon, Lord John Russell, and Sir
James Graham, to whom had been entrusted the
task of considering in the first instance, subject of course
to further discussion and revision in the Cabinet, the
substance and details of the measure.

A printed copy of the original Reform Bill has been
preserved by him, with this note on it in his own
handwriting, ' Original Reform Bill, drawn by me,
Denman.'

This, of course, does not imply that he penned with
his own hand all the clauses of the bill, nor does it
exclude the assistance of able draftsmen, to whom, on
occasions of importance, the Attorney-General has
prescriptive recourse.

The following note from Lord John Russell will
show clearly enough the nature of Denman's duties as
Attorney-General in respect to the preparation of the
Reform Bill. The hurried lines, written from the Cabinet,
are not without interest, relating as they do to the
preparation for that memorable speech of March 1,
1831, in which, calmly, lucidly, and unmoved, Lord
John unfolded to the astonished House the programme
of a political revolution.

Friday, February 25, 1831.

My dear Attorney,—I send you your Bill, which you left at the Cabinet and disappeared. I beg you will look over it, correct and add as well as you can, and let me have it by ten o'clock to-morrow morning. I will then send it to the 'Journal' office, and they may set to work with the printing, in order to be ready for Tuesday.

There seems to me a doubt whether you include *non-resident* freemen ; pray look at the clauses with this view.

The clause regarding Wales is at present very unsatisfactory. You can easily make it better, if not perfect. Perhaps it would do to say, ' The boroughs of Cardiff, &c. (naming the boroughs) shall have the additions enumerated in Schedule H '—or whatever it may be.

I sent you the schedules, but they must be worked out separately, and it will suffice if they are ready on Monday morning. Pray lose no time.

Yours truly,
J. RUSSELL.

In fact, to superintend the careful and accurate preparation of the Bill, to defend its general principles, but still more its legal details—the latter a peculiarly arduous task during the long and bitter opposition in committee, of which Croker was the leader, and the Tory lawyers, Wetherell and Sugden, the active supporters—formed a principal portion of the duties of Denman as the Whig Attorney-General.

These duties he discharged with his usual vigour and success, sometimes, as in his addresses to the House on the general question, rising into eloquence, always unwearied in assiduity.

The earliest of his speeches on Parliamentary Reform was on March 2, 1831, the night immediately succeed-

ing that on which the Bill had been introduced by
Lord John Russell, the same night on which the young
member for Calne 'electrified the House,' in the
language of honest Lord Althorp, by that brilliant
display of eloquence which forms the first in the
series of Lord Macaulay's speeches corrected by himself.

There was nothing very brilliant or very profound
in Denman's address, nothing which, when it is read in
Hansard, strikes one as particularly worthy of preservation or reproduction ; but it was manly, dignified, and
intelligent : above all, it was admirably well delivered
and consequently produced on the hearers a far greater
impression than many of those more carefully prepared discourses which are better fitted for perusal in
the closet.

One passage in particular was much admired at the
time. Lord Leveson Gower, who, on the first night of
the debate, had spoken on the other side, had won
some applause by declaring that 'the portals of the
House of Commons were not so low but that men of
intelligence and integrity might stoop to enter through
them.' Denman's reply to this was in his best manner,
full of lofty indignation and generous self-esteem,
'I never shall forget,' says one who was present,[1]
' the *Roman grandeur of tone* with which Denman said
that men of intelligence and integrity should not be compelled to stoop at all, but had a right to find their way

---

[1] A gentleman named Parker, mentioned in a note from Mrs. Wright
to Lady Denman, of March 12, 1831, relating the circumstance. Mr.
Parker represents Denman's as *the* speech of the evening.

into Parliament through the broad highway of the constitution.'   The passage is thus given in Hansard:

A noble lord, in an eloquent speech last night, had compared the close boroughs to some portal through which integrity and intelligence might enter without much stooping. He would tell that noble lord that integrity and intelligence did not wish to stoop at all, but were bent on finding their way into Parliament through the great highway of the Constitution.   When he was told that Burke and Pitt and Fox, and other illustrious characters, had owed their introduction into Parliament to the defects in the Constitution, he would reply that it was not for their happiness or glory, nor for the public benefit, that they had owed their entrance into the House to anything but the free choice of the Commons of England.[2]

In the course of the same speech he thus adverted to his own entrance into Parliament through the medium of a nomination borough (Wareham):

As the noble lord had, in language far too complimentary, referred to himself as formerly sitting in Parliament for a close borough, he would say a few words on that subject.   In the year 1818 he was given to understand that there was a wish that he should be in Parliament.   Having heard that there was a vacancy in the town which he now had the honour to represent (Nottingham) he determined to offer himself to the electors: it happened that there was no vacancy.   A seat, however, was offered to him for the borough of Wareham, and, though averse to the system, he confessed with some sense of shame that he had not had virtue to resist it. He should have respected himself more had he acted on his own opinion.   At the election of 1820 he was not elected for a close borough, but sought and obtained the suffrages of one of the most enlightened towns in England ; and when in 1826

2 Hansard, Parl. Deb., third series, vol. ii. p. 1246.

circumstances prevented him from seeking the same distinction, no close borough was prepared as an asylum for him.
There was something in such a position that an independent
spirit could ill bear; for though he was bound to express
gratitude for treatment the most kind and liberal, yet the
sense of uncertainty and dependence on others was fraught
with painful feelings. He made no complaint against those
who gave him his seat or withdrew it from him ; but, when he
contrasted his situation as member for a close borough with his
situation as member for Nottingham, which he owed to the
confidence of thousands, he felt that there was no more comparison to be made between them than between the crumbling
walls of Aldborough and the most flourishing town in England.[3]

On March 22, 1831, very shortly before the memorable division on the second reading, when the ministry
obtained a majority of one—302 for and 301 against—
Denman delivered an able, argumentative, and animated speech, which produced a considerable effect on
the House. It is essentially the speech of a debater,
a great portion of it being occupied with answers
to previous speakers, and the refutation of special
objections, which, though at the time in the highest
degree useful and effective, would naturally possess
but a feeble interest for readers of the present day.
The following passage, towards the conclusion, which
deals with considerations somewhat more general,
affords a fair specimen of the powers of the speaker :

He was astonished [he said] to see moral and religious
men strenuously contending against Parliamentary reform
with such cases as Retford, and Grampound, and Evesham
before their eyes. He was surprised to behold such men in

<hr>

[3] Hansard, Parl. Deb., third series, vol. ii. p. 1247;

such circumstances endeavouring to prevent all species of reform. He would maintain that the tendency of their arguments excluded it altogether. What else was the burthen of the seven nights' debate on the part of the opponents of the measure? What other plan did they hint at? What hope did they hold out to the People? Did the right honourable baronet [Peel] admit more than a bare possibility that he might possibly be induced as an individual to give his reluctant consent to some measure of Reform? What was known of his sentiments except a decided preference of Bassetlaw to Birmingham when an extension of elective rights was in contemplation? Some persons contended that the public voice ought to be consulted! Well, the public voice had been consulted. Others cried out that the measure was a robbery of Corporations; but the Corporations had come forward and begged to be so robbed. Others, then, had said that the bill contained clauses contrary to the rights of the City of London; but the City had met the next day, and voted not only that the measure was good, but had declared itself ready to sacrifice some of its most valued privileges for the sake of the general advantages expected from the Bill. There was scarcely an exception to the unanimity of the people, whose opinions had been so confidently challenged. The measure was brought forward to remedy the greatest evils, and never was there a time in which it could be brought forward with greater safety. There was perfect happiness in observing the present state of the public mind, compared to what it had been a few weeks before. The gentlemen opposite who so often alluded to the question of Catholic Emancipation, carried, as they said, in opposition to the petitions of the people, did not seem to act consistently when they now opposed a measure in favour of which the people had poured innumerable petitions on the table of the House. For his part he would abstain from using any argument that could be called intimidation. As he would not allow such an influence to be exercised on himself, he would not attempt to exert it over others. But the language of some

of his friends was construed into menaces.   When the opponents of the bill were told that they dare not face their constituents, it could never have been supposed that they ran
any risk of personal maltreatment, but only that the cause
of Reform was making such way throughout the country,
and that among the most intelligent part of the people—and
he would observe that that extended down very far into the
lowest class—that the gentlemen who opposed the bill could
not afterwards expect the support of their constituents.
There was nothing of violence or faction among the people;
the long neglect of real grievances, the provoking disappointment that would ensue from palliatives and half
measures—especially if times less prosperous than the present
should supervene—would in the end produce those lamentable
results which the experience of mankind has always proved
to arise from just and reasonable discontent.   In his conscience he believed that the present bill would allay those
feelings of dissatisfaction by removing their cause; that it
was not too late to apply an efficient remedy to a growing
and undeniable evil; and that by adapting our institutions
to the spirit of the times we live in, by a purer mode of
election and a truer state of representation, we should give
the best security that human wisdom ever devised for the
permanence and stability of our institutions. (*Great cheering
and loud calls of ‘ Question.’*) [4]

The majority of one in favour of the second
reading, on March 22, was followed, on April 19, by a
majority of 8 against the ministry (299 to 291) on
General Gascoigne’s motion, ‘ that the total number
of representatives for England and Wales ought not to
be diminished.’

Denman spoke on this occasion at some length, and
with his usual vigour and animation, but he rose late,

---

[4] Hansard, Parl. Deb., third series, vol. iii. p. 758 et sqq.

the House was impatient for the close of the debate, and it required all his high courage and his great powers of voice to force a hearing amidst repeated cries for a division from an assembly one half of whom were weary of a protracted discussion, and the other flushed with the anticipation of a party triumph.[5]

Three days after their victory the exultation of the anti-Reformers was changed into dismay by the memorable dissolution of April 22.

On the very day of the dissolution Denman wrote a few hasty lines from the House of Commons to his eldest daughter, Mrs. Wright:

The borough-mongers have been floundering on from bad to worse, and their absurd and factious conduct has convinced the King that Parliament ought to be dissolved. He is, I believe, at this moment on the road to perform this, the most necessary, and at the same time the most popular act any Sovereign has performed since the time of Elizabeth!

Here the writing breaks off.   Then he adds, in a hand evidently unsteady with excitement :

Summoned to the House of Peers! Our gracious King, from the throne, with the crown on his head, has pronounced the doom of the borough-mongers. His voice firm and composed, his aspect dignified and imposing. In both Houses the dying culprits struggled hard, and exhibited in death the malignity and shabbiness which have disgraced their last days. Lord Lyndhurst in particular denouncing the profligacy (!!) of dissolution.

The general election speedily followed.   The country was wild with excitement, ringing with one shout,

---

[5] See for this speech, Hansard, Parl. Deb., third series, vol. iii. p. 1678 et sqq.

'The Bill, the whole Bill, and nothing but the Bill.' Denman was returned for Nottingham without the shadow of an opposition, and the Reformers were victorious along the whole line.

Denman, writing to his wife on April 29, thus records the triumph of himself and his colleague:

About five miles out of Nottingham we were met by a large cavalcade, and a little farther on by a triumphal car drawn by six greys, in which we rode into the town, attended by many on horseback and a countless multitude on foot—a band, cheers, and high good-humour. The old Whig flags waved before us, *and some even of the old Tory banners were united in the cause of Reform.* At the top of one a figure of His Majesty as a true British tar, with the Reform Bill in his hand. The Exchange room was full to overflowing when we were put in nomination in very handsome style, and chosen with unbounded acclamations. It is now a little after two—we escape chairing, but are to be carried out of the town at three in the same triumph as before. I have been talking a good deal, but do not find myself at all fatigued.

His Majesty's Attorney-General was at this time the hero and idol of the Nottingham populace, ' lads and lambs' making the streets and market-place vocal with rough chants for ' Reform and Denman, oh.'

The results of the popular enthusiasm were soon shown in the new Parliament. The second reading of the bill was carried on July 7, by a majority of 136, (367 to 231).

Then began the protracted and wearisome battle of the schedules, which raged through half of July, the whole of August, and a portion of September.

This long and embittered struggle imposed the severest labour on all the more prominent members of the administration ; on none more than on the Attorney-General, whose attendance was constantly required throughout the whole course of the discussions, and whose unwearied diligence as a speaker on committee is amply attested by the chronicles of Hansard.[6]

'Such a summer as that of 1831,' he writes to his third daughter, Fanny (now the Hon. Lady Baynes, then a lively young lady in her nineteenth year), 'few unhappy M.P.s have ever undergone before. Our enemies run down into the country and come back refreshed, while we continue slaving on in our offices, unable to get away.'

His second daughter, Mrs. Hodgson, who was then staying with him in town, writing to Lady Denman in the middle of September, gives an account of the almost unvaried tenor of his laborious days :

We breakfast every morning about nine or half-past [this after an attendance till 2, 3, or even 4 A.M. in the House]. Just before we have finished the letters arrive. Then papa reads a little hastily—briefs or something of that sort : then he goes down to chambers, where he has a great deal to do [for he had much professional and official, as well as parliamentary business to attend to] ; then at 4 he usually comes home to dinner, and at 5 goes down to the House. I want him to run down to Lilles, where Lord Nugent has invited him, but he thinks he has too much other business to allow it.

---

[6] The committee, in 1831, on the Reform Bill, sat no less than forty times between July 12 and September 7. On all these occasions Denman was present—on almost all he spoke : he frequently had to speak more than once in the same sitting. On September 7, 1831, being the fortieth day of committee, Lord John Russell's motion that the Bill, as amended, be reported to the House, was carried with loud cheers.

At length, about a week after the above lines were written, between five and six on the morning of September 22, 1831, the motion that 'this Bill do pass' was, after a three nights' debate, carried in the Commons by a majority of 109, the numbers being 345 to 236.

Denman thus announced the result in a letter to his eldest daughter, which contained also some account of the debate:

Probably this will not be the first time of your hearing that we passed the bill between five and six this morning, 345 to 236. Lord John will carry it up to the Lords, attended by the most numerous band that ever stepped from the lobby of one House to the bar of the other. Who would have dared to believe this possible on November 1, 1830: who would have ventured to call it probable even on the 1st of last March—when the House was required to condemn and correct itself, acting as judge and executioner on its own demerits. The event I really believe to be unique in the history of the world. Scarlett truly said that nothing like it had occurred—a legislature declaring itself incompetent to discharge the functions assigned to it, without the pressure of foreign invasion or internal insurrection. Strange that he did not perceive that this peculiarity is the great glory of the measure, and holds out the greatest prospects of its benefits as well as of its permanency. For it proves that public spirit is active and energetic in England, even there where it is least expected, and where corruption has done the most to extinguish it.

As you will have discovered, I made no speech in the House during this last debate. Macaulay was sublime, perhaps a little too severe in his censure of the ex-ministers.[7] Lord Stanley's[8] refutation of Croker's clever, elaborate,

---

[7] Speech of September 23, 1831; the third speech on Parliamentary Reform printed in the collection of speeches corrected by himself.

[8] Late Lord Derby.

humorous, extravagant, and excessively overpraised speech, was most vigorous and masterly, directly to the point, full of nerve and business.   Peel's effort, highly studied and wrought up, was worthy of his character, but not of his name: by which I mean that his name is much more considerable than his character deserves that it should be.

The most remarkable thing about the debate is that the enemy boldly takes up the cry of ' No Reform!'   I believe the Lords grow reasonable, and will pass the bill.

No sooner had the pressure of his Reform Bill labours been thus suspended for a time than another and far more ungrateful task was imposed on the Attorney-General—the conduct through the House of Commons of Brougham's bill for the amendment of the law of Bankruptcy, which was brought down from the Lords on September 28.   He thus refers to it, and also to the reception by the King, at Windsor, of its illustrious author the Chancellor, in a letter written to his wife on September 29 :

I am hard at work at the Chancellor's Bankruptcy Bill, and you may see by the division yesterday (the day for introducing it into the House) what a cantankerous opposition it will meet with.   The worst is they may very likely prevent its coming on by filling up the whole evening with other things.   I cannot help it.   I am amassing my materials, and shall charge my gun with a very decent speech, whether allowed to fire it off or not.[9]

---

[9] The speech in question was 'fired off' on the next day, September 30, and is complained of by Lord Althorp in a letter to Brougham of the beginning of October as ' having been ill-opened, both as to the plan of the speech and its execution (see letter in Brougham's 'Memoirs,' vol. iii. p. 128).   Lord Althorp's admirable temper had probably, when he wrote this, suffered a little under the stress of great labour and vexatious opposition.   Denman's speech, as reported in Hansard (vol. vii., third series, pp. 895–915) does not bear out his strictures, though his want of familiarity with Bankruptcy proceedings may have rendered him less effective than usual in his exposition.

Brougham is come back, delighted with the King, who drove him all about, and showed him everything, among the rest the kitchens that had cooked the dinners of twenty-four kings, having been employed in its present form and dimensions since the time of (I think) Edward the First. Dick [his third son, Honourable R. Denman] may count the crowned heads.

The Queen does not appear very favourable to the Bill. If the Lords pass it, the tranquillity and welfare of the country are secured, and if they throw it out their triumph will be but for a time. The misfortune will be the chance of tumult in the country. But as the King has no idea of parting with his ministers in that event, nor they of deserting him, I trust the evil will be but momentary.

Brougham's Bankruptcy Bill, though in many respects a vast improvement, in point of procedure, on the preceding system, or rather no system, yet, by the great amount of new patronage it created (a Chief Judge at 5,000*l.* a year, two Puisne Judges at 3,000*l.*, and ten Commissioners at 1,500*l.*), gave an opportunity to the Tory lawyers, headed by Wetherell, to attack it with the bitterest and most relentless opposition. Denman, from the fact of his practice having been almost exclusively confined to Common Law, was not by any means so well versed as Wetherell and Sugden, both great Chancery practitioners, in the minutiæ of Bankruptcy proceedings; and it required anxious labour and close attention on his part to prepare himself adequately for the minute, harassing, and protracted discussions in Committee, which dragged their slow length along till October 18, when the bill was read a third time and passed. It was some reward to Denman for his long and laborious exertions that his old friend Merivale was appointed by the Chancellor to one of the new Commissionerships, on a salary of 1,500*l.* a year.

Meanwhile the Lords had not, as Denman in his letter of September 22 to Mrs. Wright had ventured to anticipate they would, ' grown reasonable and passed the Bill; ' on the contrary they had, after long debate, rejected it late in the morning of October 8, by the famous majority of 41—199 to 158.

Denman, being elsewhere busily occupied with his Bankruptcy Bill, was present during a part only of the great debate which preceded this memorable division. He did not hear Brougham's carefully prepared oration. In writing to Mrs. Wright, he says of it, ' I thought the Chancellor's speech read beautifully, but they tell me it was rather languid in the delivery.' In writing to his wife, he says, ' it is universally allowed to have been worthy of the occasion and of himself.' He *did* hear Lord Grey : 'Lord Grey's reply,' he tells his daughter, ' was considered the flower of the debate.' He describes himself, in writing to Lady Denman, as ' listening to it with pride,' and calls it ' a most noble speech, so clear in its reasoning, so impressive in its tone, so calm and dignified in its spirit.' This was the famous speech to which Macaulay refers in his article on Warren Hastings, when he talks of men ' listening with delight till the morning sun shone on the tapestries of the House of Lords to the lofty and animated eloquence of Charles, Earl Grey.'

The rejection of the Bill by the Lords was, as everybody knows, the signal for wild commotion throughout the country. The burning of Nottingham Castle, the murderous riots at Bristol, the revolutionary menaces of the political unions at Birmingham and elsewhere, showed the extent and fierceness of the popular exasperation.

On December 12, after a brief recess, the bill was a third time introduced into the House of Commons. On Friday (16), the debate on the second reading commenced, and did not terminate till one o'clock in the morning of Sunday (18), when, on the division, the second reading was carried by a majority of 162, in a House of 486, the numbers being 324 to 162.

With this act closed the session of 1831, the most laborious, perhaps, in the whole course of our parliamentary history

CHAPTER XX.

THE REFORM BILL—SESSION OF 1832.

A.D. 1832.   ÆT. 53.

Early in January 1832, Denman, as Attorney-General, prosecutes the Bristol rioters before a special commission—The House re-assembles on January 19, and the Bill again goes into committee—Croker in his glory—Macaulay and Croker, on March 19, in the debate on the final third reading in the Commons—Parallel between Cholera and Reform —Croker in the smoking-room of the House—Denman's letter thence to Mrs. Wright—Denman speaks on third reading, March 20—Bill, as amended, sent up to the Lords—Read a second time there, April 14— Bill in committee in the Lords—Majority against ministers on Lord Lyndhurst's motion, May 7—Grey and Brougham go down to the King at Windsor, May 8—The King accepts the resignation of the Reform ministry, May 9—Popular excitement—Duke of Wellington unable to form a Cabinet—The Grey ministry reinstated, May 18— Consequence to Denman, at this time, of permanent loss of office.   His letter to Mrs. Wright, written between the 9th and 18th of May—Contents: His feeling of anxiety for the country, and of disappointment as regards the King—Professional prospects—The Bench—The Speakership—Loss of office, how received by his wife and family—His son Joseph—Intrigues by which the fall of the Whig ministry was brought about—Lord Lyndhurst, Mephistopheles—Baring—Peel—Denman's satisfaction that the whole Cabinet had resolved on resignation— Legal gossip—Revenue case before Lyndhurst as Chief Baron—Mr. 'Rat'—Scotch appeal case before Brougham—'Poor as a rat'— Another case before Lord Lyndhurst, 'When rogues fall out, honest men come by their own'—Jeffrey (Lord Advocate) taken by Denman to see his mother—Debate on Lord Stormont's motion on the 'Conduct of the Press,' May 21, 1832—Article in 'Satirist' of May 13 brought to Denman's attention—He declines to prosecute *ex officio*—His reasons—Peel misrepresents his speech—Denman explains his views of the duty of an Attorney-General in regard to Press Prosecutions— William IV. writes to Lord Althorpe to ascertain Denman's real views

on the subject—Lord Althorpe, in consequence, writes to Denman on
May 23—Denman prepares and sends on May 24, ' A Memorial on *ex-
officio informations*—Its contents—Explanation of what he said on the
subject on Lord Stormont's motion—The real question one not so
much of feeling as expediency—Prosecution gives publicity to what
might otherwise pass unnoticed—The Attorney-General should never
take action without specific instruction in cases of personal libel—
Inconveniences of having publicly to state objections against proceeding *ex officio*—Devoted expressions of loyalty to William IV.—The
King's remarks in reply to the Memorial, May 26, 1832—The Lords
abandon their opposition to the Reform Bill—It passes the Lords on
June 4 by 180 to 22—Receives the royal assent, June 7, 1832.

AFTER a very brief respite from labour, Denman was
called upon, early in January 1832, to conduct the
prosecution, before a special commission held at
Bristol, of the prisoners charged with participation
in the frightful riots that had taken place in that city
during the previous October. Of these, besides a
crowd of minor offenders, twenty-four were capitally
indicted for having been concerned in burning or
otherwise destroying private dwellings, the gaol, the
Bridewell, and the Bishop's Palace. Out of this number
twenty-one were convicted, and four of the most guilty
executed.[1]

On January 19, 1832, the House re-assembled. The
next day the Bill again went into committee, and
Denman's Parliamentary labours recommenced almost
with the same severity as in the dog-days of 1831.
Croker, more active than ever in his malign and
bustling activity, was the Opposition hero of the
battles that raged in committee all through February
and till past the middle of March, over Midhurst and

---

[1] 'Annual Register' for 1832, p. 48 et sqq.

the Tower Hamlets, and many another borough deplored as unduly suppressed or denounced as unduly created.

Croker probably reached his parliamentary acmé in the debate on the third reading, when, on the night of March 19, 1832, he made his celebrated reply to Macaulay, comparing the progress of the Reform movement to the progress of the Cholera, which was then filling all London with alarm.

Macaulay, in the course of his speech, as reported in Hansard, had said a man would rather have the measles than the cholera, to use a homely illustration, because he would be less likely to die of the one than of the other, but if he must die of the measles why he might as well die of the cholera.[2]

Croker, who immediately followed him, seized upon this, and made, *more suo*, a most unfair but witty use of it.[3]

'The honourable gentleman,' he said, 'had likened the disease under which, according to him, the country is labouring from the corruption of the rotten boroughs to the measles, and then with singular candour declared he could find nothing with which to compare the Bill but the cholera morbus.'

And then Croker traced the progress of the pestilence along what he called the 'path of reform.' It first appeared at Sunderland, a borough created by the bill, next at Gateshead, then at Musselburgh, and then at Glasgow, all places whose representation was either first given or extended by the Bill.

---

[2] Hansard, Parl. Deb., third series, vol. xi. p. 458.
[3] Hansard, Parl. Deb., third series, vol. xi. p. 467 et sqq.

' And when it came to London, where,' he asked, ' did it first show itself? Most strange to say it still followed the traces of schedules C and D. It first displayed itself in the newly enfranchised districts of Bermondsey and the Tower Hamlets,[4] and as it advances it seems to select, with peculiar caution, the very localities which have been the subject of so much discussion in this House—Lambeth, St. Giles, Marylebone.

Really, sir, this is a most extraordinary series of coincidencies, and I think I may venture to say that the honourable and learned member has completely identified the Cholera with the Reform Bill, and in none of his metaphors has he been more happy than when he classed these two simultaneous plagues together.

Croker obtained great applause for a sally which, from its arising in the course of debate, and in immediate reply to a previous speaker, was naturally enough supposed to be an impromptu.

Denman, in the following vivacious sketch of ' Rigby,' dashed off from the smoking room of the House of Commons, for the amusement of his daughter, Mrs. Wright, a night or two after this oratorical exploit, throws some doubt upon its having been a genuine inspiration of the moment.

House of Commons Smoking-room [no date].

Croker has just assured me that he never thought of anything suggested beforehand, unless the momentary occasion reminded him of it. I told him that some people gave him credit for preparing the parallel between cholera and reform ;

---

[4] Croker took care to be right in his facts : cholera, which had first appeared in this country in Sunderland, on November 4, 1831, broke out first in London at Bermondsey and Rotherhithe, on February 10, 1832.

but *he declared it was not so.* 'How is it possible,' says he, 'that I should have anticipated the advantage which Macaulay gave me, by comparing any other mode of extinction to death by a natural cause, but Reform to 'the new, dangerous and loathsome visitation of Providence that now afflicts us under the name of cholera?'[5] This was an ingenious evasion, for, in fact, Lord Maitland had told me that, meeting Croker at dinner a day or two before the debate, the idea of tracing both of them (cholera and reform) from Sunderland to the Tower Hamlets and so to Marylebone, had been played upon by him in the same strain as afterwards in the House.

Denman spoke on the third reading (March 20), but there is nothing in his speech as reported to arrest attention, unless it be the remark, probably well-founded, ' that much of the opposition to this measure had, in his belief, proceeded from ignorance of the real feelings of the people, and this ignorance arose greatly from the state of the representation. The principal knowledge which the higher classes then possessed of the feelings of the lower was that obtained by contact with those voters who were ready to barter their privileges for the basest consideration.'[6]

On March 23, 1832, the Bill finally passed the Commons, and was then sent up, as amended, to the Lords, where, after a fortnight's debate, it was read a second time by a majority of nine, the numbers being 184 for and 175 against.

It then went into committee in the Lords, where,

---

[5] Words, as has been seen, not reported in Hansard, but just in Macaulay's style, and very probably spoken by him.

[6] Hansard, Parl. Deb., third series, vol. xi., March 20, 1832, House of Commons.

on May 7, Lord Lyndhurst, by 151 to 115 succeeded in carrying his hostile motion for postponing the consideration of the first portion of the Bill till after the disenfranchising clauses had been discussed.

The ministry treated the success of this motion as equivalent to the defeat.of the Bill, and on May 8 Grey and Brougham went down to Windsor to submit to the King the alternative of the resignation of the Cabinet, or the royal consent to an immediate creation of Peers. The King took a day to consider the point, and on May 9 accepted the resignation of the Whig ministry, and charged the Duke of Wellington with the formation of a new cabinet.

Immediately this became publicly known a storm of popular indignation as formidable as that which had shaken the country in October 1831, began to mutter and darken over the land. Fortunately, however, the crisis was not of long duration. The Duke of Wellington found it impossible to form a Government, and on May 18 the Whig ministry were back in their places, with the general understanding (now known to have been perfectly well-founded), that, if need should arise, they had the King's consent to create as many new peers as might be necessary to conquer the obstinate resistance of the Lords to the popular will.

The consequences of the Whig resignation, had it proved permanent, would have been personally very serious for Denman. He had resigned his office of Common Serjeant : the etiquette of the profession would have prevented him, after having been once Attorney-

General, from going back to practice on circuit, and he would therefore, with his numerous family, have been compelled to rely solely on the chances of metropolitan employment, a field in which, though sure to command a certain measure of success, he would yet be exposed to the competition of many formidable professional rivals. Under these circumstances it is impossible not to admire the manly spirit and elastic cheerfulness of the following letter, written from Westminster Hall to his eldest daughter, on one or other of the nine days during which the ministerial crisis continued, i.e. between May 9 and 18:

You take this whole matter, my dear child, exactly in the right view, and that all my children have done the same has been my consolation and delight. The trial has been to me so much the less severe because my personal share of it has been absorbed in two feelings of higher interest; first, the effect on the public mind and on the peace and happiness of the country; and secondly, but hardly secondly, in the deep concern I have felt for the future reign and life, the name and place in history to be occupied by my royal master. I had (perhaps with romantic folly) worked myself up to a state of loyal affection of which I should not have thought myself susceptible, and plagued myself to an unreasonable degree with the hope that any good thing that befell me would be blended with his dignity and greatness, while these were identified with the best interests, the lasting tranquillity, the unalterable attachment of the people. I could have wept at the change a few hours of caprice introduced, and am equally disappointed and grieved, whether he is conscious of his degradation, or wants the qualities by which it can be appreciated. *Miserum te, si intelligis, miseriorem si non intelligis.*

Notwithstanding the loss of my City office, and the

interruption of my professional engagements by special ones,[7] I cannot doubt that I should hold a good station at the Bar, and this is much more to my wild taste than judicial elevation. The Bench may be a desirable asylum, but while health and strength last I much prefer the exertions and rewards of this humbler position. My political friends were meditating to place me in the Speaker's chair. I would rather die. Look at La Fontaine's fable of the wolf and the house-dog.

Yet the loss of large emoluments cannot be indifferent to the father of eleven children, whom he wishes to see decently placed in the world. And they are all sensible of the disadvantage brought upon them. Instead, however, of showing the least discouragement, they have materially contributed to keep up my spirits. My lady [his wife] was a little hard to pacify just at first, but ever since, both at home and abroad, in her family and in company, she has been a very Portia. But the seasonable visit of Joe [now Admiral the Honourable Joseph Denman], has been the sunbeam of our picture. A better heart, a finer mind, more agreeable manners, and a sweeter countenance, never gladdened a parent in the child. On the day before the treason broke out in the Lords, I had settled our pecuniary arrangements, and though I warned him against some possible events, that which happened was foreseen by neither; when it came, he lost no time in undoing the obligation I had entered into.

It has been a sad business. The Duke has been fomenting a foul intrigue, and so has, I fear, one greater than he [William IV.]. Certainly his illegitimate son, the new-made earl, has been shamefully active. The two leading anti-reformers, who yielded their opinions on Reform, but could not sacrifice their resentment at the disfranchisement

---

[7] According to the etiquette of the Bar, an Attorney or Solicitor-General, after resigning his office, cannot go back to circuit practice, which, in Denman's case, would have involved a considerable loss of income.

of their boroughs—the Earl of Harrowby and Lord Wharncliffe— expressly promised their votes against the manœuvre of Mephistopheles (Lord Lyndhurst). This judicial personage has been the father of all the lies, and the contriver of all the mischief. The sending for *him* in the interregnum is the worst fact in the conduct of the unhappy Faust (the King). The acceptance of a message from him was unworthy of the military hero. The selection of so unpopular a man as Baring [8] was most fortunate for the country. Peel has not much illustrated himself by a refusal [to take the lead of the Commons] of which he is said to have shared the honour with Twiss (Horace) and Croker. I have no doubt, if the thing had gone on, all would have been overpersuaded, and after no long interval. Sir R. Inglis's manly attack struck, perhaps, the most decisive blow.

For twenty-four hours I was labouring under intense anxiety, in fear that some damaging compromise would be accepted, and though I felt no doubt that the creation of peers would have been now, as it was before, fully authorized and consented to,[9] such was my relief on hearing that the unanimous Cabinet had so honourably resolved on resignation, that I felt more grateful to Lord Grey for the step which deprived me of office than even for promoting me.

Most likely I shall get more news before I despatch this, but, unless I make some addition on that head, conclude that all is *in statu quo* up to 7 this evening.

Meanwhile, I will gossip a little. On Monday I was engaged in prosecuting a Revenue case for the Crown in Lord Lyndhurst's Court (the Exchequer, of which Lord Lyndhurst was then Chief Baron). An excise agent had been a great agent of fraud. I introduced him with great

---

[8] Proposed leader of the Commons in the projected administration.

[9] This surmise, as shown by Brougham's 'Memoirs,' vol. iii. pp. 101–104, was erroneous. Grey and Brougham went down to Windsor on May 8, laying before the King the alternative of a creation of peers or a resignation. On the 9th the King accepted the resignation, which Grey in the Lords and Althorp in the Commons announced that same evening.

pomp to the jury—with a description of himself, his family, and their general practice, ending with his name, enounced with emphasis, Mr. Ratt.[10]   On the same day a Scotch appeal was heard before Brougham, in the House of Lords, and some letter read in evidence contained the phrase, 'as poor as a rat.' 'Is not that a mistake?' said Brougham; 'is it not mouse?' Two or three counsel eagerly exclaimed, 'No, my lord, its rat in my copy.' He said it was a very odd expression, 'I thought the rats were all very rich, though they might be wholly without credit.' Yesterday, in another case, tried before Lord Lyndhurst, also for cheating the Government of duties, I had to open the evidence of an accomplice, and, with perfect innocence in this instance, observed to the jury that it was only when rogues fell out that honest men or honest governments came by their own. A general stir among the bystanders.

> 'If you mention vice or bribe,
> Men will take it for a gibe.'

His lordship's face all day indicated no happy internal feelings.   As to the two first allusions, which were malicious, it was horribly undignified in Chancellors and Attornies-General, but quite irresistible.

To this may be added that the above anecdotes show graphically enough the intense political fever of the time.

The letter concludes with a characteristic reference to his venerable mother, then in her eighty-fifth year.

I took the Lord Advocate (dear little Jeffrey) to call upon my mother and receive her consolations. I expected a line from the Essay on Man exhorting men

> 'To fall with dignity, with temper rise,'

---

[10] 'Rat' then (as indeed now), the current term for a politician who had changed sides; the real name was Raitt, pronounced as though spelt Rat.

but she was taken at a fault, which she has now repaired by sending the enclosed, half quotation and half composition [not preserved]. She is wonderfully well.

Three days after the return of the Whigs to office, May 21, 1832, an interesting debate arose on Lord Stormont's motion on the conduct of the Press.[11]

The indignation of the people at the temporary overthrow of the Reform ministry by a Tory intrigue, generally supposed to have been favoured, if not promoted, by the Court, was deep and widespread. It naturally found an echo in the Press, from the thunder of the 'Times,' in the famous leader beginning 'The Queen has done it all,' down to the inarticulate shrieking or coarse raving of the lowest organs of faction, 'the brood of clamorous and obscene birds, with those also that love the twilight.' The article specially selected by Lord Stormont for the purposes of his motion was a coarse and scandalous one from the 'Satirist' of May 13, reflecting in the grossest terms on the King and Queen for the part assumed to have been taken by them in the late crisis. William IV. was spoken of as ' the Guelf who had deceived the people,' and had better retire with all speed to the obscure land of his origin. Queen Adelaide was abused as an ' ill-favoured German woman, who, conspiring with the miscreant Cumberland, had dared to frustrate for a time the high-raised hopes of a great nation,' with a vast deal more of similar scurrilous and rabid rancour.

Lord Stormont having pointedly called the attention

[11] Hansard, Parl. Deb., third series, vol. xii. pp. 1144-1174.

of the Attorney-General to this gross abuse of the
liberty of the press, and enquired what course he
intended to take upon it, Denman, under circumstances of some difficulty, owing to the repulsive
nature of the publication complained of, rose to say
that he intended to take no official step whatever,
but to treat the infamous libel with silent and dignified
contempt.

In the course of his remarks he said :

It was his firm opinion, founded on experience, that a
political libeller thirsted for nothing more than the valuable
advertisement of a public trial in a court of justice. Triumph there made him rich, and defeat gave him all the
honours of martyrdom. Even martyrdom was found to
have its pecuniary advantages also, while it often procured
the wretched writer a much better lodging in a prison than,
when at large, he had ever been accustomed to occupy.
Allusion had been made to slanderous attacks on ladies of
the highest rank. Nothing could be more disgusting ; but
it seemed to him he would be taking a great liberty if he
prosecuted in such cases without special instructions. By
a trial in a court of justice they might sometimes be placed
in a much worse situation, for which, certainly, they would
have no reason to thank him.[12]

Denman had also in the course of his speech said
something about the regret he had felt in having to
inflict long terms of imprisonment on misguided men
for the sincere, though illegal, expression of opinions
on speculative questions of religion and politics which
they conscientiously held, and had expressed the satisfaction he experienced when the eighteen months

[12] Hansard, Parl. Deb., third series, vol. xii. p. 1151.

imprisonment to which he had been compelled to condemn Humphry Boyle had come to an end. Peel, insidiously mixing up the two very different classes of libel cases together, represented His Majesty's Attorney-General as having laid down in general terms the doctrine 'that no man ought to be prosecuted for the publication of his opinions provided those opinions are sincere.' 'Entertaining,' said the Opposition leader, 'high respect for the learned gentleman's private character, entertaining also high respect for his consistency in public life, yet I cannot conceive how he can possibly reconcile the sentiments he now avows with the duties which devolve on him as Attorney-General.' [13]

Denman, in reply, clearly enounced the views he really entertained, as distinct from those he was wrongly represented as holding.

I never said that, in my judgment, sincerity of opinion was to protect a man from prosecution. I also said that it was not my *personal* feeling which was to regulate this matter; but my feeling of what was due to the security of the public and to the honour of the Crown. My idea of the duty of an Attorney-General is this, that he is to do all that in his conscience he believes to be right, for the purpose of protecting the peace of the country, and the honour of the Crown. [14]

William IV., always very sensitive on the subject of libels affecting the royal family, and not unnaturally extremely indignant at the attacks on the Queen, was a good deal annoyed at the reluctance of Denman to

[13] Hansard, Parl. Deb., third series, vol. xii. p. 1163.
[14] Hansard, Parl. Deb., third series, vol. xii. pp. 1169–1171.

prosecute, and being mystified by some of the expressions reported to have fallen from him in the debate on Lord Stormont's motion, wrote urgently on the matter to Lord Althorpe, then Home Secretary who, in consequence, addressed the following communication to his friend and colleague, the Attorney-General:

Downing Street: May 23, 1832.

My dear Denman,—The King has written me a very strong letter on the subject of the libels. I had told him that Peel had misunderstood what you had said, and had made his speech in consequence. I must, however, quote for you the postscript of his letter, as it so directly concerns you, and probably requires you to write something in reply, but do not *send* anything till I have seen you. 'As His Majesty has understood that the Attorney-General's sentiments on this painful subject have been incorrectly given in the newspapers, he desires that the Attorney-General may be called on to state, for His Majesty's information, what they really are.' It is very difficult to do one's duty and tell the truth, and yet please a king. Our fate, however, places us in this difficulty, and, for great objects, it must be done.

Yours most truly,
ALTHORPE.

In consequence of this communication Denman immediately drew up and transmitted to Lord Althorpe, with a view of its being laid before the King, the following masterly memorial on the subject of *ex-officio prosecutions for libel*, which, owing to its value and importance, is here printed *in extenso* from his MSS.

Lincoln's Inn: May 24, 1832.

My Lord,—I am honoured with your lordship's letter of yesterday's date, which informs me that 'His Majesty, understanding that the sentiments avowed by me in the debate in the House of Commons on Monday last, on the subject of prosecutions for libel, had been erroneously reported in the newspapers, desires that I may be called upon to state for His Majesty's information what they really are.'

In humbly obeying His Majesty's commands, I beg to observe in the first place that I have not read any report of what fell from me in the debate alluded to. My statement, therefore, will have reference generally to the sentiments avowed and entertained by me, but not to the correction of language which particular reports may have ascribed to me.

The object of my speech was to expose the current fallacy that prosecutions would prevent an evil which I am fully persuaded they would aggravate in a tenfold degree. From a multitude of cases that have occurred during the last fifteen years, I wished to select a few in which former Attornies-General had forborne to prosecute libels of equal malignity with any that had recently issued from the press. This led me to refer to the long impunity of Carlile's periodical work, 'The Republican,' of which the worst was prosecuted, not by the Attorney-General, but by an Association which undertook the office they charged him with declining, but yet were generally thought to have done more harm than good by their interference. I also referred to the violent libels of the 'Morning Journal,' and other papers, in the early part of 1829, against all who supported Catholic emancipation, some of which systematically threatened the exclusion of His present Majesty from the throne. And the same line of observation necessarily pointed to the great discredit thrown upon proceedings *ex officio*, by their multiplication in less culpable instances, towards the close of the same year.

I endeavoured to trace this reluctance to prosecute shared by so many Crown lawyers, who must have been shocked and disgusted by such libels, to some general causes. Such, among others, are the encouragement held out by the law of England to free discussion in general; the consequent jealousy of the public in all that concerns the freedom of the press; the indulgence granted by juries to almost anything that may be considered as mere opinion, if supposed to be honestly advanced; the injury sustained by Government from acquittals, and the possibly greater injury arising from convictions and mock martyrdoms; the tendency of libels, thus forced into notoriety, to engender more; the apparent iniquity of punishing sometimes a mere instrument of publication, ignorant of the evil he creates, while the author, or even the actual publisher, cannot be reached by evidence; finally, the ease with which practised libellers may contrive to write the bitterest things without subjecting themselves to legal visitation.

I took great pains in my first speech, and still more in my second, after being, as I thought, very unfairly represented, to guard myself against being supposed to surrender any legal right possessed by the Crown, particularly excepting from all claim to favourable consideration writings prompting to crime, endangering the public peace, or dealing in personal slander.

This last description of libel, however, appears to me to require peculiar caution. I trust that I did justice to my own feelings by expressing in the strongest terms the contempt and indignation which publications such as these must inspire in every manly bosom. Where, in addition, loyalty is outraged, and decent respect to the most exalted persons in the realm rudely thrown away, these feelings must be far more strongly excited. But the question is not how all good men must feel on this subject: it is, whether prosecution is the proper course for putting down such offences.

Your lordship will remember that Lord Stormont, even while recommending prosecution, *acted* on the strongest motive against resorting to it: he professedly abstained from reading to the House the foulest of the libels, *from unwillingness to give them publicity.* Yet prosecution would bring them to the ears of hundreds in Court, and to the eyes of hundreds of thousands out of Court, who never otherwise would have seen or heard of them : the publisher would make his trial the occasion for bandying about and blackening the most sacred names, wounding their most endeared connections, perverting known facts, insinuating rank falsehoods, while the judge sits by powerless to stop an accused man pleading in his own defence, or adds a sting to the invectives which he seems anxious to silence.

I apprehend that it can be no part of the duty of an Attorney-General, but would be an act of unwarrantable presumption on his part, to place any persons, and especially the highest persons, in a situation like this, without instructions the most specific and direct.

The general feeling upon this subject is shown in this, that though the female connections of the nobility are perpetually thus attacked, they are never known to resort to legal measures, except for the direct assertion of positive falsehood.

If there be (as I think there is) some inconvenience in publicly stating reasons such as these for leaving libels unpunished, the necessity is created by these incessant attacks on the Government in both Houses of Parliament for declining to prosecute.[15] Indeed, not only Lord Stormont, as I have mentioned, guided his own discretion by one of the strongest reasons by which we have been influenced, but Sir Robert Peel and Sir Charles Wetherell both acknowledged the force of the objections above detailed.   It is true that they are *at all times* fit to be seriously considered before commencing prosecutions for libel; but they strike me, as they do all unprejudiced men with whom I have conversed, as peculiarly strong *at the present season, and in the present state of the public mind.*   When its agitation

---

[15] These attacks, it was suspected, and no doubt with truth, were encouraged by the Court.

has subsided, a reasonable hope may be entertained that such libels will no longer disgrace the press: if they do, the application of a remedy will be attended with less difficulty.

I conclude with expressing my humble but earnest hope that this explanation may be found satisfactory to His Majesty. The call which the King has been pleased to direct your lordship to make affords me an opportunity of adverting to a subject I could not, without arrogance, have approached in the House of Commons—I mean the personal relation in which I have the honour to stand to the King.

Besides what I owe to official duty and constitutional loyalty, I am deeply sensible of the warm gratitude by which His Majesty's kingly magnanimity,[16] displayed in my promotion, has ever bound me to him, and I have laboured by all the means in my power to endear His Majesty to his people. His gracious approval of the manner in which I executed the painful task assigned to me in the Special Commission will never be effaced from my memory; and I venture to hope that His Majesty, whether on the present occasion he may or may not think my opinion just, will give me credit for acting upon it to the best of my humble ability, and with the same ardent zeal for his happiness and honour.

The concluding lines of this statement seem to show that Denman, like the first Pitt, and other impulsive and high-minded patriots, when brought into close quarters with Royalty, was by no means insensible to 'that divinity which doth hedge a King.'

The King's reply, though courteous and guarded in its terms, clearly evinces the distaste with which His Majesty yielded to the prudent suggestions of the

---

[16] In forgetting and forgiving Denman's fierce and effective attack on him in the proceedings against Queen Caroline.

Attorney-General.   The letter, which is in the hand-writing of Sir Herbert Taylor, but signed by the King himself, runs thus :

St. James' : May 26, 1832.

The King acknowledges the receipt of Viscount Althorpe's letter of yesterday, enclosing one from the Attorney-General containing the explanation or statement of his sentiments on the subject of prosecutions for libels, which His Majesty has read with great attention.   The King assures Viscount Althorpe, and desires he will assure the Attorney-General, that the desire which he expressed for a statement of his real sentiments upon this occasion did not result from any doubt His Majesty entertained of his zeal or devotion to his service, but from feeling it right that the Attorney-General should have the opportunity of doing justice to himself in a matter in which his sentiments might have been mis-represented.

His Majesty is satisfied, from the observations his letter contains, that the Attorney-General takes a sound and reasonable view of the subject, and, much as he laments the existence of such a curse to his country as a licentious and uncontrolled Press, and of a state of things which renders the law as to libellers and agitators a dead letter, His Majesty admits that it would not be advisable to resort to proceedings which would increase, rather than diminish, the effects of so deplorable a condition of the country.

WILLIAM R.

While these and other matters were occupying, without engrossing, the attention of the House of Commons—for the House, like the nation, had its whole mind bent on the speedy passage of the Reform Bill through its final stages, till the royal assent converted it fro   a Bill into an Act—the House of Lords had had time to reconsider their position and resolve, since yield they must, to yield with as little loss of dignity as possible. The speedy return to office of the Reform ministry, armed by the Sovereign with the power, if necessary, of creating Peers *ad libitum*, and borne upwards and onwards by an irresistible tide of popular enthusiasm, had its due effect even upon the tenacious and desperate obstinacy of the Upper House. It was determined, on the wise advice of the Duke of Wellington, forthwith to give up the hopeless struggle, and desist from all further opposition to the Bill.

So, on June 4, 1832, the Bill was read in the Lords a third time and passed—180 peers recording their votes in its favour, and only 22, the staunch and faithful remnant of the ultra-Tory Opposition, appearing in the House to declare themselves 'non-content.'

On June 7 the Bill received the royal assent, and became part and parcel of the law of the land.

At this final close of the great Reform Bill struggle it may be as well to pause, reserving for the next chapter the consideration of such matters as more prominently engaged the attention of Denman in Parliament during the residue of the session of 1832.

CHAPTER XXI.

CLOSE OF SESSION OF 1832—STONY MIDDLETON—DENMAN'S POLITICAL CONFESSIONS TO MERIVALE.

A.D. 1832.   ÆT. 53.

Discussions on the Russian-Dutch loan—Case of Daniel Whittle Harvey—Debate on June 14, 1832—Denman's speech on—Bill abolishing death punishment for forgery carried through the Commons—Altered in Lords—Mr. Ewart's bill abolishing death punishment for horse-stealing and for stealing over 5*l.* in a dwelling house—Mr. Warburton's clause for opening Coroners' inquests to the public—Chancery sinecures Abolition Bill—Sugden's question in the Commons—Brougham's attack on Sugden in the Lords—The 'Bug' speech—William Brougham's explanation in the Commons—Retiring pension and salary of the Lord Chancellor fixed—Present amount of Chancellor's salary—Severe Parliamentary and forensic labours of Denman since November 1830—Stony Middleton first occupied by Denman in 1830—The house and grounds—His delight in them—Pleasant society near Stony Middleton—The Hodgsons—Arkwrights—Strutts—Duke of Devonshire—The session of 1832 terminates on August 16—Letter from Denman to Merivale of August 17—The 'traitor of Ascot Heath'—Break-up of the session—'Joe in the Snake'—Three letters to Merivale of August 24, and September 4 and 11, containing statements of Denman's political views. *First letter, August* 24: Early political opinions—Never a Republican—The greatest of all political evils—The true remedy—Instances—Paramount necessity for Reform in Parliament—Early hopes that men of all parties would concur in reform—Expectation that the Duke would take it up, as he had Catholic Emancipation—The rancorous Tory opposition to Reform a surprise to Denman—Critical position of the Whig Government—Line taken by Peel—Harsh judgment of him—Position of the Lords and the Church—The Reform agitation a consequence of the Tory opposition—Wetherell's speeches—Political unions—Physical force put down by the Whigs—Invitation to stand for Derbyshire—Brougham like Mazeppa's horse. *Second letter, September* 4: Family party at Stony Middleton—

ONE of the questions which imposed on Denman, as the principal legal member of Government in the Commons, a good deal of harassing labour during the sessions of 1831 and 1832 was that of the Russian-Dutch Loan, a question which, notwithstanding the embittered discussions and floods of Parliamentary talk to which it then gave rise, has long since ceased to have any interest, and may be stated in very few words.

In 1815 England contracted with the Emperor of Russia and the King of the Netherlands to pay interest on one third of a loan of 2,000,000*l.*, subject to the promise 'that all such payments should cease and determine, should the possession and sovereignty of the Belgian provinces at any time pass or be severed from the dominion of His Majesty the King of the Netherlands.'

The Belgian provinces, as everybody knows, did in fact become severed from the dominions of the King of the Netherlands by the successful issue of the revolution of 1830, and Belgium became a separate and independent kingdom. On June 21, 1831, the King's speech had admitted the definite separation of Holland and Belgium.

Notwithstanding this, the British Government, unwilling, probably, by refusing to pay further interest, to offend the Government of Russia, directed the Treasury to continue the payments, alleging that the event contemplated and provided for by the Treaty was a severance of Belgium from Holland by *external* force, not by *internal* revolution.

The Opposition impeached the legality of the payments, contending that the construction put by Government on the language of the Treaty was forced and erroneous, and that the event contemplated by the framers of the Treaty as that on which all such payments should cease had actually arisen.

When the matter was first brought before the House, on December 16, 1831, Denman, with probably imprudent frankness, had admitted his first impression to have been (according to what undoubtedly seems the natural construction of the clause) that the moment the possession and sovereignty of the Belgian provinces passed from the kingdom of the Netherlands, *by whatever event*, the obligation for payment of interest under the Treaty was at an end;

but, he added, ' on further consideration he and his learned friends had come to the unanimous conclusion that what was meant by both parties was the passing away of the possession and sovereignty of Belgium from Holland by *some external force*, that a separation by *any internal cause or mutual agreement* was never contemplated, and that, consequently, the obligations of the Treaty continued in full force.'

It may readily be imagined what use an indignant Opposition would make of such a vexed question as this. In one shape or another it was repeatedly brought before the House throughout the whole session of 1832, and though the views of the Government ultimately prevailed, this result was only obtained at the cost of several damaging discussions.

Another question, of a wholly different nature, which caused Denman a great deal of anxiety, was the case of the well-known Daniel Whittle Harvey, a man of singular ability, and, within his own range, one of the very best and most effective speakers in the House.

On June 14, 1832, Harvey, in a speech of consummate tact and ability, moved for leave to bring in a bill ' empowering the Court of King's Bench to compel by mandamus the Benchers of the Inns of Court to admit, or show cause why they should not admit, parties to become members of their societies, and subsequently, having passed their state of pupillage as students, to call them to the degree of Barrister of Law.'

Harvey, before coming to his own case, stated that of Wooler, who, in 1825, was refused admission *as student,* by the Society of Lincoln's Inn, on the real but unavowed ground (for no ground was ever stated, though often requested), that he was the writer or editor of an objectionable publication called ' The Black Dwarf.' Wooler applied for a mandamus to the Court of King's Bench, and failed, the Court declaring that they had no power to direct the writ, or to require the Benchers to state their reasons for refusing him admission.

Harvey's own case, shortly stated, was as follows. After having been admitted as a member of the Inner Temple, having kept terms, and, for the then required period of three years, discontinued his practice as an attorney, he was refused his call by the Benchers in consequence of two circumstances in his previous history. The first was that, having sued another attorney for libel in charging him with having purloined a document from his office, and the defendant having put in, and, in the opinion of the jury, proved a plea of justification, the jury found for the defendant, thereby, as far as their verdict went, affirming that Harvey *had* purloined the document in question. The other circumstance was a charge of having purchased for less than its value an estate from one Frost, for whom he was at the time acting as an attorney.[1]

After considering these two cases the Benchers of the Inner Temple refused to call Harvey to the Bar.

[1] Harvey, in the debate of June 14, gave, in his speech in reply, the amplest explanation and refutation of both these charges, more especially of the second. See Hansard, Parl. Deb., third series, vol. xiii. p. 673 sqq.

He then appealed to the Judges. The case was heard before them, sitting with closed doors. Brougham and Denman were Harvey's counsel, but the Judges refused to interfere with the decision of the Benchers.

Such, in outline, was the case which Harvey, with all the winning and persuasive graces of a consummate orator, laid before the House. After a fierce but effective denunciation by O'Connell of the system of closed tribunals and judgments delivered without statement of the grounds of decision, Denman rose to oppose the motion, which he did in a temperate and dignified, if not a convincing speech :

It is admitted [he said] that some enquiry into the character and fitness of those who desire to enter the Inns of Court must take place, and I wish to confine the discussion as much as possible to the mere question whether the alteration proposed by the honourable member is advisable or not. The amendment he proposes is, that a mandamus shall issue to the treasurer of the Society compelling him to return facts that may be tried by a jury, in justification of the refusal to admit an applicant to the Society or to the Bar.

My answer is that there may be good reasons for the exclusion of an individual which do not consist of facts that can be tried by a jury; that there may be good reasons, which still are not tangible, which do not admit of proof; and I think this was fully shown in the case to which allusion has been made.[2]

After a reply from Harvey of even greater ability than his opening speech, the motion was rejected,

[2] Hansard, Parl. Deb., third series, vol. xiii. Denman's speech is from pp. 659–672.

but on July 17, Government acceded to another motion of his, for appointing a Commission of inquiry into the law and practice prevailing in the Inns of Court on the application of persons seeking to become students thereof and to be called to the Bar.

Very few measures of Law Amendment were passed during this exciting and agitated session.

Denman, indeed, had the satisfaction of carrying through the Commons (on July 31, 1832) a bill for the abolition of death punishment in *all* cases of *forgery*.[3] The Lords, however, alarmed at this excess of progress, insisted on retaining the power of passing capital sentences in the two cases of Wills and Bank powers of attorney. Denman, though reluctantly, was compelled on the last day of the session to accept these amendments, and the full and final abolition of the judicial power of putting men to death for forgery did not pass the Legislature till after Denman's appointment as Chief Justice.

At an earlier period of the session he had warmly supported and assisted in passing a bill introduced by Mr. Ewart for abolishing capital punishment in cases of horse-stealing, and stealing in a dwelling-house above the value of 5*l*., remarking that in his uniform experience ' the severity of the criminal law defeated itself.'[4]

He also supported and aided in carrying, by the influence of Government, a clause introduced (in the Coroners' Bill) by Mr. Warburton, providing (contrary

---

[3] Hansard, Parl. Deb., third series, vol. xiv. pp. 969–983.
[4] Hansard, Parl. Deb., third series, vol. xiii. p. 198.

to the opinion of the judges) that all coroners' inquests should be held in public. 'His opinion,' he said, 'was that coroners' inquests should be perfectly open ; that the witnesses should be examined publicly, and all the proceedings take place without any appearance of secrecy. He looked on coroners' inquests as a kind of advertisement, calling upon all who could give any information to come forward.'[5]

One of the latest measures of which Denman took charge in the House of Commons was the bill prepared by Brougham for the abolition of Chancery sinecures.

Among the offices the abolition of which was provided for by this bill was the lucrative one of Register of Patents, then held by Scott, Lord Eldon's son. On Scott's death, Brougham, while the bill abolishing it was passing through Parliament, put his brother William into the office.

Sugden having, on July 25, 1832, asked in the House of Commons how Government explained this appointment, Brougham the next day, in the Lords, made his memorable and indecent attack on Sugden, sarcastically giving him credit for being actuated in putting his question by that heaven-born thirst for information which distinguished men 'not only from the insect which flies and stings, but from that more powerful and offensive creature, *the bug*, which, powerful and offensive as it is, can, after all, only crawl.'

The next day, the 27th, Sugden brought the matter before the notice of the House of Commons. In the

[5] Hansard, Parl. Deb., third series, vol. xiii. p. 937.

course of the discussion that ensued, Denman stated that Sugden 'must have been perfectly well aware that the appointment of William Brougham was only provisional, and that, therefore, his putting his question as he had without notice was an offensive and irritating act.'

William Brougham, the appointee, brought the discussion to a close in a few words by stating, as the fact was, that the appointment was purely provisional, made because otherwise certain deeds could not be entered, and given by the Chancellor to his brother because he was a person on whom he could most perfectly rely for throwing up the place the instant Parliament thought fit to abolish it without a word or a whisper about 'vested interests.' [6]

The Chancery sinecures bill became law before the end of the session,[7] and by one of its clauses, in consideration of the patronage given up by the Chancellor in respect to the abolished offices, very properly increased the amount of his retiring pension to 5,000$l.$, and, by an Act nearly contemporaneous,[8] a clear salary of 10,000$l.$ a year was assigned to him in lieu of all fees and emoluments to which he had been previously entitled.

For some years after this the Chancellors, in addition to the salary of 10,000$l.$ a year thus fixed by statute, used also to receive 4,000$l.$ a year as Speakers of the House of Lords. This was altered by an Act of

---

[6] Hansard, Parl. Deb., third series, vol. xiv. p. 843.

[7] As 2 and 3 Will. IV. c. 111.

[8] 2 and 3 Will. IV. c. 122.

1851, directing that the sum payable to the Lord Chancellor as Speaker of the House of Lords should form part of his salary as Chancellor, so that he should not receive more in the whole than the 10,000*l.* fixed by the statute of William IV.[9]

Since November, 1830, His Majesty's Attorney-General had had scarcely any respite from the severe pressure of Parliamentary and forensic labour, and as the summer of 1832 waxed and waned he naturally began to long for some share of relaxation and repose.

It was some two years before the period now arrived at that Denman, who had previously been in the habit of passing his Long Vacations with his family at various places in the country and on the coast, first established himself at Stony Middleton, near Bakewell, in Derbyshire, a place he had inherited from his late uncle, but which, down to 1830, had remained in the occupation of one of his uncle's tenants. It was a rough place when he first determined to make it his permanent summer residence, an old-fashioned grange or small manor house, with ill-arranged rooms and whitewashed walls,[10] having nothing to recommend it but the charming scenery in its neighbourhood. To improve the house and the grounds till he had made the one a comfortable residence and the other a beautiful combination of wood and landscape garden

---

[9] See Act 14 and 15 Vic. c. 83, § 17.

[10] Which Mr. Radford, the late tenant, had edged with a deep border of black out of respect for the memory of his deceased wife. Lord Wensleydale, even in its improved state, used to say of it that Denman must be very fond of ancestral property to like such a house.

became henceforth the most delightful employment of Denman's leisure.

Scott did not take more pleasure in planting and thinning in his more stately domain at Abbotsford, than Denman in his humble patrimony among the romantic hills of Derbyshire. His letters henceforth are full of allusions to his alterations and improvements, his building and his planting, occupations all the more enjoyable owing to the severe labours from which he escaped to take part in them.

' It was in the summer of 1830,' writes Mrs. Baillie, in her biographical sketch, ' that my brother first went to reside with his family at Stony Middleton. In this retirement he enjoyed himself completely, entering with delight into the improvement of his little domain, planting and transplanting trees with his own hand, and labouring with as much eagerness and interest as though this had been the sole occupation of his life. It was delightful to see him at these periods of relaxation, surrounded by his family, all engaged in similar pursuits, and he himself entering with ardour and affection into all their little plans and suggestions of improvement.

' The advantage he derived from a few weeks thus employed may easily be imagined. Having determined that Stony Middleton should in future be his summer residence, he found it necessary to make some additions to the house, as it was too small to accommodate his numerous family ; but these additions were very moderate, and did not at all interfere with the simple and unpretending character of the place.'

As regards society, Denman was very pleasantly situated at Stony Middleton. His old friend Francis Hodgson, who had then for some years been Vicar of Bakewell, was living with his first wife, a graceful and accomplished person, in his immediate neighbourhood; at Stoke Hall, not far off, were the Arkwrights,[11] and at St. Helen's House, Derby, the Strutts,[12] two delightful families with whom the Denmans had long been intimate; the Duke of Devonshire's palace at Chatsworth was within easy visiting range, and its princely owner was not only splendid in his hospitality, but cordial in his friendship.

The session of 1832, even after the Reform Bill struggle had been finally set at rest, threatened at one time to be almost as protracted and little less laborious than that memorable one of 1831.

Writing on July 18, 1832, to his third daughter, Fanny (now the Honourable Lady Baynes), who was then presiding over the improvements at Stony Middleton,[13] Denman complains bitterly of the anticipated

[11] Robert Arkwright, Esq , for many years the occupant of Stoke Hall, was a grandson of the well-known Sir Richard Arkwright. His wife was celebrated for the exquisite taste of her singing and her talents as a musical composer. Moore, in January 1828, visited Stoke Hall and Bakewell Vicarage, the latter in quest of information from Hodgson as to Byron (whose Life he published in 1830). In his diary from January 22 to 28, he gives a pleasant account of the Arkwrights, Hodgsons, and Strutts.

[12] Edward Strutt, Esq., long M.P. for Derby, afterwards for Nottingham, was raised to the Peerage in 1856, as Lord Belper.

[13] This lively young lady, a great favourite of her father's, had, with her brothers Richard and George—now the Judge—then a boy of eleven, been one of the pioneers of the family migration (in 1830) to Stony Middleton, when it was something like a settlement in the backwoods. She had ever since been invested with a sort of mock sovereignty

duration of the Session, and of the inveteracy of the Opposition, adding : 'They must, however, wear out their patience at last, and then I must have a real domestic leisure at Stony Middleton, with as many of you about me as possible.'

The menace, however, proved worse than the reality : Parliament, worn out with hard work and excitement, rose at length on August 16, and the next day Denman wrote as follows from town to his friend Merivale, who had already settled himself in Devonshire for the Long Vacation at his patrimonial residence, Barton Place :

I am delighted to hear of your improvements in Barton Place, and hope, in about a week, to be doing as much for the prospect out of your window at Middleton. My wife and three youngest daughters are now alone with me in Russell Square; and they will move about Monday. I go on Tuesday to prosecute the traitor of Ascot Heath,[14] and then I think of making my way into Derbyshire, *viâ* Liverpool and Manchester. I have disembarrassed myself of all electioneering ideas in that part of the world, and hope to lead a backwoodsman's life for at least a month.

Such a clearance from London of official people ! Such schoolboy happiness at our breaking-up ! and what a glorious harvest is gathering, and what a prospect of a still fine summer.

Did you see Joseph pass in the 'Snake.'[15] He was at

over the domain, and was sometimes, in consequence, as in the letter referred to in the text, addressed by her father as 'Dear little Queen.' Miss Frances Denman married in 1846, Admiral Sir Robert Lambert Baynes, K.C.B., who died 1869.

[14] Denis Collins, a mad mariner, who had shot at William IV. in June 1832, on the Ascot Heath race-course ; he was found insane, and shut up 'during His Majesty's pleasure,' i.e. for life.

[15] The 'Snake' was a vessel to which Admiral (then Lieutenant)

Plymouth a week ago, and we believe him to be at Cork, where, if he should be detained, I shall feel strongly tempted to cross the Channel and join him.

A week later Denman wrote to the same old friend the first of an interesting series of letters, which so fully and fairly exhibit the real political bias of his mind immediately before the change which was to take him out of the sphere of active party politics for ever, that it has been thought better, though rather lengthy, to give them almost in their entirety :

50 Russell Square : August 24, 1832.

My dear Merivale,—I often quiz myself for doing what seems more ridiculous than it really is under some circumstances — citing my own opinions at a former time as affording some guidance to what the truth probably is at the present time. It is in the nature of an appeal from Philip heated, to Philip in his calmer moments, from an opinion fermented into activity while the passions were at work to that which has been formed when reason was exercising an undisturbed and undisputed sway. Very true, there is in this no authority to bind another, but strong evidence to a man's self, that the best judgment he is capable of forming is that to which he is so enabled to turn back. It is one of the cases in which second thoughts are not the best; at all events, you, who ask me my present views, cannot object to my reminding you of those which I formerly entertained.

Possibly, then, you may remember Fladgate having said, many years ago, in speaking of Romilly, that he was a bigoted Republican. Walking by the dead wall of Lincoln's Inn Fields, I remember expressing to you my strong con-

Denman had been appointed before he got the ‘ Curlew.’ An unfounded report was at this time flying about that the ‘ Snake ’ had been lost.

viction that he must be mistaken, because the universal estimate of Romilly's fine understanding would be greatly depreciated by the fact being so. For to hazard all the secured benefits of an established order, from a distaste for those forms which fools alone contest; to reject the freedom which may be enjoyed under a constitutional monarchy for the purpose of an experiment whether it may not also find shelter in a fabric which, if it can be reared, will belong to an order of architecture which, in my eyes, may be more symmetrical — this is a course which would no doubt deserve many other names, but certainly that of folly in a pre-eminent degree.

The greatest of all political evils I have always thought was this — injustice deliberately perpetrated or wilfully persisted in by the State. My own opinion has uniformly been that injustice and wrong, whenever detected, ought to be instantly swept away. Like everything that prevails, it will by degrees strengthen itself by inveterate habits and factitious interests, and even the disinterested will grow in time accustomed and indifferent.

Let, then, the first moment be taken when you can bring a sufficient force to bear upon mischief. Shake off the bad principle while you may, and scan not too nicely the inconveniencies or even dangers that may result from the success of your exertions. Peel's Bill on the Currency, the repeal of the Test Act, and Catholic Emancipation are examples of what I mean.

Paramount to all these questions, great as they were, has ever been to my mind the question of Parliamentary Reform. The perpetual fraud upon the people, the audacious belying of the Constitution, the shameless effrontery and cunning with which the multiform and outrageous abuse was at once avowed and concealed, the frightful small fry of peculation daily engendered in the huge midden of corruption, the license to degrade and oppress, the charter to demoralise and plunder the mass of our countrymen—all this could not be laid bare without exciting such decided hostility as could not fail in the end to sweep away the nuisance.

I always thought that this could, and hoped it would, be done without jeopardy to any one respectable part of our institutions. You may possibly remember that in those days, while waiting till public opinion should be fully awake on this momentous subject, I reckoned on the conversion of our enemies and the co-operation of *all* the great parties in the effort to carry out an effective measure of Reform.

In the autumn of 1830 I thought the time was come, and took my seat in Parliament fully prepared to support the Duke as the Reformer with the same contentment and zeal which my friends had displayed in his favour as the Emancipator.

I was little prepared to expect, when a Government had been formed on the principle of Parliamentary Reform, when the Cabinet had agreed on a measure which the King had deliberately adopted, when the people were all but unanimous in applauding it, and it had received the sanction even of an unreformed Parliament—that we should still encounter a vexatious and sordid opposition to the very principle of Reform itself.

The consequence has arisen that, with principles the most conservative, and convinced that Reform ought to have been peculiarly of that character, I must admit our present position to be unsatisfactory, and find it difficult to lay down the course we ought to take on the wide chart of the time to come.

As a *nisi prius* advocate I am convinced that Peel would have won more verdicts than even Scarlett. His management of the '*appearances*' in a cause is consummate. He is a very able debater, a respectable speaker, an admirable head of the Home Department ; but as a statesman his deficiency is deplorable. His truckling to the half-witted arrogance of the opponents of Schedule A., when he might have shared the public confidence by supporting, and perhaps improving, the Bill, marks him out as a man of narrow views and infirm mind.[16] His appetite for keeping his party together has in fact shaken them to pieces. What blindness not to see the principle of Reform as clearly in the wretched *ex post facto* botchings of Grampound and Bassetlaw as in our Bill. His conduct deprives you of all chance of an honest Conservative Opposition to take our places. No Opposition can now turn us out but one disposed to carry Liberal opinions to a far greater length than the present Cabinet ever can dream of.

Lord Harrowby's views on arriving from the Continent, and his inconsistent vote against the second reading, while he approved of the principle of the Bill, have had results equally unfortunate. The injury, however, sustained by the Lords as a body has almost escaped notice in comparison with what the Church has received from the Archbishop's feeble, irrational, and party speech at the same period. I confess that even these disasters were immeasurably outdone by the success of Lyndhurst's clever party manœuvre in May. The unhappy effect of all is that the Conservative powers are all formidably damaged in the estimate of that public opinion without which they are all nothing, and which has learned the fatal lesson of its own irresistible power.

I strongly protest against the charge of our producing this state of things. Reform no doubt is an agitating subject, but we had no choice whether to bring it forward or not. The choice lay *not* between Reform or no Reform; *but between Reform proposed by the Government and peaceably carried through, or Reform proposed by the Clubs and hurried forward by convulsion.* I heartily lament the dangerous assemblies that have been held, and the inflammatory language that has been employed, but the senseless

---

[16] Denman lived very considerably to modify this unfavourable opinion of Peel. Peel's later career as a great financial and commercial reformer, and especially his self-denying courage in abolishing the Corn Laws, met with Denman's warm and generous sympathy and approval. It must be admitted that in Peel's obstinate resistance to Parliamentary Reform there was much to justify the severe judgment expressed in the text.

cry of reaction was a constant challenge to vehement demonstrations.

Wetherell's speeches were from the first an appeal to popular violence against the bill. Parties were so nearly balanced, and the two Houses so disqualified by the nature of the measure from judging of it dispassionately, that both parties referred their quarrel to the people, as promising fairest to be impartial arbitrators. How could you have distinguished Political Unions from Grey's Friends of the People in 1792, or (a still stronger case) Pitt's Convocation of Delegates in 1782? Even if possible, indicting a whole people is a hopeless task, but remember that the moment an organisation of force was announced, we put the scheme down by proclamation, and that everything like an overt act of violence has been prevented or punished.

I start for Liverpool to-morrow evening; *rail* to Manchester, and thence make a descent on Derbyshire, avoiding the distracted districts—those, I mean, where I have been named as a candidate.[17] Some of my supporters were so slack in requisitioning till they knew whether I would stand if invited, and I was so resolved to tell them nothing about it till invited, that both the other candidates have been making play personally, and I fear the Tory will outstrip the Whig. I am against all pledges, though I think very general ones may fairly be asked from a new candidate. I am equally against all canvassing.

The King is very gracious, and has sent a recommendation to mercy for this wretched old mariner [Dennis Collins]. My best regards to Dr. Drury,[18] in addition to the other remembrances. I will take the 'Edinburgh Review' with

---

[17] This alludes to a requisition recently set on foot inviting Denman to stand for the county at the general election after the dissolution, which was then known to be resolved on, but which did not take place till December 2.

[18] Late Head-master of Harrow; Merivale's father-in-law, then probably on a visit to Barton Place, from which his own residence—Cockwood—was not very distant.

me.   Do tell me in what Brougham resembles Napoleon, •
except in intellectual power.   I think him most like Mazeppa's
horse, and, as a member of the Useful Knowledge Committee,
am somewhat in a fright.   Are you easy ?[19]

The above letter was written just before Denman left
Town; that which follows almost immediately after his
arrival at Stony Middleton:

Middleton : September 4, 1832.

My dear Merivale,—On the 25th ult. I went by the mail
to Liverpool, which magnificent commercial town I never
visited before; thence I performed my maiden journey by
rail to Manchester—the thirty-two miles in an hour' and
twenty minutes.   The rapidity is delightful, and not at all
dazzling or confusing as to objects on each side, though part
of the way we came at the rate of a mile in two minutes.

At Manchester the rain fell, accompanied me to this
place, and lasted three days.   I found Bess [20] with her
brothers Richard and George : [21] my lady and the other five [22]
came on Thursday evening, when the weather became comparatively fair, and for the last two days has been superb.

We still have workmen about, but the house is much
improved, and almost all my experiments out of doors have
been successful.   The Arkwrights and Hodgsons are at
home : the Duke just come to Chatsworth for a long spell,
so we feel we have a neighbourhood, and the country seems
alive.

One day I went over to Buxton to concert with Fergusson
[General Sir R. C. Fergusson] our joint candidate address to

[19] Merivale, like Denman, was a member of the Committee of Useful
Knowledge.

[20] Hon. Mrs. Hodgson.

[21] Hon. Richard Denman and the Hon. Mr. Justice Denman, then in
his thirteenth year.

[22] Fanny (Hon. Lady Baynes), Margaret (Hon. Mrs. Cropper), Ann
(Hon. Mrs. Holland), Caroline Amelia (Hon. Mrs. Beresford), Lewis
(Hon. and Rev. Lewis Denman).

the electors of Nottingham, and my valediction to this county [Derbyshire] will appear at the same time. But all electioneering activity seems laid at rest for the present.

That is no reason against my returning to your important question, viz.: What course the Government intend to take, and where they are prepared to set up their standard of resistance to further innovation?

If my former prose meant anything it meant this—that as a Conservative reformer, I lamented the course adopted by the Tories in resisting the Bill, both as it affected the objects to be protected and the means of protecting them. For my part I could have been well pleased to follow the great work of Parliamentary Reform with a long repose, that we may set our House in order, not as on the eve of dissolution, but to ensure its being safely and comfortably and socially inhabited. But it is a mere delusion to expect that any great benefits can be secured for man without an incessant exertion on his part.

The spirit of reform was abroad long before the Whigs came into office; the first great benefit they have done is to gratify this just and eager expectation, without those dangerous convulsions which the nature of the evil, and the conduct of the adversary, seemed at one time to make unavoidable.

The question of retrenchment must weave itself into every vote for supplies and estimates. Taxes must be reduced; expenditure must come down: yet establishments must be maintained, and the national creditor receive his dividend. Where is the line to be drawn? What mortal can say beforehand?

You are aware that the Archbishop of Canterbury set on foot a commission for enquiring into the revenues of the Church: it must make a report, and that report must be taken into consideration, and acted on. To what extent? Will a reformed Parliament be satisfied with less than Peel's noble brother-in-law [Lord Henley] recommends? Then the Bishops must be excluded from the House of Lords, and all their incomes be cut down to 5,000*l.* a-piece, and all the revenues of Deans and Chapters be taken to augment the poorer livings, and raise the working clergy above want.

But it is possible that while all Lord Henley's *concessions* are freely accepted, the *limitations* he would impose on reform would not be so willingly received. He may be thought judicious in arguing that bishops should have *no more* than 5,000*l.* a year; but his doctrine that they ought to retain *as much* may be reckoned a mere gratuitous assumption. Great alacrity may be shown in taking the revenues of Deans and Chapters, without the same eagerness to apply them so as to give every one of the numerous poorer clergy so much as 400*l.* a year. Nor can he expect universal concurrence in the opinion that the most valuable livings should retain all their present emoluments undiminished. All may agree that ecclesiastical sinecures ought not to go beyond the lives of their present possessors; but will all consent to their lasting quite so long: particularly such as may be persuaded by his lordship's scriptural doctrine that these sinecures are the 'accursed thing,' and that the 'accursed thing' must be ' put away '? On the contrary, it is possible that every surplus may be voted a sinecure, and every sine-cure adjudged to be ' put away ' on the instant, not preserved to move the divine vengeance during the continuance of some of the best lives in the world.

Much may be said against Church robbery, and the hateful inroads of infidelity; but I much doubt whether all the religious public (no doubt a very large proportion of the community) are faithful devotees of the Church of England and Ireland. Will the Presbyterian offer up prayers for Prelacy; or the Quaker fight for it; or the Independent and old Puritan of whatever creed make largesses to support what Lord Henley calls its representation? If any of these numerous bodies (to whom may be added the Catholics, now despairing of restitution) think that our National Church has long enough enjoyed its temporal advantages, the device of a Corporation of Commissioners provides them with the most apt and ingenious machinery for their purpose.

Now remember (as Cobbett would say) these matters cannot be staved off. They must undergo discussion. The Archbishop has tabled the Church of England, and that of Ireland has taken care to challenge full investigation.

Hodgson and others have called and interrupted my pamphlet, luckily for you. I finish and despatch it, because you could not otherwise receive it till your return to London, if I reckon your time correctly.

The third and concluding letter of the series followed after a week's interval:

Stony Middleton: September 11, 1832.

My dear Merivale,—We seem equally agreed in our general principles, and in the difficulty of making a practical application of them.

The Church is inevitably first thought of when we look to the results of reform. The 'Times' the other day had a curious collection of Conservative electioneering addresses— all broaching the same idea of the necessity of changes in the Church. Only spare vested interests! say you and Lord Henley. To establish a vested interest in the 'accursed thing' which the Church must 'put away' is his lordship's affair.

But is not commutation of tithes to be immediate? If nay—nothing is done to satisfy the public mind. If yea, behold 'vested interests' set aside. And, speaking in good earnest, ought they in all cases to be spared? Supposing it true that the Bishop of London's income will be raised in ten years to 100,000$l.$ by leases falling in—ought this to be allowed? Why not? Surely for no other reason than that the interest, vested as it is, is in fact and principle a compensation for public services, and ought to bear some proportion to it. Perhaps I can draw no satisfactory line of distinction between the improvement of this property and that of a great landed proprietor. I may, indeed, argue that the latter holds his land without any such implied condition annexed; that such is the nature of property that you can lay hands on no accumulation, however exorbitant, without endangering the smallest interests of the meanest subject; introducing an agrarian law at the end of every year, month, and day—in a word, without annihilating the rights of property altogether. These distinctions may be just and reasonable in the abstract, yet they would be no barrier against the inroads of excited passions in the form of political unions, public meetings, unanimous resolves, &c.

My coarse and shadeless etching may perhaps sufficiently set forth my view of the inherent difficulties of the case. Changes must be made; you say the very principle of change, once adopted, may lead to total subversion. It makes me melancholy to think how great a card for the public was thrown away when the Tories set their faces against all reform of Parliament, *preposterously confounding abuse with establishment, and clothing infamous corruption in the robes of venerable prescription.* I lament still more that these insufferable nuisances were not permitted to be abated by the lawful authority of King, Lords and Commons, without a popular demonstration that amounted almost to mob control and dictation.

The party of the movement condemns itself by its very title. A firm government is the great aim of all political exertions; establishment the only honest end of revolution. But we must not be wafted about by mere words; there may be a great movement of parties, while the law is still supreme; there must be a perpetual readiness to improve the laws in every one of their details, while their authority and leading principles are left unimpaired.

You think we should make a defensive stand somewhere, prepared to sacrifice office, life, everything, if we cannot maintain the position. Show me a clear case of right and wrong at any period, and I hope I should not hesitate. But if I lay down an arbitrary rule of right, for purposes of conservation, what shall it profit the country? Ten to one, if the case arises, the Tories will join the Radicals to turn us out. They will have another ten days' trial, find they cannot form a government, and retire amid general derision. Into what hands will the government then pass ?   Will there be one ?

But if the Tories, contrary to their conduct on timber and sugar, give us manful support, the hypothesis being always that the people desire the change we resist, then the basis of public opinion is removed, and the edifice must rest on bayonets. What would be the consequence, what the duration of that dread repose ?

Why, then it is the duty of the present ministry to propose a still lower scale of expenditure, and a Reform in the Church as well as in the Law—each changing as little as possible. They must incorporate with the Constitution all such real improvements as may be sure to continue when once adopted, and may, by promoting the welfare, secure the confidence of the great body of the people. They must carefully watch events as they pass, and give to each measure of reform the most wholesome and permanent character of which it can be made susceptible.

I totally deny the numerous blunders you ascribe to the present ministry, and set them down to the account of ‘ Candour and Philosophy.’ Considerable awkwardness may have arisen in the parliamentary management of questions ; the budget was a clumsy business—but in the conduct of the Government nothing, I contend, with such exceptions as these, can fairly be called erroneous.   Every day's experience, every day's continuance in power (especially now that the King's heart is entirely with his ministers) will furnish new securities against the sort of faults that have given the enemy on some occasions this advantage. Still more strenuously do I deprecate the charge of deserting the cause of the public peace. Prosecutions or dragoonings must have ended in defeat and bloodshed, perhaps civil war. Nor will I submit to be told that the inflammation which made the public mind intractable grew out of Reform. The state of England in November, 1830, proves that it existed before. Nothing could allay it.   Obstinate opposition to our measures on principles adverse to all reform could only exasperate the discontent.   Oh, wretched blindness ! not to see that the stale arguments by which Canning warded off the discussion had become ten times worse than nothing the moment that discussion had begun !

The difficulty of preserving a *juste milieu* must always be great—of maintaining peace at home amidst strongly roused antagonistic feelings, and peace abroad among nations eager for violence and conquest, with a domestic cry for war raised by the very men who know in their hearts that the present ministers are the only ones who possess the power of being really conservative, but not without a generous confidence accorded by that still higher power—*Public Opinion.*

On October 7, still from Stony Middleton, Denman wrote as follows to his venerable mother, who had then for some years been an inmate of her daughter Mrs. Baillie's house in Cavendish Square.

My dearest Mother,—Though I have been rather an indifferent correspondent during the present vacation, I assure you some of my most agreeable moments have been owing to you.   Tom's [23] letters have never failed to give me an account of you, and I am as happy to receive such good tidings of you as grateful for your acts of kindness to him. He has been a most active supervisor of my affairs in town, and a full reporter of all that has passed in the family.

We have amazingly little to say for ourselves, one day having been exactly like another ; for five weeks all fair, except Friday last, which was very wet, and prevented—not us, indeed, from taking our ride, but—Mrs. Holland and her daughters from leaving the inn at Bakewell to look about

---

[23] The present Lord Denman, who spent this Long Vacation in town, watching the routine of administrative business that passed in vacation through the Attorney-General's chambers, greatly to the relief and accommodation of his father.

this beautiful country.   They had better fortune yesterday— saw Chatsworth and our own magnificent dale ; and will, I hope, be lighted to-morrow by a bright sun to the threshold of the great Peak cavern.   Some of us ride daily, and we have visited more of the beautiful scenes of this varied country than I ever saw before ; always with increasing pleasure.   We have very nearly done with workmen about the house, which has been made very convenient ; but some small improvements are projected in the garden, &c., for another year.   We have excellent neighbours, and almost more going out than I could desire.

You will be glad to hear that a cautious examination of the votes at Nottingham secures to the present members [himself and General Fergusson] a majority of at least 800 at the approaching election ; [24] most likely no opposition will be attempted.

I hope to be in London on the evening of the 19th. Shadwell is coming here for three days before that, and we shall go up to town together.   Give our united kindest love to my sister, William,[25] and all.

Your truly affectionate Son.

In his recently cited letters to Merivale, mention, it will have been seen, has been made of an invitation from the gentlemen of his native county to come forward as their representative at the general election which was to follow on the dissolution rendered necessary by the passing of the Reform Act.   In a previous letter to his daughter Fanny, written in the early part of August, he had said in reference to this invitation, ' I may be *compelled by circumstances* to

---

[24] That which was to come on after the dissolution consequent on the passing of the Reform Act, and which, owing to the many changes introduced by that measure, did not take place till December 2, 1832.

[25] Mr. William Henry Baillie, son of Dr. and Mrs. Baillie.   Denman's mother resided latterly at Mrs. Baillie's house in Cavendish Square.

accept the compliment. . I acknowledge it to be one of a most flattering nature, coming as it does spontaneously from my neighbours, without any other effort on my part than attempting to discourage it.'

The circumstances thus alluded to were no doubt those attending his rough reception by the 'lambs' of Nottingham when he, with his colleague, Sir R. C. Fergusson, went down there, in August 1832, to celebrate the final triumph of Parliamentary Reform. When Denman, on this occasion, came forward to address the people, he was greeted with groans, hisses, and imprecations. Halters were exhibited round men's necks, and there were loud shouts of 'No Denman! Burke him! Bristol him!' &c.; nay, to such an extent did the violence of the populace proceed, that, at one period, fears were entertained for his personal safety.

The cause of the popular fury was this: five men had been condemned to death under the Special Commission that sate at Nottingham in January 1832 (while the Attorney-General was engaged in prosecuting the rioters under another Special Commission at Bristol), as ringleaders in the great outbreak that culminated in the burning of Nottingham Castle. Of these five men three were executed, notwithstanding a petition for reprieve, which in twenty-four hours received 17,000 signatures; and the Whig Attorney-General (who might, it was supposed, have averted their doom) became thenceforth the object of the bitterest popular execration.

On ascertaining, however, that the feeling of the populace was not shared by the great body of the electors, Denman resolved again to try his fortunes with his old constituency, and issued, as intimated in his letter to Merivale of September 4, an address in which he presented himself to the electors a fifth time as a candidate for their suffrages, and another of the same date to the electors for the county, declining the honour of their invitation.

Subsequently, as appears from his letter to his mother of October 7, he had ascertained by reliable calculations that he and his colleagues were sure of commanding a very considerable majority, and that in all probability they would not have to encounter any opposition.

The necessity for completing, before the new writs were issued, the novel and extensive electoral arrangements consequent on the great Parliamentary changes introduced by the Reform Act, had the effect of unavoidably postponing the dissolution, which did not finally take place until December 2, 1832.

CHAPTER XXII.

APPOINTMENT AS CHIEF JUSTICE.

A.D. 1832.   ÆT. 53.

Trial at Bar of Mayor of Bristol and others—Lord Tenterden sits in court for the last time on third day of the trial, October 27—Dies on November 3, 1832—Denman appointed his successor, November 6, 1832—Reason for this expedition—Good sense and magnanimity of William IV.—Denman's letter of acknowledgment to Lord Grey—His appointment generally popular—The best since Lord Holt—Article from 'Morning Herald' on the relative claims of Denman and Lyndhurst—Letter from Denman to his wife announcing his appointment, November 7, 1832—Shadwell makes the farewell speech at Lincoln's Inn —Letter from Denman to his wife, November 14—First week as Chief Justice—Demeanour of Bench and Bar—Copley—Scarlett—Quarrel of Scarlett and Denman on Mayor of Bristol's trial—Supreme happiness of Denman's mother—Letter of congratulation from Spring Rice— Reason of the general satisfaction at Denman's appointment—Address from Master and Fellows of St. John's College, Cambridge—Deputation and address from City of London—The Chief Justice's reply.

BEFORE the dissolution of December 2, 1832 took place, an event occurred which was to lift Denman above the stormy region of party politics, and enable him to exchange the severe and anxious labours of the Attorney-Generalship for the higher dignity, and comparative, though, as in his case it proved, only comparative, leisure of the Bench.

Lord Tenterden, who for the last fourteen years had presided as Chief Justice of the King's Bench, was now in his seventy-first year, and had long been in a feeble state of health.[1]   On October 27, 1832—the third day of the trial at Bar in the Court of King's Bench of the late Mayor of Bristol and others, for alleged neglect of duty during the riots in that city of the previous year[2]—he appeared in Court for the last time; and a week afterwards, on November 3, he expired with these words on his lips—addressing an imaginary jury—' Gentlemen, you are all dismissed.'

Lord Grey, on Brougham's instant and urgent suggestion,[3] at once went down to Windsor to submit Denman's name to the King, who, ' after a short struggle,' says Brougham in his ' Memoirs,'[4] assented to the appointment; and on November 6, 1832, Denman was sworn in at the Privy Council as Lord Chief Justice of England.

Grey and Brougham were both thoroughly agreed

---

[1] Charles Abbott, born 1762, the son of a barber at Canterbury, distinguished himself at Oxford, where he gained the Latin verse prize in 1784, and the English essay prize in 1786; published his celebrated ' Treatise on Shipping,' 1802; Judge, 1816; Chief Justice of King's Bench, 1818; raised to Peerage as Lord Tenterden, 1827; died, November 3, 1832, in his seventy-first year. Foss's ' Lives of the Judges,' vol. ix. p. 68.

[2] Denman, as Attorney-General, prosecuted; the Mayor (Mr. Pinney) was honourably acquitted, the jury declaring their opinion that in a situation of great difficulty, and when deserted by those from whom he was entitled to aid and encouragement, he had conducted himself with great firmness and propriety. The prosecution, after this verdict, was abandoned against the other defendants. ' Annual Register,' vol. lxxiv. p. 51. This was the last important occasion on which Denman appeared in court as counsel.

[3] ' I was resolved,' says Brougham, ' that Denman should succeed him (Tenterden) on every ground—political, party, public, and private.' ' Memoirs,' vol. iii. p. 220.

[4] ' Memoirs,' vol. iii. p. 224.

as to the fitness of the selection; the Prime Minister stating strongly and emphatically that he had never made any appointment with greater satisfaction to himself. They were also both agreed as to the great importance of making it at once, in order, as Brougham expressed it, ‘ that not even a day might be given to the enemy to torment, or even work on, the King.’[5]

The King, who, notwithstanding this politic promptitude, had already been strongly worked on in favour of Lord Lyndhurst, though he at first showed some reluctance, yet behaved on the whole with commendable good sense and magnanimity, replying to some of those who were careful to remind him of Denman’s strong language on the Queen’s trial that ‘ he had long since forgiven all that, and almost forgotten it.’

Denman, on receiving through Brougham an intimation from the Prime Minister that the appointment had been made, wrote the following letter of acknowledgment to Lord Grey :

My dear Lord,—Having just received your Lordship’s communication from the Lord Chancellor, I cannot delay the expression of my most grateful feelings for the kindness you have uniformly shown me, and most eminently on the present occasion.

Conscious of many deficiencies, I trust I am neither wanting in gratitude, nor in the just pride that ought to accompany such an elevation; and I persuade myself that the only way I can ever hope to prove these sentiments will be that most agreeable to your lordship.

It must be by a constant endeavour to discharge the new

---

[5] ‘Memoirs,’ vol. iii. p. 222. Letter from Brougham to Lord Grey of November 5, 1832.

duties to which I am called with diligence, zeal, and fidelity ; so that the public may be loath to censure the appointment, and its authors may neither feel shame nor regret for having placed their confidence in me,

I have the honour to be,
My dear Lord,
Yours most faithful and obliged,
T. DENMAN.

To the Earl Grey.

With the Liberal party, with the public, and with Westminster Hall generally, the appointment was from the first highly popular ; it was regarded as the just reward of professional eminence and unswerving political integrity. Even the more moderate of the Tories had little to say against it ; it was only the old ' Mumpsimus ' party—the party of Cumberland, Eldon, and Wynford—who indulged in suppressed murmurs of pious indignation at the scandal involved in elevating to the highest seat of Judicature a hot political partisan—an ultra-Liberal, if not even something worse— who had libelled one ' gracious sovereign ' as a ' Nero,' and branded another as a ' slanderer.'

Time was soon to show that since the days of Lord Holt no better appointment of a chief magistrate had ever been made in England.

The following article from the ' Morning Herald,' which appeared just before the appointment had been made public, and when a rumour was being industriously circulated that Lord Lyndhurst, not Denman, was to be the new Chief Justice, is well worthy of insertion, as a sample of the reasonable public opinion of the time on the respective claims of the two men, and as a proof of the high estimation which Denman then enjoyed among moderate men of all parties :

There requires no argument to prove the necessity of filling with a man of superior legal abilities, and purity of character, the vacancy which the death of Lord Tenterden has occasioned in the first judicial situation of the department of Common Law; but though all persons will agree, or affect to agree, in the abstract principle, *detur digniori,* yet it appears there is some difference of opinion, or rather opposition of feeling, as to who is the more worthy of the candidates for this high and responsible appointment.

When it is known, as the public already know, that the present Attorney-General and Chief Baron are the only individuals whose claims have been put in competition for the Chief Justiceship of the King's Bench, there cannot, we should think, be any real or reasonable doubt as to the superiority of the claims preferred upon the part of the former. We leave out of question the custom or *etiquette* which establishes a sort of equitable prescription, if we may so call it, to such an office in favour of the Attorney-General for the time being. We are aware that custom has sometimes been broken in upon, and we think it ought to be whenever a departure from it ensures the appointment of a more respectable and efficient Chief Justice than a rigid adherence to official routine could supply. In the present instance, however, the claims which the Attorney-General has by virtue of his office are greatly strengthened by those personal merits which constitute his best ˙recommendation to a station of such serious trust and exalted dignity.

In this question the adjustment of the conflicting claims of individuals is of little moment compared with the great consideration which involves the impartial, fearless, and honest administration of justice, and thereby affects the interests of the whole nation. If the fountain of justice be impure, how can the streams that issue from it be expected to flow in that clear and stainless current which reflects the pure image of the law?

Of Lord Lyndhurst the country knows a great deal. Far more distinguished as a politician than either a lawyer or a judge, his name is connected with some instances of unhappy celebrity. He may be pure on the judgment seat; we neither say nor insinuate aught to the contrary; but certainly his political character does not bear that stamp of principle and consistency which is calculated to inspire the public with confidence; and where there is not confidence, the highest talent—the greatest legal attainments—fail to make upon the public mind the impression which is favourable to the moral authority of the judicial office. If Lord Lyndhurst held the scales of justice with the exact severity of a modern Aristides, it would still be recollected that in ambition he was a Proteus, and that his path to power was through the wreck of all political consistency.

Sir Thomas Denman has also united the character of the politician, in some degree, with that of the lawyer; but how different a picture does his political life present! Having adopted certain principles which his judgment approved, he has stood by them, through evil and good report, with a steadiness which forms a striking contrast to the facility with which his learned rival has put off the doctrine of one day to suit the purpose of another. We have occasionally differed from opinions laid down by Sir Thomas Denman since he came into office; but when we thought him in error we have regretted it rather as an instance of the fallibility of human judgment than as any proof of a conscious deviation from admitted principle. He never argued in favour of one set of opinions or measures only to prove his versatility in refuting his own reasons, and falsifying his own predictions. Long did his professional fortunes seem to wither beneath the chilling shade of court neglect; yet no impatience of party persecution caused him to fling off the badge of disqualifying fidelity, and purchase speedy promotion at the expense of honourable fame.

As a judge, at least in a court of criminal jurisdiction, the present Attorney-General made a high and deserved reputation. His conduct on the Bench of the City Court, when he presided as Common Serjeant, was distinguished by the exercise of those qualities which give the laws a moral influence, and preserve the passionless dignity of justice. With all his talents and various legal acquirements, the late Lord Tenterden wanted one essential attribute for the judgment seat—amenity of manners. His disposition was more overbearing than one expects to find in a man of superior understanding; and his temper, at times, was exceedingly harsh and morose. In this respect Sir Thomas Denman is not likely to imitate the bad example which his distinguished predecessor gave to men in judicial authority. The courtesy of his deportment and the kindliness of his manners seem part of his nature, and not dependent upon circumstances or situation. His administration of his high duty may, therefore, be expected to be as dispassionate as it will be impartial; for his long proved integrity is the best guarantee that he will not venerate the pretensions of rank, or riches, or power, more than the claims of justice—or, by any admixture of political feeling with the opinions of the judge, pervert the law, and ' sully the spotless purity of the ermine.'

It is not unimportant, also, to recollect that in the King's Bench are tried those great cases of political libel in which it is particularly requisite that the presiding judge should not be one who stands in that situation with the public in which he thinks the freedom of opinion a very dangerous privilege, and one which ought to be cut down with an unsparing hand. There is a trial for libel against the press on record of which we will not say more at present than that it was conducted in a most unprecedented manner. We are quite sure that such a proceeding could not be sanctioned under the judicial authority of Sir Thomas Denman, who will greatly disappoint us if he does not always recollect that the glory and usefulness of justice perishes when 'legal redress' becomes the pretext for political persecution.

Lady Denman, who had been prevented by an attack of illness from accompanying her husband to town at the end of the Long Vacation, and who was then at Buxton, received from him the following announcement of his promotion, the day after he had been sworn in at the Privy Council.

November 7, 1832.

My dearest Love,—I can hardly believe my eyes and ears, though they agree in telling me I am Chief Justice of England.

I most sincerely and anxiously hope that the office may not be depreciated in my hands, and that I may in some degree justify the partiality of my friends. Their cordial encouragement is delightful. Lord Grey and Brougham have behaved with a simplicity and kindness worthy of great men.

Shadwell made the farewell speech on my leaving Lincoln's Inn, with earnest and affectionate eloquence; but I am not sure whether my reception by the judges (especially those of my own court) has not gratified me more than all the rest.

Great exertions will be wanted to preserve so much confidence and attachment.

Your ever faithful and affectionate husband.

Another letter to Lady Denman, written a week later, runs as follows:

November 14, 1832.

Dearest Love,—This afternoon completes my week's service, which has been as decently performed, I believe, as any reasonable person could expect. My time and thoughts have been most fully occupied, and what gives me now a little leisure is that some cases in which I was concerned at the Bar, and can take no part now, are being heard by the other judges.

I am delighted to think you are on your way home, but I beg you not to exert yourself too much in travelling. Every change that will be necessary, as engaging a butler and keeping a coach, I have put off till you come.

The patronage of my office has been immensely reduced,[6] but I hope to find a very good provision, as the reward of useful employment, for Tom and Archer.[7]

It is highly gratifying to see the manner in which my promotion has been received, not only by the Bar but by the Bench. My four brethren in this court[8] behave with all imaginable kindness, giving all possible assistance, and, between ourselves, I believe not a little happy that they escape a severer chief.

Copley[9] carries it off with perfect good humour ; though he pretends to state a promise of Lord Grey's in his favour, which is, of course, pure fiction.

Scarlett also contrives to put a tolerable face on it, though we have not yet quite recovered from our quarrel on the Bristol case.[10]

---

[6] By the Act of 1825, 5 and 6 G. IV. c. 82.

[7] Denman's eldest son (the present Lord Denman) was appointed by him Marshal and Associate. Sir Archer Croft, Bart., the eldest son of his sister Margaret—Lady Croft—became one of the Masters of the Court of King's Bench.

[8] Littledale, Patteson, James Parke (afterwards Lord Wensleydale), and Taunton.

[9] Lord Lyndhurst had used all his influence to obtain the appointment for himself.

[10] The trial of the Mayor of Bristol, in which Denman led for the Crown and Scarlett for the defence. The altercation between them is thus referred to by Brougham in a letter of November 3 to Lord Grey— 'Denman's attack on Scarlett you may have heard spoken of as *ferocious* ; but *all* admit it was deserved, and was purely in retaliation of a most wanton attack on us all. I hear there never was anything more savage, but nobody blames it.' ('Memoirs,' vol. iii. p. 221.) Denman and Scarlett met not long afterwards (on Denman's first judicial circuit) at Sir George Philip's, Weston, near Warwick, where a complete reconciliation took place.

You may suppose that my mother is supremely happy; she looks younger and handsomer than ever, and has written the best penned of all the congratulations I have received.

The letter from his venerable mother thus referred to is unluckily not to be found among his papers, and, indeed, of the many written expressions of joy and satisfaction which he must have received on his elevation to the Chief Justiceship hardly any have been preserved. One of the few is the following from the late Lord Monteagle (then the Right Honourable Thomas Spring Rice), which so well expresses what was then the almost universal feeling with regard to Denman's appointment that it may be well inserted here:

Treasury, November 7, 1832.

My dear Lord Chief Justice,—Though you will be overwhelmed with congratulations, I cannot for the life of me remain passive. I assure you that among the many friends who have admired and respected you, and who now rejoice at your triumph, there are few who feel more warmly than myself.

Your elevation to the highest dignity in your own branch of the law, *without having once turned to the right hand or the left, or having ever faltered in the cause of the People*, is a noble example to the Bar, and it is refreshing to think that we are able to add to the small capital stock of really patriotic judges.

And now I shall leave you, with the earnest hope that your future course may be as gratifying as its outset has been distinguished.

Believe me always,
With every good wish, most truly yours,
T. Spring Rice.

Lord Monteagle, in the passage printed in italics, precisely expressed the sentiment then uppermost in all men's minds as to the promotion of Denman. He had been elevated to his present position 'without having once turned to the right hand or the left, or having ever faltered in the cause of the People;' and so it came to pass that all honest and true men everywhere rejoiced at his appointment with a pure and disinterested joy, which is not often called forth in a similar degree on a similar occasion.

The address which follows, from the Master and Fellows of his old college—St. John's, Cambridge—has been treasured up with peculiar care. To Englishmen who have made their way in the world, few circumstances are more gratifying than to find themselves not forgotten in the place where they have received the moral and intellectual training that has in a great measure conduced to their success.

St. John's College, Cambridge: February 15, 1833.

My Lord,—The Master and Fellows of St. John's College most respectfully present to your Lordship, as a late member of their society, their cordial congratulations on your recent elevation to the high and important office of Lord Chief Justice of His Majesty's Court of King's Bench.

They rejoice that the early promise which your Lordship gave of future eminence, whilst you were a student within their walls, has been so fully realised; and that the eloquence, zeal, and ability which you have exhibited in the exercise of an arduous profession has been rewarded with this distinguished mark of your Sovereign's confidence, at a time of life when you may be permitted, under the blessing of Divine

Providence, to look forward to a long career of honour and usefulness.

(Signed)   J. WOOD, Master,

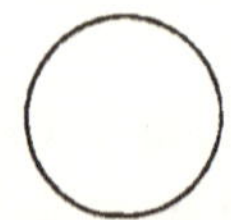

The Seal of the College.

On the 4th of the preceding month of January a deputation from the City of London had attended the Chief Justice at his house in Russell Square, and presented to him the following address :

My Lord,—On the advancement of your Lordship to the high and important office of Lord Chief Justice of England, the Lord Mayor, Aldermen, and Commons of the City of London, in Common Council assembled, on behalf of the whole body of citizens, are anxious to offer their heartfelt congratulations to one with whom they have long been nearly connected by the ties of public duty and personal esteem.

The high opinion which was entertained of your Lordship's character and talents led to your being placed in the office of Common Serjeant of the City of London ; your able performance of its duties, and a nearer acquaintance with your estimable qualities, had greatly endeared you to the citizens of London, when your appointment to fill the office of His Majesty's Attorney-General, at the same time that it deprived us of your services, was a gratifying sanction of the choice we had made ; and we rejoice in your Lordship's recent elevation, not merely from the interest which we take in your Lordship's honour and welfare, but from the satisfaction which we feel that so important an office has been conferred upon one of whose talents, integrity, and enlarged views we have had the most favourable experience, and whose character is highly esteemed by the whole country.

That your Lordship may live long to preside over the

administration of justice, to assist in introducing into it those improvements of which it may be found susceptible, and to enjoy the esteem of the wise and good, is, my Lord, our most earnest wish and prayer.

Signed by order of the Court,

H. WOODTHORPE.

The new Chief Justice returned the following answer :

My Lord Mayor and Gentlemen,—No language can do justice to the sense which I entertain of the high and extraordinary compliment paid to me by the City of London. The presentation of such an address, unanimously voted in the Court of Common Council, is the last and greatest in a long train of acts of kindness, every one of which is far beyond my desert, and only to be equalled by my gratitude.

The honour of being enrolled among the freemen of London was enhanced by every circumstance that could render it most desirable. It was shared with illustrious colleagues,[11] and on the most trying occasion bore testimony not only to individual conduct, but to a principle of unquestionable truth and immense importance—the connection between the rights and liberties of every subject, and the fearless discharge of the duty of an advocate.

In exercising afterwards in my favour the privilege of conferring rank at the Bar, you at the same time placed me in the judicial seat. Cheered by your generous confidence, I entered upon that career of service : the warm approval with which you hailed its close gives me the right to boast that eight years experience had in no degree diminished your favourable opinion.

The kind expressions with which you greet me now, at the commencement of a far weightier task, encourage me to hope that I may not be found altogether unworthy the favour with

---

[11] Brougham and Lushington.

which a gracious King has regarded me, nor wholly disappoint the expectations of that enlightened country to which it is our pride and happiness to belong. And among all the motives that can spur to faithful and zealous exertion, none has more influence in my breast than the hope that my fellow citizens of London may never feel shame, nor incur just censure, for the unexampled favour they have been pleased to bestow upon me?

CHAPTER XXIII.

SIR THOMAS DENMAN, CHIEF JUSTICE.

A.D. 1833.   ÆT. 54.

Puisne Judges of Court of King's Bench on Denman's accession—Littledale—Parke—Patteson—Taunton—Denman's relations as Chief with
the other judges of his court—Extract from letter to Rev. R. W.
Vevers—Pleasant picture of judicial harmony—Denman from the first
popular as a judge—His judicial qualifications—Emoluments of the
Chief Justiceship—Verbal understanding with Brougham on appointment—Denman throughout the whole term of his office only drew
8,000*l.* instead of 10,000*l.* a year—*Query,* what went with the difference?—Present salaries of Chief Justices not fixed till 1851—Denman's
great and successful exertions to clear off arrears—Severe judicial
labours—He keeps up his interest in literature—Letters to his son-in-
law, Mr. Wright, on his translation of the 'Inferno,' Jan. 1, 1833; and
remarks on merits of the translation—General impression of the
'Inferno'—The two great episodes—Francesca and Ugolino—Interest
inspired by Dante—Desire to know the facts of his life and times—
Dante's style—The allegorising commentators—Death of Denman's
mother, January 29, 1833—Her character—Affection and attentions of
her son—Denman's first judicial circuit, the Midland—Spring
Assizes, 1833—His son George goes the same circuit as Judge forty
years later in Spring Assizes of 1873—Curious coincidences of time—
Impression produced by Denman as Judge on his first circuit—Correspondence when on circuit—Extracts from letters to Lady Denman
from Lincoln and Warwick—To his daughter Margaret, on 'getting
poetry by heart,' &c.—Denman on Northern Circuit, Summer Assizes,
1833—Extract from letter to Mrs. Baillie from York—To Lady
Denman from Carlisle—Durham described—Hospitalities of the Prince-
Bishop—Newcastle—From Newcastle to Carlisle—Scottish mountains, &c.—To Lady Denman from Appleby—Brougham Hall—Lowther Castle.

WHEN Denman was appointed Chief Justice of the King's Bench, the Puisne Judges of that Court were Littledale, James Parke, Patteson, and Taunton.

Littledale has been well characterised by Lord Campbell as ' the most acute, learned, and simple-minded of mankind '—a thorough lawyer, and nothing but a lawyer—an infant in the ways of the world, and taking so little interest in anything beyond the narrow range of his profession, that in days when politics were at fever heat he once quaintly, but truly, described himself to a friend as being ' of the politics of a special pleader.' [1]

Parke, afterwards Lord Wensleydale, was a judge of first-rate ability, who in his long career (eight-and-twenty years) of judicial service, discovered no failing except an excess of subtlety, leading at times to a sacrifice of the substance of justice to the forms of procedure. He only sate for about a year-and-a-half in the King's Bench after Denman became Chief, having been moved to the Exchequer in Easter Term, 1834. In 1826 he had been engaged on the opposite side to Denman on the memorable trial of the Queen, having been selected, owing to the great legal reputation he had even then acquired, to assist as junior counsel the law officers of the Crown. [2]

---

[1] Sir Joseph Littledale, born 1707; senior wrangler, 1787; called t Bar, 1793; Judge of King's Bench, 1824; retired, 1841; died, 1842, æt. 75. Foss's ' Lives of the Judges,' vol. ix. p. 220.

[2] James Parke; born 1782; fifth wrangler and senior medallist, 1803; called to Bar, 1813; Judge of King's Bench, 1828; Baron of

Patteson, who had been appointed a judge of the King's Bench in 1830 [8] (two years before Denman became Chief), did not resign till two years after him, in 1852. Between him and Denman there subsisted the closest and most loving friendship, only to be severed by death. He was, perhaps, take him altogether, one of the very best and ablest judges that ever sate in Westminster Hall, the only drawback being his deafness, the increase of which led to his retirement after a service of two-and-twenty years. His judicial character is traced with truth and eloquence in the following passage from the farewell address pronounced by Sir Alexander Cockburn, now Chief Justice, then Attorney-General, on the occasion of his retirement from the Bench. 'Though we lose you, your memory will yet remain among us, assuming its proper position among those revered names which dignify this place and this Hall, and will be cherished by us, not more for that vast and varied learning by which all have profited, and which all have admired, than for that untiring love of justice and truth, and that hatred of oppression and wrong, that unflinching integrity of purpose, that simplicity and singleness of heart, and that benevolent kindness of nature which leave us in doubt whether we should more revere the judge or love the man.' On Littledale's retirement in 1841 Patteson became Senior Puisne Judge, and his ready

Exchequer, 1834; retired, 1856, and then created Lord Wensleydale; died, 1868, æt. 86. Foss's 'Lives of the Judges,' vol. ix. p. 231.

[8] As one of the three additional judges created under the Act of that year.

learning and sound judgment were of inestimable service to the Chief Justice.[4]

The fifth judge of the Court in 1832 was Sir Elias Taunton, who, like Patteson, had been appointed as an additional judge in 1830. He died suddenly in 1835, and made way for Sir John Taylor Coleridge, of whom more hereafter. Sir E. Taunton had the reputation of being an extremely learned lawyer, and was by no means an incompetent judge.[5]

The perfect temper and admirable tact of Denman soon effaced whatever prejudice, on political grounds, might have been at first entertained towards him by some members of his Court, and very little time had elapsed before he was on terms of cordial brotherhood with the whole of them.

At a somewhat later period, after the place of Parke had been supplied by Williams, and that of Taunton by Coleridge, Denman, writing to his brother-in-law, the Rev. R. Vevers, gave the following pleasing picture of the mode in which he and his colleagues worked together:

Yesterday was a very busy day, the last of the term, when we sit late, do an unusual quantity of work, and dine together at my house. We rose at seven in court, sate at dinner till near eleven, and had a joyous compotation. Four excellent

[4] Sir John Patteson; born 1790; called to the Bar, 1821 (having previously practised some years as a special pleader); Judge of King's Bench, 1830; retired, 1852; died, 1861, æt. 71. Foss's 'Lives of the Judges,' vol ix. p. 235.

[5] Sir William Elias Taunton, born 1773; English prize essay at Oxford, 1793; called to the Bar, 1799; King's Counsel, 1822; Judge of King's Bench, 1830, died, 1835, æt. 62. Foss's 'Lives of the Judges,' vol. ix. . 96.

and honourable men, of the most varied qualities, but always on the best terms, agreed with me that the time between our meeting on November 2 and parting now appeared like a single day—a strong proof of our uninterrupted harmony, resulting from the consciousness on our own part, and confidence with regard to each other, that no wish or idea exists among us but the earnest desire to come to a just conclusion on every case before us. The four sitting in court last term (Littledale, Patteson, Williams and I) were equally divided yesterday in an important political case (the Ipswich Bribery)—discussed it frequently without an angry word or untoward thought. This must be allowed to be a happy course of life, more especially when we have good reason to hope that our work is well done, and the Bar and the public fully satisfied with us.[6]

With the public and the profession Denman was from the first a favourite. His dignified presence, his majestic voice, the precise and impressive eloquence of his language, his admirable impartiality, his never-failing courtesy, made him the object alike of respect and affection. As a constitutional and criminal lawyer his merits were of the highest order, and, if less versed than some of his learned brethren in the subtleties of special pleading and the ponderous erudition of the Reports and Year Books, he more than made up for the deficiency by his anxious and unremitting solicitude to try every case on its merits, and by his uniform preference of substantial justice to technical formality.

The emoluments of the Chief Justiceship of the King's

---

[6] This letter towards its close contains an expression which almost reads like a presentiment; he speaks of the appointment as an honourable and ample provision for the rest of his life, unless he be disabled from continuing to fulfil its duties '*by palsy.*'

Bench when Denman acceded to the office were, as fixed by Act of Parliament in 1825, 10,000*l.* a year.[7] In 1830 a Committee of the House of Commons, of which Mr. Baring (afterwards Lord Ashburton) was chairman, had reported in favour of the reduction of various salaries. In consequence of this report the salaries of several of the chief officers of State were reduced, and there was an understanding that the salaries, *inter alia*, of the Chief Justices should also be reduced as fresh appointments were successively made. When Brougham intimated to Denman that he was to be Chief Justice of the King's Bench he said: ' You understand that you take the office with notice,' to which Denman replied, ' I presume that the salary will be reduced, as that of the Irish Chancellor has been, from 10,000*l.* to 8,000*l.* a year.'[8]

It was on this footing, accordingly, that Denman always sent in his claims to the Treasury, and during the whole term of his office drew, not 10,000*l.* a year, as he was by law entitled to have done, but 8,000*l.* a year, in accordance with the understood arrangement.[9]

Owing to Brougham's omission, no measure was then introduced for reducing the salaries of the Chief

[7] 6 G. IV. c. 82, 83, and 84.

[8] From a letter written by Denman to Mr. Justice Coleridge on July 25, 1846, in reference to a discussion which took place in the House of Lords, on July 14, 1846, on the subject of the Chief Justices' salaries.

[9] In consequence of Brougham's omission to introduce an Act fixing the salaries, the public derived no benefit from Denman's self-denial, the sum of 10,000*l.*, as fixed by the Act of 1825, being still borne yearly on the estimates until the year 1851, when an Act was passed, as stated in the text. It would be a curious enquiry what went with the difference, amounting in the seventeen years, Denman's tenure of office, to something like 34,000*l.*

Justices, nor was any such act passed till after Denman's retirement, when, in 1851, the salary of the Chief Justice of the Queen's Bench was fixed at 8,000*l.* a year, and those of the Chief Justice of the Common Pleas and of the Chief Baron of the Exchequer, at 7,000*l.* a year each, at which amounts they now respectively stand.[10]

Denman had no sooner been appointed Chief Justice than the Court of King's Bench, both in Banc and at Nisi Prius, felt the benefit of his fresh energy, great capacity of labour, and single-hearted devotion to the service of the public.   Owing to the Court of Common Pleas being in those times closed to general professional competition,[11] and to the comparative judicial inefficiency (before the accession of Lyndhurst, Parke and Alderson) of the Court of Exchequer, the great mass of legal business had for some time gravitated towards the Court of King's Bench, the files of which had, in consequence, become heavily encumbered with arrears.   To reduce these Denman set to work, in his own phrase, ' like a dragon,' commencing early and protracting the sittings of the Court till a late hour in the evening, earnestly bent on destroying what he termed, in a subsequent letter to his daughter, Mrs. Wright, ' *that gigantic monster called Arrear.*'

By steady perseverance in this arduous task, regardless alike of the murmurs of the profession and of his own ease, and mindful only of the interests of the

[10] 14 and 15 Vic. c. 41. The retiring pension of the Chief Justice of the Queen's Bench is fixed at 4,000*l.* a year, those of the other two at 3,750*l.* a year.

[11] Not thrown open till 1847.

public, he at length succeeded, not however without a severe strain on his constitution, in almost entirely clearing away the encumbering mass, and leaving his Court more free from arrears than it ever had been within living memory.

The public were not ungrateful for his exertions, and nothing probably contributed to set him higher in general estimation as a laborious, conscientious, and most efficient Chief Magistrate.

Notwithstanding the pressure of his judicial labours Denman kept alive and vigorous his taste for and interest in literature.

The husband of his eldest daughter, Mr. Ichabod Charles Wright, had, shortly before his father-in-law's appointment as Chief Justice, published his admirable translation of Dante's 'Inferno.' Even those who may not entirely agree with the Chief Justice in his criticisms can hardly fail to read with some interest the following extracts from letters written by him on the subject to the young and gifted translator:

January 1, 1833.

The first thing I do this year is to thank you, my dear Wright, for your unexpected and *forbidden* [12] present; no arrival was ever more seasonable. It came in the middle of dinner on Saturday : adjourning early to the drawing-room I read a full third to my lady and Elizabeth.[13] We made the same progress the next day, and last evening finished the translation.

This is a fair proof that it reads well. It is clear, easy, spirited, flowing—and another epithet of more importance

---

[12] Denman had insisted on purchasing his copy from the publishers.

[13] Hon. Mrs. Hodgson. Denman was a most admirable reader.

than all the rest must be added—interesting. The author-ship and circumstances may have contributed somewhat to this ; but they would have acted as a drawback if any great faults had appeared, and still more if the translation had been heavy. The language is good, pure, undefiled English ; the quality of style that most attracts me is the freedom and boldness, I am tempted to say, the business-like fidelity, with which the translator leaps into the same boat as the poet, and shares the toil and danger of the adventurous voyage. No retracting, no flinching, no pausing to consider whether he has wisely embarked, but a loyal confidence in the guide who leads you into such unheard-of scenes, peopled by such weird inhabitants.

As to Dante himself, I now know much more about him than I did when I got up from dinner on Saturday. I can now take a comprehensive view of the entire effect of the poem, and am rather at a loss to describe the impression produced.

Francesca and Ugolino are undoubtedly the two eyes of the great picture, though other parts contain groups and figures, and snatches of landscape, too, worthy to be placed on the same canvas. These two wonderful and unrivalled scenes, so opposite in their subjects, possess the same merits —pre-eminently that of uncommon delicacy of taste—evinced by their breaking off just at the right moment. This quality is the more striking from the strange nature of the materials on which the poet has chosen to exercise his pure, lofty and fastidious mind. The high-wrought perfection of these two passages deepens the contrast with the rude and almost grotesque design of the work.

Dante's merit surely consists not so much in accomplishing an ingenious design as in triumphing over such immense difficulties. The respect, the interest, the strong emotion, he inspires, make one desirous to enter into all his feelings and have all his secrets disclosed. Hence our greediness for all anecdotes of the states and chiefs of whom he writes ; hence also, I am convinced, the desire to ascribe an esoteric meaning to his plain language. I long to grow familiar with all his facts, and though I do not expect to be ever caught by his supposed mystic meanings, I no longer despise and wonder at those who are.

Your successfully accomplished task bids fair to do what nothing has accomplished yet—naturalise Dante in England. Hitherto we have regarded him with a sort of gloomy and distant veneration, and have been well content to keep aloof from his intimacy: our letters of introduction have been formal and ceremonious, and only placed us more effectually at a distance, but you have really brought us together.

In another letter, written a little later to the same correspondent on the same subject, Denman thus expresses his appreciation of Dante's style :

I doubt whether any writer exceeds Dante in style. All his words are select and weighty; the structure of his sentences is simple and natural; the divisions, pauses, and cadence most gratifying to the ear; the unstudied majesty and natural freedom of his march bespeak a lofty character, full of spirit and decision.

Of the allegorising theories of some of the commentators, especially Rosetti, he thus writes :

That line of speculation seems to me not only very uninteresting, but degrading to the magnificence of the poet's genius. Very possibly he might write for some confined and temporary purpose, and think his hidden mysteries more important than his broad pictures of passion and the human heart. So may Spencer have preferred his allegory to his Una. So may some great painter have intended primarily a half idolatrous devotion to some fabled saint when he unfolded the history of his imagined life on the canvas; but if, while pursuing in his own thoughts this meaner worship, the muse, guiding his unconscious hand, made him the instrument for rousing the strongest and tenderest sympathies of all posterity, depend upon it posterity will take no more interest in the theme he thought he was immortalising than in the scaffolding which was employed to lift the dome of St. Peter's into the clouds.

Among all the sentiments of just self-satisfaction which Denman derived from his high and honourable appointment, few were of a purer or more pleasurable nature than the thought that his beloved and venerable mother had been spared to witness the deserved elevation of her son. She just lived to see him Lord Chief Justice of England, and then, in less than three months after his accession to office, on January 19, 1833, at the house of her daughter, Mrs. Baillie, with whom she had long been an inmate, she expired a few days before the completion of her 86th year, ' loving and loved,' writes Mrs. Baillie, ' to the last moment of her life.'

She was a very admirable person, of rare virtue and considerable talent, to whose constant tenderness, enlightened superintendence, and watchful care her son was no doubt greatly indebted for the high qualities and engaging manners which made him so eminent and so beloved.

He repaid her love by the fondest attachment and the most unremitting attention. ' It was beautiful,' writes Mrs. Baillie, ' to witness his attention to this venerable parent. The higher his rank became, and the more elevated his position, the more he seemed anxious to show her duty and affection ; and during the short period that she was spared after he became Lord Chief Justice he seemed almost jealous if she received from any other than himself that assistance which her infirmities required. Highly did he estimate her character, and deeply did he lament her death, and sweetly did his wife and family unite with him in showing their affectionate attentions to the last moments of his mother's life.'

The first judicial circuit travelled by the new Chief Justice, in the Spring Assizes of 1833 (his companion being Mr. Justice Bosanquet),[14] was his own old circuit—the Midland—and it must have been a source of high gratification to him to revisit, as Chief Justice, those well-known assize towns which he had for so many years frequented, first as a comparatively unemployed barrister, then as a successful and celebrated advocate.[15]

The impression he produced as a judge on this his first circuit, both on the public generally and on all concerned in the administration of the law, was a deep sentiment of unqualified veneration and esteem. 'The Lord Chief Justice,' writes Mr. Sawbridge, a gentle-

[14] Sir John Bernard Bosanquet, born 1773; called to Bar, 1800; Serjeant-at-Law, 1814; King's Serjeant, 1827; Judge of Common Pleas, 1830; retired, 1842; died 1847, æt. 74. Foss's 'Lives of the Judges,' vol. ix. p. 149.

[15] Just forty years later, in the Spring Assizes for 1873, his fourth surviving son, George (raised to the Bench as the Hon. Mr. Justice Denman in November 1872), also went as judge the Midland Circuit. Mr. Justice Denman, in the course of his charge to the grand jury at Derby, adverted to the circumstance with feeling and eloquence. He mentioned also the following curious coincidences in point of time. 'Forty years,' he said, ' had elapsed from the birth of Lord Chief Justice Denman when I was born (1779 to 1819); forty years elapsed between the time when Lord Chief Justice Denman was called to the Bar and the time when I was called to the Bar (1806 to 1846); and forty years elapsed between the time when Lord Denman was raised to the Bench and the time when I was raised to the Bench (1832 to 1872).'

man of the county of Northampton, ' appears to have pleased and gratified everybody.   I hear nothing but praises of his eloquence, of the propriety of all he said and did, and of the kindness and attention of his manner.'   Mrs. Baillie has collected and preserved some extracts to the same effect from the provincial journals of the time, from which the following may be cited as describing, with considerable correctness, those traits of demeanour and manner which distinguished him throughout his whole judicial career, and invariably produced a strong impression upon all who saw and heard him on the Bench.   ' His appearance is strikingly prepossessing ; his figure is tall, and his head of fine and noble expression ; his features massive, yet mild in their aspect, and for the most part bearing an expression of well-bred suavity which renders it difficult for the spectator to believe that such a man has ever been led away into the use of harsh and intemperate language.   His voice is clear, loud, and manly, yet mild and persuasive in its tones, and his enunciation is remarkably clear and distinct.'

On his judicial circuits Denman did not neglect the practice he had observed as a barrister, of keeping up, amid all the pressure of business, a frequent correspondence with his wife and the numerous members of his family.   Among the few letters of this kind that have been preserved relating to the Spring Circuit of 1833, the following, written to Lady Denman from Lincoln, is one of the earliest :

I have been completely confined to the Court all the week, till after post-time yesterday ; but everything was then cleared away except one case of murder, which my brother Bosanquet is now trying. All things have gone on extremely well ; the attendance of magistrates and grand jurors very large. We had more than forty guests at our dinner, including the Lord Lieutenant (Lord Brownlow) and Lord Winchelsea, whom, to my surprise, I found to be a very agreeable man. Sir Charles [16] attended, in excellent looks and spirits, and with good reports of all at home and abroad. We have a brilliant day, and hope for a delightful ride to Newark. We enter Nottingham exactly at noon to-morrow.

Just before the close of the circuit he writes to his wife from Warwick :

With great sorrow I write to retract my engagement of coming home so soon. The business has been extremely heavy, and much remains to be done. I am writing in Court, while my brother Adams [17] is rending the hearts of the jury by a pathetic appeal. We had a most magnificent banquet at Warwick Castle, and Lord Warwick paid us the unprecedented honour of dining with us and a very full attendance of magistrates. The Bar came yesterday, to the number of more than sixty—about twice as many as were here in my time, and I fear three times as many as receive even a single guinea for their travels on the circuit. To-day they have invited us to a turtle dinner in honour of my pro-motion. I am told I cannot get through my own work before Friday night, and I shall be bound then to stay on and assist my brother judge. In this case I should leave on Saturday evening, and get home on Monday. But I must contrive to write again, so God bless you and all.

The dinner referred to in the foregoing letter as given by the Bar at Warwick forms the subject of an

[16] Sir Charles Anderson of Lea, Lady Denman's maternal uncle.

[17] Mr. Serjeant Adams, a well-known member of the Midland Circuit. As all the Judges, on their promotion, become Serjeants, ' brother ' is the style in which they address Serjeants in Court.

unanimous resolution in the Circuit Book (dated Derby, March 31, 1833); the last but one in its pages which relates to Lord Denman—the final one being the record of Mr. Whitchurst's letter, and Lord Denman's reply, on his retirement from the Bench in 1850, which will be given subsequently among the addresses presented to him on that occasion.

Either while still on circuit, or soon after his return to town, he found time, early in April, to despatch to his fourth daughter, Margaret, now the Honourable Mrs. Cropper, then a young lady in her 18th year,[18] a few lines which will illustrate what has been said in an earlier chapter as to the delightful and improving nature of his intercourse with his daughters. Miss Margaret Denman was at the time staying with Mr. and Mrs. Enfield, old friends of her father's, who had just written to him in high praise of her lively talents and winning manners.

How can I sufficiently thank your host and hostess [he writes] for all their kindness. The former sent me a delightful letter, written on Sunday, which nothing but the urgent pressure of time prevented me from acknowledging. Mrs. Enfield's certificate is still more satisfactory, and she can do nothing more kind than to find employment for your mind, and promote its cultivation.

Do you ever get poetry by heart? I do not think it desirable to load the memory with vast quantities, but some of the most beautiful passages may be learned with the highest pleasure, and will be treasured up through life as the most precious of all possessions. I mean to commend to

---

[18] Born 1815; married, first, 1841, Henry William Macaulay, Esq. (brother of Lord Macaulay); he died 1846; secondly, 1848, Edward Cropper, Esq., of Swaylands, near Penshurst, in Kent.

your perusal Milton's 'L'Allegro' and 'Il Penseroso,' and advise you to learn all the former from 'Haste thee, nymph,' &c., and all the latter from 'Come, pensive nun.' You will thank me for this counsel fifty years hence.

I expect great things from you, dear Margaret, not only from my own observation, but from the eulogies of Mr. and Mrs. Enfield, and from Mrs. Arkwright's wish for your company. Some of these days you will, perhaps, yourself know the feelings of a parent ' blessing when he reads the praises of his child.'

In the Summer Assizes of 1833, the Chief Justice, in company with Mr. Baron Bolland, his competitor in 1822 for the office of Common Serjeant, presided on the great Northern Circuit.

Denman was much pleased by the splendour and hospitality of his reception at York, as appears by the following extract of a letter written thence on July 27, 1833, to his sister Mrs. Baillie:

Nothing can exceed the general good humour and hospitality, and it delights me to have formed acquaintance with this great county. We have been made much of. Lord Feversham sends us a buck; Lord Fitzwilliam a whole paradise of pine-apples, melons, and grapes. The High Sheriff, a young Catholic of very old family, after loading us with favours, has taken leave of us in a letter of thanks. The Bishop of Durham [19] will be our next host; a prince of the Church whose judges (not the King's) we are within his palatinate.

From Carlisle he writes to his wife a letter which may be inserted in full, as being of more general interest than usual. It was written in the days before railroads, when judges of an active habit of body still

____
[19] Then Dr. Van Mildert.

frequently kept up the old custom of riding on horse-back from one circuit town to another.

Carlisle: August 6, 1833.

Dearest Love,—I am so grateful for your delightful letters, and so much annoyed by the disappointment you so feelingly describe, that I am resolved to seize even a few stray moments to tell you that all are well,[20] and to pursue our ' travel's history' since I last gave you our proceedings up to the end of York.

I left Court that evening between 7 and 8, dined, and then rode alone to Easingwold,[21] the hottest ride I ever underwent. Next morning the staff joined; we were then fifty-three miles from Durham, and thought it not right to drive into that episcopal city in the day time, too late for the abbey service, but early enough for the palace dinner: so we dined quietly *téte-à-téte* at a pretty country inn of great celebrity in these parts, called Rushyford, and entered Durham just as the moon was growing bright.

How can I paint the magnificent situation of that lofty town. I was the more enchanted from never having heard it fully praised—a succession of bold ridges covered with dwarfish wood, then the abbey planted at the top of the last and highest hill—massive, grand, and simple. Immediately under its walls a river running between woody banks in wild beauty, almost equalling the Derwent.

The Bishop (Van Mildert), formerly preacher of Lincoln's Inn, extremely courteous and hospitable, attended us to his Courts (for we are his judges here, and not the King's) and placed me at his right hand in his castle hall for three days successively at dinner, with gown and wig. On Wednesday evening we parted with great cordiality.

---

[20] His eldest son, the present Lord Denman, and his third son, the Hon. Richard Denman, were both with him on circuit; the first as Associate, the second as Judges' Marshal.

[21] Some seventeen or eighteen miles north of York; it adjoins Sterne's Parish of Coxwould.

VOL. I.   F F

It is seventeen miles from Durham to Newcastle. I rode as far as Lambton Castle (Lord Durham's seat), a very elegant modern structure, with a terrace of extraordinary beauty. It was dark when we reached Gateshead, on the south bank of the Tyne—a kind of suburb of Newcastle. Both the Sheriff of the county and the Mayor of Newcastle came out to meet us. We passed through countless multitudes to the Mansion House, where we were entertained till Sunday at 1 P.M. (Bolland had left the evening before); and again had dinner two days running—venison, gowns, wigs, and above 150 people each day. The present mayor is Mr. Brandling; he took me a charming ride about the country, through green lanes, before dinner on Saturday.

Yesterday, after service at the crumbling church of St. Nicholas, we drove along the south bank of the Tyne to Hexham, through soft and beautiful scenery; then, reaching the centre of the island in this narrow part of it, we came down on Carlisle from a wild, high point, and found the west still softer and more cultivated, and much nearer harvest, than the east.

We thus escaped a public dinner, and, finding a good fire not unpleasant, I had the pleasure of discovering that my criminal calendar here consisted but of nine cases—the first for stealing a lamb, another for stealing a hen, 'value ten-pence,' a third for ' larceny of eight copper halfpennies,' and nothing much more serious.

I think I must give Newcastle a letter by itself. I was delighted with that ancient and picturesque, but active and improving town.

We had the Scottish mountains in prospect at sunset as we came westward—very noble and grand ; and we are now so near the border that I think I must take the mare some morning and make a raid into our neighbours' county. We are now assembling at breakfast, so I conclude with all the loves and good wishes that can come from the most affectionate of husbands.

The last letter preserved among those he wrote on this circuit is to Lady Denman, from Appleby. The following is an extract:

I have had some pleasant travelling since I last wrote—a morning visit to Corby castle, a most beautiful place on the banks of the Eden; a long ride from Carlisle to Brougham Hall, and a most happy repose there with the dear old lady [22] and her eldest daughter, who were full of kind enquiries and remembrances touching you and yours. I had infinite pleasure in looking over the improvements, which are most judicious, and form a solid, handsome, and well-proportioned house and grounds.

After a delightful sauntering morning there, we had a buckram wig and gown dinner at Lowther Castle [Lord Lonsdale's], where also much kindness was manifested respecting you. The Earl was extremely civil, and led me among his fir-groves and grass-terraces overlooking the Lake Mountains.

Addendum.

The following letter from George IV. to the late Duke of Wellington, supplied by the courtesy of his Grace the present Duke, was received too late for insertion in the text, but is added here as a note to vol. i. p. 310. It is very characteristic of the writer, and shows the strength and persistency of his animosity against Denman.

Royal Lodge: November 9, 1829.

My dear Duke,—As it is impossible for me on account of the state of my eyes to write a letter by candle-light, I am under the necessity of having recourse to an amanuensis to convey to you my sentiments upon the subject of your letter just received.

[22] Mrs. Brougham, the gifted and venerable mother of the illustrious Harry Brougham.

I must express to you my extreme surprise, my dear Duke, that you should suggest to me that I should either decline to receive the Recorder's report to-morrow, or submit to the indignity of receiving the Common Serjeant to fulfil the duties of the Recorder upon the occasion, when you cannot fail to know the insult which I have received from that individual, and you ought to know the firmness of my character in not bearing an insult from any human being with impunity. A provision has been made for the fulfilment of the Recorder's duties, in the event of his indisposition, in the appointment of Mr. Serjeant as Deputy-Recorder for that express purpose, and I desire that he should attend in that capacity rather than defer the report, he having already officiated in that character. I must express a hope that this will be the last time that I shall be troubled relative to Mr. Denman, as no consideration will ever induce me to admit that individual into my presence.

I remain, my dear Duke,
Your sincere friend.

P.S. Mr. Peel will accordingly announce to the Deputy-Recorder that he will be required to officiate to-morrow.

The King to Field-Marshal the Duke of Wellington.

END OF THE FIRST VOLUME.

LONDON: PRINTED BY
SPOTTISWOODE AND CO., NEW-STREET SQUARE
AND PARLIAMENT STREET

39 PATERNOSTER ROW, E.C.
LONDON: *March* 1873.

GENERAL LIST OF WORKS

PUBLISHED BY

Messrs. LONGMANS, GREEN, READER, and DYER.

History, Politics, Historical Memoirs, &c.

Estimates of the English Kings from William the Conqueror to George III. By J. LANGTON SANFORD, Author of 'Studies and Illustrations of the Great Rebellion' &c. Crown 8vo. price 12s. 6d.

The History of England from the Fall of Wolsey to the Defeat of the Spanish Armada. By JAMES ANTHONY FROUDE, M.A.

    CABINET EDITION, 12 vols. cr. 8vo. £3 12s.
    LIBRARY EDITION, 12 vols. 8vo. £8 18s.

The English in Ireland in the Eighteenth Century. By JAMES ANTHONY FROUDE, M.A. late Fellow of Exeter College, Oxford. In Two Volumes. VOL. I., 8vo. price 16s.

The History of England from the Accession of James II. By Lord MACAULAY:—

    STUDENT'S EDITION, 2 vols. crown 8vo. 12s.
    PEOPLE'S EDITION, 4 vols. crown 8vo. 16s.
    CABINET EDITION, 8 vols. post 8vo. 48s.
    LIBRARY EDITION, 5 vols. 8vo. £4.

Lord Macaulay's Works. Complete and uniform Library Edition. Edited by his Sister, Lady TREVELYAN. 8 vols. 8vo. with Portrait, price £5. 5s. cloth, or £8. 8s. bound in tree-calf by Rivère.

Memoirs of Baron Stockmar. By his Son, Baron E. VON STOCKMAR. Translated from the German by G. A. M. Edited by MAX MÜLLER, M.A. 2 vols. crown 8vo. price 21s.

Varieties of Vice-Regal Life. By Major-General Sir WILLIAM DENISON, K.C.B. late Governor-General of the Australian Colonies, and Governor of Madras. With Two Maps. 2 vols. 8vo. 28s.

On Parliamentary Government in England : its Origin, Development, and Practical Operation. By ALPHEUS TODD, Librarian of the Legislative Assembly of Canada. 2 vols. 8vo. price £1. 17s.

The Constitutional History of England since the Accession of George III. 1760—1860. By Sir THOMAS ERSKINE MAY, K.C.B. Cabinet Edition (the Third), thoroughly revised. 3 vols. crown 8vo. price 18s.

The History of England, from the Earliest Times to the Year 1865. By C. D. YONGE, Regius Professor of Modern History in Queen's College, Belfast. New Edition. Crown 8vo. 7s. 6d.

Lectures on the History of England, from the Earliest Times to the Death of King Edward II. By WILLIAM LONGMAN. With Maps and Illustrations. 8vo. 15s.

The History of the Life and Times of Edward the Third. By WILLIAM LONGMAN. With 9 Maps, 8 Plates, and 16 Woodcuts. 2 vols. 8vo. 28s.

History of Civilization in England and France, Spain and Scotland. By HENRY THOMAS BUCKLE. New Edition of the entire work, with a complete INDEX. 3 vols. crown 8vo. 24s.

Realities of Irish Life. By W. STEUART TRENCH, late Land Agent in Ireland to the Marquess of Lansdowne, the Marquess of Bath, and Lord Digby. Fifth Edition. Crown 8vo. 6s.

The Student's Manual of the History of Ireland. By M. F. CUSACK, Authoress of 'The Illustrated History of Ireland.' Crown 8vo. price 6s.

A Student's Manual of the History of India, from the Earliest Period to the Present. By Colonel MEADOWS TAYLOR, M.R.A.S. M.R.I.A. Second Thousand. Crown 8vo. with Maps, 7s. 6d.

The History of India, from the Earliest Period to the close of Lord Dalhousie's Administration. By JOHN CLARK MARSHMAN. 3 vols. crown 8vo. 22s. 6d.

Indian Polity; a View of the System of Administration in India. By Lieut.-Col. GEORGE CHESNEY. Second Edition, revised, with Map. 8vo. 21s.

A Colonist on the Colonial Question. By JEHU MATHEWS, of Toronto, Canada. Post 8vo. price 6s.

An Historical View of Literature and Art in Great Britain from the Accession of the House of Hanover to the Reign of Queen Victoria. By J. MURRAY GRAHAM, M.A. 8vo. price 12s.

Waterloo Lectures; a Study of the Campaign of 1815. By Colonel CHARLES C. CHESNEY, R.E. late Professor of Military Art and History in the Staff College. Second Edition. 8vo. with Map, 10s. 6d.

Memoir and Correspondence relating to Political Occurrences in June and July 1834. By EDWARD JOHN LITTLETON, First Lord Hatherton. Edited, from the Original Manuscript, by HENRY REEVE, C.B. D.C.L. 8vo. price 7s. 6d.

Chapters from French History; St. Louis, Joan of Arc, Henri IV. with Sketches of the Intermediate Periods. By J. H. GURNEY, M.A. New Edition. Fcp. 8vo. 6s. 6d.

Royal and Republican France. A Series of Essays reprinted from the 'Edinburgh,' 'Quarterly,' and 'British and Foreign' Reviews. By HENRY REEVE, C.B. D.C.L. 2 vols. 8vo. price 21s.

The Imperial and Colonial Constitutions of the Britannic Empire, including Indian Institutions. By Sir EDWARD CREASY, M.A. &c. With Six Maps. 8vo price 15s.

The Oxford Reformers—John Colet, Erasmus, and Thomas More; being a History of their Fellow-Work. By FREDERIC SEEBOHM. Second Edition. 8vo. 14s.

A History of Greece. Drawn from Original Authorities, and designed chiefly for the use of Colleges and Schools. By the Rev. GEORGE W. COX, M.A., late Scholar of Trinity College, Oxford; Author of 'The Aryan Mythology' &c. [*In the Press.*

The History of Greece. By C. THIRLWALL, D.D. Lord Bishop of St. David's. 8 vols. fcp. 28s.

The Tale of the Great Persian War, from the Histories of Herodotus. By GEORGE W. COX, M.A. late Scholar of Trin. Coll. Oxon. Fcp. 3s. 6d.

The Sixth Oriental Monarchy; or, the Geography, History, and Antiquities of Parthia. Collected and Illustrated from Ancient and Modern sources. By GEORGE RAWLINSON, M.A. Camden Professor of Ancient History in the University of Oxford, and Canon of Canterbury. With Maps and Illustrations. 8vo. price 16s.

Greek History from Themistocles to Alexander, in a Series of Lives from Plutarch. Revised and arranged by A. H. CLOUGH. Fcp. with 44 Woodcuts, 6s.

History of the Romans under the Empire. By Very Rev. CHARLES MERIVALE, D.C.L. Dean of Ely. 8 vols. post 8vo. price 48s.

The Fall of the Roman Republic; a Short History of the Last Century of the Commonwealth. By the same Author. 12mo. 7s. 6d.

Encyclopædia of Chronology, Historical and Biographical: comprising the Dates of all the Great Events of History, including Treaties, Alliances, Wars, Battles, &c.; Incidents in the Lives of Eminent Men, Scientific and Geographical Discoveries, Mechanical Inventions, and Social, Domestic, and Economical Improvements. By B. B. WOODWARD, B.A. and W. L. R. CATES. 8vo. price 42s.

The History of Rome. By WILHELM INNE. English Edition, translated and revised by the Author. VOLS. I. and II. 8vo. 30s.

History of European Morals from Augustus to Charlemagne. By W. E. H. LECKY, M.A. 2 vols. 8vo. price 28s.

History of the Rise and Influ-ence of the Spirit of Rationalism in Europe. By the same Author. Cabinet Edition (the Fourth). 2 vols. crown 8vo. price 16s.

God in History; or, the Progress of Man's Faith in the Moral Order of the World. By the late Baron BUNSEN. Translated from the German by SUSANNA WINKWORTH; with a Preface by Dean STANLEY. 3 vols. 8vo. 42s.

Introduction to the Science of Religion: Four Lectures delivered at the Royal Institution of Great Britain in February and March 1870; with a Lecture on the Philosophy of Mythology and an Essay on False Analogies in Religion. By F. MAX MÜLLER, M.A., Professor of Comparative Philology at Oxford. [*In the Press.*

Socrates and the Socratic Schools. Translated from the German of Dr. E. ZELLER, with the Author's approval, by the Rev. OSWALD J. REICHEL, B.C.L. and M.A. Crown 8vo. 8s. 6d.

The Stoics, Epicureans, and Sceptics. Translated from the German of Dr. E. ZELLER, with the Author's approval, by OSWALD J. REICHEL, B.C.L. and M.A. Crown 8vo. 14s.

The English Reformation. By F. C. MASSINGBERD, M.A. late Chancellor of Lincoln. 4th Edition. Fcp. 8vo. 7s 6d.

Three Centuries of Modern His-tory. By CHARLES DUKE YONGE, Regius Professor of Modern History and English Literature in Queen's College, Belfast. Crown 8vo. 7s. 6d.

Saint-Simon and Saint-Simonism; a Chapter in the History of Socialism in France. By ARTHUR J. BOOTH, M.A. Crown 8vo. price 7s. 6d.

The History of Philosophy, from Thales to Comte. By GEORGE HENRY LEWES. Fourth Edition, corrected and partly rewritten. 2 vols. 8vo. 32s.

The Mythology of the Aryan Nations. By GEORGE W. COX, M.A. late Scholar of Trinity College, Oxford. 2 vols. 8vo. price 28s.

Maunder's Historical Treasury; comprising a General Introductory Outline of Universal History, and a Series of Separate Histories. Fcp. 8vo. price 6s.

Critical and Historical Essays contributed to the *Edinburgh Review* by the Right Hon. Lord MACAULAY :—

STUDENT'S EDITION, crown 8vo. 6s.
PEOPLE'S EDITION, 2 vols. crown 8vo. 8s.
CABINET EDITION, 4 vols. 24s.
LIBRARY EDITION, 3 vols. 8vo. 36s.

History of the Early Church, from the First Preaching of the Gospel to the Council of Nicæa, A.D. 325. By the Author of 'Amy Herbert.' New Edition. Fcp. 8vo. 4s. 6d.

Sketch of the History of the Church of England to the Revolution of 1688. By the Right Rev. T. V. SHORT, D.D. Lord Bishop of St. Asaph. Eighth Edition. Crown 8vo. 7s. 6d.

Essays on the Rise and Progress of the Christian Religion in the West of Europe. From the Reign of Tiberius to the End of the Council of Trent. By JOHN EARL RUSSELL. 8vo. [*In the Press.*

History of the Christian Church, from the Ascension of Christ to the Conversion of Constantine. By E. BURTON, D.D. late Regius Prof. of Divinity in the University of Oxford. Fcp. 8vo. 3s. 6d.

History of the Christian Church, from the Death of St. John to the Middle of the Second Century; comprising a full Account of the Primitive Organisation of Church Government, and the Growth of Episcopacy. By T. W. MOSSMAN, B.A. Rector of East and Vicar of West Torrington, Lincolnshire. 8vo. price 16s.

Biographical Works.

The Life of Lloyd, First Lord Kenyon, Lord Chief Justice of England. By the Hon. GEORGE T. KENYON, M.A. of Ch. Ch. Oxford. With Portraits of Lord and Lady Kenyon from Sketches by Sir Thomas Lawrence. 8vo. [*Nearly ready.*

Memoir of the Life of Admiral Sir Edward William Codrington; with Selections from his Private and Official Correspondence, including Particulars of the Battles of the First of June 1794 and Trafalgar, the Expeditions to Walcheren and New Orleans, War Service on the Coast of Spain, and the Battle of Navarin. Edited by his Daughter, Lady BOURCHIER. With Two Portraits, Maps, and Plans. 2 vols. 8vo. price 36*s*.

Life of Alexander von Humboldt. Compiled, in Commemoration of the Centenary of his Birth, by JULIUS LÖWENBERG, ROBERT AVÉ-LALLEMANT, and ALFRED DOVE. Edited by Professor KARL BRUHNS, Director of the Observatory at Leipzig. Translated from the German by JANE and CAROLINE LASSELL. 2 vols. 8vo. with Three Portraits, price 36*s*.

Autobiography of John Milton; or, Milton's Life in his own Words. By the Rev. JAMES J. G. GRAHAM, M.A. Crown 8vo. with Vignette-Portrait, price 5*s*.

Recollections of Past Life. By Sir HENRY HOLLAND, Bart. M.D. F.R.S., &c. Physician-in-Ordinary to the Queen. Third Edition. Post 8vo. 10*s*. 6*d*.

Biographical and Critical Essays, Reprinted from Reviews, with Additions and Corrections. By A. HAYWARD, Esq. Q.C. 2 vols. 8vo. price 28*s*.

The Life of Isambard Kingdom Brunel, Civil Engineer. By ISAMBARD BRUNEL, B.C.L. of Lincoln's Inn, Chancellor of the Diocese of Ely. With Portrait, Plates, and Woodcuts. 8vo. 21*s*.

Lord George Bentinck; a Political Biography. By the Right Hon. B. DISRAELI, M.P. Eighth Edition, revised, with a new Preface. Crown 8vo. 6*s*.

Memoir of George Edward Lynch Cotton, D.D. Bishop of Calcutta, and Metropolitan. With Selections from his Journals and Correspondence. Edited by Mrs. COTTON. Second Edition, with Portrait. Crown 8vo. price 7*s*. 6*d*.

The Life and Travels of George Whitefield, M.A. By JAMES PATERSON GLEDSTONE. 8vo. price 14*s*.

The Life and Letters of the Rev. Sydney Smith. Edited by his Daughter, Lady HOLLAND, and Mrs. AUSTIN. New Edition, complete in One Volume. Crown 8vo. price 6*s*.

The Life and Times of Sixtus the Fifth. By Baron HÜBNER. Translated from the Original French, with the Author's sanction, by HUBERT E. H. JERNINGHAM. 2 vols. 8vo. 24*s*.

Essays in Ecclesiastical Biography. By the Right Hon. Sir J. STEPHEN, LL.D. Cabinet Edition. Crown 8vo. 7*s*. 6*d*.

The Life and Letters of Faraday. By Dr. BENCE JONES, Secretary of the Royal Institution. Second Edition, with Portrait and Woodcuts. 2 vols. 8vo. 28*s*.

Faraday as a Discoverer. By JOHN TYNDALL, LL.D. F.R.S. New and Cheaper Edition, with Two Portraits. Fcp. 8vo price 3*s*. 6*d*.

Leaders of Public Opinion in Ireland; Swift, Flood, Grattan, O'Connell. By W. E. H. LECKY, M.A. New Edition, revised and enlarged. Crown 8vo. 7*s*. 6*d*.

Life of the Duke of Wellington. By the Rev. G. R. GLEIG, M.A. Popular Edition, carefully revised; with copious Additions. Crown 8vo. with Portrait, 5*s*.

Dictionary of General Biography; containing Concise Memoirs and Notices of the most Eminent Persons of all Countries, from the Earliest Ages to the Present Time. Edited by WILLIAM L. R. CATES. 8vo. price 21*s*.

Letters and Life of Francis Bacon, including all his Occasional Works. Collected and edited, with a Commentary, by J. SPEDDING. VOLS. I. to VI. 8vo. price £3. 12*s*. To be completed in One more Volume.

Felix Mendelssohn's Letters from *Italy and Switzerland,* and *Letters* from 1833 to 1847, translated by Lady WALLACE. With Portrait. 2 vols. crown 8vo. 5*s*. each.

Musical Criticism and Biography, from the Published and Unpublished Writings of THOMAS DAMANT EATON, late President of the Norwich Choral Society. Selected and edited by his SONS. Crown 7*s*. 6*d*.

Lives of the Queens of England.
By AGNES STRICKLAND. Library Edition,
newly revised; with Portraits of every
Queen, Autographs, and Vignettes. 8 vols.
post 8vo. 7s. 6d. each.

Apologia pro Vita Sua; being a History of his Religious Opinions. By JOHN
HENRY NEWMAN, D.D. of the Oratory of
St. Philip Neri. New Edition. Post 8vo.
price 6s.

Memoirs of Sir Henry Havelock,
K.C.B. By JOHN CLARK MARSHMAN.
People's Edition, with Portrait. Crown 8vo.
price 3s. 6d.

The Rise of Great Families, other
Essays and Stories. By Sir BERNARD
BURKE, C.B., LL.D. Ulster King-of-Arms
Crown 8vo. price 12s. 6d.

Vicissitudes of Families. By Sir
J. BERNARD BURKE, C.B. Ulster King-of-
Arms. New Edition, remodelled and en-
larged. 2 vols. crown 8vo. 21s.

Maunder's Biographical Trea-
sury. Thirteenth Edition, reconstructed and
partly re-written, with above 1,000 additional
Memoirs, by W. L. R. CATES. Fcp. 8vo. 6s.

Criticism, Philosophy, Polity, &c.

On Representative Government.
By JOHN STUART MILL. Third Edition.
8vo. 9s. crown 8vo. 2s.

On Liberty. By JOHN STUART MILL.
Fourth Edition. Post 8vo. 7s. 6d. Crown
8vo. 1s. 4d.

Principles of Political Economy.
By JOHN STUART MILL. Seventh Edition.
2 vols. 8vo. 30s. or in 1 vol. crown 8vo. 5s.

Utilitarianism. By JOHN STUART
MILL. 4th Edit. 8vo. 5s.

Dissertations and Discussions. By
JOHN STUART MILL. Second Edition.
3 vols. 8vo. price 36s.

Examination of Sir William
Hamilton's Philosophy, and of the principal
Philosophical Questions discussed in his
Writings. By JOHN STUART MILL.
Fourth Edition. 8vo. 16s.

The Subjection of Women. By
JOHN STUART MILL. New Edition. Post
8vo. 5s.

Analysis of the Phenomena of
the Human Mind. By JAMES MILL. A
New Edition, with Notes, Illustrative and
Critical, by ALEXANDER BAIN, ANDREW
FINDLATER, and GEORGE GROTE. Edited,
with additional Notes, by JOHN STUART
MILL. 2 vols. 8vo. price 28s.

Principles of Economical Philo-
sophy. By H. D. MACLEOD, M.A. Barrister-
at-Law. Second Edition, in Two Volumes.
VOL. I. 8vo. price 15s.

A Dictionary of Political Econo-
nomy; Biographical, Bibliographical, Historical, and Practical. By H. D. MACLEOD,
M.A. VOL. I. royal 8vo. 30s.

A Systematic View of the Science
of Jurisprudence. By SHELDON AMOS,
M.A. Professor of Jurisprudence to the
Inns of Court, London. 8vo. price 18s.

The Institutes of Justinian; with
English Introduction, Translation, and
Notes. By T. C. SANDARS, M.A. Barrister-
at-Law. New Edition. 8vo. 15s.

Lord Bacon's Works, collected
and edited by R. L. ELLIS, M.A. J. SPED-
DING, M.A. and D. D. HEATH. New
and Cheaper Edition. 7 vols. 8vo. price
£3. 13s. 6d.

A System of Logic, Ratiocinative
and Inductive. By JOHN STUART MILL.
Eighth Edition. 2 vols. 8vo. 25s.

The Ethics of Aristotle; with Essays
and Notes. By Sir A. GRANT, Bart. M.A.
LL.D. Third Edition, revised and partly
re-written. [In the press.

The Nicomachean Ethics of Aris-
totle. Newly translated into English. By
R. WILLIAMS, B.A. Fellow and late Lecturer Merton College, Oxford. 8vo. 12s.

Bacon's Essays, with Annotations.
By R. WHATELY, D.D. late Archbishop of
Dublin. New Edition. 8vo. 10s. 6d.

Elements of Logic. By R. WHATELY,
D.D. late Archbishop of Dublin. New
Edition. 8vo. 10s. 6d. crown 8vo. 4s. 6d.

Elements of Rhetoric. By the same
Author. New Edition. 8vo. 10s. 6d. Crown
8vo. 4s. 6d.

English Synonymes. By E. JANE
WHATELY. Edited by Archbp. WHATELY.
5th Edition. Fcp. 3s.

An Outline of the Necessary
Laws of Thought: a Treatise on Pure and
Applied Logic. By the Most Rev. W.
THOMSON, D.D. Archbishop of York. Ninth
Thousand. Crown 8vo. 5s. 6d.

Causality; or, the Philosophy of Law Investigated. By GEORGE JAMIESON, B.D. of Old Machar. Second Edition, greatly enlarged. 8vo. price 12s.

Speeches of the Right Hon. Lord MACAULAY, corrected by Himself. People's Edition, crown 8vo. 3s. 6d.

Lord Macaulay's Speeches on Parliamentary Reform in 1831 and 1832. 16mo. price ONE SHILLING.

A Dictionary of the English Language. By R. G. LATHAM, M.A. M.D. F.R.S. Founded on the Dictionary of Dr. S. JOHNSON, as edited by the Rev. H. J. TODD, with numerous Emendations and Additions. 4 vols. 4to. price £7.

Thesaurus of English Words and Phrases, classified and arranged so as to facilitate the expression of Ideas, and assist in Literary Composition. By P. M. ROGET, M.D. New Edition. Crown 8vo. 10s. 6d.

Three Centuries of English Lie- rature. By CHARLES DUKE YONGE, Regius Professor of Modern History and English Literature in Queen's College, Belfast. Crown 8vo. 7s. 6d.

Lectures on the Science of Lan- guage. By F. MAX MÜLLER, M.A. &c. Foreign Member of the French Institute. Sixth Edition. 2 vols. crown 8vo. price 16s.

Southey's Doctor, complete in One Volume, edited by the Rev. J. W. WARTER, B.D. Square crown 8vo. 12s. 6d.

Manual of English Literature, Historical and Critical with a Chapter on English Metres. By THOMAS ARNOLD, M.A. New Edition. Crown 8vo. 7s. 6d.

A Dictionary of Roman and Greek Antiquities. With about 2,000 Engravings on Wood, from Ancient Originals, illustrative of the Industrial Arts and Social Life of the Greeks and Romans. By ANTHONY RICH, B.A., sometime of Caius College, Cambridge. Third Edition, revised and improved. Crown 8vo. price 7s. 6d.

A Sanskrit-English Dictionary. The Sanskrit words printed both in the original Devanagari and in Roman letters; with References to the Best Editions of Sanskrit Authors, and with Etymologies and comparisons of Cognate Words chiefly in Greek, Latin, Gothic, and Anglo-Saxon. Compiled by T. BENFEY. 8vo. 52s. 6d.

A Latin-English Dictionary. By JOHN T. WHITE, D.D. Oxon. and J. E. RIDDLE, M.A. Oxon. Third Edition, revised. 2 vols. 4to. pp. 2,128, price 42s.

White's College Latin-English Dictionary (Intermediate Size), abridged from the Parent Work for the use of University Students. Medium 8vo. pp. 1,048, price 18s.

White's Junior Student's Com- plete Latin-English and English-Latin Dictionary. Revised Edition. Square 12mo. pp. 1,058, price 12s.

Separately { ENGLISH-LATIN, 5s. 6d.
{ LATIN-ENGLISH, 7s. 6d.

An English-Greek Lexicon, containing all the Greek Words used by Writers of good authority. By C. D. YONGE, B.A. New Edition. 4to. 21s.

Mr. Yonge's New Lexicon, English and Greek, abridged from his larger work (as above). Square 12mo. 8s. 6d.

A Greek-English Lexicon. Compiled by H. G. LIDDELL, D.D. Dean of Christ Church, and R. SCOTT, D.D. Dean of Rochester. Sixth Edition. Crown 4to. price 36s.

A Lexicon, Greek and English, abridged for Schools from LIDDELL and SCOTT's *Greek-English Lexicon*. Fourteenth Edition. Square 12mo. 7s. 6d.

The Mastery of Languages; or, the Art of Speaking Foreign Tongues Idiomatically. By THOMAS PRENDERGAST, late of the Civil Service at Madras. Second Edition. 8vo. 6s.

A Practical Dictionary of the French and English Languages. By Professor LÉON CONTANSEAU, many years French Examiner for Military and Civil Appointments, &c. New Edition, carefully revised. Post 8vo. 10s. 6d.

Contanseau's Pocket Dictionary, French and English, abridged from the Practical Dictionary, by the Author. New Edition. 18mo. price 3s. 6d.

New Practical Dictionary of the German Language; German-English, and English-German. By the Rev. W. L. BLACKLEY, M.A. and Dr. CARL MARTIN FRIEDLÄNDER. Post 8vo. 7s. 6d.

Historical and Critical Commen- tary on the Old Testament; with a New Translation. By M. M. KALISCH, Ph.D Vol. I. *Genesis*, 8vo. 18s. or adapted for the General Reader, 12s. Vol. II. *Exodus*, 15s or adapted for the General Reader, 12s. Vol III. *Leviticus*, Part I. 15s. or adapted for the General Reader, 8s. Vol. IV. *Leviticus*, Part II. 15s. or adapted for the General Reader, 8s.

Miscellaneous Works and *Popular Metaphysics.*

An Introduction to Mental Phi-losophy, on the Inductive Method. By J. D. MORELL, M.A. LL.D. 8vo. 12s.

Elements of Psychology, containing the Analysis of the Intellectual Powers. By J. D. MORELL, LL.D. Post 8vo. 7s. 6d.

Recreations of a Country Parson. By A. K. H. B. Two Series, 3s. 6d. each.

Seaside Musings on Sundays and Weekdays. By A. K. H. B. Crown 8vo. price 3s. 6d.

Present-Day Thoughts. By A. K. H. B. Crown 8vo. 3s. 6d.

Changed Aspects of Unchanged Truths; Memorials of St. Andrews Sundays. By A. K. H. B. Crown 8vo. 3s. 6d.

Counsel and Comfort from a City Pulpit. By A. K. H. B. Crown 8vo. 3s. 6d.

Lessons of Middle Age, with some Account of various Cities and Men. By A. K. H. B. Crown 8vo. 3s. 6d.

Leisure Hours in Town; Essays Consolatory, Æsthetical, Moral, Social, and Domestic. By A. K. H. B. Crown 8vo. 3s. 6d.

Sunday Afternoons at the Parish Church of a Scottish University City. By A. K. H. B. Crown 8vo. 3s. 6d.

The Commonplace Philosopher in Town and Country. By A. K. H. B. 3s. 6d.

The Autumn Holidays of a Country Parson. By A. K. H. B. Crown 8vo. 3s. 6d.

Critical Essays of a Country Parson. By A. K. H. B. Crown 8vo. 3s. 6d.

The Graver Thoughts of a County Parson. By A. K. H. B. Two Series, 3s. 6d. each.

Miscellaneous and Posthumous Works of the late Henry Thomas Buckle. Edited, with a Biographical Notice, by HELEN TAYLOR. 3 vols. 8vo. price 2l. 12s. 6d.

In the Morningland, or the Law of the Origin and Transformation of Christianity; Travel and Discussion in the East with the late Henry Thomas Buckle. By JOHN S. STUART-GLENNIE, M.A. Post 8vo. [*In May.*

Short Studies on Great Subjects. By JAMES ANTHONY FROUDE, M.A. late Fellow of Exeter College, Oxford. 2 vols. crown 8vo. price 12s.

Miscellaneous Writings of John Conington, M.A. late Corpus Professor of Latin in the University of Oxford. Edited by J. A. SYMONDS, M.A. With a Memoir by H. J. S. SMITH, M.A. LL.D. F.R.S. 2 vols. 8vo. price 28s.

The Rev. Sydney Smith's Mis-cellaneous Works. Crown 8vo. price 6s.

The Wit and Wisdom of the Rev. SYDNEY SMITH; a Selection of the most memorable Passages in his Writings and Conversation. Crown 8vo. 3s. 6d.

The Eclipse of Faith; or, a Visit to a Religious Sceptic. By HENRY ROGERS. Twelfth Edition. Fcp. 8vo. 5s.

Defence of the Eclipse of Faith. By HENRY ROGERS. Third Edition. Fcp. 8vo. price 3s. 6d.

Lord Macaulay's Miscellaneous Writings:—
LIBRARY EDITION, 2 vols. 8vo. Portrait, 21s.
PEOPLE'S EDITION, 1 vol. crown 8vo. 4s. 6d.

Lord Macaulay's Miscellaneous Writings and SPEECHES. Student's Edition, in One Volume, crown 8vo. price 6s.

The Election of Representatives, Parliamentary and Municipal; a Treatise. By THOMAS HARE, Barrister-at-Law. Fourth Edition, adapting the proposed Law to the Ballot, with Appendices on the Preferential and the Cumulative Vote. Post 8vo. price 7s.

Chips from a German Workshop; being Essays on the Science of Religion, and on Mythology, Traditions, and Customs. By F. MAX MÜLLER, M.A. &c. Foreign Member of the French Institute. 3 vols. 8vo. £2.

A Budget of Paradoxes. By AUGUSTUS DE MORGAN, F.R.A.S. and C.P.S. of Trinity College, Cambridge. Reprinted, with the Author's Additions, from the *Athenæum.* 8vo. price 15s.

The Secret of Hegel: being the Hegelian System in Origin, Principle, Form, and Matter. By JAMES HUTCHISON STIRLING, LL.D. Edin. 2 vols. 8vo. 28s.

Lectures on the Philosophy of Law. Together with Whewell and Hegel, and Hegel and Mr. W. R. Smith; a Vindication in a Physico-Mathematical Regard By J. H. STIRLING, LL.D. Edin. 8vo, price 6s

As Regards Protoplasm. By J. H. STIRLING, LL.D. Edin. Second Edit., with Additions, in reference to Mr. Huxley's Second Issue and a new PREFACE in reply to Mr. Huxley in 'Yeast.' 8vo. price 2s.

Sir William Hamilton; being the Philosophy of Perception: an Analysis. By J. H. STIRLING, LL.D. Edin. 8vo. 5s.

The Philosophy of Necessity; or, Natural Law as applicable to Mental, Moral. and Social Science. By CHARLES BRAY. Second Edition. 8vo. 9s.

A Manual of Anthropology, or Sience of Man, based on Modern Research. By CHARLES BRAY. Crown 8vo. 6s.

On Force, its Mental and Moral Correlates. By CHARLES BRAY. 8vo. 5s.

Time and Space; a Metaphysical Essay. By SHADWORTH H. HODGSON. 8vo. price 16s.

The Theory of Practice; an Ethical Inquiry. By SHADWORTH H. HODGSON. 2 vols. 8vo. price 24s.

Ueberweg's System of Logic and History of Logical Doctrines. Translated, with Notes and Appendices, by T. M. LINDSAY, M.A. F.R.S.E. 8vo. price 16s.

The Senses and the Intellect. By ALEXANDER BAIN, LL.D. Prof. of Logic in the Univ. of Aberdeen. Third Edition. 8vo. 15s.

Mental and Moral Science: a Compendium of Psychology and Ethics. By ALEXANDER BAIN, LL.D. Third Edition. Crown 8vo. 10s. 6d. Or separately: PART I. *Mental Science*, 6s. 6d. PART II. *Moral Science*, 4s. 6d.

A Treatise on Human Nature; being an Attempt to Introduce the Experimental Method of Reasoning into Moral Subjects. By DAVID HUME. Edited, with Notes, &c. by T. H. GREEN, Fellow, and T. H. GROSE, late Scholar, of Balliol College, Oxford. 2 vols. 8vo. [*In the press.*

Essays Moral, Political, and Literary. By DAVID HUME. By the same Editors. 2 vols. 8vo. [*In the press.*

Astronomy, Meteorology, Popular Geography, &c.

Outlines of Astronomy. By Sir J. F. W. HERSCHEL, Bart. M.A Eleventh Edition, with 9 Plates and numerous Diagrams. Square crown 8vo. 12s.

Essays on Astronomy. A Series of Papers on Planets and Meteors, the Sun and sun-surrounding Space, Stars and Star Cloudlets; and a Dissertation on the approaching Transit of Venus: preceded by a Sketch of the Life and Work of Sir J. Herschel. By R. A. PROCTOR, B.A. With 10 Plates and 24 Woodcuts. 8vo. price 12s.

Schellen's Spectrum Analysis, in its Application to Terrestrial Substances and the Physical Constitution of the Heavenly Bodies. Translated by JANE and C. LASSELL; edited, with Notes, by W. HUGGINS, LL.D. F.R.S. With 13 Plates (6 coloured) and 223 Woodcuts. 8vo. 28s.

The Sun; Ruler, Light, Fire, and Life of the Planetary System. By RICHARD A. PROCTOR, B.A. F.R.A.S. Second Edition; with 10 Plates (7 coloured) and 107 Woodcuts. Crown 8vo. price 14s.

Saturn and its System. By R. A. PROCTOR, B.A. 8vo. with 14 Plates, 14s.

Magnetism and Deviation of the Compass. For the use of Students in Navigation and Science Schools. By JOHN MERRIFIELD, LL.D. F.R.A.S. With Diagrams. 18mo. price 1s. 6d.

Air and Rain; the Beginnings of a Chemical Climatology. By ROBERT ANGUS SMITH, Ph.D. F.R.S. F.C.S. Government Inspector of Alkali Works, with 8 Illustrations. 8vo. price 24s.

The Star Depths; or, other Suns than Ours; a Treatise on Stars, Star-Systems, and Star-Cloudlets. By R. A. PROCTOR, B.A. Crown 8vo. with numerous Illustrations. [*Nearly ready.*

The Orbs Around Us; a Series of Familiar Essays on the Moon and Planets, Meteors and Comets, the Sun and Coloured Pairs of Suns. By R. A. PROCTOR, B.A. Crown 8vo. price 7s. 6d.

Other Worlds than Ours; the Plurality of Worlds Studied under the Light of Recent Scientific Researches. By R. A. PROCTOR, B.A. Third Edition, revised and corrected; with 14 Illustrations. Crown 8vo. 10s. 6d.

Celestial Objects for Common Telescopes. By T. W. WEBB, M.A. F.R.A.S. New Edition, revised, with Map of the Moon and Woodcuts. Crown 8vo. price 7s. 6d.

A New Star Atlas, for the Library, the School, and the Observatory, in Twelve Circular Maps (with Two Index Plates) Intended as a Companion to 'Webb's Celestial Objects for Common Telescopes.' With a Letterpress Introduction on the Study of the Stars, illustrated by 9 Diagrams. By RICHARD A. PROCTOR, B.A. Hon. Sec. R.A.S. Crown 8vo. 5s.

Maunder's Treasury of Geography, Physical, Historical, Descriptive, and Political. Edited by W. HUGHES, F.R.G.S. With 7 Maps and 16 Plates. Fcp. 8vo. 6s.

A General Dictionary of Geography, Descriptive, Physical, Statistical, and Historical ; forming a complete Gazetteer of the World. By A. KEITH JOHNSTON, F.R.S.E. New Edition, thoroughly revised. [*In the press.*

The Public Schools Atlas of Modern Geography. In Thirty-one Maps, exhibiting clearly the more important Physical Features of the Countries delineated, and Noting all the Chief Places of Historical, Commercial, and Social Interest. Edited, with an Introduction, by the Rev. G. BUTLER, M.A. Imperial quarto, price 3s. 6d. sewed; 5s. cloth.

Nautical Surveying, an Introduction to the Practical and Theoretical Study of. By JOHN KNOX LAUGHTON, M.A. F.R.A.S. Small 8vo. price 6s.

Natural History and *Popular Science.*

Popular Lectures on Scientific Subjects. By H. HELMHOLTZ, Professor of Physiology, formerly in the University of Heidelberg, and now in the University of Berlin, Foreign Member of the Royal Society of London. Translated by E. ATKINSON Ph.D. F.C.S. Professor of Experimental Science, Staff College. With many Illustrative Wood Engravings. 8vo. price 12s. 6d.

Introduction to Experimental Physics, Theoretical and Practical ; including Directions for Constructing Physical Apparatus and for Making Experiments. By A. F. WEINHOLD, Professor in the Royal Technical School at Chemnitz. Translated and edited (with the Author's sanction) by B. LOEWY, F.R.A.S. With a Preface by G. C. FOSTER, F.R.S. Professor of Physics in University College, London. With numerous Wood Engravings. 8vo. price 18s.

Natural Philosophy for General Readers and Young Persons; a Course of Physics divested of Mathematical Formulæ and expressed in the language of daily life. Translated from Ganot's *Cours de Physique,* by E. ATKINSON, Ph.D. F.C.S. Crown 8vo. with 404 Woodcuts, price 7s. 6d.

Mrs. Marcet's Conversations on Natural Philosophy. Revised by the Author's Son, and augmented by Conversations on Spectrum Analysis and Solar Chemistry. With 36 Plates. Crown 8vo. price 7s. 6d.

Ganot's Elementary Treatise on Physics, Experimental and Applied, for the use of Colleges and Schools. Translated and Edited with the Author's sanction by E. ATKINSON, Ph.D. F.C.S. New Edition, revised and enlarged ; with a Coloured Plate and 726 Woodcuts. Post 8vo. 15s.

Text-Books of Science, Mechanical and Physical. Edited by T. M. GOODEVE, M.A. and C. W. MERRIFIELD, F.R.S. Small 8vo. price 3s. 6d. each :—

1. GOODEVE's Mechanism.
2. BLOXAM's Metals.
3. MILLER's Inorganic Chemistry.
4. GRIFFIN's Algebra and Trigonometry. GRIFFIN's Notes and Solutions.
5. WATSON's Plane and Solid Geometry.
6. MAXWELL's Theory of Heat.
7. MERRIFIELD's Technical Arithmetic and Mensuration. KEY, by the Rev. JOHN HUNTER, M.A.
8. ANDERSON's Strength of Materials.
9. JENKIN's Electricity and Magnetism.

Dove's Law of Storms, considered in connexion with the ordinary Movements of the Atmosphere. Translated by R. H. SCOTT, M.A. T.C.D. 8vo. 10s. 6d.

The Correlation of Physical Forces. By Sir W. R. GROVE, Q.C. V.P.R.S Fifth Edition, revised, and Augmented by a Discourse on Continuity. 8vo. 10s. 6d

Fragments of Science. By JOHN TYNDALL, LL.D. F.R.S. Third Edition. 8vo. price 14s.

D

Heat a Mode of Motion. By JOHN TYNDALL, LL.D. F.R.S. Fourth Edition. Crown 8vo. with Woodcuts, price 10s. 6d.

Sound; a Course of Eight Lectures delivered at the Royal Institution of Great Britain. By JOHN TYNDALL, LL.D. F.R.S. New Edition, with Portrait and Woodcuts. Crown 8vo. 9s.

Researches on Diamagnetism and Magne-Crystallic Action; including the Question of Diamagnetic Polarity. By JOHN TYNDALL, LL.D. F.R.S. With 6 Plates and many Woodcuts. 8vo. 14s.

Principles of Animal Mechanics. By the Rev. SAMUEL HAUGHTON, F.R.S. M.D. Dublin, D.C.L. Oxon. Fellow of Trinity College, Dublin. 8vo. price 21s.

Lectures on Light, Delivered in America in 1872 and 1873. By JOHN TYNDALL, LL.D., F.R S. Professor of Natural Philosophy in the Royal Insitution of Great Britain. [In the press.

Notes of a Course of Nine Lectures on Light, delivered at the Royal Institution, A.D. 1869. By J. TYNDALL, LL.D. F.R.S. Crown 8vo. 1s. sewed, or 1s. 6d. cloth.

Notes of a Course of Seven Lectures on Electrical Phenomena and Theories, delivered at the Royal Institution, A.D. 1870. By JOHN TYNDALL, LL.D. F.R.S. Crown 8vo. 1s. sewed, or 1s. 6d. cloth.

Light Science for Leisure Hours; a Series of Familiar Essays on Scientific Subjects, Natural Phenomena, &c. By R. A. PROCTOR, B.A. Second Edition, revised. Crown 8vo. price 7s. 6d.

Light: its Influence on Life and Health. By FORBES WINSLOW, M.D. D.C.L. Oxon. (Hon.) Fcp. 8vo. 6s.

Professor Owen's Lectures on the Comparative Anatomy and Physiology of the Invertebrate Animals. Second Edition, with 235 Woodcuts. 8vo. 21s.

The Comparative Anatomy and Physiology of the Vertebrate Animals. By RICHARD OWEN, F.R.S. D.C.L. With 1,472 Woodcuts. 3 vols. 8vo. £3 13s. 6d.

Kirby and Spence's Introduction to Entomology, or Elements of the Natural History of Insects. Crown 8vo. 5s.

Strange Dwellings; a Description of the Habitations of Animals, abridged from 'Homes without Hands.' By J. G. WOOD, M.A. F.L.S. With a New Frontispiece and about 60 other Woodcut Illustrations. Crown 8vo. price 7s. 6d.

Homes without Hands; a Description of the Habitations of Animals, classed according to their Principle of Construction. By Rev. J. G. WOOD, M.A. F.L.S. With about 140 Vignettes on Wood. 8vo. 21s.

The Harmonies of Nature and Unity of Creation. By Dr. G. HARTWIG. 8vo. with numerous Illustrations, 18s.

The Aerial World. By Dr. GEORGE HARTWIG, Author of 'The Sea and its Living Wonders,' 'The Polar World,' &c. 8vo. with numerous Illustrations.
[In the press.

The Sea and its Living Wonders. By the same Author. Third Edition, enlarged. 8vo. with many Illustrations, 21s.

The Tropical World; a Popular Scientific Account of the Natural History of the Equatorial Regions. By the same Author. New Edition, with about 200 Illustrations. 8vo. price 10s. 6d.

The Subterranean World. By the same Author. With 3 Maps and about 80 Woodcut Illustrations, including 8 full size of page. 8vo. price 21s.

The Polar World: a Popular Description of Man and Nature in the Arctic and Antarctic Regions of the Globe. By the same Author. With 8 Chromoxylographs, 3 Maps, and 85 Woodcuts. 8vo. 21s.

A Familiar History of Birds. By E. STANLEY, D.D. late Lord Bishop of Norwich. Fcp. with Woodcuts, 3s. 6d.

Insects at Home; a Popular Account of British Insects, their Structure, Habits, and Transformations. By the Rev. J. G. WOOD, M.A. F.L.S. With upwards of 700 Illustrations engraved on Wood. 8vo. price 21s.

Insects Abroad; being a Popular Account of Foreign Insects, their Structure, Habits, and Transformations. By J. G. WOOD, M.A. F.L.S. Author of 'Homes without Hands' &c. In One Volume, printed and illustrated uniformly with 'Insects at Home,' to which it will form a Sequel and Companion. [In the press.

The Primitive Inhabitants of Scandinavia. Containing a Description of the Implements, Dwellings, Tombs, and Mode of Living of the Savages in the North of Europe during the Stone Age. By SVEN NILSSON. 8vo. Plates and Woodcuts, 18s.

The Origin of Civilisation, and the Primitive Condition of Man; Mental and Social Condition of Savages. By Sir JOHN LUBBOCK, Bart. M.P. F.R.S. Second Edition, with 25 Woodcuts. 8vo. 16s.

An Exposition of Fallacies in the Hypothesis of Mr. Darwin. By C. R. BREE, M.D. F.Z.S. With 36 Woodcuts. Crown 8vo. price 14*s*.

The Ancient Stone Implements, Weapons, and Ornaments, of Great Britain. By JOHN EVANS, F.R.S. F.S.A. 8vo. with 2 Plates and 476 Woodcuts, price 28*s*.

Mankind, their Origin and Des-tiny. By an M.A. of Balliol College, Oxford. Containing a New Translation of the First Three Chapters of Genesis; a Critical Examination of the First Two Gospels; an Explanation of the Apocalypse; and the Origin and Secret Meaning of the Mythological and Mystical Teaching of the Ancients. With 31 Illustrations. 8vo. price 31*s*. 6*d*.

Bible Animals; a Description of every Living Creature mentioned in the Scriptures, from the Ape to the Coral. By the Rev. J. G. WOOD, M.A. F.L.S. With about 100 Vignettes on Wood. 8vo. 21*s*.

Maunder's Treasury of Natural History, or Popular Dictionary of Zoology. Revised and corrected Edition. Fcp. 8vo. with 900 Woodcuts, price 6*s*.

The Elements of Botany for Families and Schools. Tenth Edition, revised by THOMAS MOORE, F.L.S. Fcp. with 154 Woodcuts, 2*s*. 6*d*.

The Treasury of Botany, or Popular Dictionary of the Vegetable Kingdom; with which is incorporated a Glossary of Botanical Terms. Edited by J. LINDLEY, F.R.S. and T. MOORE, F.L.S. Pp. 1,274, with 274 Woodcuts and 20 Steel Plates. Two PARTS, fcp. 8vo. 12*s*.

The Rose Amateur's Guide. By THOMAS RIVERS. The Tenth Edition, revised and improved. Fcp. 8vo. price 4*s*.

A Dictionary of Science, Literature, and Art. Fourth Edition, re-edited by the late W. T. BRANDE (the Author) and GEORGE W. COX, M.A. 3 vols. medium 8vo. price 63*s*. cloth.

Maunder's Scientific and Literary Treasury; a Popular Encyclopædia of Science, Literature, and Art. New Edition, in part rewritten, with above 1,000 new articles, by J. Y. JOHNSON. Fcp. 6*s*.

Loudon's Encyclopædia of Plants; comprising the Specific Character, Description, Culture, History, &c. of all the Plants found in Great Britain. With upwards of 12,000 Woodcuts. 8vo. 42*s*.

Handbook of Hardy Trees, Shrubs, and Herbaceous Plants; containing Descriptions, Native Countries, &c. of a selection of the Best Species in Cultivation; together with Cultural Details, Comparative Hardiness, suitability for particular positions, &c. Based on the French Work of Messrs. DECAISNE and NAUDIN, intitled 'Manuel de l'Amateur des Jardins,' and including 720 Woodcut Illustrations by Riocreux and Leblanc. By W. B. HEMSLEY, formerly Assistant at the Herbarium of the Royal Gardens, Kew. Medium 8vo. 21*s*.

A General System of Descriptive and Analytical Botany: I. Organography, Anatomy, and Physiology of Plants; II. Iconography, or the Description and History of Natural Families. Translated from the French of E. LE MAOUT, M.D. and J. DECAISNE, Member of the Institute, by Mrs. HOOKER. Edited and arranged according to the Botanical System adopted in the Universities and Schools of Great Britain, by J. D. HOOKER, M.D. &c. Director of the Royal Botanic Gardens, Kew. With 5,500 Woodcuts from Designs by L. Stenheil and A. Riocreux. Medium 8vo. price 52*s*. 6*d*.

Chemistry, Medicine, Surgery, and *the Allied Sciences*.

A Dictionary of Chemistry and the Allied Branches of other Sciences. By HENRY WATTS, F.C.S. assisted by eminent Scientific and Practical Chemists. 5 vols. medium 8vo. price £7 3*s*.

Supplement, Completing the Record of Discovery to the end of 1869. 8vo. 31*s*. 6*d*.

Contributions to Molecular Physics in the domain of Radiant Heat; a Series of Memoirs published in the Philosophical Transactions, &c. By JOHN TYNDALL, LL.D. F.R.S. With 2 Plates and 31 Woodcuts. 8vo. price 16*s*.

Elements of Chemistry, Theoretical and Practical. By WILLIAM A MILLER, M.D. LL.D. Professor of Chemistry, King's College, London. New Edition. 3 vols. 8vo. £3.

    PART I. CHEMICAL PHYSICS, 15*s*.
    PART II. INORGANIC CHEMISTRY, 21*s*.
    PART III. ORGANIC CHEMISTRY' 24*s*.

A Course of Practical Chemistry, for the use of Medical Students. By W. ODLING, M.B. F.R.S. New Edition, will 70 new Woodcuts. Crown 8vo. 7*s*. 6*d*.

A Manual of Chemical Physiology, including its Points of Contact with Pathology. By J. L. W. THUDICHUM, M.D. 8vo. with Woodcuts, price 7s. 6d.

Select Methods in Chemical Analysis, chiefly Inorganic. By WILLIAM CROOKES, F.R.S. With 22 Woodcuts. Crown 8vo. price 12s. 6d.

Chemical Notes for the Lecture Room. By THOMAS WOOD, F.C.S. 2 vols. crown 8vo. I. on Heat, &c. price 5s. II. on the Metals, price 5s.

The Handbook for Midwives. By HENRY FLY SMITH, B.A. M.B. Oxon. M.R.C.S. Eng. late Assistant-Surgeon at the Hospital for Women, Soho Square. With 41 Woodcuts. Crown 8vo. price 5s.

The Diagnosis, Pathology, and Treatment of Diseases of Women; including the Diagnosis of Pregnancy. By GRAILY HEWITT, M.D. &c. Third Edition, revised and for the most part re-written; with 132 Woodcuts. 8vo. 24s.

Lectures on the Diseases of Infancy and Childhood. By CHARLES WEST, M.D. &c. Fifth Edition. 8vo. 16s.

On Some Disorders of the Nervous System in Childhood. Being the Lumleian Lectures delivered before the Royal College of Physicians in March 1871 By CHARLES WEST, M.D. Crown 8vo. 5s

On Chronic Bronchitis, especially as connected with Gout, Emphysema, and Diseases of the Heart. By E. HEADLAM GREENHOW, M.D. F.R.S. Physician to and Lecturer on the Principles and Practice of Medicine at the Middlesex Hospital. 8vo. price 7s. 6d.

On the Surgical Treatment of Children's Diseases. By T. HOLMES, M.A. &c. late Surgeon to the Hospital for Sick Children. Second Edition, with 9 Plates and 112 Woodcuts. 8vo. 21s.

Lectures on the Principles and Practice of Physic. By Sir THOMAS WATSON, Bart. M.D. Physician-in-Ordinary to the Queen. Fifth Edition, thoroughly revised. 2 vols. 8vo. price 36s.

Lectures on Surgical Pathology. By Sir JAMES PAGET, Bart. F.R.S. Third Edition, revised and re-edited by the Author and Professor W. TURNER, M.B. 8vo. with 131 Woodcuts, 21s.

Cooper's Dictionary of Practical Surgery and Encyclopædia of Surgical Science. New Edition, brought down to the present time. By S. A. LANE, Surgeon to St. Mary's Hospital, &c. assisted by various Eminent Surgeons. 2 vols. 8vo. price 25s. each.

Pulmonary Consumption; its Nature, Varieties, and Treatment: with an Analysis of One Thousand Cases to exemplify its Duration. By C. J. B. WILLIAMS, M.D. F.R.S. and C. T. WILLIAMS, M.A. M.D. Oxon. Post 8vo. price 10s. 6d.

The Climate of the South of France as suited to Invalids; with Notices of Mediterranean and other Winter Stations. By C. T. WILLIAMS, M.D. Physician to the Hospital for Consumption at Brompton. Second Edition, with an Appendix on Alpine Summer Quarters and the Mountain Cure, and a Map. Crown 8vo. price 6s.

Anatomy, Descriptive and Surgical. By HENRY GRAY, F.R.S. With about 410 Woodcuts from Dissections. Sixth Edition, by T. HOLMES, M.A. Cantab. With a New Introduction by the Editor. Royal 8vo. 28s.

The House I Live in; or, Popular Illustrations of the Structure and Functions of the Human Body. Edited by T. G. GIRTIN. New Edition, with 25 Woodcuts. 16mo. price 2s. 6d.

Quain's Elements of Anatomy. Seventh Edition [1867]. Edited by W. SHARPEY, M.D. F.R.S. Professor of Anatomy and Physiology in University College, London; ALLEN THOMAS, M.D. F.R.S. Professor of Anatomy in the University of Glasgow: and J. CLELAND, M.D. Professor of Anatomy in Queen's College, Galway. With upwards of 800 Engravings on Wood. 2 vols. 8vo. price 31s. 6d.

The Science and Art of Surgery; being a Treatise on Surgical Injuries, Diseases, and Operations. By JOHN ERIC ERICHSEN, Senior Surgeon to University College Hospital, and Holme Professor of Clinical Surgery in University College, London. A New Edition, being the Sixth, revised and enlarged; with 712 Woodcuts. 2 vols. 8vo. price 32s.

A System of Surgery, Theoretical and Practical, in Treatises by Various Authors. Edited by T. HOLMES, M.A. &c. Surgeon and Lecturer on Surgery at St. George's Hospital, and Surgeon-in-Chief to the Metropolitan Police. Second Edition, thoroughly revised, with numerous Illustrations. 5 vols. 8vo. £5 5s.

A Treatise on the Continued Fevers of Great Britain. By CHARLES MURCHISON, M.D. New Edition, revised.
[*Nearly ready.*

Clinical Lectures on Diseases of the Liver, Jaundice, and Abdominal Dropsy. By CHARLES MURCHISON, M.D. Physician to the Middlesex Hospital. Post 8vo. with 25 Woodcuts, 10s. 6d.

Copland's Dictionary of Practical Medicine, abridged from the larger work, and throughout brought down to the present state of Medical Science. 8vo. 36s.

Outlines of Physiology, Human and Comparative. By JOHN MARSHALL, F.R.C.S. Surgeon to the University College Hospital. 2 vols. crown 8vo. with 122 Woodcuts, 32s.

Dr. Pereira's Elements of Materia Medica and Therapeutics, abridged and adapted for the use of Medical and Pharmaceutical Practitioners and Students. Edited by Professor BENTLEY, F.L.S. &c. and by Dr. REDWOOD, F.C.S. &c. With 125 Woodcut Illustrations. 8vo. price 25s.

The Essentials of Materia Medica and Therapeutics. By ALFRED BARING GARROD, M.D. F.R.S. &c. Physician to King's College Hospital. Third Edition, Sixth Impression, brought up to 1870. Crown 8vo. price 12s. 6d.

Todd and Bowman's Physio-logical Anatomy and Physiology of Man. With numerous Illustrations. VOL. II. 8vo. price 25s.
VOL. I. New Edition by Dr. LIONEL S. BEALE, F.R.S. in course of publication, with numerous Illustrations. PARTS I. and II. price 7s. 6d. each.

The Fine Arts, and *Illustrated Editions.*

Grotesque Animals, invented, described, and portrayed by E. W. COOKE, R.A. F.R.S. F.GS. F.Z.S. in 24 Plates, with Elucidatory Comments. Royal 4to. 21s.

In Fairyland; Pictures from the Elf-World. By RICHARD DOYLE. With a Poem by W. ALLINGHAM. With 16 coloured Plates, containing 36 Designs. Folio, 31s. 6d.

Albert Durer, his Life and Works; including Autobiographical Papers and Complete Catalogues. By WILLIAM B. SCOTT. With Six Etchings by the Author and other Illustrations. 8vo. 16s.

Half-Hour Lectures on the His-tory and Practice of the Fine and Ornamental Arts. By. W. B. SCOTT. Second Edition. Crown 8vo. with 50 Woodcut Illustrations, 8s. 6d.

The Chorale Book for England: the Hymns Translated by Miss C. WINKWORTH; the Tunes arranged by Prof. W. S. BENNETT and OTTO GOLDSCHMIDT. Fcp. 4to. 12s. 6d.

The New Testament, illustrated with Wood Engravings after the Early Masters, chiefly of the Italian School. Crown 4to. 63s. cloth, gilt top; or £5 5s. morocco.

The Life of Man Symbolised by the Months of the Year in their Seasons and Phases. Text selected by RICHARD PIGOT. 25 Illustrations on Wood from Original Designs by JOHN LEIGHTON, F.S.A. Quarto, 42s.

Cats and Farlie's Moral Em-blems; with Aphorisms, Adages, and Proverbs of all Nations: comprising 121 Illustrations on Wood by J. LEIGHTON, F.S.A. with an appropriate Text by R. PIGOT. Imperial 8vo. 31s. 6d.

Sacred and Legendary Art. By Mrs. JAMESON. 6 vols. square crown 8vo. price £5 15s. 6d. as follows:—

Legends of the Saints and Mar-tyrs. New Edition, with 19 Etchings and 187 Woodcuts. 2 vols. price 31s. 6d.

Legends of the Monastic Orders. New Edition, with 11 Etchings and 88 Woodcuts. 1 vol. price 21s.

Legends of the Madonna. New Edition, with 27 Etchings and 165 Woodcuts. 1 vol. price 21s.

The History of Our Lord, with that of His Types and Precursors. Completed by Lady EASTLAKE. Revised Edition, with 13 Etchings and 281 Woodcuts. 2 vols. price 42s.

Lyra Germanica, the Christian Year. Translated by CATHERINE WINKWORTH, with 125 Illustrations on Wood drawn by J. LEIGHTON, F.S.A. Quarto, 21s.

Lyra Germanica, the Christian Life. Translated by CATHERINE WINKWORTH; with about 200 Woodcut Illustrations by J. LEIGHTON, F.S.A. and other Artists. Quarto, 21s.

The Useful Arts, Manufactures, &c.

Gwilt's Encyclopædia of Archi-tecture, with above 1,600 Woodcuts. Fifth Edition, with Alterations and considerable Additions, by WYATT PAPWORTH. 8vo. price 52*s.* 6*d.*

A Manual of Architecture : being a Concise History and Explanation of the principal Styles of European Architecture, Ancient, Mediæval, and Renaissance ; with their Chief Variations and a Glossary of Technical Terms. By THOMAS MITCHELL. With 150 Woodcuts. Crown 8vo. 10*s.* 6*d.*

History of the Gothic Revival; an Attempt to shew how far the taste for Mediæval Architecture was retained in England during the last two centuries, and has been re-developed in the present. By C. L. EASTLAKE, Architect. With 48 Illustrations (36 full size of page). Imperial 8vo. price 31*s.* 6*d.*

Hints on Household Taste in Furniture, Upholstery, and other Details. By CHARLES L. EASTLAKE, Architect. New Edition, with about 90 Illustrations. Square crown 8vo. 14*s.*

Geometric Turning : comprising a Description of the New Geometric Chuck constructed by Mr. Plant of Birmingham, with Directions for its use, and a Series of Patterns cut by it; with Explanations of the mode of producing them, and an Account of a New Process of Deep Cutting and of Graving on Copper. By H. S. SAVORY. With 571 Woodcut Illustrations. Square crown 8vo. price 21*s.*

Lathes and Turning, Simple, Me-chanical, and Ornamental. By W. HENRY NORTHCOTT. With about 240 Illustrations on Steel and Wood. 8vo. 18*s.*

Perspective ; or, the Art of Drawing what one Sees. Explained and adapted to the use of those Sketching from Nature. By Lieut. W. H. COLLINS, R.E. F.R.A.S. With 37 Woodcuts. Crown 8vo. price 5*s.*

Principles of Mechanism, designed for the use of Students in the Universities, and for Engineering Students generally. By R. WILLIS, M.A. F.R.S. &c. Jacksonian Professor in the Univ. of Cambridge. Second Edition ; with 374 Woodcuts. 8vo. 18*s.*

Handbook of Practical Tele-graphy. By R. S. CULLEY, Memb. Inst. C.E. Engineer-in-Chief of Telegraphs to the Post-Office. Fifth Edition, revised and enlarged ; with 118 Woodcuts and 9 Plates. [8vo. price 14*s.*

Ure's Dictionary of Arts, Manu-factures, and Mines. Sixth Edition, re-written and greatly enlarged by ROBERT HUNT, F.R.S. assisted by numerous Contributors. With 2,000 Woodcuts. 3 vols. medium 8vo. £4 14*s.* 6*d.*

Encyclopædia of Civil Engineer-ing, Historical, Theoretical, and Practical. By E. CRESY, C.E. With above 3,000 Woodcuts. 8vo. 42*s.*

Catechism of the Steam Engine, in its various Applications to Mines, Mills, Steam Navigation, Railways, and Agriculture. By JOHN BOURNE, C.E. New Edition, with 89 Woodcuts. Fcp. 8vo. 6*s.*

Handbook of the Steam Engine. By JOHN BOURNE, C.E. forming a KEY to the Author's Catechism of the Steam Engine. With 67 Woodcuts. Fcp. 8vo. price 9*s.*

Recent Improvements in the Steam Engine. By JOHN BOURNE, C.E. New Edition, including many New Examples, with 124 Woodcuts. Fcp. 8vo. 6*s.*

A Treatise on the Steam Engine, in its various Applications to Mines, Mills, Steam Navigation, Railways, and Agriculture. By J. BOURNE, C.E. New Edition ; with Portrait, 37 Plates, and 546 Woodcuts. 4to. 42*s.*

Treatise on Mills and Millwork. By Sir W. FAIRBAIRN, Bart. F.R.S. New Edition, with 18 Plates and 322 Woodcuts. 2 vols. 8vo. 32*s.*

Useful Information for Engi-neers. By the same Author. FIRST, SECOND, and THIRD SERIES, with many Plates and Woodcuts. 3 vols. crown 8vo. 10*s.* 6*d.* each.

The Application of Cast and Wrought Iron to Building Purposes. By the same Author. Fourth Edition, with 6 Plates and 118 Woodcuts. 8vo. 16*s.*

The Strains in Trusses Computed by means of Diagrams ; with 20 Examples drawn to Scale. By F. A. RANKEN, M.A. C.E. Lecturer at the Hartley Institution, Southampton. With 35 Diagrams. Square crown 8vo. price 6*s.* 6*d.*

Mitchell's Manual of Practical Assaying. New Edition, being the Fourth, thoroughly revised, with the recent Discoveries incorporated. By W. CROOKES, F.R.S. With numerous Woodcuts. 8vo.
[Nearly ready.

Bayldon's Art of Valuing Rents and Tillages, and Claims of Tenants upon Quitting Farms, both at Michaelmas and Lady-Day. Eighth Edition, revised by J. C. Morton. 8vo. 10s. 6d.

On the Manufacture of Beet- Root Sugar in England and Ireland. By William Crookes, F.R.S. With 11 Woodcuts. 8vo. 8s. 6d.

Loudon's Encyclopædia of Gar- dening: comprising the Theory and Practice of Horticulture, Floriculture, Arboriculture, and Landscape Gardening. With 1,000 Woodcuts. 8vo. 21s.

Practical Treatise on Metallurgy, adapted from the last German Edition of Professor Kerl's *Metallurgy* by W. Crookes, F.R.S. &c. and E. Röhrig, Ph.D. M.E. 3 vols. 8vo. with 625 Woodcuts, price 4l. 19s.

Loudon's Encyclopædia of Agri- culture: comprising the Laying-out, Improvement, and Management of Landed Property, and the Cultivation and Economy of the Productions of Agriculture. With 1,100 Woodcuts. 8vo. 21s.

Religious and Moral Works.

The Speaker's Bible Commen- tary, by Bishops and other Clergy of the Anglican Church, critically examined by the Right Rev. J. W. Colenso, D.D. Bishop of Natal. 8vo. Part I, *Genesis*, 3s. 6d. Part II. *Exodus*, 4s. 6d. Part III. *Leviticus*, 2s. 6d. Part IV. *Numbers*, 3s. 6d. Part V. *Deuteronomy*, 5s.

The Outlines of the Christian Ministry Delineated, and brought to the Test of Reason, Holy Scripture, History, and Experience. By Christopher Wordsworth, D.C.L. &c. Bishop of St. Andrew's. Crown 8vo. price 7s. 6d.

Christian Counsels, selected from the Devotional Works of Fénélon, Archbishop of Cambrai. Translated by A. M. James. Crown 8vo. price 5s.

Eight Essays on Ecclesiastical Reform. By various Writers; with Preface and Analysis of the Essays. Edited by the Rev. Orby Shipley, M.A. Crown 8vo. 10s. 6d.

Authority and Conscience; a Free Debate on the Tendency of Dogmatic Theology and on the Characteristics of Faith. Edited by Conway Morel. Post 8vo. 7s. 6d.

Reasons of Faith; or, the Order of the Christian Argument Developed and Explained. By the Rev. G. S. Drew, M.A. Second Edition, revised and enlarged. Fcp. 8vo. 6s.

Christ the Consoler; a Book of Comfort for the Sick. With a Preface by the Right Rev. the Lord Bishop of Carlisle. Small 8vo. 6s.

The True Doctrine of the Eucha- rist. By Thomas S. L. Vogan, D.D. Canon and Prebendary of Chichester and Rural Dean. vo. 18s.

The Student's Compendium of the Book of Common Prayer; being Notes Historical and Explanatory of the Liturgy of the Church of England. By the Rev. H. Allden Nash. Fcp. 8vo. price 2s. 6d.

Synonyms of the Old Testament, their Bearing on Christian Faith and Practice. By the Rev. Robert B. Girdlestone, M.A. 8vo. price 15s.

Fundamentals; or, Bases of Belief concerning Man and God: a Handbook of Mental, Moral, and Religious Philosophy. By the Rev. T. Griffith, M.A. 8vo. price 10s. 6d.

An Introduction to the Theology of the Church of England, in an Exposition of the Thirty-nine Articles. By the Rev. T. P. Boultbee, LL.D. Fcp. 8vo. price 6s.

Christian Sacerdotalism, viewed from a Layman's standpoint or tried by Holy Scripture and the Early Fathers; with a short Sketch of the State of the Church from the end of the Third to the Reformation in the beginning of the Sixteenth Century. By John Jardine, M.A. LL.D. 8vo. 8s. 6d.

Prayers for the Family and for Private Use, selected from the Collection of the late Baron Bunsen, and Translated by Catherine Winkworth. Fcp. 8vo. price 3s. 6d.

Churches and their Creeds. By the Rev. Sir Philip Perring, Bart. late Scholar of Trin. Coll. Cambridge, and University Medallist. Crown 8vo. 10s.

The Problem of the World and the Church Reconsidered, in Three Letters to a Friend. By a Septuagenarian. Second Edition, revised and edited] by James Booth, C.B. Crown 8vo. price 5s.

An Exposition of the 39 Articles, Historical and Doctrinal. By E. HAROLD BROWNE, D.D. Lord Bishop of Ely. Ninth Edition. 8vo. 16s.

The Voyage and Shipwreck of St. Paul; with Dissertations on the Ships and Navigation of the Ancients. By JAMES SMITH, F.R.S. Crown 8vo. Charts, 10s. 6d.

The Life and Epistles of St. Paul. By the Rev. W. J. CONYBEARE, M.A. and the Very Rev. J. S. HOWSON, D.D. Dean of Chester. Three Editions :—

LIBRARY EDITION, with all the Original Illustrations, Maps, Landscapes on Steel, Woodcuts, &c. 2 vols. 4to. 48s.

INTERMEDIATE EDITION, with a Selection of Maps, Plates, and Woodcuts. 2 vols. square crown 8vo. 21s.

STUDENT'S EDITION, revised and condensed, with 46 Illustrations and Maps. 1 vol. crown 8vo. 9s.

Evidence of the Truth of the Christian Religion derived from the Literal Fulfilment of Prophecy. By ALEXANDER KEITH, D.D. 40th Edition, with numerous Plates, in square 8vo. 12s. 6d.; also the 39th Edition, in post 8vo. with 5 Plates, 6s.

The History and Destiny of the World and of the Church, according to Scripture. By the same Author. Square 8vo. with 40 Illustrations, 10s.

The History and Literature of the Israelites, according to the Old Testament and the Apocrypha. By C. DE ROTHSCHILD and A. DE ROTHSCHILD. Second Edition. 2 vols. crown 8vo. 12s. 6d. Abridged Edition, in 1 vol. fcp. 8vo. 3s. 6d.

Ewald's History of Israel to the Death of Moses. Translated from the German. Edited, with a Preface and an Appendix, by RUSSELL MARTINEAU, M.A. Second Edition. 2 vols. 8vo. 24s. Vols. III. and IV. edited by J. E. CARPENTER, M.A. price 21s.

England and Christendom. By ARCHBISHOP MANNING, D.D. Post 8vo. price 10s 6d.

Ignatius Loyola and the Early Jesuits. By STEWART ROSE. New Edition, revised. 8vo. with Portrait, 16s.

An Introduction to the Study of the New Testament, Critical, Exegetical, and Theological. By the Rev. S. DAVIDSON, D.D. LL.D. 2 vols. 8vo. 30s.

Commentary on the Epistle to the Romans. By the Rev. W. A. O'CONNOR, B.A. Crown 8vo. price 3s. 6d.

The Epistle to the Hebrews; With Analytical Introduction and Notes. By the Rev. W. A. O'CONNOR, B.A. Crown 8vo. price 4s. 6d.

A Critical and Grammatical Com- mentary on St. Paul's Epistles. By C. J. ELLICOTT, D.D. Lord Bishop of Gloucester and Bristol. 8vo.

Galatians, Fourth Edition, 8s. 6d.

Ephesians, Fourth Edition, 8s. 6d.

Pastoral Epistles, Fourth Edition, 10s. 6d.

Philippians, Colossians, and Philemon, Third Edition, 10s. 6d.

Thessalonians, Third Edition, 7s. 6d.

Historical Lectures on the Life of Our Lord Jesus Christ : being the Hulsean Lectures for 1859. By C. J. ELLICOTT, D.D. Fifth Edition. 8vo. 12s.

The Greek Testament; with Notes, Grammatical and Exegetical. By the Rev. W. WEBSTER, M.A. and the Rev. W. F. WILKINSON, M.A. 2 vols. 8vo. £2. 4s.

The Treasury of Bible Know- ledge; being a Dictionary of the Books, Persons, Places, Events, and other Matters of which mention is made in Holy Scripture. By Rev. J. AYRE, M.A. With Maps, 15 Plates, and numerous Woodcuts. Fcp. 8vo. price 6s.

Every-day Scripture Difficulties explained and illustrated. By J. E. PRESCOTT, M.A. I. *Matthew* and *Mark*; II. *Luke* and *John*. 2 vols. 8vo. price 9s. each.

The Pentateuch and Book of Joshua Critically Examined. By the Right Rev. J. W. COLENSO, D.D. Lord Bishop of Natal. Crown 8vo. price 6s.

PART V. Genesis Analysed and Separated, and the Ages of its Writers determined 8vo. 18s.

PART VI. The Later Legislation of the Pentateuch. 8vo. 24s.

The Formation of Christendom. By T. W. ALLIES. PARTS I. and II. 8vo. price 12s. each.

Four Discourses of Chrysostom, chiefly on the parable of the Rich Man and Lazarus. Translated by F. ALLEN, B.A. Crown 8vo. 3s. 6d.

Thoughts for the Age. By ELIZABETH M. SEWELL, Author of 'Amy Herbert.' New Edition. Fcp. 8vo. price 5s.

Passing Thoughts on Religion. By Miss SEWELL. Fcp. 3s. 6d.

Self-examination before Confirmation. By Miss SEWELL. 32mo. 1s. 6d.

Thoughts for the Holy Week, for Young Persons. By Miss SEWELL. New Edition. Fcp. 8vo. 2s.

Readings for a Month Preparatory to Confirmation, from Writers of the Early and English Church. By Miss SEWELL. Fcp. 8vo. 4s.

Readings for Every Day in Lent, compiled from the Writings of Bishop JEREMY TAYLOR. By Miss SEWELL. Fcp. 5s.

Preparation for the Holy Communion; the Devotions chiefly from the works of JEREMY TAYLOR. By Miss SEWELL. 32mo. 3s.

Bishop Jeremy Taylor's Entire Works; with Life by BISHOP HEBER. Revised and corrected by the Rev. C. P EDEN. 10 vols. 8vo. price £5. 5s.

Traditions and Customs of Cathe"drals. By MACKENZIE E. C. WALCOTT, B.D. F.S.A. Præcentor and Prebendary of Chichester. Second Edition, revised and enlarged. Crown 8vo. price 6s.

Spiritual Songs for the Sundays and Holidays throughout the Year. By J. S. B. MONSELL, LL.D. Vicar of Egham and Rural Dean. Fourth Edition, Sixth Thousand. Fcp. price 4s. 6d.

Lyra Germanica, translated from the German by Miss C. WINKWORTH. FIRST SERIES, the *Christian Year*, Hymns for the Sundays and Chief Festivals of the Church; SECOND SERIES, the *Christian Life*. Fcp. 8vo. price 3s. 6d. each SERIES.

Endeavours after the Christian Life; Discourses. By JAMES MARTINEAU. Fourth Edition. Post 8vo. price 7s. 6d.

Travels, Voyages, &c.

Rambles, by PATRICIUS WALKER. Reprinted from *Fraser's Magazine*; with a Vignette of the Queen's Bower, in the New Forest. Crown 8vo. price 10s. 6d.

Slave-Catching in the Indian Ocean; a Record of Naval Experiences. By Capt. COLOMB, R.N. 8vo. with Illustrations from Photographs, &c. price 21s.

The Cruise of H.M.S. Curaçoa among the South Sea Islands in 1865. By JULIUS BRENCHLEY, M.A. F.R.G.S. 8vo. with Map and Plates. [*Nearly ready.*

Six Months in California. By J. G. PLAYER-FROWD. Post 8vo. price 6s.

The Japanese in America. By CHARLES LANMAN, American Secretary, Japanese Legation, Washington, U.S.A. Post 8vo. price 10s. 6d.

My Wife and I in Queensland; Eight Years' Experience in the Colony, with some account of Polynesian Labour. By CHARLES H. EDEN. With Map and Frontispiece. Crown 8vo. price 9s.

Untrodden Peaks and Unfrequented Valleys; a Midsummer Ramble among the Dolomites. By AMELIA B. EDWARDS, Author of 'Barbara's History' &c. With a Map, and numerous Illustrations from Designs by the Author; Engraved on Wood by E. Whymper. Medium 8vo. uniform with Whymper's ' Scrambles in the Alps.' [*Nearly ready.*

How to See Norway. By Captain J. R. CAMPBELL. With Map and 5 Woodcuts. Fcp. 8vo. price 5s.

Pau and the Pyrenees. By Count HENRY RUSSELL, Member of the Alpine Club. With 2 Maps. Fcp. 8vo. price 5s.

Hours of Exercise in the Alps. By JOHN TYNDALL, LL.D., F.R.S. Third Edition, with Seven Woodcuts by E. Whymper. Crown 8vo. price 12s. 6d.

Cadore or Titian's Country. By JOSIAH GILBERT, one of the Authors of the 'Dolomite Mountains.' With Map, Facsimile, and 40 Illustrations. Imp. 8vo. 31s. 6d.

The Dolomite Mountains. Excursions through Tyrol, Carinthia, Carniola, and Friuli. By J. GILBERT and G. C. CHURCHILL, F.R.G.S. With numerous Illustrations. Square crown 8vo. 21s.

Travels in the Central Caucasus and Bashan, including Visits to Ararat and Tabreez and Ascents of Kazbek and Elbruz. By DOUGLAS W. FRESHFIELD. Square crown 8vo. with Maps, &c., 18s.

Life in India; a Series of Sketches shewing something of the Anglo-Indian, the Land he lives in, and the People among whom he lives. By EDWARD BRADDON. Post 8vo. price 9s.

The Alpine Club Map of the Chain of Mont Blanc, from an actual Survey in 1863—1864. By A. Adams-Reilly, F.R.G.S. M.A.C. In Chromolithography on extra stout drawing paper 28in. × 17in. price 10s. or mounted on canvas in a folding case, 12s. 6d.

History of Discovery in our Australasian Colonies, Australia, Tasmania, and New Zealand, from the Earliest Date to the Present Day. By William Howitt. 2 vols. 8vo. with 3 Maps, 20s.

Visits to Remarkable Places: Old Halls, Battle-Fields, and Scenes illustrative of striking Passages in English History and Poetry. By the same Author. 2 vols. square crown 8vo. with Wood Engravings, 25s.

The Rural Life of England. By William Howitt. Woodcuts by Bewick and Williams. Medium 8vo. 12s. 6d.

Guide to the Pyrenees, for the use of Mountaineers. By Charles Packe. Second Edition, with Maps, &c. and Appendix. Crown 8vo. 7s. 6d.

The Alpine Guide. By John Ball M.R.I.A. late President of the Alpine Club. Post 8vo. with Maps and other Illustrations.

The Guide to the Eastern Alps, price 10s. 6d.

The Guide to the Western Alps, including Mont Blanc, Monte Rosa, Zermatt, &c. Price 6s. 6d.

Guide to the Central Alps, including all the Oberland District, price 7s. 6d.

Introduction on Alpine Travelling in general, and on the Geology of the Alps, price 1s. Either of the Three Volumes or Parts of the *Alpine Guide* may be had with this Introduction prefixed, price 1s. extra.

Works of Fiction.

The Burgomaster's Family; or, Weal and Woe in a Little World. By Christine Müller. Translated from the Dutch by Sir J. Shaw Lefevre, K.C.B. F.R.S. Crown 8vo. price 6s.

Popular Romances of the Middle Ages. By the Rev. George W. Cox, M.A. and Eustace Hinton Jones. Crown 8vo. 10s. 6d.

Tales of the Teutonic Lands; a Sequel to 'Popular Romances of the Middle Ages.' By George W. Cox, M.A. and Eustace Hinton Jones. Crown 8vo. price 10s. 6d.

Novels and Tales. By the Right Hon. Benjamin Disraeli, M.P. Cabinet Editions, complete in Ten Volumes, crown 8vo. price 6s. each, as follows :—

Lothair, 6s.	Venetia, 6s.
Coningsby, 6s.	Alroy, Ixion, &c. 6s.
Sybil, 6s.	Young Duke, &c. 6s.
Tancred, 6s.	Vivian Grey, 6s.

Contarini Fleming, &c. 6s.
Henrietta Temple, 6s.

Cabinet Edition, in crown 8vo. of Stories and Tales by Miss Sewell :—

Amy Herbert, 2s. 6d.	Katharine Ashton, 2s. 6d.
Gertrude, 2s. 6d.	
Earl's Daughter, 2s. 6d.	Margaret Percival, 3s. 6d.
Experience of Life, 2s. 6d.	Laneton Parsonage, 3s. 6d.
Cleve Hall, 2s. 6d.	Ursula, 3s. 6d.
Ivors, 2s. 6d.	

Becker's Gallus; or, Roman Scenes of the Time of Augustus. Post 8vo. 7s. 6d.

Becker's Charicles: Illustrative of Private Life of the Ancient Greeks. Post 8vo. 7s. 6d.

Tales of Ancient Greece. By the Rev. G. W. Cox, M.A. late Scholar of Trin. Coll. Oxford. Crown 8vo. price 6s. 6d.

Wonderful Stories from Norway, Sweden, and Iceland. Adapted and arranged by Julia Goddard. With an Introductory Essay by the Rev. G. W. Cox, M.A. and Six Illustrations. Square post 8vo. 6s.

The Modern Novelist's Library:
Melville's Digby Grand, 2s. boards; 2s. 6d. cloth.
———— Gladiators, 2s. boards; 2s. 6d. cloth.
———— Good for Nothing, 2s. boards; 2s. 6d. cloth.
———— Holmby House, 2s. boards; 2s. 6d. cloth.
———— Interpreter, 2s. boards; 2s. 6d. cloth.
———— Kate Coventry, 2s. boards; 2s. 6d. cloth.
———— Queen's Maries, 2s. boards; 2s. 6d. cloth.
———— General Bounce, 2s. boards; 2s. 6d. cloth.
Trollope's Warden 1s. 6d. boards; 2s cloth.
———— Barchester Towers, 2s. boards; 2s. 6d. cloth.
Bramley-Moore's Six Sisters of the Valleys, 2s. boards; 2s. 6d. cloth.

Poetry and *The Drama.*

Ballads and Lyrics of Old France; with other Poems. By A. LANG, Fellow of Merton College, Oxford. Square fcp. 8vo. price 5s.

Moore's Lalla Rookh, Tenniel's Edition, with 68 Wood Engravings from Original Drawings. Fcp. 4to. 21s.

Moore's Irish Melodies, Maclise's Edition, with 161 Steel Plates from Original Drawings. Super-royal 8vo. 31s. 6d.

Miniature Edition of Moore's Irish *Melodies,* with Maclise's Illustrations (as above), reduced in Lithography. Imp. 16mo. 10s. 6d.

Lays of Ancient Rome ; with *Ivry* and the *Armada.* By the Right Hon. LORD MACAULAY. 16mo. 3s. 6d.

Lord Macaulay's Lays of Ancient Rome. With 90 Illustrations on Wood, Original and from the Antique, from Drawings by G. SCHARF. Fcp. 4to. 21s.

Miniature Edition of Lord Ma- caulay's Lays of Ancient Rome, with Scharf's Illustrations (as above) reduced in Lithography. Imp. 16mo. 10s. 6d.

Southey's Poetical Works, with the Author's last Corrections and Copyright Additions. Library Edition. Medium 8vo. with Portrait and Vignette, 14s.

Goldsmith's Poetical Works, Illustrated with Wood Engravings from Designs by Members of the ETCHING CLUB. Imp. 16mo. 7s. 6d.

Poems. By JEAN INGELOW. 2 vols. Fcp. 8vo. price 10s.

> FIRST SERIES, containing 'DIVIDED, 'The STAR'S MONUMENT,' &c. Six-' teenth Thousand. Fcp. 8vo. price 5s.
> SECOND SERIES, 'A STORY of DOOM,' 'GLADYS and her ISLAND,' &c. Fifth Thousand. Fcp. 8vo. price 5s.

Poems by Jean Ingelow. First Series, with nearly 100 Illustrations engraved on Wood. Fcp. 4to. 21s.

Bowdler's Family Shakspeare cheaper Genuine Edition, complete in 1 vol. large type, with 36 Woodcut Illustrations, price 14s. or in 6 pocket vols. 3s. 6d. each.

Horatii Opera, Library Edition, with Copious English Notes, Marginal References and Various Readings. Edited by the Rev. J. E. YONGE, M.A. 8vo. 21s.

The Odes and Epodes of Horace ; a Metrical Translation into English, with Introduction and Commentaries. By Lord LYTTON. Post 8vo. price 10s. 6d.

The Æneid of Virgil Translated into English Verse. By the late J. CONINGTON, M.A. New Edition. Crown 8vo. 9s.

Rural Sports &c.

Encyclopædia of Rural Sports ; a Complete Account, Historical, Practical, and Descriptive, of Hunting, Shooting, Fishing, Racing, &c. By D. P. BLAINE. With above 600 Woodcuts (20 from Designs by JOHN LEECH). 8vo. 21s.

The Dead Shot, or Sportsman's Complete Guide ; a Treatise on the Use of the Gun, Dog-breaking, Pigeon-shooting, &c. By MARKSMAN. Fcp. 8vo. with Plates, 5s.

A Book on Angling: being a Complete Treatise on the Art of Angling in every branch, including full Illustrated Lists of Salmon Flies. By FRANCIS FRANCIS. New Edition, with Portrait and 15 other Plates, plain and coloured. Post 8vo. 15s.

Wilcocks's Sea-Fisherman: comprising the Chief Methods of Hook and Line Fishing in the British and other Seas, a glance at Nets, and remarks on Boats and Boating. Second Edition, enlarged, with 80 Woodcuts. Post 8vo. 12s. 6d.

The Fly-Fisher's Entomology. By ALFRED RONALDS. With coloured Representations of the Natural and Artificial Insect. Sixth Edition, with 20 coloured Plates. 8vo. 14s.

The Ox, his Diseases and their Treatment ; with an Essay on Parturition in the Cow. By J. R. DOBSON, M.R.C.V.S. Crown 8vo. with Illustrations, 7s. 6d.

A Treatise on Horse-shoeing and Lameness. By JOSEPH GAMGEE, Veterinary Surgeon, formerly Lecturer on the Principles and Practice of Farriery in the New Veterinary College, Edinburgh. 8vo. with 55 Woodcuts, 15s.

Blaine's Veterinary Art: a Treatise on the Anatomy, Physiology, and Curative Treatment of the Diseases of the Horse, Neat Cattle, and Sheep. Seventh Edition, revised and enlarged by C. STEEL. 8vo. with Plates and Woodcuts, 18s.

Youatt on the Horse. Revised and enlarged by W. Watson, M.R.C.V.S. 8vo. with numerous Woodcuts, 12s. 6d.

Youatt on the Dog. By the same Author. 8vo. with numerous Woodcuts price 6s.

Horses and Stables. By Colonel F. Fitzwygram, XV. the King's Hussars. With 24 Plates of Woodcut Illustrations, containing very numerous Figures. 8vo. 15s.

The Dog in Health and Disease. By Stonehenge. With 73 Wood Engravings. New Edition, revised. Square crown 8vo. price 7s. 6d.

The Greyhound. By the same Author. Revised Edition, with 24 Portraits of Greyhounds. Square crown 8vo. 10s. 6d

Stables and Stable Fittings. By W. Miles, Esq. Imp. 8vo. with 13 Plates, 15s.

The Horse's Foot, and how to keep it Sound. By W. Miles, Esq. Ninth Edition, with Illustrations. Imp. 8vo. 12s. 6d.

A Plain Treatise on Horse-shoeing. By the same Author. Sixth Edition, post 8vo. with Illustrations, 2s. 6d.

Remarks on Horses' Teeth, addressed to Purchasers. By the same. Post 8vo. 1s. 6d.

The Setter; with Notices of the most Eminent Breeds now extant, Instructions how to Breed, Rear, and Break; Dog Shows, Field Trials, and General Management, &c. By Edward Laverack. With 2 Portraits of Setters. Crown 4to. 7s. 6d.

Works of Utility and *General Information.*

Chess Openings. By F. W. Longman, Balliol College, Oxford. Fcp. 8vo. 2s. 6d.

The Theory of the Modern Scientific Game of Whist. By William Pole, F.R.S. Mus. Doc. Oxon. Fifth Edition, enlarged. Fcp. 8vo. price 2s. 6d.

A Practical Treatise on Brewing; with Formulæ for Public Brewers, and Instructions for Private Families. By W Black. Fifth Edition. 8vo. 10s. 6d.

The Theory and Practice of Banking. By Henry Dunning Macleod, M.A. Barrister-at-Law. Second Edition. entirely remodelled. 2 vols. 8vo. 30s.

Collieries and Colliers: a Handbook of the Law and Leading Cases relating thereto. By J. C. Fowler, Barrister. Third Edition. Fcp. 8vo. 7s. 6d.

Modern Cookery for Private Families, reduced to a System of Easy Practice in a Series of carefully-tested Receipts. By Eliza Acton. Newly revised and enlarged; with 8 Plates, Figures, and 150 Woodcuts. Fcp. 6s.

Maunder's Treasury of Knowledge and Library of Reference: comprising an English Dictionary and Grammar, Universal Gazetteer, Classical Dictionary, Chronology, Law Dictionary, Synopsis of the Peerage, Useful Tables, &c. Fcp. 8vo. 6s.

Pewtner's Comprehensive Specifier; a Guide to the Practical Specification of every kind of Building-Artificer's Work: with Forms of Building Conditions and Agreements, an Appendix, Foot-Notes, and Index. Edited by W. Young, Architect. Crown 8vo. 6s.

M'Culloch's Dictionary, Practical, Theoretical, and Historical, of Commerce and Commercial Navigation. New Edition, revised throughout and corrected to the Present Time; with a Biographical Notice of the Author. Edited by H. G. Reid. 8vo. price 63s.

Hints to Mothers on the Management of their Health during the Period of Pregnancy and in the Lying-in Room. By Thomas Bull, M.D. Fcp. 8vo. price 5s.

The Maternal Management of Children in Health and Disease. By Thomas Bull, M.D. Fcp. 8vo. price 5s.

How to Nurse Sick Children; containing Directions which may be found of service to all who have charge of the Young. By Charles West, M.D. Second Edition. Fcp. 8vo. 1s. 6d

Notes on Lying-In Institutions; with a Proposal for Organising an Institution for Training Midwives and Midwifery Nurses. By Florence Nightingale. With 5 Plans. Square crown 8vo. 7s. 6d.

Blackstone Economised; being a Compendium of the Laws of England to the Present Time. By D. M. Aird, of the Middle Temple, Barrister-at-Law. Post 8vo. 7s. 6d.

The Cabinet Lawyer; a Popular Digest of the Laws of England, Civil, Criminal, and Constitutional. Twenty-third Edition, corrected and brought up to the Present Date. Fcp. 8vo. price 7s. 6d.

A Profitable Book upon Domestic Law. Essays for English Women and Law Students. By Perkins, Junior, M.A. Barrister-at-Law. Post 8vo. price 10s. 6d.

A History and Explanation of the Stamp Duties; containing Remarks on the Origin of the Stamp Duties and a History of the Stamp Duties in this Country from their Commencement to the Present Time. By Stephen Dowell, M.A. Assistant-Solicitor of Inland Revenue. 8vo. price 12s. 6d.

Willich's Popular Tables for Ascertaining the Value of Lifehold, Leasehold, and Church Property, Renewal Fines, &c. with numerous useful Chemical, Geographical, Astronomical, Trigonometrical Tables, &c. Post 8vo. 10s.

INDEX.

SPOTTISWOODE AND CO., PRINTERS, NEW-STREET SQUARE, LONDON.